Adventures of Bobby

Bob Schwinger

Emmie + Peter,
Hope you enjoy this novel
Bob Schwinger

AmErica House
Baltimore

ISBN: 1-58851-823-X
PUBLISHED BY AMERICA HOUSE BOOK PUBLISHERS
www.publishamerica.com Baltimore
Printed in the United States of America

Acknowledgments

Thanks to my wife, Debbie Condello, for her constant support, to my son, Nicholas Schwinger, for contributing his story, "Don't Underestimate the Little Guy," to Caryn McVoy, Randy Udall, and Michael Shephard whose comments convinced me to change the manuscript from a novel/essay to a novel, and to Ruth Kirschbaum and Beth Sturgeon for proofing the grammar and spelling.

Part I

Chapter 1

My mother held me on her lap while my father drove to her parents' house. Her long, brown hair was pulled back into a ponytail, accentuating her high cheekbones and full lips. She had a thin layer of fat, so no matter where I touched her she felt soft. My father, in contrast, was thin and muscular with a round, cheerful face. They both had a deep tan and were healthy and vibrant. We stopped at a gray, two-story Victorian house. As my father got my bag out of the back, once again, I pleaded with my mother. "Please, mommy, don't leave me with grandma and grandpa. I want to go with you. Please, let me stay with you."

She looked at me with her soft brown eyes and said, "I'm sorry, Bobby. I wish you could come, but it just won't work this time."

The three of us were now on the cracked concrete walk leading through the gate in the wrought iron fence that surrounded the house. Fragrance from the flowers all along the front fence thickened the air. My father sneezed. I stopped as we were about to step through the gate, tightened my grip on my mother's hand, leaned back, and jerked her toward our car.

"I'm not going. I won't go. You can't make me."

"Bobby, it's all right. We'll be back. We've left you before, many times." Then softly to herself, "Maybe too many times for only being six years old." Again to me, "What is it? Why don't you want to stay?"

"I don't know. I just don't want you to leave."

To my mother my father said, "Of all the times, why does he have to pull this now? We don't have time for this."

My father came from behind, grabbed my left hand, and pulled me up the walk.

My mother caught up and put her hand on his shoulder. "Tom, let go. Come on. You're not the only one with needs in this family. Something's really upsetting Bobby, and I want to know what it is. And so should you!"

5

"He's just trying to manipulate us. His friend Ryan does this all the time to his parents, and they give in. Bobby is just trying it out on us. I'm not falling for it. I'm not going to be manipulated by a child. Let's get going!"

He glared at me with his icy blue eyes then jerked me up to the steps. I yanked my hand out of his, grabbed my mother's arm with both hands, and started crying.

I heard him say, "Boy, he's really putting on the act now."

My mother turned on my father. "Do you have to be so rough? Look what you've done now! You could at least try to be a little understanding!"

"I'm doing the best I can. We've got a lot to get done. This is not a good way to start."

"He's not acting. I can tell. Something is really bothering him. Ever since we told him about this trip, weeks ago, he's wanted to be near us all the time. I've never known him to want to be so close."

"Yeah, you don't have to tell me. He's been on top of me ever since. I can't get anything done."

She sat on the steps and pulled me onto her lap. "What is it, honey? Why don't you want us to go? We won't be gone long. Not more than any of the other times. What is it? Don't you want to stay with grandma and grandpa? Would you rather stay with one of your cousins?"

Forcing the words, I said, "No. It's not that. I just don't want you to go. I don't know why. I feel that I'll never see you again. I feel that we'll never go home again. Please, don't go."

She looked up at my father. "Maybe we shouldn't go, Tom. I haven't felt good about this trip either."

He raised his voice. "I can't believe this! We have to go!"

"Then maybe we should take Bobby with us. Stay a few more days if we have to."

He stomped his feet. "No! No! No! We've got a lot of work to get done. You have your photo essay to finish. They've already extended your deadline. The boat is ready. The crew is waiting. I can't have him around pulling his tricks, and who knows if the wind picks up. The sea is calm now. We've got to get out there, pinpoint that sunken ship, and get back. We have to get this done to get paid. The bills are piling up."

6

"Well, yeah, I guess so. You don't even know if there's a ship down there.

"I hate to leave Bobby feeling this way," she sighed.

She gently turned my face toward hers. "Believe me, Bobby. Trust me. We'll be back as soon as we can.

Her warmth and softness and the kindness in her voice comforted me. I stopped crying and said, "I still don't want you to go. Maybe daddy can go, and you stay here. Let's go home, mommy."

"I'm sorry, Bobby. Your daddy is right. We have a lot of work to do, and there will be no one to take care of you. You wouldn't have any fun. After a day you will have wished you had stayed here. Your cousin Eddie is coming over this afternoon. You can swim in the pool together. Really, Bobby, you'll have a lot more fun staying here than going with us. All we're going to do is work."

"I still don't want you and daddy to go."

She brushed her hand through my hair. "Before you know it, we'll be back. We'll be gone four, five days at the most."

The screen door slammed. My grandmother, a petite woman with solid gray hair and recessed, brown eyes, peered down at us from the top of the steps and said, "What's going on? I thought you had to get going?"

"We do. It's just that Bobby doesn't want us to leave."

She stuffed her hands in the pockets of her plaid apron. "Does he ever?"

"No. But it's different this time."

Still standing on the walk, arms folded across his chest, my father said, "Yeah, he's putting up more of a fuss."

My grandmother said, "Here, bring him here. It's easiest if you just go and don't drag it out."

"I suppose you're right. But I still don't feel good about this. Come on, Bobby, let's go to grandma."

She placed my hand in her mother's hand. My grandmother led me over to her rocking chair, sat down, tried to pull me onto her lap; but I stepped to the side.

My mother hugged me, gave me a kiss, and said, "Have a nice time, Bobby. We'll be back soon. I promise. As soon as possible. We love you."

She then gave me another kiss and turned to go. But before she made it to the stairs, I dove, wrapped both arms around her leg and started crying, "No. Don't go. I won't let you."

My grandfather, a husky man with deep wrinkles in his face and dull black eyes, burst onto the porch through the screen door. He was a retired boss from a steel mill. He yelled, "What the hell's going on here? I've been watching from the window. My kids never did anything like this. Never allowed it. That's all there was to it. He's spoiled. Plain and simple goddamned spoiled. For Christ's sake, Clare, you'll be here all day at this rate. Go. Go on. Let go, Bobby!"

"Now, Daddy!"

"Now Daddy nothing. Let her go, Bobby. I said, let her go."

I squeezed my arms around her leg as tightly as I could. My grandfather grabbed my leg and yanked me toward the door. My mother fell backward on the floor.

My grandfather yelled, "Now look what you've done! If you had let her go, this wouldn't have happened. You okay, Clare?"

"Now don't blame him."

My grandfather reached down to help her up.

My mom gave him a quick look. "No, no thanks. You've been enough help already. Oh, my knee." She was now standing, leaning against the rail and rubbing her knee.

My father came forward and said, "Are you all right, honey?"

"Yes, I'm fine. Bobby, come here."

I started to crawl to my mom as she stepped toward me, but her father stepped between us.

"Time to get going, Clare. You can have one last goodbye and then you and your husband leave. That's all you can do."

"But..."

"But nothing. Enough is enough! Now say goodbye and be gone. Everything will be fine if you would just leave. Don't worry. Now go."

My mother said, "I don't like this."

"Neither do I," said her father. "Things have got to change if you want us to watch him again. Now, goodbye. Drive safely."

My mother gave me a hug and kiss, set me on my grandmother's lap and walked away with my father. I had given up and stopped crying. Partway down the walk my parents stopped, talked, and glanced back at me several times. My mom blew me a kiss and said, "I love you. We'll be back soon."

My father grinned and said. "Now you behave yourself, Bobby. See you in a few days."

They turned, rushed to the car, and as they drove away, my mother blew me another kiss.

Sadness overwhelmed me after they left. I didn't do anything: didn't swim in the pool, didn't play with my cousins, didn't go fishing, didn't bake with my grandmother, didn't even watch cartoons. I just lay on the floor and in bed, sat on the porch and watched cars go by in hopes of seeing my parents. But they didn't come. My grandfather yelled at me for not doing anything, but not often because I stayed away from him. Grandma tried to encourage me to do something to get my mind off of them, but it was of no use. At least I wasn't acting up; I wasn't acting at all.

On the night of their expected return, I sat up out of my sleep wide-awake. My heart was pounding. I sat for a long time staring into the darkness; tried to lie down and go back to sleep, but my eyes wouldn't close. My mind was racing. Slowly, emptiness filled the room. I began to feel separate from everything and then I became afraid. I walked out into the living room and found my grandmother in her chair alone, crying.

For some reason, I felt that I needed to comfort her. My fear passed as I crawled up onto her lap, wrapped my arms around her neck and said, "It'll be all right, grandma. Everything will be all right."

She held me away from her, looked deeply into my eyes, then she drew me against her breasts, which heaved heavily.

"What's a matter, grandma. Why so sad?"

She didn't answer. Her silence brought back my fear and separateness. I felt something terrible had happened, something she would never be able to fix.

Slowly one by one she forced her words. "Bobby, I just got a call from the police. They said your parents were killed in a car wreck."

"No. No. Mommy, Daddy coming back. They not dead. They coming back."

"I'm sorry, Bobby. I'm really sorry. But, they won't be coming home."

I held onto her and cried.

Chapter 2

Shortly after my parents' deaths, my grandfather delivered me to Aunt Alice and Uncle Jake. They already had eight kids. After being told not to play in mud puddles, I couldn't resist a nice one on the way home from school one day. It was big and warm and almost deep enough for me to float. I was having the time of my life when I looked up and saw Aunt Alice, on her way home from downtown, standing over me.

"How many times have we told you not to play in mud puddles? Get out! Look at you now! Those are your good school clothes. I've got enough kids to take care of without you making a mess of yourself."

"I'm sorry. I promise, I'll never do it again!"

"Get out! Now!"

I got out and gave her a big smile.

"Oh, you and that grin. You've won me over before but not this time."

A few days later I was dropped at Aunt Sharon's. She met us in front of her clean concrete driveway. She wore a plain, blue dress and her hair in a bun. She was tall and thin and had a long skinny neck. A forced smile, as she said hello to Aunt Alice and shook her hand, cracked her face. She looked down at me with cold, scrutinizing eyes.

As Alice drove away, Sharon grabbed me by my shirtsleeve and marched me into the garage.

I jumped as she shot the air with a loud, shrill voice. "Here," she pointed with her long, bony finger, "before you come into the house leave your shoes right here on the mat."

I kicked them onto the mat.

"No, not like that! Place them next to each other off to one side. Where am I supposed to put my shoes!?"

"Come on," she yelled, "hurry up!" She pushed me through the door and led me into a bedroom. The walls were white. There was a single bed in the corner and beside it a dresser. That was it.

"This is your room." She said as she opened the dresser drawer.

"Open your suitcase!"

Before I reached the button, she shouted, "God you're slow." She snatched the suitcase out of my hand, placed it on the bed, and opened it.

"Good God. What a mess! Who did this!?"

"I don't know."

"Don't lie to me. I catch you lying and I'll take a stick to you. Now tell me, who did this?" She looked at me as though she already had the stick in her hand.

"I guess Aunt Alice did it." I lied again.

She stared at me with a suspicious, evil eye. "You will be neat here. None of this stuff. Do you hear me?"

"Yes."

"I mean what I say."

She pulled a pair of pants out of the suitcase. "The bottom drawer is for pants only. Second drawer for shirts and sweaters, and the top drawer underwear and socks." She started folding and putting my clothes away. "Don't you just throw your clothes in here. I want them folded and put away neatly just like this. Don't think you can get away with anything. Nothing gets past me."

She scowled. "What? What is it? What do you want now?"

Sheepishly I said, "Could I have something to eat?"

"Hungry already, huh?"

"I haven't eaten yet."

"Come on."

She led me by the arm into the kitchen, pulled out a chair at one end of a small, rectangular, white table, and shoved me into it.

"You sit here. That will be your chair. What do you eat? Never mind, this isn't a restaurant. You'll eat whatever I make."

She set a tuna fish sandwich and bowl of vegetable soup in front of me complete with place mat and napkin. She stood over me, arms locked on her flat, bony chest, and corrected me as I ate. Part way through eating, my stomach became so knotted-up that I couldn't eat anymore, even though I was still hungry. I sat back in the chair and looked out the window at a couple hummingbirds drinking slowly from a feeder. I wished I were one of them.

She shoved the plate against my chest. "We don't waste food in this house. You eat everything on your plate, even if you have to sit here all afternoon."

I managed to swallow everything without puking on her.

Wasn't long before I felt like a captured invader in a foreign land. And I was only a little kid. I couldn't move without her jumping on me. Everything I did disrupted her mysterious order. Not knowing how to move without being criticized can be hard on a little boy; take my word for it. I was constantly on the verge of tears.

One afternoon she ordered me to peel carrots for some chicken soup. She spread newspaper on the counter and said, "Make sure all the peels land on the paper. Here are the carrots and peeler. I have to go check the wash. I'll be right back. Remember, on the paper."

I flipped the peels off the paper, on the counter, on the wall, even turned around and shot some on her shiny, spotless floor. I was laughing and peeling like crazy when she re-entered the kitchen.

She jammed her hands on her hips and yelled. "What do you think you're doing?" She grabbed my arm, and yanking the peeler out of my hand, gashed it.

I screamed, "Leave me alone! Leave me alone!" I smeared blood across the counter as I swept everything onto the floor. I ran out the door crying.

She caught me before I got out of the driveway, dragged me to her car as I fought her, shoved me inside; and without saying a word but glaring at me most of the way, drove to Aunt Patsy's and Uncle Ed's, and dumped me on the curb.

Both Ed and Patsy had big empty holes. Everything they had fell into their holes. Even their kids seemed to be falling into their big empty holes. They had one of the biggest houses in town with a lot of empty rooms filled with stuff. Yet, when I was there, they were talking about buying a bigger house because their house just wouldn't do anymore. Almost every day they bought something new, especially Aunt Patsy. Shortly afterward it would begin to slip into their big empty holes and disappear. Then they would go out and buy more and more things to try to fill their holes, but everything would just fall out of sight. Sometimes, if you dared to get close enough to their holes, you could here a voice screaming, "Give me more. Give me more." One

13

day Uncle Ed was complaining about what he didn't like about their cars, and then the next day there were two new cars in the driveway, and they too began to slide through the blacktop into the emptiness. If Ed and Patsy could have somehow owned the entire world, I'm sure it would have disappeared into their big empty holes, leaving them lost in space with nothing else to buy.

One day my cousin Eddie was showing me his trophies while I was sitting on his bed. Eddie was small, lean; had brown eyes and dusty brown hair. He talked with a whine, almost as though he were begging, and rarely made eye contact. He was always moving; even when he sat, he jiggled his legs. His bedroom was at the other end of the house from his parents' bedroom.

"This one here, isn't it nice. I got this one when I was only seven years old. Got it for coming in first in my first freestyle swim race."

He passed some ribbons lying on his dresser as he walked toward some more trophies.

I said, "What are the ribbons for?"

Without looking back, he said, "Nothing. Hey, look at this one, this big one. Won first place for a relay race in the state finals. I'm really a good swimmer, and you know, last year in baseball, I hit three home runs. This year I'm going to hit more than anyone."

"Let's go outside and play." I said.

"No. Stay here. Don't you want to see more of my trophies?"

"No. Let's go outside."

"I bet you don't have any trophies. I bet you've never even been in a swim meet." He laughed at me.

That night we went to a swim meet. All along the way Uncle Ed was telling him what to do. "Remember when you push off, as soon as your hands leave the edge of the pool, start stroking as hard and as fast as you can. Don't look around at the other kids. Keep your head back so the water flows along the side of your face. Last swim meet you could have had first if you hadn't started looking around. You've got to keep your body straight and streamlined to cut down the water resistance. Can you remember that, or should I write it on your trunks?"

"I can remember."

"Stoke with all your strength. Count to yourself, 'one two, one two, one two,' just as your coach taught you." He went on and on and on all the way to the meet.

I watched Eddie's frail frame walk alone to the edge of the pool. Not talking to anyone, he jumped into the pool and curled up at the edge. The whistle blew and off went the racers, kicking and stroking as if their lives depended on it. Eddie quickly fell behind, and the more he fell behind, the more he started to look around at the other kids, so by the end, his head was rocking from side to side. He took fourth out of eight. He quickly walked, head down, to the side of the pool and slipped into the showers.

No one talked all the way home, except right before we got out of the car, his father said, "Learn to keep that head straight, or else I won't take you to anymore swim meets. I can't be proud of a loser."

After that day, I let Eddie show me all his trophies and everything else he had ever won. We spent hours in his room. For as long as I stayed at his house, which wasn't long, I went to all his swim meets and cheered for him. He won a couple of races while I was there, but most of the time he'd finish somewhere in the middle, which really displeased and aggravated my aunt and uncle.

They weren't satisfied with Eddie trying his best to please them. They always wanted him to do better, to try harder, to perform as he could not perform. Sometimes he chewed his fingernails so much that his fingers bled.

And so, my cousin Eddie (I still feel for him), despite the many trophies he won, he still felt that he had failed his parents. It wouldn't have been so bad if they had accepted him at other times, walked up and kissed him when he was just sitting on the couch or taken him swimming just for the fun of it or told him that they loved him; no, the only attention he got was when he won.

Eddie wasn't the only one. That day made such an impression on me that I watched my cousins and their parents all the time. You could say they became my objects of study. I became very quiet, almost manageable, and would sit on the sidelines and watch. My objects of study soon objected to my study of them. I had become too quiet. I was seeing too much. People are afraid of others, no matter what their age, who see too much.

One day, shortly after the swim meet, I was playing with some dolls in the yard; Uncle Ed, yes, Uncle Ed. Well, more like, no, Uncle Ed, no. Uncle Ed looked a lot like my mother's father, short, stocky, hard, deep-set eyes: a frown at home, a smile for his friends. He was well liked; maybe he would not have been if others had known what he was like at home. He retained the childlike quality of rapidly changing emotions. He would be smiling and laughing, then see something he didn't like and explode with anger and start screaming, and then, just as quickly, shake his head and start joking around. He would often pause in mid-sentence, sometimes for a long time, then resume with what he was talking about or talk about something completely different. Once he sent a piercing fear through me that I have never again experienced. Eddie and I had left some cars we had been playing with in a long closet in the basement. There was a stiff hard chair that faced one of the long blank walls. Later, I went back to get our cars. I could barely see, but found the cars anyway, and while I was kneeling on the floor picking them up, I felt someone's presence, and turning to my left, only inches from me, Uncle Ed was sitting in the chair. He didn't look at me, didn't move, and just stared as though he were dead. I left as quietly as I could. I trembled for the rest of the day. Since then, he has always given me the strangest look.

Anyway, that day in the yard he stood over me and yelled. "What the hell are you doing playing with dolls? Put them back! You're a boy, aren't you? Or do you want to be a girl? Oh no, don't tell me I have a queer boy living under my roof."

"I was pretending they were my brothers and sisters."

"Oh, I don't believe my ears. I must be hearing things. Do that again if you can."

I continued to play quietly with my head down.

"I said talk again!"

"About what?"

"Different words this time! I never knew you knew so many words."

"I did."

"Don't get smart with me."

"I'm not."

"What are you looking at all the time?"

"The world around me."

"I said don't get smart! You know what I mean. You don't talk like you used to. You sit and watch us."

"I don't have family of my own, so I watch yours. Whose else do I have to watch?"

"What do you see?"

"Oh, I don't know."

"Don't give me that shit! I can see your mind registering. I'm ordering you to tell me." He grabbed me by the arm, jerked me up, and twisted me toward him.

"Okay! Okay! Let go of my arm!"

"Don't tell me what to do." His squeeze tightened. "Tell me."

Hurt and angry, I spoke without caring about the consequences.

"You never ask Eddie how he feels. All you want him to do is win those stupid races. You should be happy to have a boy who tries as hard as he does to please you. Will he ever win enough races for you? Do you think he really wants to be in those races?"

"Who the hell do you think you are? Who do you think you are talking to? It's none of your business how I raise my kids. Insolent little shit. You should be grateful for having a roof over your head."

"You should be like me. I don't have a family and neither should you."

He raised his arm. "You fuckin', little, wiseass bastard. You are a bastard son, aren't you? What do you know? When I'm with my kids, I don't care where we are; I don't want you around. You'll eat alone, play alone; you're not a part of my family. You've got no business thinking what you're thinking."

I said, "Why get mad at me. I only did what you wanted me to. Why ask a question if you don't want an answer?"

He slapped me across the face to the ground. "One more word out of you, Bobby, and you'll regret it. Shut that stupid mouth of yours." He stomped off.

I cried quietly to myself, "I'm not stupid. I'm not a bastard. Mommy Daddy, where are you?"

Chapter 3

Next day I was loaded into the back seat of Uncle Ed's car. I didn't know where I was going; how far away I would be taken, or if I was to be delivered to another relative, stranger, or taken to an orphanage. I was afraid that I had run out of relatives and would be taken to a place where I would never be wanted and never feel at home. All I knew was that I was in a back seat alone being taken somewhere with what few clothes I had thrown beside me. I was trying not to cry, but couldn't control myself. I was lucky Aunt Patsy was there, or else Uncle Ed probably would have hurt me. In a short while, we stopped in front of a brown house surrounded by an unmowed, weedy lawn.

Ed got out of the car, opened my door, glared at me and sneered, "Get your stuff! Hurry up! The sooner I get rid of you the better."

Aunt Patsy raised her voice. "Ed!"

"Don't Ed me. Come on kid; time to tell someone else how to raise their kids."

I grabbed what clothes I could. As I stepped out of the car, some of them fell on the ground. Patsy came around the back of the car and helped me.

"Here, Bobby, I'll get the rest for you."

Ed laughed. "Why bother. He probably doesn't like any of the things we bought him anyway. He sure knows the meaning of gratitude."

Patsy stuffed some clothes in Ed's folded arms. "Here, carry these."

He spread his arms apart, letting the clothes fall to the ground. "I've done all I'm going to do."

Patsy lowered her eyebrows. Her face went pale as she said, "Good! That's just fine! Could you once, just once in your life, stop acting like a child?"

Ed pressed Patsy against the car. "Watch it! You always feel real brave when we're at your big brother's. Remember, you're going home with me." He squeezed her arms as he glared in her eyes. Then he stepped back, threw his arms in the air, and laughed, "Oh, what the hell. Why am I getting so angry? Sure, come on Bobby let's go see your new home."

He picked the clothes off the ground. Patsy winked at me and smiled. Together, as one little happy family, we walked up the front walk.

Unlike Uncle Ed's, the sidewalk to my new home was cracked, short and narrow. From the car, the house looked well kept, but as we got closer, it was plain to see that much of the paint was falling off, and as we stepped onto the worn wooden porch, our shoes scraped off some surface rot. The bottom of the screen door was broken, and holes in the screen were patched with gray tape.

Ed rolled his eyes and said, "Yep, this is your brother's house all right. Things don't change around here." He banged on the screen door and yelled, "Anybody home?"

A clear voice from inside, "Come in."

We stepped inside to find Uncle John, dressed in a jean shirt and pants, setting a book on a glass coffee table as he rose off the couch. His pale, round face lit up when he saw his sister. "Well, hello sis. Good to see you."

She smiled and said, "Good to see you too. Wish it were under better circumstances."

They gave each other a warm, close hug. Ed twitched his neck, put his hand on John's shoulder, pulled him away from Patsy, and shoved his hand into his.

Ed grinned and laughed, "Well, if I didn't know better I'd think you were making a pass at my wife. How's it going, old buddy?"

In a solemn voice John replied, "Oh, you came along too. Hello Ed."

"Well, isn't that one hell of a welcome. What's wrong with me?"

"If you don't know by now, then you'll never know."

Patsy stepped between them. "Now, let's not start." She put her hands on both of them. "Don't you know how it hurts me to see the two most important men in my life not get along. Come on, please, let's put it aside. Do it for me. Okay? Me and Bobby."

Ed glanced down at me, looked coldly at his wife, and said, "I'll do it for you. But, on second thought, I'd rather leave. Come on, let's go. I've already had enough. The kid is here.

"Where is he anyway? There's that rascal over by the door." Ed laughed the laugh of power and revenge, reached back, grabbed me by the arm, and jerked me through the air to Uncle John. "Make yourself at home, Bobby. Because this is it. How do you like it?"

I lowered my eyes on the speckled brown, shag carpet and stepped behind John.

Uncle John put his arm around me and said, "It's okay, Bobby. He won't hurt you anymore. If I had only known."

Ed smiled, laughed, then set his hard dark eyes on Uncle John as anger distorted his face. "If you had only known what? Hey Bobby, go outside and play. Your uncles are going to have a man to man talk."

I didn't want to go outside. Although I was still terrified of Uncle Ed, I wanted to hear what they were going to say about me.

Adults always think, no matter how you feel or what's going on around you, that you're always in the mood to play, that you have a little play switch inside your head just itching to be turned on. And yet, at other times, they would talk about me in front of others as though I didn't exist, as though I were a dog, a stone without feelings.

I grabbed John's hand and pulled it to me.

He looked down at me, smiled, and said, "I think you and I are thinking the same thing. Come, let's sit on the couch."

He put his arm around me. "You know, Bobby, my parents shielded me, not completely of course, from the world. And I did much the same to my children. There are just certain things children should not see or hear. But then, when the child grows up and begins to move about, he is confused by this new world, by the strange things he sees people say and do, and he can go through life at odds believing that somehow the world has changed, usually for the worse. The world is as good and as bad as it always has been. So, Bobby, as long as you live with your Uncle John, I'll let you experience the world, within reason that is."

He laughed and hugged me.

Then his face lost expression as he turned toward Ed. "For your information, Bobby is in my care now. It's not your place to tell him what to do. Please, sit down."

"Yeah, I'll sit down all right. On the porch where the air is fresh."

Ed gave John a dirty look and slammed the door as he went onto the porch. He crossed in front of the windows to the end of the porch, dragged a white plastic chair back across next to the screen door, dropped himself into it and yelled, "Hurry up and say what you want to say, Patsy."

Patsy was tall, but still much shorter than her brother, thin and good looking except for the fear in her hazel eyes. She threw her hands in the air and plopped in the worn, gray armchair across from John. She grabbed the hem of her tight, red dress and wiggled it down, then crossed her slender legs, dropped her arms over the side of the chair, threw her long, brown hair back, and sighed, "Why does everything have to be so hard? Why can't we just have a nice little chat? Are all families like this? Is there any peace? I would just love, I really would, I'd love to just sit here and talk and smile and laugh and just have a good time together as we used to.

"Where's Marty anyway?"

"She took Cindy to the dentist to have her braces adjusted. She should be here by now."

"Oh good. I'd love to see her.

"Here, Bobby, come here and sit on my lap for a minute." I looked up at Uncle John. He smiled and nodded his head.

She leaned forward, arms outstretched, and said, "Please, Bobby. For me, please?"

I thought her request strange because she had never asked me to sit on her lap at her house. Reluctantly I walked over, sat on her lap sideways with my head down, and looked at patterns in the rug.

In a quiet voice she said, "I'll miss having you around, Bobby. If it were up to me, you would still be staying with us. But, it's for your own good. I think you'll be much happier here with John and Marty."

Without looking up, I said, "I think so too."

"I'm sorry about what happened. I really feel bad. I'm sorry I couldn't protect you. I'm barely able to protect myself and my own children."

Ed charged through the screen door. "I heard that! It's all my fault, again! I'm the one to blame. Bullshit! If you'd just put your foot down once in a while, things wouldn't get so out of control for me to take care of them. You're such a pansy, Patsy. You let the kids run all over you.

"I'm not going to stand around and let the kids, anybody's kid, mouth off to me. He even had Eddie mouthing back, telling me, just the other night, that he's not coming to dinner because he doesn't feel like it. I made him feel like it soon enough. And that's why Bobby is here. Because he mouths off and does as he damn well pleases. I won't have it! And you shouldn't have allowed it either. If you had been just a little bit firm, things wouldn't have gotten this far. So don't go blaming me!"

By then he was standing over her yelling.

In a subdued, tearful voice she said, "Yes, Ed. You are right. It's all my fault. It's all my fault that you are such an angry person. It's all my fault that you are humiliating me in front of my brother."

Uncle John stood tall, pulled back his broad shoulders and stuck out his massive chest. "Sis, you don't have to protect yourself in my house. And you don't have to try to protect Bobby anymore either. You're under my roof now. I won't put up with this crap in my house."

Ed interrupted, "So that's what you call this run-down shack."

"As a matter of fact, no," said John, "this is my home. A word you don't know the meaning of."

John jabbed his finger at Ed. "Nothing is wrong with you. No, it can't be your fault. Well, open your eyes because it is. You're the only reason Bobby is here. Yeah, that's right. For Christ's sake, he lost his mother, lost his father; he's all alone in the world, and what did you do? Did you think about caring for him? Hell no! You knocked him around. Don't look at me like that. I know. Look at me like that again, and I'll show you what it feels like to get knocked around."

Ed glared at Patsy with dagger eyes. I felt afraid for her.

John continued, "You know what it is? It's not that Bobby mouths off. Like all children, he probably tells the truth. That's what you can't stand. Why don't you do everybody a favor and go get some therapy?"

"I'm not taking this shit from you."

Uncle John turned to me. "Bobby, you don't need to experience everything. I was wrong. You've seen enough of Ed and his anger.

"I'll be more than happy to care for you. You're welcome here and you can rest assured that no one here will hurt you." He turned to Patsy. "I'm sorry it happened this way."

With a subdued voice she said, "That's all right. What else should I have expected. I've stopped believing in miracles."

"Let's go," Ed ordered. "The job is done. The kid is here. I didn't want to come to begin with. Come on, get up Patsy. Let's go."

"I'll meet you in the car."

"No you won't! You're leaving now."

Patsy eased me onto the floor. "Bye, Bobby. I'm sorry. I really am."

She followed her husband to the door, but as he stepped through the doorway, John stepped between them, shut the inside door, and locked it.

Ed yanked open the screen door, shook the door knob, kicked the door and screamed, "Open the goddamn door. Goddamnit, open it."

John yelled, "I'm talking to my sister for a minute. Don't worry; we won't say a thing, no, not one single thing about you. I'd hate for you to feel paranoid."

Ed laughed and slammed the screen door.

Patsy drooped her arms over her brother's shoulders and laid her head on his chest. He put his arms around her narrow waist.

In a soft, desperate voice she said, "I don't know how much more of this I can take. He's just getting more and more angry. I don't know what it is. I just don't. He's making more money than he can spend. I don't know what pressure he's under, but it's something.

"Every day he comes home he seems to be more and more upset. He paces around the house. He's like a caged animal. I just feel so trapped and afraid. I just don't know anymore. I can't live like this much longer. Every time we talk, he gets mad. And I don't know why.

"Someday, I'm afraid; oh, I don't know. I'm afraid all the time. He was so sweet to me when we first met. But, now, he doesn't love me. And I've lost all love and respect for him. John, what am I going to do? What am I going to do?"

"You need to get away from him."

"I know. But I can't. He'll follow me wherever I go. He's said that."

"You can always come stay with us."

"How could I with the kids? There's hardly enough room for your family."

"We'll make room."

Patsy turned and looked out the window. "Oh, he's standing there staring at the house. Am I going to hear about it now. I'd better go."

"Has he hit you?"

"No. He probably would have if I didn't have so many brothers."

She hugged her brother, kissed his cheek, then smiled and said, "Don't be surprised if I show up at your door soon. Real soon."

She stepped away. Her eyes were red; her mouth quivered.

"If it's that bad just stay here now. I'll take care of everything," John said.

"Oh no, not now. You've got Bobby and all, and oh, I'd better go."

John opened the door for her. "Take care, sis. I'll call you later. Be careful. If anything happens let me know. Okay?"

"Yeah, sure."

Uncle John took her by the arm. "I'm serious."

"I will. Really, I will."

"You'd better."

"Don't worry, John; I will."

"You be careful now."

"Talk to you later. Bye." Patsy said as she took his hand.

"Later."

Patsy cautiously walked out to the car. Ed gave her the silent look of death. Without looking at him, she walked around his car and got in. Ed stood for a while staring at the house, then threw open the car door, jumped inside, slammed the door, and raced off.

Partly to me, partly to himself John said, "I'm worried about my sister. She's in a dangerous situation. I saw that in Ed from the very beginning. I even warned Patsy about it, but she was carried away by him, and I just didn't think it would ever get this bad."

Chapter 4

John plopped on the couch next to me and gave me a hard hug.

"Well, Bobby, welcome to your new home. Come on, little buddy, let's get you settled in."

Still frightened from the last few days and by what had just happened, I said in a weak voice, "Okay."

He grabbed my things that Ed had thrown on the couch, turned right in front of the kitchen, took a few steps into a narrow hallway then right through a doorway into a bedroom. I followed behind feeling that it was all make-believe.

He dumped the clothes on a lower bunk bed, sat, and said, "This is my son Dave's room. He's away at college. Boy, it's been so long since we've had a little one in the house. Here, you can sleep on the bottom bunk. It's comfortable. Want to try it out?" He gave the bed a hearty pat.

His voice came from far off in the distance. I lifted my eyes off the rug to his outstretched arms dangling in the air, long fingers, his crooked teeth and thin parched lips; looked up to his glazed, lifeless, blue eyes that hung in a sickening pink blur. I froze. I didn't want to go to him, didn't want to go back to Uncle Ed's, didn't want to go anywhere I'd been, but desperately wanted to go somewhere. I didn't know it at the time, at least not consciously, but I wanted to go home.

I lowered my eyes onto the carpet hoping that everything would go away.

I was flying a kite in a wide-open field on a cool, breezy day. The kite went higher and higher. The string was reeling out faster and faster. The string came to an end on the spool, but luckily it was tied tight. I pulled the spool to my chest as hard as I could. The kite lifted me off the ground and carried me away.

"Come here, Bobby." He paused. "It's okay." Pause. "I won't hurt you."

I heard him stand up. I stepped back. I heard him sit back down.

"I'm really sorry, Bobby. If I had known you could have come here instead of staying with Ed. Marty and I discussed it. We did and thought you'd be happier living with some of your cousins the same age as you. It was a mistake. I'm sorry. Marty and I should have known."

I heard a woman's soft, clear voice say, "There you two are. I finally made it. I took Cindy over to Wendy's house. I wish I'd been here when you came, Bobby, but, oh, what's wrong!?"

John said, "Too much of Ed."

The soft, clear voice, "I was afraid of that."

The soft voice put her arms around me from behind and said, "You remember me, don't you?"

Eyes still on the carpet, "No."

"I most certainly remember you."

Silence.

The soft voice took my hand. "Come with me. I bet you're hungry, huh?"

"Sort of."

"Well, why don't we go out in the kitchen together and make us something to eat. How does that sound?"

"Okay. I guess."

She led me into the kitchen which formed an L shape with the living room.

"How about a grilled cheese sandwich, tomato soup, and let's see, grapes?"

I couldn't speak.

"You know what I need? I need some bread. Could you be my little helper and, right over there by the toaster, could you get me some bread?"

I got her the bread.

"Thank you."

Silence.

"I don't know about you, but I feel like getting out. I was in the house and in town all morning. How about we go for a little boat ride after lunch. Get out of here for a while. What do you say, Bobby."

I looked up at her and was stunned by the intensity in her blue-grey eyes. I immediately looked down. What hit me and what I'll always remember about Aunt Marty was the penetrating look in her eyes. They saw everything. The world passed through her eyes. When she looked at me I lost all protection. And when I looked into her eyes, as I did before looking away, I felt I was passing through them — my feelings, thoughts, everything past and future. She had eyes from which you could not hide. The intensity in her eyes frightened me, yet, at the same time, I felt she cared about me.

She turned around. I looked up her straight back, broad shoulders, black hair that waved down to the center of her back, and felt relieved that she wasn't looking at me; but suddenly she turned around, looked me straight in the eye without saying anything, and I disappeared.

Uncle John strolled into the kitchen, placed his hands on Marty's hips and asked, "Am I included in this feast?"

She leaned back against him, "Of course."

Uncle John turned to me, "Hey Bobby, would you help me set the table? I can show you where everything is."

I no longer felt so far away. "Sure."

We carried the plates, silverware, etc. out to a round wooden table in the corner of the L between the kitchen and living room.

Soon the air was filled with the smell of food and lively talk.

John said, "How'd everything go at the dentist office?"

"Everything went fine. Another five hundred dollars. Her teeth are straightening out at the rate he thought they would. She'll look so much better when they're straight. I'm glad we're doing it, although it's money we don't need to spend. She'll feel so much better about herself, as if she doesn't feel pretty good about herself now. I'm happy about how our kids are turning out. They're really pleasant to be with."

"Yes. They're great kids, if I must say so myself."

"Next time you'll have to come to the dentist with us and watch him adjust her braces. He takes this little..."

Marty went into a long detailed explanation of how Cindy's braces were adjusted. Uncle John listened with interest. They talked all during lunch. John only said a few things about my arrival.

Marty did most of the talking about her conversations with friends in town, the way the town square was being redone, the wind as it came up and died down, and the swirling clouds of dust that spun through a parking lot. And that was how it was in their house. Never did they seem bored with each other's talk, never talked to fill an empty space or a yawn. And I wasn't surprised later on in life when I read some of John's writing to find Marty's descriptions.

At the end of lunch, Marty said, "I was thinking of taking Bobby to Willow Lake. Would you like to come?"

"Oh, let me think." John paused, stared at his hands as he fiddled with a fork. "No, I think I'd rather stay home and read and try to get some writing done. Do you mind?"

"No. Well, it would be nice to be together, but I understand. Your free time is limited. So we can get going and be back before dark, would you mind cleaning up?"

John looked around. Instead of lunch for three, it looked as though thanksgiving dinner for fifty had been prepared.

John grinned. "Are you serious? I'll do the dishes if you put everything away. What did you use all this stuff for?"

"Oh, I don't know. You know me."

She put her hand on mine. "Come on, Bobby, help me, okay?"

We put everything away. She got a paper bag from between the white refrigerator and white metal cabinet, grabbed some peaches and apples out of the bottom of the fridge, put them in the bag, filled water bottles, grabbed a jacket, told me to get one, kissed her husband; and as we were leaving, said, "See you later, honey."

He turned around at the sink, swayed from side to side and said softly, "I'll be here ready, willing and wanting."

She threw her right hand out, laughed, and away we went.

After a short drive we were sauntering through some woods on a narrow path. The air was fresh and cool from the previous night's rain. Fallen leaves on that early autumn afternoon were soft under our feet. Within the green foliage were flashes of bright red, orange, and yellow that signaled the coming of winter. A sudden gust blew leaves far off into the distance.

Marty veered left into a small cluster of pines. She bent down amidst some short broad plants and said, "Look here, Bobby." She pulled back some leaves, and there at the fork in the stem hung a yellow fruit the size of an egg. "Here. Would you like to try one? They're called May apples. They're quite tasty." She picked another one and ate it. I bit off a tiny piece.

"Well, do you like the way it tastes."

"They're good. I like it here."

As she glanced around, a thoughtful look came upon her face.

"Yes. So do I. We used to come here often; I mean our family, but now Dave's off to college, and Cindy would rather be with her friends; and your Uncle John, he'll come with me sometimes, but he's really not here when he does come. I come by myself, but it's much nicer having someone along. I'm alone a lot. Yes," she paused, "I have fond memories of this place when the kids were young."

She looked at me, rubbed my hair with her hand, then her thoughtful look was suddenly replaced by a lightness as her eyes lit up, and she smiled.

"Soon winter will be here." She took my hand and led me toward the lake. "The lake will freeze, and we'll be able to go ice-skating, build a fire, have hot chocolate. Lots of people come here then. The ice freezes smooth, like glass, and at times, on a cold, clear, sunny day, the snow will blow off the trees and come sparkling down with the colors of the rainbow. I don't know what time of year is most beautiful here. I really love the winters.

"Then in the spring, life just jumps out of the ground and..."

She talked all the way to the water about the seasons at the lake. And with every step not only did I feel we were getting closer to the lake but farther away from Uncle Ed.

Huge weeping willow trees, bordering the lake, hung lazily into the water. Their massive roots slithered all over the bank and up on land. Tied to one of these roots with a manila rope was a small, green, wooden rowboat. Marty held the boat against the roots as I climbed in. We pushed off, slid through the curtain of dangling willow branches, and quietly glided onto the lake.

The small lake was all ours. We were near the shallow end where a creek fed the lake. Marty would pull on the oars, lift them into the boat, and then look over the side for a while. Of course, I looked over the side with her and saw, not as though I had never looked into the water before, but, with her that day and many days afterward, I saw a whole other world. The seaweed swayed in the breeze of the water caused by the boat, and in that sway fresh water shrimp, small fish, beetles, crabs, and a few large fish darted about, just as my thoughts and feelings were darting about in the sways rippling through my life.

Once again, I was with someone new, and I was worried about whether they would like me or not, and how long I would be with them, for I feared that my new parents would not be unlike those in the past.

Everything below me was where it belonged, that was their home, and although the water was cold to my hand, I wanted to be with them.

"Aunt Marty, can I go in? Please?"

"Really?"

"Yeah."

"Sure. I guess. Take off your clothes. Those are the only ones we have with us."

I jumped in up to my chest. The water took my breath away. Dove in, felt the seaweed slide by, jumped up, dug my feet into the mud, and continued being a kid. I swam over toward the stream where it spread softly into the lake, sat in its warm waters and piled mud onto my legs. Some ducks, floating down the creek, spotted me and flew away. Marty glided next to me.

"Years ago, Bobby, this creek flowed headlong into the lake, creating a deep hole just about where you are sitting now. Slowly over the years the creek has brought down silt and dirt along its meandering path and created this small alluvium. Eventually our little creek down here will recede leaving behind its memory in the form of a swamp. Since I was a little girl, I've been watching the lake change. Year after year people come here, and I listen to them, and over and over I hear them say how it is just as they remembered it. Ta ha. Just as they remembered it! Just as the sun is the same every morning when it rises. It never feels the same. Nor are we the same day after day. Change is what gives things meaning; it forms characteristics. This creek, this lake, your life, my life; because mine when I was your age was not much different than yours; it may all seem haphazard, but somewhere in there's a thread, some meaning, a stream running through it carrying down experiences, and oh, you're so young. Why am I saying these things?

"Come on, hop in; let's get back before it gets dark."

She smiled, reached out her hand, and pulled me headlong, mud and all, into the boat. Quietly we rowed back toward the sleepy willows.

As we crossed the lake plants waved up through the mirrored surface. My aunts and uncles, Uncle Ed, everything was gone behind except for Aunt Marty, the boat and the lake. I leaned back against the rail and gazed at the willows. A spider's thread drifted vertically out of the willows and seized my attention. The silvery thread slowed as it passed in front of me. Through this thread was an opening to another world, and through it, I saw a silver lake that had never been seen by anyone else. All was peaceful, the willows hung in silence, fish glided through the swaying weeds; and as I looked up, the thread was still hanging through the sky, slowly drifting away, and I felt that things would get better. It floated away and disappeared in the shadows along the shore.

After holding the boat while Marty tied it up, I climbed onto a submerged root and washed off the mud. Marty took my hand, pulled me out, and helped me dress. Hand in hand we walked quietly back to the car, not without snacking at a persimmon tree on the way.

After she put me to bed that night, I lay for a long time thinking about her and the lake, and slowly but surely, in spite of my efforts, the strangeness of someone else's room crept in on me. The banners, the high stark dresser, pictures of strangers on the wall, the plain closet doors behind which something had to be hiding, the misty light coming through the partially drawn blinds, and the mess piled in the corner made me feel separate and alone. I saw a light beneath the door, and at first afraid of even moving, I finally stood, stared, then slowly opened the door and followed the light down the hall past the kitchen to its source in the living room. There beneath a lamp was Uncle John sitting at a long desk looking out the picture window. The outside light was on.

Still being a quiet observer, I stood and watched for what seemed to me a long time, and as I did, I felt a peacefulness coming from Uncle John. Slowly it made everything feel close again. I quietly lay on the couch and watched him: watched him write, lean back in his chair, tilt forward, write furiously for a while, stare out the picture window, rest his head on his arms, then raise up and write some more.

Now, as I sit here writing, I clearly remember those moments of watching him and feeling his serenity, being awed by seeing someone for the first time in my short life sitting alone without the television, thoroughly absorbed in what to me was a mysterious activity. That was my first and strongest influence to write.

Although, I didn't want to write, I wanted to be able to make a room feel that way.

Rested my head on my arm, and while watching John and feeling secure in the pool of calmness surrounding him, I slowly settled into sleep.

I dreamt someone was chasing me in a long white hall. At the end of the hall was a door. My legs were heavy, my knees ached. I tried with all my strength to run fast, but I could hardly lift my legs. I felt him getting closer and closer. Reached the door, slammed it behind me, bolted it, and ran straight across a barren white room to another door. I leaned against the door trying to catch my breath. He started pounding on the door behind me, harder and harder. The room began to shake. The door flew open against the wall. I rushed through the door and bolted it. The pounding started right away, and before I got halfway across the room, it started shaking, and the door slammed against the wall, and he was right behind me when I slammed the other door, locked it and ran; and that door slammed against the wall, and I barely made it through the next door, bolted it, and trudged across with leaden legs, looked up for the next door, but there wasn't one. The room was shaking violently; the door behind me crashed against the wall, and the room was shaking harder and harder, and as I staggered toward the wall, I felt him right behind me, his breath on my neck. He grabbed my shoulder, and I woke.

Someone was shaking my shoulder and saying, "Bobby, Bobby, wake up. You're having a bad dream. Bobby, look at me. Can you open your eyes? Bobby, look at me. Bobby, are you awake? I can't tell. Bobby, wake up! It's okay! It's okay!"

"No. No. Get away."

"Bobby, wake up! It's all right. You're having a bad dream."

"No. No. Oh, where am I?" I was partly in the dream, somewhat conscious of my surroundings, which were still foreign.

"You're at Uncle John's and Aunt Marty's. Remember you came here this morning. This is your first day here. You went to the lake today with Marty. Do you remember?"

"Oh."

"Come here, Bobby. Sit on my lap."

He pulled me onto his lap. Slowly he rocked me and stroked my hair as a room in a house in a town on a planet wobbling through space came back to me.

Softly he said, "Bobby, do you know where you are?"

"Oh, I think so. Yeah, now I remember. Another strange place."

"Soon I hope we won't be strangers to you, and maybe someday you'll call this place home. But for now, let's get you back to bed."

"No. I don't wanna go back in there. I don't wanna be alone in there."

"Would you like to sleep out here on the couch? I plan to be up for a while, so you won't be alone. I understand the way you feel. Sometimes I even get scared in my own room."

"Yeah, please let me sleep out here."

John fluffed a pillow, put it under my head, floated covers over me, and gave me a kiss goodnight. I slipped from Uncle John's peacefulness to the peacefulness of sleep.

Chapter 5

I enjoyed living with Uncle John and Aunt Marty. Moving in with them brought me great relief. After you fall and scrape your knee, the first thing you do is race home for your mother to make the hurt go away. I had fallen and was hurting at Ed's. John and Marty made most of the hurt go away. Not that they gave me a lot of love and attention. They didn't. But they were nice and did make me feel protected, and I felt, shortly after I arrived, that they would not hurt me. That, by itself, made me feel at home in their home.

Fall quickly stripped nature of her color. Winter settled in, and so did I. I became more and more comfortable at their place, made friends in the neighborhood, and was able to tolerate school. What seemed like overnight, spring re-dressed mother nature with her usual springtime colors.

One cool, spring night Marty went out with some of her friends to the movies while, as what happened every Tuesday night, Uncle John had a card game. Usually, I was put to bed or told to go play in my room before John's friends came over, but this night I was determined to be a part of the action, so I became an agreeable, little helper. Never left John's side. So when I heard the usual, "Time for bed now, Bobby," I was ready with endearing eyes, a sweet smile, and a pleading voice, "Uncle John, could I please stay up? Please!? I've done everything you said, and you know what you said when I first came here that I should experience...what'd you say anyway?"

"Why you little bugger." He gazed down at me with amused eyes as he brushed his hand over my hair. "Experience the world as it is. Okay, you can stay up for a while, but, and I mean it, when I say time for bed, you go to bed. Right?"

Smiled my brightest smile. "You know it, Uncle John."

Al was the first to arrive, or more correctly, to appear what seemed out of nowhere. He was so quiet that both John and I suddenly noticed him sitting at the dining room table. He was there, small and pale, staring at his hands as he rubbed them together. He wore gray pants and a light blue shirt with dark blue stripes. It was buttoned tight around his neck. I wondered how he breathed. He jerked his head up as though shocked that someone would talk to him when John spoke with his usual friendliness.

"Hey Al, what'd you do — float out of the ceiling? I didn't even hear you come in."

In a dead serious tone, "This really isn't me. It's a mirage." He smirked.

"Really, where'd you come in?"

"Right through the front door."

"For Christ's sake, somebody could rob me while I'm home and I'd never know it. Want a beer?"

"No thanks." Al returned his eyes to his hands.

"What's wrong? You don't look like you're feeling up to snuff?" John leaned back against the counter.

Al sighed, "Oh nothing."

John mimicked Al, "Oh nothing." He retrieved his usual voice. "Right! I know you. You know me. We're friends. Come on, what's wrong?"

He stared at his hands without responding then looked up. "Oh, I'm just not feeling too great. My stomach has been bothering me."

"Well here, want a glass of milk?" John turned toward the refrigerator. "Maybe this will help."

"Sure."

John poured the milk in a glass as he walked toward Al and set it down in front of him. "This should make you feel better. You up for a game?"

"Of course. I look forward to this every week. It's one of the only times I get out."

"Good."

The house vibrated as in stomped Roger, letting the screen door slam behind him. Not only his size but his mouth made you aware of his presence. Everything about him was big, especially his jean overalls. I believed he was Santa Claus's jolly younger brother.

He rubbed his hands together, smiled and boomed, "I hope you boys went to the bank today because I'm feeling awful lucky. I feel so lucky that it's gonna break my heart to clean out you two unfortunate souls."

"So tell me, John," Roger slapped him on the shoulder, "what goodies did Marty fix for us tonight?"

"Just feast your eyes on this."

"Hmmm, this looks so good I might feel bad about takin' all your money."

As he chomped on an egg salad sandwich, he noticed me standing next to John.

"Hey Bobby, what are you doing up?"

"I'm gonna take all your money."

Roger looked at John. "What kinda influence you havin' on this kid anyway." He stared down at me from ten stories and waved his tree limb arms toward my room. "Nighty night, Bobby boy. Off to bed."

Uncle John patted me on the head. "I told him he could stay up for a while to see a bit of the real world."

Roger bit off half a donut and mumbled, "Come on, you're not serious. Are you?"

"Yeah. It's part of his education to see how people really are. Don't worry. He won't get in the way."

I poked Roger in his beach ball stomach and said, "Is that real?"

"No! Nothing is real except the dreams in your sleep, so you'd better go to bed."

Uncle John took a swig of his beer, smiled, and said to Roger, "He writes some great little stories. Bobby, go get one of your stories and read it to Roger for me."   ·

"Sure."

Standing tall against the refrigerator, I read, "Don't underestimate the little guy. Once upon a time there was a mommy, daddy, and baby flea. A blackbird came out of the sky and ate mommy and daddy. The baby flea hopped on a hawk. The hawk flew by the blackbird. The flea hopped off the hawk on the blackbird. Ever since then the blackbird had fleas. The end."

Uncle John slapped Roger on the back. "I just love his stories. That's a new one, isn't it?"

"Yeah. I wrote it after school."

Roger shook his head as he stuffed his mouth with potato chips. "All right. All right. Let's play cards. Where's Carl?"

The question was the message and in walked Carl.

Carl walked with an easy rhythmic stride. He was tall, lanky, and had a calm, youthful, handsome face. He always wore colorful clothes. He played the piano and usually wore sunglasses, even at night. John and he wrote songs together. John usually wrote the words, Carl the music. John's house was Carl's second home.

Uncle John lit up. "Hey buddy, you're just the man we've been looking for. Hope you brought a lot of money because Roger plans on taking us to the cleaners."

Carl responded in his cool, casual way. "Every man needs a dream to keep him going."

Roger puffed, "Dream! Reality man, I'm talking reality."

Carl picked up a carrot stick. "Well then, let's have a dose of reality. Maybe it will wake me up."

The fact was that Carl usually piled up the chips.

The game began. A lot of joking around, food and beer consumed, and every so often a "read em and weep" followed by "I'll be crying all the way to the bank."

Just as things started to get going Uncle John sent me to bed.

I was still suffering from feelings of separation in that strange room and was having quite a few nightmares; slept on the couch as much as I slept in that bedroom. So I lay there listening to them through the paper thin walls and wishing that I were a grown-up too. Not only to play cards late at night, but adults, I mistakenly thought, weren't afraid to be alone in someone else's room. But slowly, in spite of their noise and my craving to hear every word, I fell asleep.

Suddenly, I was woken by loud laughter. At first I thought it was morning, but after hearing the familiar voices coming through my sleepy haze, I realized that the card game was still happening. Adults had all the late night fun. I went out into the hallway, stood there awhile, then crawled behind the couch to the other end and watched.

Roger glanced up from his cards and asked my uncle, "So what's Florence have for us this time?"

Roger was one of the plumbers at the place where John worked. John was a salesman.

"I don't know if she'll have anything."

"What do you mean? I thought it was in the bag?"

40

"Well," John laughed to a himself, "it was until I opened my big mouth."

Roger frowned and said, "Why? What'd you say this time!?"

John glanced up at the ceiling, looked a little embarrassed, and said, "Well, I basically told her her priorities were screwed up."

Everyone looked shocked at John.

Roger: "No!"

John: "Yes."

Roger leaned forward and gave him a disgusted look. "What the hell did you say? You're supposed to be getting us jobs, not losing them. That's your job. I needed that job. I can't afford any slack time between jobs. Let's have it. Give me the whole story."

John kept his eyes on his cards. "We're standing there. She's as neat as can be in her blue suit, sparse makeup, and short gray hair. I look around. Everything is clean, neat and orderly, and so disgustingly perfect. The cleaning lady, to whom I've never heard Florence speak, is behind us waxing the floor. Florence says she wants to redo her bathroom. She doesn't like it anymore. She wants to move things around, replace fixtures, larger tub — the whole nine yards. As usual, she really doesn't know what she wants, just something different. She's bored with it, as with everything else. So, she asks me for ideas.

"I look around, and it looks ten times better and bigger than mine or anyone else's I know, so I told her so. I told her I thought it was very functional; for Christ's sake we redid it just four years ago, and that I thought it'd be a waste to redo it."

Roger threw his arms up in the air. "What does it matter to you? If she wants to throw money our way, let her. She's got tons of it. Those people up on the hill are our life blood. No matter what the economy is doing, they've always got something for us. What are you trying to do?"

John turned to Carl who wore a big proud smile. Al was staring wide-eyed in disbelief with a naughty boy smirk on his face.

"So she says in her condescending way that I've put up with all these years..." John paused. "You know, that's it really. I'm just not going to put up with it anymore. They think they're so much better than everyone else. They're better at self-deception. As I was walking up their flagstone driveway, Florence's husband Jack calls to me from the garage. He always likes to bullshit. Lonely old man. So he's in there among his truck and two cars sweeping the floor in his stained clothes, and I said, 'What are you doing, Jack? Trying to get the good housekeeping award for the cleanest garage in town?'

"'Just trying to clean up a bit before we head down to the beach house for the summer.'

"I told him he was a lucky man."

He leaned on his broom handle and said, 'Luck has nothing to do with it. Just hard work and using my mind a little bit. That's the trouble with people now days. They don't want to work. They want everything given to them. They want their rent paid for, their kids taken care of, their medical bills paid while they sit around on their asses all day. It's driving our country deeper and deeper into debt. I don't know how they have any self-respect. What kind of example are they setting for their kids? Their kids will just do the same thing. We're raising a whole generation of welfare cheats. If I had my way, I'd end the program today. There was never welfare when I was young, and we got along just fine! You have to be responsible for yourself. A person has to learn to take care of himself.'

"Usually I keep my mouth shut, but his self-righteous hypocrisy really irritated me. So I said to him, 'Yeah, there are some who are abusing the system. So what? That happens in every system. There just aren't enough jobs for everyone, and besides that, many jobs don't pay enough to live. Anyway, a lot of those on welfare are single mothers with children. They need some help.'

"Then he takes his broom handle and pokes it up and down and says, 'They should be sterilized — the whole lot of them. The young girls too before they have a dozen kids at my expense.'

"That just set me off, so I said, 'You know, this wanting something for nothing is the essence of this economy; it's what built this country. Everyone is looking for a way to make money without working. That's the whole idea behind capitalism. Capitalize on others' labor. I do most of the bidding, and I know what they're paying us and what they're charging customers like you. They're paying us about half. Even after taxes and workmen's comp they're still making between ten to fifteen dollars an hour on each one of us. They don't earn that money. They're stealing it as far as I'm concerned, yet they think they're working real hard for it. Some people sit around and figure ways to take from the government, others sit in their offices and think of ways to shaft their employees. There's no difference. Life in this country is one big scam.'"

Roger interrupted, "All right, all right already. I'm familiar with your thoughts on that. Get on with it. What did you say to the old lady?"

"Don't worry. I'll get there.

"Everyday I go to work I get robbed. But if someone were to rob me on the street that would be illegal. The robber on the street, well hell, he's only being honest as far as I can tell. He's not trying to deceive anyone by trying to make others believe that he is earning his ill-gotten gain. There are two kinds of crime in this country — legal and illegal crime, and legal crime is far worse, like the crime of being exploited at work, because so many people are fooled into believing that it isn't crime, and they just go along with it and let themselves get taken everyday. Not only that, they feel thankful that they've got a job where they can go get taken. Then there are all those other people, so-called criminals, who aren't fooled and take it as a justification for all kinds of crimes. The only difference between legal and illegal crime is that those who commit legal crime have power. You either take or get taken. It's simply impossible to make a lot of money by yourself. Those with money have either directly or indirectly stolen money from others."

Carl smiled and said, "Oh man, John's on a roll now. Hey John, have another beer."

"Don't mind if I do." John took a long drink then said, "I didn't say all that to ole Jack. Some of it maybe, I'm not sure. I don't remember too well. But what I did say made him mad.

"He glared at me and snarled, 'Like hell it's a scam. Money earned in a business is not stolen; it's honest, well deserved profit for successfully running an organization and taking a risk. It's the return on the investment of money and energy. Why else be in business? "To earn what a wage earner earns? They're satisfied with what they get. If they want more, they should go in business for themselves and see what it's like. It's a hell of a lot of work. I know. I ran my company for over thirty years. It was my baby. Many years I barely made a dime. So don't give me that crap that it's the same as being on welfare.'

"I gave him a big grin, patted him on the shoulder and said with my easy going salesman voice, 'Don't get me wrong, Jack. I wasn't talking about you. I was talking about business in general. I'm in one of my cynical moods, that's all. You have always been fair with us.'

"We small talked a bit, and as I walked toward the house, I could feel him watching me."

Roger shook his head. "Oh man, I can't believe it. Maybe I don't want to hear what else you said to Florence. Yeah, I do. Come on, let's have it."

"That's what she said." John laughed.

"Yeah right," Roger said sarcastically. "I bet she said, let me have it.'"

"Really though, that's what she said, 'I don't want to hear it.' That's what she said in her hoity-toity voice with her hands on her hips. She said, 'I want ideas. Can't you understand? I want to change it. I don't like the way it feels. Give me some ideas!'

"Yeah, she orders me just like that. So I looked her right in the eye, smiled and said, 'I have a wonderful idea for you. Why don't you take what you'd spend on a new bathroom remodel and give it to someone who doesn't have a bathroom or give it to a charity or do something that would benefit someone in need.'"

Roger looked at John in disbelief and ran his soiled, callous hand across his forehead. "What right do you have to judge what she's doing? It's none of your goddamn business what she does with her money. And besides that, man, she is helping someone. She's helping us. You know as well as I do that those bathroom remodels are mostly labor. And by upgrading her fixtures, she's helping provide jobs for those who manufacture those things. What's the big deal? What's wrong with that?"

John spoke sincerely, "The big deal is the big questions. I'm sorry if I screwed things up for you. She's put off, but I can smooth things over and get the job back. But you know, while she was wondering what to do with her bathroom, I was standing there, as I've been standing everywhere lately, with questions going through my mind. I'm in the middle of my life, and what am I supposed to do — waste the rest of it selling plumbing fixtures? Am I only a replaceable little fixture in this gigantic economic machine? Is that the essence of my life — to play a meaningless role in the movement of mostly useless goods and services?

"We've all been herded into cities, driven into debt, and made dependent on companies to fill our needs. We're all babies sucking the industrial tit. Worse than babies because they grow up to be independent, except nowadays they'll grow into another kind of dependency. Dependency on money. Money, money, money. Money to fill our needs. Isn't that a joke? Our needs! Our needs have been fulfilled a long time ago. Now the game is to fill manufactured needs so that the machines can keep going all the time.

"You know, the other day while I was in the mart standing in line looking in everyone's carts, looking at all the junk they were wasting their money on, all the stuff they were conned into buying by salesmen like me; I was thinking to myself — what if by some miracle everyone decided to live a simple real life, or if people became magically self-actualized, like my sister Iris, and just bought what they really needed. There'd be an economic collapse. Isn't that a sad statement about the times in which we live? Become a real live human being, and everything will go to hell. But, why worry? We'd rather be tooled into fools by industry. Be false to be. Be good, little, obedient producers and consumers.

"We're just appendages to machines. Gone is our humanity. Instead of machines freeing us from the threat of desperation, the threat of desperation is used to keep us slaves to machines. Step in line, boy. Play your part, obey your boss, and you'll receive money to live in this ridiculous world. Who am I to judge? I stepped in line. I've got to sell people plumbing supplies, then they'll give us their money, and then we can take some of it and give the rest to our suppliers; and then they can give it to the manufactures so they can pay their bills, keep their machines going, and pay their employees so they can go buy junk at the mart.

"I'm trapped in this self-perpetuating madness just as everyone else. Madness feeds madness. But, some of the stuff I sell is good. Take a good cast iron sink. You take good care of it, and it'll last for generations. But man, what about those guys making and selling all that planned obsolescence junk or junk that nobody needs — all that created market garbage; or geez, what about those guys creating new product lines, new gadgets that don't serve any real purpose except to move the flow of money from other companies to theirs. Where's the meaning in their lives? But why knock it? That's progress. That's the glorious benefits of competition. That's the way of the highest standard of living on earth. Whose standard? That's what I'd like to know. Not mine, that's for sure."

Uncle John jumped up, raised his eyes and arms upward as though beseeching the one above, and in a high-pitched, mocking voice said, "What is the purpose of our lives? Wake up, make it, sell it, go home, buy some of it, enjoy a temporary fixation, watch it break, throw it away, go to sleep, wake up, who am I?, what am I doing here?, go back to work, make it up again, get off, and search for another fixer-upper. We're hooked on junk. Either junk or death."

In a deep voice pretending to talk into a hand held microphone, he addressed his friends, "And which do you choose, my fellow men?"

John stumbled over to Roger and shoved his fist in front of Roger's mouth.

Roger shoved his hand away and roared, "I choose life, and I'd be able to choose it more easily if you'd stop mixing politics with your job."

John laughed and took a long drink of beer. I wondered why card playing always made him thirsty.

"You know, John," Roger went on, "you dwell too much on what you don't like about your life. Compared to all the people in the world, you've got it made. Goddamn, look around you, look at what you've got. There aren't any wars here, no famine. You live in a nice house. You ain't rich but you're not hurting for anything. You've got a lovely wife. Your son is doing well in college. Your daughter isn't in trouble. You've got that cute little wise-ass living with you now. Man, do you know, right now, how many people in this world are starving? You should go live with them, then you'd appreciate what you have. Or just live with me. Joan and I haven't been able to have children. It's just us and her sick mother and piles of doctor bills.

"Maybe your life isn't as meaningful as you'd like it to be, but hell, that's a minor problem compared to what a lot of other people are going through."

John grinned. "Yeah Roger, you're just a down-to-earth kind of guy. It's guys like you who keep the world stable. Can't rock the boat with you in it."

Roger rubbed his stomach and said, "Heh, I don't think I like that."

"Just kidding, big guy."

"You're always bitching about how you can't stay home and write all the time, but I know, I know for a fact you wouldn't be happy staying home alone writing. You're a people person. You like to talk too goddamn much. Wouldn't be long before you'd be out feeding somebody a line of bullshit. That's why you have these card games. You don't give a shit about cards. Am I right or what?"

"Maybe."

Carl, with his head resting on his hand, spoke in a calm voice. "It's difficult not to ponder one's role in a society that has gone astray. Why, just today, while I was watching my students work on their problems, I was wondering for what was I preparing them. Is teaching just indoctrination into this industrial, consumptive society? Or am I helping them to become better human beings, whatever that means? I try to present math as more than balancing a checkbook, that it's a way to organize information, solve problems, and make predictions, but today, as I was looking at those kids, I felt guilty that I was leading them blindly into a world that is not good for them and preparing them to only make it worse.

"I sympathize with your feelings, John. They are disturbing enough without considering the fact that our way of life is destroying the world. For us to survive in this economic system means the death of most everything else. And I, for the life of me, can't figure out a solution. Everyone needs a job, and as you said, a job means constant production and consumption which means using up the world. Perhaps we are the germ that will kill the earth. And that's what was really on my mind today as I was watching my kids. Am I training them to follow the status quo and continue this destruction, or will they be braver than our generation and create a better way to live. I hope the latter, but I doubt it. You know what they talk about much of the time? Shopping!

"I can't wait until next year when I teach music." Carl smiled. "That's going to be so much fun."

John drank and paced. "What's it all for? Why is it happening? Are all these animals dying and becoming extinct just so we can keep our cities lit at night? So we can parade around town in the latest styles? So we can isolate ourselves in big houses filled with stuff? So everybody can own a few cars? Are we really that pathetically vain and insecure that without all the latest things we feel like a worthless failure, and our self-esteem dries up like water in the desert? That's what it is — all those ridiculous consumer items and all those ads drilling into our heads that without this stuff, these trophies, that's what they are — junk trophies, we are nothing." John switched to his high mocking voice. "Step right up and win these junk trophies and in the eyes of your fellow man you will be viewed as a success, a winner, a person deserving to belong to the human race, even though, underneath your five hundred dollar, three-piece suit, feelings of absolute worthlessness and guilt reign.

"It's really sad how far we have strayed from our real needs. We've built concentric walls, around and around, and in the center lies the lonely child buried in the gold mine of his most precious worthless self. And while we cry for love and the touch of another living, breathing human being, we wander in the vast emptiness called modern civilization, trying to get attention from a distance. Maybe that's it. Maybe that's the cause of our meaningless, destructive way of life, maybe we've forgotten what we really need and how to go about getting it."

Carl took a long drag on his cigarette, leaned back, and spoke with his melodic voice, "Yeah, I wonder about it all myself. It seems that deep, dark, menacing tones are rising up and drowning out the sweet melodies of life. I don't mean to condone what is occurring, but in nature death is often followed by rebirth. New songs are born. Stars explode to give birth to a new generation of stars and planets, continents submerge as others rise to support new life forms, out of a decaying apple on the ground grows a new tree. I don't know but I'm awed by nature and I just feel that we are witnessing some profound change, even though we seem to be, on the surface, responsible for it all. Well guys, that's my deep thought for the evening."

Roger rose, slammed his cards on the table, and roared, "Who gives a shit?! We're the superior species. Nothing compares to us. Other animals don't have a chance; that's how successful we are. Cave men had their asses chewed by bears. A bear gets near me, and I'll blow his goddamn head off. You guys moan and groan about the extinction of species. Who the hell cares?! Maybe you and a handful of other fools, but the rest of us don't. For Christ's sake, it's the inevitable consequences of evolution. Species take care of themselves without concern for those around. I'm gonna take care of myself no matter what the consequences. What, do you think a pack of wolves worries about whether they'll drive caribou into extinction? Fuck no! And neither should we."

Roger raised his arms in the air and shouted, "Homo sapiens are the winners. Winner take all. I'm proud to be on the winning team. My message to all the other species is that they'd better smarten up if they want to live on this planet."

John leaned across the table poised as a cat ready to pounce. "That's an awfully cold-hearted thing to say. How can you say that? I'm no fool. You're the fool! Even if you don't give a shit about the preciousness of life, we are doing ourselves in. We won't survive our own destruction. You..."

Roger grinned. "Gotcha! Got ya real good this time, Johnny baby. Pay back time for the other day when you had me crawling all over hell in that tiny crawl space, scraping my back on the bottom of the joists..."

John quipped, "Yeah, what were they — about four feet off the ground?"

"I'll ignore that. All the time I'm crawling around getting filthy dirty, trying to find the shut off valve, he's standing on top of it out in the yard with a big, shit-eating grin on his face."

Roger smiled from ear to ear. "So what do you guys say, did I get him or what!?"

Carl unglued his sunglasses and said, "You fell all the way to the floor, Jonathan."

John stood frozen with his mouth open.

Roger laid his heavy arms on the table and looked at John. "I can't believe it! I'm disappointed; really, that was too easy." He laughed. "No, but honestly, tell me John, did you really think I felt that way? I thought you knew me better than that."

John took a long drink out of his can of beer, paused, and said, "Well, yeah, I know you pretty well, but you do get off the wall sometimes. Like now."

"You're still pissed off. Ha, I'm loving every minute of this."

John walked over to the counter and shoved a pickle in his mouth. "All right. Okay. Have a good time at my expense. Here, this will make you feel even better. I admit it. You got me. Big time."

Roger stood up. "That's music to my ears." He attacked the pickles, pointed at John, and said, "Now to set the record straight, I don't care as much as you do. I don't, honestly, think about it much. I'm just a guy trying to survive in this world he has found himself in. I didn't create this society. I didn't make the rules and I can't change them either. Like this card game here, I'm just trying to play out my life as best I can. And, you know as well as I do ol' buddy, I don't like to see anything get hurt, except for salesmen who lose jobs on me."

He punched John into the wall, rubbed his stomach and said, "All this serious discussion has rekindled my appetite. Think I'll sample a few more of Marty's goodies."

"Yeah, sounds good to me. I need something to soak up all this beer." John burped a mighty burp.

"Hey John," Carl sang out, "mind if I play?"

"Be my guest."

They ate to the boogie woogie except for Al who sat alone at the end of the table with his head hung.

Uncle John went to him, put his hand on his shoulder, and said, "Looks like you're not feeling any better. You've been awfully quiet."

In a tense voice, "My stomach is killing me. Sorry I haven't been much fun. I can't afford to get sick."

"Have you been to the doctor?"

"No. Haven't had time. I can't miss work. I've probably got some bug. I'll go away soon. I mean — it'll go away soon."

"Weren't you sick last week, too?"

"Yeah."

"Same thing?"

"Well, yeah, only now it's worse."

"You better go to the doctor. Here, we never finished. Here's the pot."

John yelled, "Hey guys, I'm giving the pot to Al for the doctor. Okay?"

Heads nodded. Al pushed the money back into the center of the table. "No. Don't!"

"Yeah. Here, take it." John crammed the money in Al's pocket.

Al got up. "Time to go, I guess. Thanks. Sorry I wasn't any fun." He walked toward the door holding his stomach.

John put his arm over his shoulder. "Can you make it all right? Need a ride?"

Al sighed, "No."

At the doorway, which I couldn't see from behind the couch, I heard a pat on the shoulder. Then Al said in his tight voice, "You're a good friend, John. A good friend."

I heard footsteps, car door slam, and a car drive away. Uncle John stood alone by the door for quite a while. Carl continued to play the piano. John returned to eat, drink, and talk with Roger. I went to sleep.

Chapter 6

The next day after picking me up from school, Marty drove to where John worked. It was a long, gray building with pipes piled everywhere. The left side of the building was a warehouse, which took up most of the building; the right contained a service counter and offices. When we walked inside, I was struck with how plain and barren it looked: all gray, metal counter, and behind it rows of shelves loaded with cardboard boxes. It was duller than my school. I didn't think anything could ever get that dull. There were a couple men getting supplies, and at the far end, Al was leaning against the counter holding his stomach and looking much worse than the previous night.

Uncle John came out of a door across from Al, waved to us and said, "Oh, I'm so glad you're here." Then he turned to Al, "Come on, Al. Marty's here. I made an appointment for you."

Without looking up, Al moaned, "It's not necessary. I'll feel better soon."

"Yeah, right. You've been saying that for weeks. Here Marty, take his arm."

As Marty took Al's arm, the owner came through the same door as John. He wore gray pants, white shirt with sleeves rolled up, and a thin dirty mustache under his long nose. He was thin, tall and had a long large head that was out of proportion with the rest of his body.

He talked fast. "Going to the doctor, Al? All you've probably got is gas. What's your old lady been feeding you lately — beans morning, noon and night? Well, go anyway. Hurry up! You're not making me any money standing around holding your guts. Get better and get back to work! I need you on the job. We've got a lot of orders to fill."

He rushed past us and disappeared in the shelves.

We dropped Al off at the doctor's. Marty wanted to stay, but Al insisted that she leave. His wife was to pick him up after she got off work.

After dinner, while we were still sitting around the table, John said to Marty, "I wonder what they found out about Al."

"I don't know. Why not give him a call?"

There was no answer.

Uncle John kept his hand on the phone after hanging up. A frightened, worried look seized his face. "Where could they be? I hope nothing is seriously wrong. Boy, maybe they're at the hospital."

He called, and after getting transferred about ten thousand times, finally reached Al's wife, Wendy.

"How's Al doing? Is he all right?" Pause. "No." Pause. "Surgery! I can't believe it." Pause. "We'll come down and wait with you." Pause. "Are you sure?" Pause. "Well, that's good the rest of his family is there. We'd probably just be in the way anyway. Let us know if we can help in any way."

John eased himself into his chair. He was silent for a moment, then raised his head. His face was flushed and his mouth quivered as he talked. "You just never know what's going to happen in this world, do you? Al's not doing well. Wendy said he may not make it. There's a blockage in his intestines. Poison has been leaking into his body.

"Even after the blockage is removed, it may, well, poison has been leaking so long that he may with surgery and all, it may be too late. For Christ's sake, all he was worried about was his job, losing time from work, having goddamn Hexel mad at him for taking time off; and now, he may lose his life. If he dies, it won't be from intestinal poisoning but from the poison of humiliation. There isn't a day that Hexel doesn't humiliate him in one way or another."

Marty said quietly, "He could have stood up for himself. He could have gone to work for someone else. I'm not justifying what Hexel did, but Al did make the choice to stay there and take it."

"No. No, he couldn't have left. Al has his weaknesses, and he can't do anything about them. We are what we are from birth until death. People don't change except for the worse. I'm losing my belief in the human ideal and the possibility of achieving it. No. Hexel knew what he was doing and took pleasure in it."

He slammed his fist on the table. "The hell with him and his goddamn plumbing! He should be the one in the hospital!"

John did go to the hospital that night and was with Al when he died.

My uncle mourned the death of his friend. Besides mourning the loss of his friend, he mourned the loss of what little faith he had left in the way of life in his hometown. Then, without telling anyone, he dug up the entire backyard and planted a garden. But, as everyone knows, a garden doesn't pay the bills, so every day my favorite uncle would don his best suit and search for a job.

One day after coming home from school, I swung open the kitchen screen door and stepped inside. The screen door bounced off the back of my sneaker and closed quietly. I heard my aunt and uncle talking in the living room. I was surprised to hear my uncle's voice, for he usually came home late after looking for a job. I stood quietly next to the refrigerator and listened.

John, "...where to look anymore. I've been to every place I can think of. There's not much going on in this old town anymore. The old industries are either dead or dying from outside competition. Besides that, I've been told by more than one place that I'm too old. Too old! Christ, I'm only in my forties. As far as I'm concerned, I'm in my prime. I guess planned obsolescence isn't just applied to machines."

"I'll get a job." Marty said. "That'll help some. I could go back to doing secretarial work or retail. Most married women work these days. It's not like it used to be."

"I know. Still, I don't want you to."

"I don't mind. I've certainly got the time. Why don't you want me to go back?"

"Because, well, uh, I am shocked that I feel this way, more frightened really, but I will feel as though I've failed as a man. I know that may sound strange coming from me because I'm always complaining about how meaningless my job is, but somewhere along the way it got embedded in me that a man isn't much of a man if he can't provide for his family."

"You'll always be a man to me.

"It doesn't surprise me how you feel. Maybe you've forgotten," she laughed, "but I have met your family. You don't have to feel you're less of a man. It's simply more expensive to live nowadays."

"Isn't that ironic though — feeling worthless by not having a worthless job?"

"Your job isn't worthless. What a mess there'd be without plumbing. It's necessary." She laughed.

"Yeah right! Come on now, how many toilets does a person need to take a shit? I have yet to meet someone with more than one ass. I don't mind doing what's essential, but two, three, four, five bathrooms. Give me a break. Stop wasting my time."

"Maybe you're writing will get published."

"With this time off I've accomplished a great deal."

"Well, that must feel good."

"It does."

"What else is bothering you? I can tell there's something else."

"You know what I've been feeling? Today, on the way home, I drove down Wadson. Dirty kids playing in the streets, burned out buildings, empty buildings' windows all broken, drunks passed out in the entry ways, kids, Bobby's age, selling drugs on the corner; and I felt — I haven't felt this way in a long time — but I felt helpless and alone. None of us are safe from that. I could see it happening to us. Christ, I've only been out of work a couple months, and we've already put a huge dent in our savings. And whom could we turn to for help? If we can't make it on our own, who will support us? Who would help us keep our home? It's a goddamn crime. We've almost got this place paid off, and if we'd start missing payments — if I can't find a job — we'll lose it. The market is so bad we wouldn't be able to sell it before they took it. And then where the hell would we go?

"We've got our friends and families, but when it comes right down to it, we don't have anyone but ourselves. They wouldn't carry us until I got back on my feet. It's a very lonely, helpless feeling. How separated we are from each other! What a sad world we live in. Poor Al. I can understand why some guys blow their brains out. It's not the poverty; it's the feeling of being a failure, because even if it's caused by circumstances beyond one's control, a man still blames himself."

"You aren't alone, you have me."

"Yes, I have you. We have each other and that's about it."

"Someday," she said, "we'll look back on this time and laugh about how foolish we were to worry. Something will come up; I'm sure of it."

"I wish I was sure.

"It's not just that there's not much out there, it's that I don't know if I want to work anymore. The only reason to work is to not lose what we have. I am also seething with resentment. Who am I anyway? Does anyone really know who they are? I doubt it, because we are not supposed to exist as we are. From the moment we arrive in this world, others pressure us into changing to please them, to do tricks. And so we deny what we are and try to fit into their plan. Then we get dumped on the school assembly line, and before we know it, we're on our way to becoming a specialized member of this repressive, industrial madness. And if you aren't moldable, for whatever reason, either you don't or can't perform properly, then you aren't wanted; worse than that, you don't deserve to exist. You haven't earned the right to exist because you haven't distorted yourself the way those in power want you to be distorted. We learn from birth not to exist as we are. And that is what was going through my mind as I was driving through the poor section is that nobody cares about them because they aren't performing properly, and therefore, they deserve to be poor. They've failed at earning the right to exist because they aren't playing the game in this absurd, production, consumptive society!

"All my life I've done what was expected of me, and now, after all these years, I wonder just who I am. What are my real interests? What do I believe in? Down through all the walls I've built up, through all my fabricated behavior, who am I? or where am I, for that matter? And these feelings are what scare me about getting a job because it's all been a waste of my life, and I don't want to waste the rest of my life. I want to live my life, live who I am, but until now, someone has been living it for me. And if I try to live my life, find out who I am, there's a real possibility that I may end up in the poor house. This all just makes me so mad. I feel like a caged animal, only instead of a cage I'm trapped within myself."

Marty said, "I'm shocked with this sudden outburst. I know you feel this way, but, oh, umm, I didn't realize you were this unhappy. Has life with me been a waste?"

"No, not at all. I love you more than ever.

"I've also been thinking about something else."

"What?"

"Bobby."

"What about Bobby?"

"We can't afford to raise him. Dave's college tuition is due again next month. Cindy has yet to go through college. It's getting more and more expensive every year. I just don't know where the money is going to come from for them, let alone for Bobby, too.

"I love him as much as you do and I hate to see him go, but we have a life to live. What do you think?"

"I think it would be a real setback for him. He's been tossed around so much, and what Ed did to him; and now, when he's just starting to feel at home here, for him to readjust to another place, I think it would be devastating for him. He'd really be hurt."

My blood ran into the floor. Tears swelled in my eyes.

Marty's voice pleaded. "You're the only father he's had since their death. He adores you, and for him to think that you don't want him — and he'd sense that I know be crushed. He'd really feel rejected. He's like my own child to me. I couldn't bear to see him hurt like that.

"I love him too much. No. No. I'm dead set against it. I'll work just so he can stay with us."

"I don't want him to be hurt either, but I don't want the responsibility of raising another child or the pressure. I'm done raising kids. I've been looking forward to when our kids would be on their own, and we can have our life back again. Not that I don't love them and haven't enjoyed raising them, but we have to have a life after children, and now with Bobby, hell, I'll be pushing sixty by the time he's on his own. I'm sorry, but I just can't do it."

"You're troubled about being alone without any help from others, and yet, you want to do just that to Bobby. I'll raise him. You go about your existential worries. Don't worry about us."

In a deep, mean voice John said, "Not in this house you won't!"

Marty raised her voice. "What do you mean by that!?"

"Just what I said. I'm dead serious. I'm not raising anymore kids! I'm not here to save every damn orphan that walks across my threshold. Nothing against Bobby, but I'm done. I've already spoken to Iris. She'd love to take care of him. And she's got the means. Larry left her sitting real pretty."

Marty screamed, "What!? You've spoken to her before saying anything to me? I thought we talked everything out?"

In a sarcastic tone, "What the hell do you think we're doing now? Playing poker?"

"You're not going to want to hear this but you're drinking too much. When you drink your view of the world becomes bleak, and you get mean. Oh, woe is me. Poor John can't find a job, so he's got to come home and drink everyday. Do yourself a favor. Stop it or else you will be alone."

"Go to hell. I'll drink as much as I want. It's one of my only pleasures in life now. This one's empty."

I heard a can hit the wall.

"I think I'll have another right now."

Before I could move, John came around the corner and spotted me. I froze. He went pale as a guilty look came over his face. He lowered his head, but as he raised it, his face was red and his eyes fierce. I was scared. I backed into the door and started to crumble.

He yelled, "You've been standing here all this time?"

I muttered, "Yes."

"For Christ's sake, can't I even have a talk with my wife in private? Your eyes and ears are everywhere. What the hell do you think you're doing?"

Marty came around the corner and screamed, "Now don't take it out on him."

She walked toward me and in her soft voice said, "Bobby, I'm so sorry you heard that. Oh no, this is terrible. Come here, Bobby." She reached out her arms.

I broke into tears, raced out the door, hopped on my bike, and blurry eyed hit the tree at the end of the driveway, got up and started running down the sidewalk. I could barely hear Marty behind me yelling, "Bobby, Bobby come back here."

Randy and his little brother, sitting on the porch, yelled, "Hey Bobby, where're you going so fast?" I ran past Mrs. Sass pushing her baby in a stroller. In an alarmed voice, she yelled, "Bobby!" Looked up and saw through a picture window my friend, Don, sitting on his father's lap reading a book. Turned my head away only to see Nancy, whom I liked at the time, playing jump rope with her mom and dad. She saw me and smiled. I covered my face with my hands, ran faster, tripped over a crack in the sidewalk, and fell. I lay crying.

Marty placed her hands on my back and said, "We're so sorry. We really are. We do love you. You okay? Come, let's get up." She slid her hands under my arms and lifted me.

I turned, put my arms around her neck, and cried, "Don't get rid of me. Please! I'll do anything you want. I won't get in the way."

She hugged me. "Don't worry. We still want you. Oh, I'm so sorry. I'm so sorry. Come, let's go home."

She put her arm over my shoulder. We walked to her home. I was afraid to go back, but had no choice. Where else was I to go?

Days later they talked it over again without my presence and decided that I should live with Aunt Iris. Together they told me their decision, and as Marty had predicted, I was devastated. I felt that they really didn't like me anymore and had lied to me about how they felt, were getting rid of me just as everyone else had, were dumping me on some poor, old lady who would soon tire of me and probably abandon me in an orphanage, and that would be my end. I hid from them in my cousin Dave's room.

Uncle John soon warmed me to him, which wasn't hard because I was yearning for him to be kind to me again and tell me that they had changed their minds and wanted me to live with them forever. I waited and waited for him to say it. Every time he opened his mouth, I expected him to say it. But while I was waiting, my unsuspecting little mind was being sold on the idea of living with Aunt Iris. He kept on telling me how nice Aunt Iris was, how beautiful her house was, that behind her house was a national forest, a lake, a stream to go fishing in; and just a short walk out her backyard was the ocean, with miles of open beaches and cute little hermit crabs scurrying about, sea shells, sea gulls and all kinds of other creatures; and I'd be able to go swimming and body surfing and ocean fishing; and not far down the beach was a marina where Iris kept her sailboat, and she'd teach me how to sail.

He kept on telling me how nice her neighbors were and that there were lots of kids to play with, and how Aunt Iris liked to travel; and she would take me to many beautiful places that I never dreamed existed; and besides having the ocean nearby, she lived in one of the unique places in the world where the mountains meet the ocean, and when you went out her backyard, if you turned the opposite way to go to the sea, you'd head right into the mountains; and Aunt Iris wasn't an old, broken down heifer, oh no, she could out hike most anyone around.

Every day he'd have something new to tell me about Aunt Iris and where she lived. He showed me photographs of her, her house, the surrounding area; and one night we watched home movies of some of John's and Marty's visits to her house. Every day he was more and more excited about my new life to come. He even told me he wished he was I, just so he could live in a place like that. He kept on telling me that they weren't getting rid of me, that they loved me more than ever and were sending me on a wonderful adventure that I'd never be able to have if I stayed with them. So when it came time to leave, which was a couple weeks after I got caught in the kitchen listening to them, I was so excited that I couldn't sleep. John had sold me so well that I was convinced Aunt Iris's was the best place on earth to live.

Chapter 7

The next day we drove forever in the morning. Of course, they told me it was a full day's trip to her house, clear across the state they said. But as far as I could see, we hadn't gone anywhere. The land was still as flat as at their house: same trees, same corn fields, same gas stations, same kinds of houses. We even passed a house that was exactly the same as theirs, the same color paint, everything.

"Don't worry, we'll get there." Marty would say after I'd ask how much longer.

I began to doubt that the place where Iris lived would be any different from the place I was supposedly leaving behind. Where were the mountains? Where was the ocean? Where was the sand? Where was my belief and trust in Uncle John and Aunt Marty? Slipping away as I sank alone in the back seat and stared at the two adults sitting close together in front of me. The same two adults who had control and were taking me to a place that was supposedly best for myself. I shed John's excitement, became suspicious, and started to worry that everything they had told me was a lie, and that I was alone again being taken to a strange place, maybe not even to John's sister's, but to a stranger's or an orphanage, or maybe to be sold or maybe to be left in a cornfield. Maybe they didn't even know where, just somewhere far enough from their house where no one would ever find out who dropped me off, and I'd be without any family, and then what would happen to me? I wore myself out worrying and sank back away from everything into sleep.

"Bobby, Bobby look!" Marty's voice punctured my sleep.

"What?" Still sleepy I looked up at her.

"Look outside. I don't want you to miss this." She exclaimed in her usual cheerful voice.

There were the large, rising foothills my uncle had told me about.

Marty turned around. "Isn't this beautiful?"

"Yes, Aunt Marty. It really is."

"Just wait! From here it only gets more and more beautiful."

Long, slanting, tiered hills reminded me of the long, rounded humps I once had made in a sandbox. I started jumping around on the inside.

We were going to Aunt Iris's! We were going to the ocean! They really were taking me to one of the best places on earth! John's big, fat car cruised up those long, tired hills, gliding from one to the other and weaving its way through their curves and valleys. There were no more corn fields, no more gas stations, no more houses to remind me of the other houses I'd been in — just endless grass. Every so often there'd be a creek or pond, and I'd wonder if they were alive with fish.

Marty turned around. "Look through the windshield way off in the distance."

I leaned over the front seat. "What?"

"Come up here. You don't have to be alone back there."

I climbed between them. She put her arm around me. "Look at the horizon. See its jaggedness? It's kind of misty, but can you see the mountains? They're like dark shapes in the mist."

"You mean those dark clouds way out there?"

"Dark clouds?" John laughed. "Those are mountains, Bobby. Before you know it, we'll be going through them."

The inclined plains bubbled up in front of us. The grasslands gave way to small trees, then larger ones, as the car sailed up the side of a hill and glided down the other. The sandy hills were smooth, rounded, and covered with sparse trees at first, but as we got higher the trees thickened and got bigger, and the hills became rockier with cliffs, canyons, and rock formations jutting out of the sides and tops. These hills just kept on getting larger and taller and more rocky.

We came around a long curve, and Marty, her arm still around me, nudged me forward and said, "Now look up there. This alone is worth the drive."

The mountains were everywhere. I never thought anything could be so big or stand so tall. They went up into the clouds, which were drifting around and through the dark gray, snow sprinkled peaks. Down below dark green evergreens and light aspen trees took over, which, from our distance, looked like a carpet with shades of green drifting through. These mountains were wise and serene and held within themselves the secrets of the world.

The mountain peaks cracked horizontally as giants rose up, wearing the peaks as crowns. They stretched and yawned as though waking from a long, deep sleep. They danced in a line around the mountaintops, jumped over the canyons, and rolled down some of the valleys. The leader sprinted ahead, scooped up a giant snowball, whipped it at the other kings, knocking them down into a valley. He folded his arms across his chest and thundered with laughter, which echoed throughout the mountains and set off some avalanches. The other kings jumped up with snowballs and knocked the lead king, still deep in laughter, headlong into a deep canyon. He bounced back out as though covered with springs. He attacked all the other kings with a flurry of snowballs. That started a huge snowball fight. Soon the kings grew tired of it and sat facing us on the mountaintops. They waved to me. I waved back. Slowly they sank into the mountains, leaving behind their ragged crowns as mountain peaks.

We drove up a winding road beside a creek then left the creek as we followed switchbacks cut into the mountainside. Up and up we went, back and forth to the top of a mountain where we pulled off at a scenic overlook. We got out of the car and walked to the edge of the mountain. John kicked a rock over the side. It crashed down to the bottom of the world.

He put his arm over my shoulder, pulled me to him, and said, "Here we are at the top of the world, little buddy. I told you we'd get here, didn't I? So, what do you think?"

Standing exposed and unprotected on top of the mountain as a sharp, cold wind blew through me, I felt terribly alone. It was as though Uncle John and Aunt Marty weren't even there. I wanted to run and hide in a warm compartment; I wanted to be held and wanted.

I grabbed his hand with both of mine and said, "I don't know, Uncle John. It's so beautiful. I've seen pictures of mountains before, but now, on top looking out over everything,-what is that way over there? It looks as though the sky sinks into a deeper blue?"

"That's the ocean, Bobby. It looks like the sky, but the ocean is a slightly different color because it is reflecting the sky. Boy, the ocean sure looks calm."

"Oh yes, I see! I see! Uncle John, you mean that's the ocean?" I pointed.

"Yes, it sure is."

"Well then, where is Aunt Iris's?"

"Look over this way to our left." He gently turned my head with his hands. "See how the mountains drop down, and there at the very end, see that little lake, that tiny patch of blue?"

"Yeah."

"Well, right over that hill — it's hard to see that it's a hill from here — between it and the ocean is where your new home will be. Just as I told you."

"Uncle John?"

"What, Bobby?"

I squeezed his hand tighter. "Why do I have to live there? Why can't I stay with you? I promise, I won't do anything you don't want me to."

John knelt down, put his hands on the sides of my chest and said, "Bobby, now you may not understand this, but I think it will be best for all of us. We'll miss you, we really will, and I know you'll miss us, but in the long run you'll be much happier with Iris. My sister is a great person. She is genuinely kind. This will be your permanent home. You won't be going from house to house anymore, not knowing if the next day you'll be moved or not. Just look out there, Bobby. This is a better, much more beautiful place for a child to grow up than in that broken down old town in which I live. Trust me, Bobby, you'll be much happier here. Aunt Iris will take good care of you."

"I guess I don't have any choice."

I turned away from Uncle John, pulled a photograph of my parents (which I always carried with me) out of my pocket, got in the back seat, and stared at the photo.

In silence we drove down the mountain to Aunt Iris's.

We stopped on a sandy road in front of a weathered, gray shingle, saltbox house sitting all by itself. The house was set back from the road and was hard to see. It looked deserted. Fruit trees in front were scattered in tall, weedy grass. There weren't any flowers or shrubs or landscaping of any kind. The jagged line, where the grass met the road, reminded me later of the coastline. As we walked along an overgrown, river rock path onto a small front porch, sand ground between my feet and the stones.

I breathed deeply the fresh salt air, and felt that John and Marty had really brought me to an unusual place in the world. I turned around and gazed at the horseshoe shaped mountain range. My feelings of being alone had fallen away on the way down the mountains, and so, that gone and a completely new place, I once again was excited about my new home.

Uncle John rang the doorbell. We waited. He rang the bell again. No answer.

He grinned and said, "I bet I know where she is."

We walked around back in search of Aunt Iris. My eyes were overwhelmed with color, and my nose with sweet fragrances. Her huge back yard was filled with trees, bushes, flowers, and vegetables of all kinds. Tiny paths weaved throughout the vegetation. You couldn't walk without plants brushing up against you.

We finally found Aunt Iris, surrounded by flowers, sound asleep on the ground. She was wearing a light blue, flowered smock. Her face was without wrinkles, smooth and soft, and covered with a peachy fuzz.

At one moment she looked old, but then, at another, she looked like a child. They could have just left me with her. She looked so peaceful that I thought it a shame to wake her. For some reason, even though she was a stranger and I had no idea what she was like, I felt close to her. I felt I had finally found someone who would want me.

John spread out his arms, lifted them up, and said, "Just as I thought."

He knelt down and shook his sister by the shoulder. "Iris, it's me — John. Wake up!"

He stood up, turned to Marty, and said, "That's my sister for you — asleep in the grass. Many times when she was young, mother would call and call her, and finally we'd have to go out looking for her and we'd find her sleeping somewhere in the meadow. Then, when she got older, she'd sleep with her boy friends in the tall grass." He laughed.

He gently rocked her with his hand and said, "Iris, Iris wake up. Dinner time!"

She slowly raised and rubbed her eyes.

"Have you forgotten about us coming?"

"No. Of course not!" She snapped. "What do you think, I'm getting old and senile like the rest of my relation?" She slapped his leg.

He turned to Marty. "Those two oughta get along just fine.

"Well, it looks like I need to get the wheelchair out of the car."

Iris pursed her lips, lowered one eyebrow while raising the other, and said, "Oh yeah!? I'll wheelchair you right into my neighbor's yard. You should talk! Pretty soon with all that beer you drink you'll need a wheelbarrow for that." She poked him in the stomach.

John grinned. "Speaking of which, you wouldn't by any chance have a few cold ones in the fridge for your dear brother, now would you? It's been a long, hot, dry drive."

"Of course! First thing I did when I heard you were coming was buy a keg."

"All right. Okay. I'm getting the message from all sides. I'll slow down — tomorrow."

John walked into the house.

Again Iris rubbed her eyes. Then she looked up, grabbed me by the shirt tail, and pulled me over to her. "So, you're Bobby. Last time I saw you you were just this high." She raised her hand about a foot off the ground. "You're quite grown up. Would you please help me up?"

She placed her hand on my shoulder and slowly raised herself.

We weaved through the plants and sat on a swing on the back porch.

John and Marty sat beside us in white wicker chairs.

Marty started. "This hasn't been easy. It's one of the hardest things I've ever done, but, um, well Bobby, here we are. This is your new home and your new parent."

Iris pulled me up onto her lap. "You don't remember me, do you? I'm not surprised. I saw you last at your parents' funeral, God bless their souls, and only a couple times before that when you were very young. I've heard you can be a handful to take care of. Is that true?"

"I don't know. I'm not a handful for me."

She laughed so hard that she almost knocked me to the floor.

Iris looked at John and Marty and said, "I have a good feeling about this." She then turned to me. "I feel we will enjoy each other's company. It's been so long since I've cared for a child. This will be a new adventure for me, for us. It'll be nice to have you around. I've been alone since, God bless his soul, Bill died. I could use a little life in mine.

"Hey," she stood as she lowered me to the floor, "let's go to the beach and have dinner and watch the sunset. I've got everything ready. What do you say, Bobby, wouldn't you love to see the ocean?"

"I sure would."

Everyone looked affectionately at me. There was a hurt in Marty's and John's eyes.

We followed Iris as she scurried through her garden into a meadow and up a hill. When we got to the top, the ocean was right there in front of us. We stopped. It went on forever and ever in all directions.

Iris put her arm around me, pulled me next to her and said, "There it is, Bobby. It goes all over the world. It keeps the earth alive."

"I bet it does."

I was dazed, no, bombarded; my eyes with the deep evening blue of the ocean splashing everywhere with sparkling white, my ears with the rhythmic sounds of the waves gliding up on the sand, my nose with the fresh salt air, and the rest of my body with the cool, ocean breeze sailing and swirling around me. I had imagined that the ocean was just bigger than a lake, just water everywhere, but there was a mysterious power to it, and it drew me to itself. I felt that somehow, somewhere, the ocean was my home.

Marty yelled, "Let's go in."

Like four kids we ran into the water. We swam for a while, and then the adults got out, spread a blanket, and talked. And of course, the child stayed in the water, forgot about the adults, played in the sand, looked at the sea shells, played with kids he did not know, and wondered about his new world. The adults called him out for dinner many times, but he didn't come until he was shivering.

The sky became a flaming red, then eased back to a pinkish orange as the sun sank below the ocean, creating the transitional twilight that is loved by some and feared by others. A mysterious deep, dark blue dipped into the pink creating wavy bands of purple.

Iris held my hand on our way up the hill. We stopped as before at the top and looked at the ocean.

She squeezed my hand and said, "I'm glad you've come, although I can't say I'm happy about how you got here. This is your home now, Bobby. Believe me, please, as your Uncle John has tried to assure you, this will be your home. You won't be going anywhere else to live, unless of course, you decide to."

I took her hand in both of mine. "I hope so, Aunt Iris. I don't ever want to move again."

That night, she put me to bed in a soft blue room with a single bed against the wall, a tall chest of drawers, and a dresser. She hadn't decorated it except for photographs and paintings that she told me my mother had done. She thought that I'd like to decorate the room myself. When I first saw the room, I felt it was mine.

She sat on my bed, tucked the covers around my neck, kissed me on the forehead, and said, "Would you like me to tell you a good night story?"

I looked into her trusting, blue eyes. "Yes, please."

"Once upon a time there was a wood duck family that lived in a tree beside a pond. When the ducklings were ready to leave the nest, mother wood duck flew down into the pond at the base of the tree and quacked for them to jump. At first they were afraid to jump, but they wanted their mother, so one by one they jumped into the pond.

"Woody was the last to jump, but as he hopped toward the hole in the tree, a fierce wind blew him back, and rain came pouring down. A nearby river overflowed the pond and swept away the wood duck family.

"Next morning when the sky was clear, Woody peeped for his mother. But she didn't call back. He peeped again. She didn't answer.

"For the entire day and through the night, he sat alone and every so often would peep for his mom, but she never quacked back.

"The next day when Woody looked out, the waters had receded leaving the pond as before. Woody was lonely and hungry. He peeped for his mom. She still did not answer. He looked down at the pond. It was a long way down.

"He said to himself, 'If my brothers and sisters could, then so can I.'

"He jumped, flapping his tiny wings, went down into the water and bounced up to the surface like a cork.

"He ate some algae and then started looking for his family. He looked and he peeped.

"Other animals, hearing his lonely peeping, knew he was alone. A snake in the grass followed Woody as he swam along the shore.

"Woody hopped onto the shore.

"The snake raised his head, lashed out his tongue, and said, 'Please, do not be afraid. I mean no harm. Have you lost your family?'

"'They were washed away in a rain storm.'

"'What is your family like?'

"'I have a mommy and a daddy and seven brothers and sisters.'

"'Oh dear me, I just saw a family like that by a pile of rocks. Quick, hurry, follow me before they leave.'

"The snake quickly slithered through the tall grass, while woody bounced behind. But when they came to the rocks, there weren't any wood ducks.

"Woody sighed, 'No one's here.'

"The snake's eyes gleamed, and once again, he lashed out his tongue. 'They were over on the other side of the pile. Go look!'

"Woody hopped ahead of the snake, flipped over a rock, and when he looked up, the snake's unhinged mouth shot at him. Woody jumped, flapped his little wings with all his might, and for the first time in his life, he flew. Not far but far enough.

"'Whew,' Woody said to himself as he tumbled onto the ground, 'I will never believe a snake again.'

"Woody kept on hopping along and peeping. A dark shadow passed over him. It passed over him again, only this time it was bigger.

"Again, and even bigger. Again, and the shadow stayed on him. He heard a shriek, and without looking up, he ran into a thick, tangled clump of wild roses. A hawk crashed into the rose bush, and fiercely flapping its wings, tore at the top of it with its claws, shrieked, and then flew away. Woody stayed huddled in the bush for a long time and peeped.

"In the rose bush he smelled the rich, muddy odor of a pond. He plodded toward the smell, for he was tired and hungry, and when he got to the water, he saw a wood duck family nearby in some reeds. He jumped in the water, his heart beating rapidly, and raced over to them. But when he swam up to the other ducklings, they attacked him and pecked at him viciously, and yelled, 'Go away! Go away! You don't belong in our family.'

"Woody swam to the shore with his head hung, climbed into a clump of grass, and cried. He was not hungry anymore.

"Another shadow passed over him. Again and again, bigger and bigger. Woody wiggled down into the clump of grass. He closed his eyes. He heard the loud flapping of wings, a splash in the water, a clump, clump, clump onto the shore, and then his daddy's voice, 'Woody, is that you in there?'

"'Yes Daddy, it's me.' Woody bounced out of the grass.

"'Oh,' Woody's dad pulled him next to him with his wing, 'I've been looking all over for you.'

"'I'm so happy you found me,' said Woody as he nestled into his dad.

"And everybody lived happily ever after."

I stared at her for a while and said, "That's a sad story because I will never find my family."

She took my hand. "No. Not as he did, but you may and probably will find others who will love and protect you and make you feel at home. I hope you will feel that here."

"I hope so too."

I fell asleep holding her hand.

John and Marty stayed for a few days. The evening they left we were standing on the front porch. John wore blue shorts and a Hawaiian shirt. Marty was dressed in a black lace blouse and a black skirt. I was holding Aunt Iris's hand, and even though I had become fond of them, they had already become, in my mind, another set of parents that had gotten rid of me.

John kneeled in front of me and said, "Well Bobby, I guess we'll be going now. This isn't a goodbye because we'll come back to see you."

He asked, "Will you do me a favor?"

"What?"

"Keep on writing your stories, okay?"

"Okay."

He stood, turned to Marty, and said, "Ready to go?"

"I guess."

She looked at me. Her mouth was quivering. Her eyes were red. She hugged me, lifted me up, and then simply said, "Take care, Bobby. I'll miss you. We'll stay in touch, don't worry."

They said goodbye to Iris. Usually they walked side by side, but this time Marty walked behind John with her head lowered.

Chapter 8

Next morning after putting on plaid shorts and a white T-shirt, I walked through the living room into Iris's large kitchen, sat at a wooden table, and waited for breakfast just as I had at all my other so-called relatives. Only this time, my waiting was in vain.

Finally, I made some toast, and as I was finishing it, Iris wobbled out of her room into the kitchen dressed in a plain purple, cotton robe and sat next to me.

"Well," she pushed her messy hair out of her face, "I see you found something to eat. Good. Whenever you're hungry, just help yourself. Don't wait for me. You might starve if you do." She laughed.

"I love to watch animals, in real life and on television, and one thing I'm always impressed with is how soon newborns learn to feed themselves. Sometimes immediately after birth they're feeding themselves, but intelligent human beings, golly, it takes years, sometimes never. I know some men who still won't feed themselves. The wife goes away for a few days, and the hubby goes out to eat.

"What I'm saying is that you'll have to fend for yourself. They'll always be food here. I'll take care of that, and maybe, if our hunger coincides, we'll eat together but, well…"

She rested her chin on her hand and stared out the back window.

After a while she said, "It took some time for me to adjust to my husband's absence after he died. He was orderly. Every minute of each day was planned. When I first met him, I loved that in him because he got so much accomplished. Much of it was a waste of time now that I look back, but to him it was important, and it really helped me complete things. I'd be doing a dozen different things, and hardly anything would ever get finished, but after I met him, well…" She leaned back in her chair and with both hands threw her messy hair behind her head. "Anyway, after a while it became hard for me to breathe, so that after his death I fell back into my old patterns. Now there's no reason, usually, for me to be anywhere or do anything at any certain time unless I wish it."

I couldn't think of anything to say. She looked at me Aunt Marty style. I scanned the table for more toast.

She raised up and asked, "Well, what do boys your age like to do?"

"Play."

"Play? Hmmm, this could be play or work, all depending on how you look at it. How would you like to transfer some plants from the greenhouse to the garden?"

"Sure. Whatever you want."

She gave me a look more penetrating than Aunt Marty's and said, "I'd love you to help me. I'll just grab a banana, then get dressed; and if you want to look around, I'll meet you in the greenhouse."

In her freestanding greenhouse were plants in all shapes and conditions — tall, short, lush green, burned out brown, all mixed up, on benches, on the ground, and hanging from wires.

Suddenly from behind, "Here."

I jumped.

"Oh, sorry. I didn't mean to scare you." She put her hand on my shoulder. "Are you okay?"

"Yeah. I just didn't expect you so soon."

She hugged me and said, "These zucchini plants are ready to go. Squash can't take a frost. We're past that now. I hope so anyway. Would you please help me carry out this flat? And oh, I almost forgot, here are some yellow squash plants." Her face lit up as though finding a treasure.

That was the beginning of our many days together in the garden.

Being in the garden with her, I remember her carefulness, the look on her face, her faint smile, her intense concentration over a simple procedure; and I remember more than anything feeling like one of those plants. For on that day I felt a feeling, which only grew more and more, of being cared for as never before in a way that let me grow into a world that I never knew existed. With the passing of time, I felt freer to do what I wanted, even though what I wanted was to be with Aunt Iris and do whatever she was doing.

As I was watering the squash plants with a hose, Iris said, "Here, let me see that." She reached her hand toward me.

I gave her the hose. She grinned her ornery grin, pointed it straight up, leaned her head back, and opened her mouth.

"Ahhh, that feels good. It's so hot."

It was already hot that morning, and the spray did feel good. I started laughing, spread out my arms, and began twirling around.

The water still pouring down on us, she said, "What do you say, Bobby? How would you like to go sailing?"

I stopped twirling. "Sailing? Sure. Whatever you want to do is fine with me."

"Well," she turned off the hose, "let's go. We'll just pack up right now and go."

I went into my room, got out a pair of shorts, T-shirt, a pair of pants and threw them on the bed. Then I stood there wondering what you packed to go sailing. I was still staring at my clothes when she knocked on the door.

"Ready to go?"

"No."

"What's wrong?" She came in, wearing tan khaki pants, a white blouse, and a straw hat tied firmly under her chin.

"Is this enough?" I said without looking at her.

"No," she said cheerfully. "I didn't think you owned sailing clothes, so I took the liberty of buying you some. Here," she reached on a shelf in the closet and handed me an armful of clothes, "this is all you'll need.

"I'm so excited about teaching you how to sail. Soon we'll be gliding across the water."

On the front porch, we dropped our clothes in a red wagon with tall wooden sides. She grabbed the handle and said, "That should do it. I don't own a car, so we'll just pull this down to the marina. It's not far."

She yanked the wagon through the air onto the sidewalk and scurried down the road so fast that I had to double step most of the way to keep up with her.

At the sleepy marina we pulled the wagon on a long white dock and stopped at a long, slick, white sailboat. A burly man with a full bristly beard and tattooed arms emerged from the small cabin and bellowed, "She's all ready for another season, Iris. In tiptop shape.

"We got her repainted, the sail mended, and, well, we found a little dry rot in the stern and took care of that for you too. She's a fine boat." He slapped the top of the cabin.

"Thank you, Joe. I wish I was aging as well as she."

"Oh ma'am, you don't·look a day over forty."

"What a gentleman you are."

"Need some help getting her out to sea?"

"Thank you, but I don't think so. I brought my first mate with me." She put her hand on my shoulder.

"So I see. Well mate, you couldn't have a better captain."

"So many compliments!" Iris grinned at Joe. "You must be looking for a pretty big tip."

"Nope; only being honest.

"Have a safe voyage. Be sure to contact us if you change your schedule. Good sailing to you."

"Thank you, Joe." She handed him some money.

"Well, gee," Joe's eyes bulged. "I didn't realize I gave you that many compliments. Thank you, Iris."

The dock shook as he tramped away.

"Here Bobby, let's put everything in the cabin. Then would you take the wagon up to Joe at the shop?" She pointed back to where we entered the marina.

"Sure."

When I returned, the boat was untied. Iris was sitting in the stern holding the handle of a small outboard motor.

She waved. "Come back here and sit next to me."

I gladly obeyed.

She placed my hand on hers. "You'll get a feel for steering the boat by following my hand. Just move the handle opposite to the way you want to go. We'll steer together until we clear the break wall, and then, if you feel you've got the hang of it, I'll set the sails, while you steer us along the coast. Okay?"

"I guess. But what if I can't steer?"

"Then we'll steer together until you can. There is no hurry. It's not hard. Anyway, I have the feeling you'll be a fast learner."

Once past the boulder break wall she stood up and said, "Can you handle her?"

Not wanting to disappoint her, I said, "Yes, I think so."

Soon I started bouncing up and down in my seat, then stood up and yelled, "How'm I doin', Aunt Iris?"

"Great, Bobby. You're doing just great!"

A few minutes later, Iris yelled back, "Are you ready?"

"Ready for what?"

"Ready to sail!"

She raised the sail, and the boat thrust forward cutting through the waves, which had been lazily lapping up against the boat, and throwing them off to the side.

She tied off the sail, turned off the motor, and said, "Come up to the steering wheel. Now I'll show you how to navigate with the wheel."

She sat behind the wheel. I sat in front of her. Once again, she placed my hands on hers.

I held myself away from her. As she turned the wheel to the left, her right arm and breast rubbed across my back. I pulled myself up closer to the wheel. She turned to the right, touched me again, and although I moved away again, her touch was comforting. Wasn't long before I started moving toward her until I was leaning against her.

"So first mate, how do you like sailing?"

"I love it!"

I was excited.

Slowly the land slipped below the horizon. There we were, Aunt Iris and I, alone on the spacious sea, away from the hard land, away from the streets and buildings and noise and all the people, away from my aunts and uncles, free from everything except the confines of our tiny craft. The past sunk into the depths and all there was, all there had ever been, was Iris and I in a sailboat sailing across the endless ocean. The waves grew larger as the troughs deepened, but they didn't rock the boat as it cut through them like a knife.

Iris pointed to her right and exclaimed, "Look Bobby, there are some dolphins!"

A bunch of them were arching through the water, leaving behind a momentary sign of their presence. Soon our paths met as they swam beside our boat. I leapt onto the back of one of them and rode the dolphin like a horse. We dove into the water, rose up for a breath of moist ocean air, then dove down deeper than before. Longer and deeper we dove, higher and higher we jumped as we swam beyond the horizon with the rest of the pod. We took a deep breath then dove to the bottom of the ocean where there were many more dolphins. They were rolling on the bottom playing chase in the weeds, zooming around, knocking into each other, somersaulting through the water, and soaring up through the water as a group, then flying down again, and curving up just before hitting the bottom. We started zooming around with some of them.

We soared up to the surface, flew out of the water in a long high arch, and headed back toward Iris's boat. Just as we were about to ram the side, he dove underwater as I jumped over the rail right back into Iris's lap. She didn't even notice that I had been gone.

Suddenly, a gust of cross wind leaned the boat almost onto its side.

Iris said in a calm, quiet voice, "Just keep holding the wheel straight."

She jumped up, ran over to the mast, and started, what seemed to me, dancing around the boat. She'd pull a rope tighter, hop over and swing around a wooden bar, and then another strong wind would blow, and she'd bop around a pole, and tie off another rope.

I held the wheel as hard as I could. After a while, I started moving it to see what it would do, and before long, I knew how to move it to help Aunt Iris. For the rest of the way to the island, she ran the sails, while I steered. Every now and then she'd yell: "How's it going? You're doing well. Starboard side," and point to the right.

We sailed into a cove surrounded by bright green marsh grass and, like two seasoned sailors, slid alongside a long gray dock. After we tied off the boat, Iris jumped up onto the thick planks, reached down to me, grabbed my hand, pulled me up and said, "You did great! You've pretty much got the hang of it, don't you?"

"Yeah, I think so. That was so much fun. I can't wait till we sail back."

She put her arm around me as we began to walk toward land on the long dock. "I liked sailing the first time, too. I don't believe I have ever gone when I didn't enjoy it. Oh, there have been times when I've gotten caught on a rough sea and wished I hadn't gone, but even then, the challenge has made me a better sailor. You'll never get to be a good sailor, a sailor that can handle all kinds of conditions, if you only go out when the sea is relatively calm."

I smiled, looked up at her, and said, "I'd like to become a good sailor too."

We stepped off the dock onto a sandy path that curved through tall marsh grass. Aunt Iris got a pensive look on her face; a look that I soon became familiar with, and said, "Sailing is a lot like living. Each has taught me much about the other. You can prepare yourself the best you can, but once you leave toward your destination, you never know what may happen. You may start on a rough or calm sea, but on the way it is bound to change. A strong wind may rise up and send you sailing in your direction, and then suddenly, it may change direction and become furious and drive huge waves against you and cause you to fear for your life. Then, after a while, the wind may die down, and there will be a lull in your journey, but eventually the wind will pick up again, and you'll be on your way through its unexpected changes. But no matter how strong the wind blows or from what direction, we can't see it; we can only feel it and see the results of its power; just as with life we can feel it, we can feel it surging through our bodies and feel its presence in the world around us and we can see the results of its power, but it remains hidden from our sight. And that's what makes living and sailing alike.

"You have to feel your way along and try to set your sail so no matter from what direction the wind blows, even if it blows dead against you, you'll move toward your destination. But sometimes," she laughed, "it doesn't hurt to throw in the anchor and rest.

"Does that make any sense to you, Bobby?"

"Yeah, sort of. But best of all I like doing the steering wheel."

She laughed and hugged me.

The marsh grass gave way to shorter grass and widely spaced pine and oak trees. We came up to a gray cottage with a screen porch and a deck off to our left side. An old man and woman were sitting under an umbrella at a table on the deck.

The man, dressed in blue shorts, a plaid shirt and sporting a cigar, stood up, and yelled, "Iris, you're here! I was just about to walk out on the dock to look for you."

He hurried off the deck, gave Iris a big hug, and said, "It sure is good to see you. Did you have a good sail?"

"Yes, it was good, thanks to my first mate."

She patted me on the shoulder.

The man held out his wrinkled, weathered hand. "I take it you're Bobby. It's good to meet you. I'm Jack, and this," he turned, "is my wife, Carol."

A plain woman, wearing a simple beige dress, stepped forward, extended her hand, and said, "It is nice to meet you. I've heard so much about you."

Feeling lively from sailing, I shook her hand and said, "Nice to meet you too, although I haven't heard much about you."

She shook herself up like a chicken, scrutinized me with dark, expressionless eyes, and said, "Nothing more refreshing than a child's honesty."

Then she spread her arms and sighed, "Oh Iris, it is so good to see you again."

"Yes, it's wonderful to see you too. I've been thinking about you."

They hugged warmly.

We stayed with Iris's friends for a few days. Each day we woke early in the morning, packed for the day, and drove a short distance to the ocean side of the island where the waves were big and came from the other side of the world.

The first day Iris spent with me. She taught me how to body surf and played in the sand and water with me. It was like playing with another kid. Toward the end of the day, some adults and their kids came along whom Iris knew, so during the rest of our beach days, I played with those kids, while Aunt Iris, shaded with her friends under colorful beach umbrellas, read, painted pastel ocean scenes, and talked. Every now and then she would go for a long swim and then ride in with the waves.

One evening, Aunt Iris and I were strolling along the shore holding hands. The tide was low. Gentle waves sparkled as they broke on a sand bar, rolled up again in deeper water and sparkled again upon hitting the shore. We walked through the water onto the sand bar.

The sun, slowly descending into the water, ignited the sky in a fiery red.

Iris pointed to the right of the sun and said, "Out there was where your parents were working before they died. There's a reef out there.

They visited me on their way back. They told me how upset you were when they left. They were anxious to get back to you, especially your mother. She really felt bad about leaving you. She said you felt you would never see them again.

"Why did you feel that way, Bobby?"

"I don't know." Suddenly I felt sad, and my insides began to churn. She looked at me as though trying to look into my brain. "Do you remember being upset?"

"No."

"You don't?"

"No. Honest. I don't."

She paused. Carefully forming her words, she said, "Do you remember that day?"

"No."

"Do you remember staying with your grandparents?"

"No. Please, Aunt Iris, don't keep asking me. Please, don't. I don't remember." I started crying as words burst out of me. "I want to be like other kids. I want parents, my parents. Parents I've been told I once had. I want to be able to remember my parents. No. No. I never had parents. People say I had parents. But I never did. I don't know what to believe. Everyone talks of my parents, but I don't know what they're talking about. I'm here. That's all I know. I keep on being tossed around by people who say they're my aunts and uncles, but I don't know. Everyone is a stranger. Please Aunt Iris, tell me the truth, are you my aunt? Did I really have parents? Did I really belong to someone?"

She held me. "Yes. I am your aunt. I'm your mother's oldest sister. You did have parents. Those are your parents you're always looking at in that picture."

"What were they like?"

"Your mother was the baby in our family. She could have been my child. Because she was the last child Mother bore, she treasured your mother and gave her a great deal of love and attention. And even though the rest of us children were envious, we treated her as though she was special and always looked out for her. Your mother was sensitive, quiet; usually only spoke when she had something to say.

"Your mom always had many friends. She was likeable and easy going, even though she kept to herself. Even in a crowd, you could tell she was off in her own little world. Like you, she loved the outdoors and used to go on long camping trips. Your mother was a great lover of animals. She was always bringing home what she thought were stray dogs and cats. She read a fair amount and painted. I taught her to paint. She painted those ocean pictures in your room.

"Clare always, even as a child," Iris's voice broke as her eyes watered, "used to think and ask about death. Many times when she would be lost in thought, I'd know she was thinking about death. Maybe somewhere she knew she would meet death at an early age."

Iris wiped her eyes and cleared her throat. "It was a magical moment when your mother and father met. Clare was staying with us, my husband and me, in the same house as now, and we were standing on a dock at the boatyard, same one as this morning, talking to each other, and your mother, with her back to the ocean, stops in mid-sentence, turns all the way around, and fastens her eyes on your father whom she had never seen before. He was standing up with his foot on the rudder.

"Golden brown tan, his brown wavy hair blowing in the breeze, he looked just as if he were Neptune's son. We never even finished what we were talking about. She watched him all the way in, and unlike her usual shy self, she walked right over to where he was landing, stood there, and waited for him. When he pulled in, she introduced herself and asked him to dinner that night right in front of the woman with him.

"They were together ever since.

"Your father loved the ocean. He was a natural sailor. He taught me to sail. He was the one who instilled the love of sailing in me, both by learning from and watching him. He was so graceful. It was a beautiful sight to watch him glide through the wind. No matter how fierce or conflicting the winds, he could move his craft through it with ease and use the wind to his advantage.

"Your father wanted to remain a boy. He really never grew up.

"Not that he was immature. He was more mature than most men. What I mean is that he never grew up the way society wants boys to grow up. He should have been born on an island, long ago, when

84

surviving was a way of life, before it became separated into work. Your father worked at the boat yard sporadically. Then he worked on fishing boats, then salvaging, and that's what he was doing at the end. If it hadn't been for your mother's income as a photojournalist, they would have never kept the bills paid. But, in a way, that was an admirable characteristic of your father's. He was free. He roamed where he chose to roam, and that was on the great wide-open seas. It was not in vain, for on his last trip out to sea he did find that old sunken ship. It's been a fight, but it looks as though you'll get most of the money.

"Has this stirred up any memories?"

Her descriptions were so vivid in my mind that I became confused about their origin. Finally I said, "No."

"Well," she gave me a hug, "maybe someday, if you find a home, you'll remember them."

"What do you mean? I have a home with you now, don't I"

"Yes. I didn't mean that. I meant a home inside yourself. Right now you're too young to understand, but when you're older, I'll explain it to you. Okay?"

"Okay."

The next day we sailed back home.

That summer she taught me how to sail. Now, whenever I think of Aunt Iris I can't help think of sailing, and when I'm sailing alone, I always feel as though she is there with me, silently helping me guide my craft through the wind, just as she helped guide me through life.

Chapter 9

As the years passed, I grew to love Iris more and more. She became my best friend, and even now in my heart, she is still my best friend. She was right, after telling the story of the wood duck, in saying that I could develop feelings with others that I had or would have had with my parents.

At the beginning of my stay with her, I followed her around like a duckling and did anything she asked just to be with her. She never had to tell me to come along; I would just be there. And never once can I remember her telling me to get away or losing patience with me for being so close. It was as though she expected it. Over time this simple need to be with someone who treated me kindly developed into a love. I loved being with her at the ocean, hiking in the mountains, holding her hand, talking to her, being allowed to sit in on conversations with her friends, watching her paint and being taught by her to paint and to play the piano, sitting on the porch in the evening quietly looking at her garden, joking around; but most of all, even more than sailing, well no, but just as much, I loved watching and working with her in her garden. She had a vibrant, lush garden and treated the plants as though they were her children. She would touch them and look after them every day and gaze upon them with pride and affection. I came to feel that one of the reasons I was happy was because she treated me like a flower in her garden.

Slowly her presence filled the front of my mind similar to the way thoughts center around a person with whom one falls in love. I didn't consciously think of her or of things we had done together as one in love, but somehow she had entered me, and I had a feeling of myself and beside it, a sense of her. This sense was with me all the time, wherever I went, and is still with me only in a weaker way.

Sometimes this sense would become powerful, and I would yearn for her and become afraid of losing her and would stop whatever I was doing and run home. Many times, when playing with my friends, especially if they were fighting or putting each other down or calling each other names or saying how much they hated their parents, or were being yelled at by their parents, I'd get anxious and run home to Iris, often without saying goodbye. And I'd wonder why did I bother being with my friends or with anyone else for that matter when I was happiest with Aunt Iris. So, even as a teenager, I spent most of my time with her.

Early one summer morning, Aunt Iris, Uncle John, and I were kneeling side by side loosening the soil around some beets. Years before Uncle John had become financially successful as a writer, but not before going deeply into debt, and he and Aunt Mary moved near us. We spent a lot of time together, so I became overly familiar with his rantings and ravings. Well, honestly, I swallowed his words. Although he hurt me by getting rid of me, I still, in my child's heart, admired him and wanted him to want me again. Anyway, Iris got a little wild with her spade and sliced off the side of a beet. She pressed the piece against the beet, but it fell off. She then wiped the dirt off the piece of beet, ate it, and pushed dirt up against the beet.

"It'll heal," she said. "Healing is an amazing process. Just think if things didn't heal themselves. Everything would have died out a long time ago." She raised her arms and curved them down to her side. "Everything wants to live, and each life, the billions of microorganisms in this soil," she lifted a handful of soil and let it fall between her fingers, "this ant, the moss growing on the north side of that mighty oak; they're all tied together with each other and the lives of other living things. They all need each other to survive.

"Isn't it great to be a part of it all? It's like being a part of an unfolding miracle.

"I've always loved learning about how nature operates. It's intriguing, but you don't feel its beauty as you do being out here in the midst of it all. It's the mystery that makes life inviting, makes me feel awe, makes me feel as though I'm in the middle of something that is beyond belief. Healing is one of those amazing mysterious processes. It's not hard to understand the mechanics of it, but the process of living things returning themselves to wholeness — that is mysterious. It's one of the many ways life asserts itself."

"Yes, it is," said John. "It is truly amazing. Too bad there's so much in need of healing."

In the distance started the deep roar of engines. John stood, cocked his head, listened, then said angrily, "There they go, those sonufabitches-destroying another beautiful place on earth. Why can't they just leave things as they are? You know, that's just what we need around here, a bunch of tourists spreading around their boredom and discontent. Mankind won't be happy until the world is covered with buildings."

Iris sighed, "Well, we did what we could. Can't say we didn't put up a fight."

"Yeah, I guess. Too bad there wasn't something else we could have done, but for the life of me, I couldn't figure out what else to do.

"Too bad we couldn't have found a sympathetic soul in power. Oh well, you're right. We did what we could.

"You know, Iris, I get called almost everyday about that parcel we bought right in the middle of the development. It's really throwing a wrench in their plans. On their plot plan, they have a hotel designed to go on that spot. I just wonder how high their offers will go. The other day I got another call from big, bad Harry. He wanted to know if I was ready to deal. I told him I'd be glad to help him out anyway I could, but was in partnership with my sister, and my hands were tied until she got back from her trip to the North Pole. Then he said in his rude, demanding way, 'When the hell is she going to be back?' I said, 'I don't know, she hitchhiked.' I started laughing, and he slammed down the phone. Every time he calls I give him a different story.

"It's a beautiful piece of land — the low wind-swept dunes, the golden sand, the soft green ocean grass, and those bright red wild roses. I love to watch the grass wave in the wind. It's as though a giant, invisible hand is running through it.

"They'd better get used to its natural beauty, that's all I've got to say. It'll be there far longer than they."

Later that day I walked alone to where the tourist complex was being built. The complex was located at the end of Iris's little section of town beyond the marina. Iris's part of town, once a fishing village, still had a small fishing industry, but was now mostly the home for retirees, writers, and painters. There was a general store, mechanic shop, and a few art galleries and restaurants. A person with few needs could hole up there like a snail without ever again crawling out into the rest of the world.

Thousands of times I heard Uncle John call our capitalistic economy a death machine, and I knew what he meant, but it was just another piece of information to me, like saying smoke is black. Perhaps my new understanding was because I had reached a level in my development as a child where I was able to grasp the meaning of his words and relate them to real events in the world, or maybe it was because I was watching the destruction of a place I really loved, a place where we used to go all the time and swim and fish and admire from the sailboat. All those words of Uncle John's that were swarming through my brain suddenly fell into place with my feelings, and although I felt exhilarated at the sudden shift in my mind, I was sad about losing one of my best friends, and I hated those men and their machines.

I walked toward the river feeling stranger by the moment as my childish way of seeing things continued to shed and came upon a chemical factory spewing poisons into the air, and all around it the ground was black. Not far away on the river was another factory that was turning the river a rust color for miles with its sewage. The whole area stunk of chemicals, rotten seaweed, and dead fish that lined the shores. If I had continued south for thousands of miles, I would have seen the same thing over and over again until I came upon vast fires and armies of bulldozers destroying the earth's great forests and exterminating thousands upon thousands of species of plants and animals. Through the years, Aunt Iris and I were sad, but not surprised that there were fewer birds and butterflies in her garden.

I walked through a parking lot outside a mall where others were loading their cars with all kinds of useless junk. Walked out of the warm, summer sun and refreshing salt air into the mall's air conditioned non-air and fluorescent lights. The place was swarming with people as if it were the best of all possible places. In the endless hallway, lined with every store imaginable, were waterfalls, fish ponds, plastic plants, and tall, real plants searching for a way through the skylights. People were dumping junk in their carts, sitting comatose on benches; kids were racing around, and women were screaming at their kids as they dragged them along. And everybody, whether they were with someone or not, was talking. "Good to see you. What a beautiful day! How are you doing? Great, just great! I know I really don't need this, but golly, how can I pass up the price. I'll use it someday. Good. Great. Have a nice day. Got to run." The chatter, bouncing off the hard surfaces, crammed the place with noise and drove me toward the exit. Some friends of mine, standing and talking outside a music store, waved me over. I waved back from the other side and left.

Out the back of the mall, I weaved my way through a maze of cars until I came to the edge of a new suburb. The suburb was not new to me. I had been there many times before, but with my eyes continuing to open, it looked different. The houses went deep, but looked shallow. As I entered, it seemed like an extension of the mall, only nothing was for sale except people's lives. It reminded me of Uncle Ed's suburb. Fear murmured through me as everything became distant. Bright green, weedless, chemical lawns were neatly edged and bordered; clean solid sidewalks turned at right angles to each house, and along the walks were flowers and ornamental bushes, and these turned at right angles at the front of the houses and along the sides. For shame if grass or weeds had found a home in the flowerbeds, so in between the plants was black plastic covered with tree bark. All the different houses were from a magazine cover — clean windows, curtains in the windows, tight paint, solid roofs, clean red bricks (no weeds or small trees growing in the gutters on these houses), two car solid door garages; and although there were welcome mats on the front stoops, fences and brick walls enclosed all the homes. I didn't see any signs of life. In all this neatness, cleanliness, and order, I began thinking of Uncle Ed and felt that it was all a cover, an attempt to hide what was really there by displaying the opposite. I felt, not without shuddering, that the polite, fashionably dressed people who inhabited these houses surrounded by beautiful lawns and flowers were unhappy and decaying on the inside, and that if the anger contained in those house were to escape, it would kill every kid in town.

Time has a way of bringing things to the surface. A small infected cut, bandaged and ignored, will grow with infection until the bandage rots off, exposing the swollen red flesh that will not only threaten the loss of a limb but the person's life.

It wasn't a far walk to the old part of town which, in its day, was the spiffy, new part of town. Here the houses were broken down, paint was falling off, weeds were growing in the cracks of the sidewalks, large trees had heaved the sidewalks, patches had turned the streets into ugly mosaics, bricks and rocks had fallen out of the houses and fences and lay on the ground, and wooden fences were decayed and partly torn down. And yet, there was a beauty in the realness of this part of town where decay was not shameful. People had not locked themselves inside. They were out on the porches staring blankly into space, on the curb where old men were pissing in the gutter except for one who was pissing on a baby in a stroller in front of a bar, on the street corner where they stood around beside a boarded up building, and on the lawns where some had finally given up and died.

As healthy plants will grow out of a decaying pile of leaves, children were playing in front of an old brick, apartment building that had recently suffered a face-lift. I wondered, what will these kids be like? Will they also have their world of make-believe torn away by time? Will time do that to me, too? But, it wasn't really time, I thought, it was that events unfolded in time.

As I walked back to Aunt Iris's, I felt the innocence of my childhood slowly die and a thorny vine begin to grow that tangled through my mind with questions and confusion. The quick destruction of nature by the industrial age had begun only a couple hundred years ago, about six thousandths of one percent of Homo sapiens existence.

Why did I, out of all the time of our species existence, have to be born during the reign of the industrial death machine? Uncle John wondered the same thing about himself. Everyday in the paper or on the news there was something about a species going extinct or rivers becoming more polluted, the air getting worse, another forest being cut down, and on and on, day after day, and I felt that it would only be a matter of time, just as if you were to slowly cut off pieces of a person, that the earth herself would die and become extinct. I had developed a love of nature thanks to Aunt Iris. What would I have to look forward to in the future — the loss of what I loved? The present is hard when loss is at both ends of time.

As I passed the new tourist development, the bulldozers and men were gone. There, a couple hundred feet above high tide, were long grass huts that stretched along the shore. Young Indian braves were racing their long boats out in the ocean. A few others farther out were fishing. Women, gathered in groups amongst their huts, were talking and cooking and watching their children, most of whom were playing in the surf. And there I was, a little boy, playing in the surf with the rest of the kids. The sun began to set, and I returned to our hut and sat on my mother's soft lap and ate corn and lobster that had washed up on shore during the previous night's storm.

After we ate I stayed in my mother's lap as we watched the sun sink into the sea.

I turned, and as I walked back to Aunt Iris's, I thought about those men and their machines and about what I had been told about my parents, about how they struggled, were squeezed by debt and took risks that they should probably not have taken, and how they too were dependent on the machines for their survival and how their dependency, not a car, killed them. That thought only made me more angry, which in turn fueled more thoughts and questions.

Why, I kept on asking myself, why was all this destruction taking place? Uncle John's answers kept on going through my mind, but still, I thought there had to be more to it than that. If people were so creative, which there was no arguing against, then why couldn't they create a way of life that wasn't destructive? Maybe, I thought, people had come here from another planet but they forgot it consciously and unconsciously were trying to make the earth like their home planet where life was sustained by chemicals we call pollutants, and everything grew in the shape of triangles, rectangles and squares. Then I began to doubt that the damage was an unavoidable part of industrial development. I felt that deep in people's hearts they were proud of their destruction because they had finally subdued their last competitor and brought her to her knees.

And as conquerors often take pleasure in torturing those they conquer, people seemed to enjoy a similar sadistic pleasure in torturing mother earth by scarring her face and slowly killing off her children. As these feelings swirled through my head and as I looked at everyone drive to work every day, drive home, smile at each other, act concerned, say the same things over and over again; I felt somehow they had become numb, that they didn't care about themselves, other living things, their children's future, and in their state of pathetic numbness, they had lost their value for life and would do anything for a buck.

Maybe I could have seen some value in the destructive way of life if it had created happiness. Even when I was young, I knew that happiness was something to go after; that's why I clung to Aunt Iris.

Just being with her made me happy. But the normal way of life brought unhappiness. You can tell a lot about people by looking at them when they think no one is looking, as when they're driving alone in a car. Some look thoughtful, a few content, some vacant, but most look weary and unhappy. As I watched them, which I did more and more after my growing up walk through town, I thought how could it be otherwise? How could their disregard for life not find its way into their lives? Isn't life the same all over? They were overworked, running all over the place, wanting companionship yet stabbing each other on the upward climb, suffering with the diseases of pollution, plagued with guilt, crammed into buildings and narrow streets, pressured under debt, and constantly worrying about making it and losing their jobs if they couldn't keep up. And this, it was advertised, brought out the best in people; helped make them into steely, tough survivors, the kind of human beings needed to insure a strong economic future. Only convinced me that they did not know what was best for themselves.

A baby knows deep within its heart (even a baby cow knows this) that it needs others to survive. Somehow this precious piece of information was lost in growing because the weariness of loneliness showed through the unselfconscious adult face. You could see the lonely child walled inside trying to reach through to be touched and caressed. Yet, how could there be loneliness with the most complex, worldwide communication system in the history of the world, people crawling all over the place, sardine can jammed bars and restaurants, constant talking (you could hardly find a quiet place in town), all kinds of clubs and organizations, parties every night, a phone in everyone's pocket, radio, and TV?

Why, the question kept going through my mind, if the accepted way of life was producing unhappiness and destroying the world, why couldn't it be changed? Everything else was changing so fast that it was hard to stand up. Somehow efforts produced results opposite to those intended. Why was achieving the opposite so widespread? Many times after someone would tell me they were taking the high road into town, I'd return later only to find them squirming in a ditch with their head stuck in a culvert. Why, in having a lot was little had, in trying to be close did the gap widen, in seeking fulfillment was emptiness found, in the pursuit for meaning was guilt and uselessness the reward; why, in winning was what was most precious lost, in becoming educated were ways to become creatively bankrupt learned, in trying to be found was the way lost, in trying to be something did someone become nothing, and why, in fleeing from the void, did so many fall into it?

Before I realized this contrariness, I thought something was wrong with my hearing. I even had it tested. After I found out it wasn't my hearing, I started making a game of trying to figure out what others would really do in contrast to what they were saying. I'd usually end up entertaining many different scenes. It soon became automatic. When someone spoke to me, I would hear many different things. That's when I had my hearing checked for the second time.

Hearing many different things didn't limit itself to when others spoke of their intentions, but when they spoke to me about anything at all. My world really began to expand. A simple question over the phone, "What are you doing?" would echo with: "I'm bored, are you doing anything interesting? Are you sitting around daydreaming as usual? I'm lonely Bobby, come over and see me, please? I'm hungry, invite me over for dinner because I'm broke. Would you do something with me? Say you will. I'm afraid to ask because I'm afraid you'll say no. Why don't you get out of the garden and do something worthwhile for a change? There is nothing to do, is there? When it's all quiet, when I've got nothing to do and no one is around, I think there is nothing to do in life. Come over! Please! I'm afraid of my own mind."

Surrounded by this sea of insanity was Iris's island of sanity.

She knew about the things that troubled me. Actually, I'm not sure if my perceptions were hers or mine. Yet, she went about her life as though the world were perfect. As long as I knew her, she enjoyed living. Why wasn't she upset by the loss of what she loved? Why wasn't she like everyone else? Even Uncle John, who shared in many of her beliefs and perceptions, was not as happy as she was. He was angry, Iris wasn't. Where did she get her strength?

Barren islands rise out of the sea. Soon dead sea life washes up on shore and decays into soil, birds come to make their home, seeds and bugs ride in on the wind, and sea animals climb ashore to stay for a while and some even evolve into permanent land animals. With time, the once lifeless island is teeming with life. Unlike those islands, Aunt Iris's island didn't seem to be sustained from the outside. She was more like a mighty oak whose roots sink deeply into fertile ground. What was her source of vitality and happiness?

I tried not to think about this stuff all the time. Didn't have much luck. Oh, I was able to push these thoughts down for a while, but they'd always come back stronger than before and cram my packed brain even tighter, causing me to suffer with constipation of the brain. I needed relief! What if life was the way others lived it? What would I do? Even though I didn't like what I saw, I didn't know how things should be. I hadn't traveled to other cultures; wasn't much of a reader. Yet, I felt others really hadn't looked at life. To look at yourself in the mirror, you have to look directly into it; they seemed to be staring into the toilet.

Chapter 10

Early one morning I was yanked out of my sleep by mind cramps. I got up, staggered through the house looking for Aunt Iris, and finally found her sitting on her swing in the gazebo. Everyone should have someone like Aunt Iris to turn to, no matter what their age.

I opened my mouth, and everything poured out. "What am I gonna do, Aunt Iris? Everybody seems so unhappy. Everything is dying. No one seems to care, and I keep on thinking and thinking about it, and I can't figure out why. Why are things this way? I don't want them to be this way. I'm afraid. I'm happy with you, but I'm afraid that once I get on my own, I'll become like everyone else and be unhappy too. I don't want that to happen to me. I don't want to contribute to the destruction of the world. What's life all about, Aunt Iris?"

She gently placed her hands on my temples, tilted my head, parted my hair, and peered at my skull as though looking for fleas on a dog.

"You sure have a lot going on in there. How's it all fit in there? I've never met anyone like you." She hugged me and laughed. "You're funny. Here it is in the wee morning hours, and you wake up and the first thing you do is ask me those kinds of questions. I suppose you want answers right now?"

"Yeah."

"Well, I'll tell you, Bobby, there's nothing quite like life. I've never seen anything like it in all my life. Stick around. You'll find it'll be worth your while."

I've been sticking around ever since.

Later that day while I was sitting in the garden wondering if I could possibly find something better than life, Aunt Iris sat next to me and said, "Come on, Bobby, let's go to the ocean. There's more to life than how others live it."

"Yeah, let's go. That's a great idea, Aunt Iris."

We put on our suits, got towels, and walked out through the backyard on our well-beaten path to the ocean. Our town was built upon the dirt and rocks that were part of a mountain range that was slowly sliding into the sea. The dirt and rock that had fallen off the mountain sides left behind cliffs that ran along the coast. The cliffs were composed of red sandstone streaked horizontally by wavy bands of white sandstone. You could see as many things in those cliffs as you could in clouds. They were easy to see from the beach and complemented the water's fluidity. Beyond the cliffs toward the mountain peaks were hundreds of square miles of high altitude rolling hills and plateaus. Those areas facing south were arid and covered with tough, hardy vegetation, whereas those on the north side were lush and gentle to the eye and touch. Simply by walking a few hundred yards from one side to the other, you felt as though you were walking from one climatic zone to another. Many towns and villages thrived in those hills.

Behind Iris's backyard was a huge meadow through which flowed a stream to the ocean. Many adventures could be had just by walking, well, just by looking out her backyard. The path going out Aunt Iris's backyard divided into three when it came to the stream. One way it went straight over a plank bridge, through a meadow, and became lost in a deep, dark wood. My friends and I played often in those woods. I came to know them very well. No matter how far we went in those woods, we always found our way back. The path to the left followed the meandering stream for a few miles to a pool at the base of a cliff. This was the stream's resting place after falling out of a slit in the canyon wall. It fell as a thin line a few hundred feet, hit protruding rocks, and showered the rest of the way down. That was another favorite spot. If you weren't familiar with the area you would have thought, upon looking up from the pool, that there was no way, unless you were an experienced mountain climber, to climb the cliff. But there was a way, very stair like, that zigzagged across the cliff's face. At the top was a lake fed by that same stream. The lake sat in a small, lush valley. The area, at one time, had been the home of native folk. There was an old orchard and many vegetable plants that had gone wild and spread throughout the native vegetation. Iris and I never needed to take any food or water when we went there, just our clothes and sleeping bags. We would usually enjoy a couple weeks there.

Once we spent the entire summer. It was our second home, a very lovely place. For as peaceful and beautiful as it was and still is, I was always surprised that more people didn't go there. Everyone knew of it. But this day, after walking out her back yard past the large familiar rock next to which a spring bubbled and flowed down into the stream, we didn't take a left toward the cliff, but went right, with a hippity hop, and followed the stream toward the ocean. The stream, before disappearing under a sand dune, narrowed and deepened and fell as one for about ten feet, made a great turbulence, then surged over itself down underneath.

Up to the top of the dune we climbed. The ocean spread endlessly before us. My eyes followed the shore line north around a curve of a thin, golden peninsula, which pulsating in the heat of the sun, disappeared and reappeared in the blue sea. We bounded down the dune and joined the stream where it bubbled out of the sand. The ocean sparkled; I did the same inside.

"Come on, Aunt Iris, let's go." We dropped our towels and ran into the surf.

The ocean was relatively calm that day. After swimming awhile, we sat at the water's edge and let the waves lap onto our legs. The water was cool and refreshing, and the air smelled rich.

Iris turned to me and said, "How do you feel, Bobby?"

"I feel good, although I am still troubled."

"Why do you feel good?"

I gave her a quizzical look. "What do you mean?"

"Just what I said. Why do you feel good?"

"Because I'm having a good time swimming with you."

"What else? Now don't give me a general answer just to pacify me. Really, I want to know. Give me specific reasons why you feel good."

"Are you serious?"

"Yes."

I watched the water rise over our legs and then recede, and said, "It's a beautiful day. The water is just right — not too cold, not too warm; although, I wouldn't mind some big waves. I'm with you. And I haven't been thinking of my parents."

"What is it about me that makes you feel good?"

I gave her another funny look.

"Seriously, Bobby, this is not idle talk. Trust me."

I looked out to the horizon. "You are kind to me. I feel secure with you. I feel loved by you."

"I do love you." She put her arm over my shoulder, pulled me to her, and let go. "Do you think my love for you will last?"

"I hope so. I'll do anything I can to make it last."

"What if you were here with Uncle Ed, would you still feel good?"

"Of course not. Not unless he were being nice to me, but if he were, he wouldn't be my Uncle Ed."

She raised her knees and wrapped her arms around them. "So am I right in saying that, besides it being a beautiful day, the main reason you feel good is because you are with me and feel loved by me?"

"Yes." I shook her knees with my hand. "What are you getting at?"

"I'm trying to lead you into answers to your questions. I could answer them from my outlook on life, but if I can lead you into answering them yourself, then it will mean more to you. So, if you please, follow me along even though the answers to some of my questions will seem obvious."

"Gladly." I immediately became attentive.

"Why does my love for you make you happy?"

"Why? It just does. That's the nature of love."

A snail washed up between us. Iris picked it up as it withdrew into its shell.

"Yes, that's true. But there's a reason why happiness is essential to love's nature.

"What if I kept this snail out of the water?"

"It would die."

Iris rose, walked to some bushes behind us, tore off a leaf, and sat next to me. "What will happen to this leaf?"

"It will shrivel up."

"And what if I tore one of those bushes back there out by the roots and threw it on the ground?"

"It would also die."

"And a child, if he or she had parents or had someone, but did not receive any love and affection: no touching, no being talked to, nothing — what would happen to the child?"

"The poor thing would probably die, and if it did live, it would have so many problems that life would probably not be worth living."

100

"Why?"

"Because the child would have been deprived of what it needed to live."

"Before the child died, he or she would have been unhappy. Wouldn't you say?"

"I'd say that was an understatement. It would suffer as few do. Sorrow would slowly suck away its life."

"So what we can say about unhappiness is that it is a result of not receiving what we need to live in all the complex ways in which we live — nourishment, warmth, love, companionship, stimulation, et cetera, et cetera."

"Sure."

"But if the snail was returned to the water," Iris rolled the snail back into the ocean, "and the leaves stayed on the bush, and the bush in the ground, and the child was fed and cared for in a loving way, they would live, would they not?"

"Yes."

"And the child would be happy in being fed and loved. Would he not?"

"Sure. Of course. That's common knowledge."

"So what can we say about the nature of love?"

"It helps keep us alive, and in the process, produces happiness."

"Yes, good. We are this far along. Our greatest desire is to live, of course, and this also is the desire for love, although at times the desire for love is greater, for death is often sought when love is lost, the pain being that great. Every living thing is rooted in existence by being joined with other things, and for us human beings, love is the main force that joins our being to being itself. As blood carries life throughout the body, love carries life through the human race. Being in this flow of love produces the experience of happiness, among other things. So the craving for love is not just for love, but for life. And each of us, just as a snail washed ashore will seek the ocean, strives with all our abilities to be loved."

"Would you like me to agree that it is true?" I asked.

"Not necessarily."

"Well, I'll agree that the truth is that it was said."

"Feeling a little playful, are you?"

"True words if I ever heard any."

"Tell me, Bobby, if these words are true. Since we all have been loved and suffered losses and rejections, some more of one and less of the other, we all experience a mixture of happiness and unhappiness."

"Yes. Our days are colored in different shades of gray."

"So here we are with the rest of mankind trying to maintain an existence under siege. We have our pleasures, our little comforts, fond memories and friends, all of which we try to harbor from stormy pains and sorrows that life pounds us with. And this, my thoughtful young man, is what seems to occupy our lives."

"Well, Aunt Iris, my thoughtful old woman," I stood up and threw a rock into the ocean, "I was hoping for an answer with more meaning. I've seen the little picture you just painted over and over again, and it's one I don't want to be in, but unfortunately I am."

I continued, "Is that all there is to life- shielding our little bit of happiness from sources of unhappiness? What a disappointment if that's what life is all about. Are we to be cheated and constantly teased by not being able to share in life's joy and beauty? No, I don't believe it. Life is too grand to be that small."

"I don't think that either. I wouldn't have started this conversation if I thought that! "Seeing that you place yourself in that little picture, what have you done in your life to gain happiness and avoid unhappiness?"

"Come on, Aunt Iris! You know as well as I what I've done. Probably more since you can be more objective."

"Yes, I know, but I want to hear it from you. Please, humor your dear, old aunt."

"Really!?"

"Please? Oh, you're going to blush. You're so cute when you blush. Oh, some more. How'd that happen? Oh yes, I know what you're thinking. You're thinking since you're so cute you don't have to do anything to be loved. That's it, isn't it?"

Just then out of nowhere a huge wave rose up, wrapped itself around me and dragged me out to sea. I raised up my arm and gasped, "Help, help, I'm getting carried away."

I let the wave pull me out and under. Slowly I glided to the surface, swam back, and sat beside her.

The tide had lowered since the beginning of our talk. Shells and multi-colored rocks, little worlds unto themselves, were now being rolled up onto the sand and washed back down. Beneath them were other mysterious worlds rolling around in the deeper water, barely visible, momentarily showing themselves before being drawn down into the dark depths.

I watched the shells and stones and ran my hands through the sand as I spoke. "My happiness is being cared for by you. When I first came to live with you, I was afraid of what might happen to me if you would not have wanted me, so I did whatever you wanted. I expected, from past experiences, that you too would be mean. But soon I learned otherwise.

"I cherish your love. I really do. What would have happened to me if you hadn't wanted me? It scares me to think about it. But why should I worry about that now? That's not what happened, and now that I'm almost twenty, I don't need to worry about getting stuck with someone mean. Never again will I get dumped on some stranger's lawn.

"Well, to get back to your question. What have I done? Like everyone else, I've sought happiness and avoided her mean and ugly mate. When I was younger, it was hard because I didn't have much control over where I was and with whom. Although, some things I did luckily got me to a better place. When I dumped the carrots on the floor at Aunt Sharon's and talked back to Uncle Ed, I was trying to gain some control over my life by expressing myself. But then, with John and Marty, I did as they wanted as I do with you because living with them was great compared to what I had been through. Although, I used to hide when John got angry. He never got angry at me except for the time I got caught eavesdropping in the kitchen, but still, it was upsetting just being around his anger.

"I see my life as steps upward to you. Some steps I took, and others lady luck lifted me over. But now, I feel that it's entirely up to me what my future will be.

"There's another thing I've done, well, this is confusing; I've blocked the memory of my parents but not voluntarily, like diving into the water. Something traumatic happened. I guess it's best that I don't remember because it would be too painful for me to experience, but I don't know if the loss is worth it. There's a big empty hole in my life. Sometimes I am overwhelmed with...how can I describe it? It's like a numbing despair mixed with fear. It terrifies me. So, that's something I've supposedly done that has made me happy. No, not happy; it has only relieved me of a great unhappiness by replacing it with another kind of unhappiness." I wiped my eyes.

"I want to remember my parents, where we lived, what they were like — everything before their death. But, well, it's a dream. It's impossible. What happened happened, and it can never be reclaimed." I began rocking front to back as I rubbed my hands hard on my legs. I started crying.

Iris put her arm around me. "Thank you, Bobby, for opening up with me. I really didn't expect it. You've said more than your words.

"Should we resume this conversation some other time?"

"No, it's fine. A cry a day keeps the shrink away." I laughed.

"At least you have a sense of humor about it.

"Do you think others want the same as you?" Iris asked.

"Yes. Basically."

Iris said, "Would you say, since others feel that way, that we all have the same wants and desires?"

"I suppose. Exactly what wants and desires?"

"To love and be loved. Not to suffer through hurt, loss, rejection, and to regain what has been lost."

"Yes. I would. That's what scares me. I don't see myself as different from others in that respect. Maybe even worse in some ways.

"I don't want to be this way! It is not living to have a big hole in my life and to be clinging to you in reaction to a deep fear of loss and abandonment. I want to enjoy living in this great big, wide world. I'm not now. That's why I've come to you. I have my happiness right here in this small place by the ocean with you, but I don't want this to be my only place of happiness and to waste my life guarding it against invasion like Aunt Sharon. That's not living to me. But that is what I see life for me and others as being. I do not know of anything else. That's what scares me.

"I feel as though I'm — everyone appears to me to be this way — stuck in a room, and in this room, I have a few cherished possessions but I can't really enjoy them because I'm frantically repairing the walls that are constantly being cracked and broken by dangerous things trying to break through. It never ends. The walls never stay sealed.

"Fitting in, showing off, staying in style, always having a new car like Uncle Ed, being on the defensive, hating, filling time, the insatiable hunger for money and power; all those activities are just sealing walls — the endless, fruitless, sealing of walls.

"Oh, I don't know." I said. "I guess it's worthwhile to protect against loss, but, at the same time, I feel it's a waste of life because the threat never ends. It only gets put off until a later day when maybe it can find satisfaction through a weakness. Often, what appears to be a threat is not, except for being a reminder of something painful in the past. The past cannot be changed, only added to, and so, my God, really, is this what life is all about? Sealing walls?

"What determines what is in our rooms and what is trying to break through? Fate? Chance? It doesn't seem fair. If warm rays shine upon your birth, and you're loved and appreciated, and there you stay, and your life goes on that way as a stick floating down a gentle river; you're one of the happy few who can enjoy life in this big, round, jovial world, but if not, which is usually the case, a person comes to a quick end, alone in a tiny room, sealing cracks that will only reappear. And maybe, just maybe, if you can steal a scrap of time, a tiny bit of pleasure can be had in between sealing.

"All the development, all the consumer items, all the marvelous technological advances, all the things your brother John complains about — they are all ways to seal walls. They're all a big waste. A lot is done, but what is gained?"

An excited look seized Iris's face. "Is all futile? Is it futile to seek love, futile to avoid cruelty, futile to stand up against criticism, futile to fight one's enemy, futile for the infant to seek the warmth and nourishment of its mother, futile to stay out of closets after having been locked in them as a child? Futile to fight and strive to have needs met? Aren't these things the substance of life?"

"Yes and no, or maybe just yes. I'm not sure. Striving is a part of life, not always of living though. Few of us can have our needs met by sitting in the woods like the Buddha. No, what you said isn't futile, but it is when love found cannot be received or when cruelty is avoided by being cruel or when the faster you run the closer it gets or when

105

standing up to criticism is automatic, or by fighting an enemy that really isn't one or craving mother's teat when you're forty, or staying out of closets when the fear is really not of closets."

"I see." Iris gave me one of her mind searching looks and then stared out across the ocean.

"Imagine, Bobby, that these ocean waves are waves of time. Here we are on this present shore watching the future roll in, welcoming the good fortune it brings and buttressing ourselves, if we have the strength, from ill fortune. And as the present waves roll back out, they change future waves by undercutting and making them larger and more powerful, or by smashing up against them and reducing them, or by hesitating on the beach and reinforcing the future. Eventually, present waves dissipate back out into the past. Those great experiences of love and closeness float on the surface and are easily washed ashore, whereas those that have hurt are dragged down by the undertow into the deep, dark depths where they roll around and swirl upward through the surface.

"Mankind stands here on the shore of time trying to anticipate and control future waves, which is a great feat and usually futile, for waves change constantly as they move toward shore.

"Here, see that big wave cresting out there?"

"Yeah."

"Let's watch it. There it goes rising up on the sand bar, turning to the east, sinking down in deeper water, whoops — got swallowed by that one from behind. Oh, this could be a big one. Here it comes; there's a good size one before it rolling back out; slam, knocked the force out of it, didn't it?"

"Sure did." That once big wave was now a big ripple gliding across our feet.

"Yet, some who are blessed with relatively calm seas have a fair amount of success in enjoying life and withstanding whatever storms that crash into their world, and others of wealth and power defiantly build fortresses on the sand that, hopefully, will withstand the most violent storms. Then there are others who no matter how they dance and dodge every so often get knocked flat on their back, and then there are those unfortunate ones who, after continually getting hammered into the sand, finally lose their resilience and get bashed to pieces. No matter how secure one's world, there's always that chance, more so than not, for terrible storms constantly gather on future's vast expanse, that powerful waves of destruction, dredging painful memories up from the bottom, will crash into the present and shatter a person's world."

"As when my parents died."

"Yes. And yours wasn't the only world that was shattered."

"What I've said is similar to your metaphor of sealing walls, isn't it?"

"Yeah. The kind of life I'd like to grow out of."

Iris stood and ran her foot through a wave as it slid across the sand. "Imagine again with me that the present is where the waves of time touch the shore. When high tide floods the shore, the present can feel close, at times overwhelming, and yet at low tide at a shallow beach, the present can feel miles away, ephemeral, like a dream.

"Anyway, where time touches the shore is our contact with it, and through this place enters our experiences and knowledge. The future cannot be known because, like that wave, we don't know what it will be until it gets here, and the past, well there is nothing to know there because it doesn't exist. The past is only distorted memories.

"Imagine that all these experiences that occur in our contact with time are an expression of our relationship with being. Pleasant experiences of love, affection, play, touching, a beautiful day, a satisfying meal, friendship and the like are our connection with being. All those experiences are communications of the amount in which we share and result in our own sense of being. On the other side, all those experiences that come through the present that reduce and remove us, such as rejection, loss, ridicule, deprivation, hatred, ugly surroundings, and things like that, are the extent to which our being is separate from being. Although it feels as though they separate us, and in a way they do, it's more that they are an expression of our distance from being. Instead of things happening in time that are the cause of our being enhanced or reduced, they are expressions of our relationship to being or lack of it. Events in time are not the cause, but carry with them expressions of a state. Can you imagine that?"

I said, "Yes, I think so. Let me see. Individuals have a certain closeness and distance to this abstract being of yours. What happens to us in this world represents that closeness and distance. Events do not, from what I gather, cause closeness or distance. So if circumstances and events don't, what does?"

"The individual, but we'll get to that in a moment.

"So," she continued, "if experiences are a result of our relationship to being, would trying to alter the present to cause changes in the future alter our relationship to being?"

"Put that way — no."

"It would be a futile effort. Right?"

"Yes. Now, let me ask you a few questions." I said.

"Closeness to being, I understand, because of what experiences it comprises, is the cause of happiness."

"Yes."

"And distance is the cause of unhappiness. Right?"

"That's how I see things."

"Well," I said, "people plan for things to happen in the future that will make them happy: new car, new friends, getting reunited with a loved one, going on vacation, climbing the social ladder, enjoying a day at the beach, making more money, finding a mate. These things make them happy, don't they?"

"They will be a source of genuine happiness if they are an expression of closeness to being or an expression of moving closer, but it will only be a fading, empty happiness if it is not — if it masquerades as such. Receiving genuine affection has its share of happiness, but it can also be a source of unhappiness and disappointment when the expectation, whether conscious or unconscious, is the end of all feelings of not being loved. Shallow, short lived happinesses, especially those resulting from possessions, are such because a painful feeling is only momentarily numbed.

"I'm surprised at your question," she said. "It's as though you want to defend activities that I know you feel are a waste."

I laughed. "Not at all. I just wanted to hear your answer.

"From what I understand, to become happier and feel that efforts are not futile and that life is not being wasted, somehow one needs to move closer. You must have done this then or have hopes of doing it."

With sincerity she said, "I believe I have moved closer."

She continued, "Now, let's imagine that our relationship to being can be changed. Then a person could, if he or she knew how, move closer, and as a result, become truly more happy and secure."

"Now I see where you're going, Iris. So this is the way you've found your peace of mind in this troubled world. Will you tell me how you have achieved your peace of mind, or is it a secret?"

"No," she said, "it's not a secret. I haven't taken you this far only to stop. Although, hearing about it and experiencing it for yourself are two different things. If there is a secret, it lies in between those two.

"In trying to understand or find the source of something, much can be learned about the source, even before it is found, by investigating those things for which it is responsible in creating. Would you agree with that?"   .

"I suppose. Could you give me an example?"

"Sure. Well, let me think a moment." She paused and ran her foot back and forth through the sand.

"Say we wanted to know where sand came from. At first, that would be easy — the grinding up of rocks by the action of waves. Then, if we were curious enough, we'd wonder what was the make-up and origin of rocks and water, and this would lead to molecules and atoms. And in finding where they came from, we may need to find out the composition and origin of the earth, which would lead us to the stars and from the stars to the galaxies and from there to the origin of the universe. In our investigations, we would learn much about how things form and decay, and from this obtain clues about the ultimate origin of sand. Does that help?"

"I see what you mean," I said.

"If we were to trace back our experiences, those within and outside of us, we would understand them better, understand what they have done to us, our reaction to them, and possibly find their source. And if we understood how they came to be, then it would not be much of a step in figuring out how they could be enhanced or diminished."

I said, "I'm not sure I agree. Many people seem to understand or at least know the cause of how they came to be what they are, yet feel helpless at being able to change what they don't like about themselves."

"That is what is troubling you? You also feel helpless?"

109

"Yes, Iris. Many times I am carried away by feelings I have no control over."

"If you found the source of those feelings, do you think you could gain control over them?"

"I'm not sure." I paused. "Only if I actually gained control over their source and eliminated it. But, oh hell, right now I can't even get near them. I don't want control if that means repression because in the long run my repressed feelings will gain control over me as they do now."

"So you would rather not be repressed?"

"In one way, yes; another, no. Everything has its purpose.

"Repression seems to remove distracting, painful memories and feelings so we can function and survive, but the price is high because so many other abilities are taken away, and it creates a bomb that can easily explode, as what seemed to happen to Uncle Ed when Aunt Patsy divorced him, and he tried to kill her. But then, no, I would not like to be repressed. No, that's putting it mildly; I would love to be unrepressed if what was repressed ceased to bother me. But that's impossible, except in the imagination."

"Maybe not. Let's see how far our imaginations can take us.

"Since the mind devotes a great deal of energy in repressing itself and developing an elaborate defensive system, it would be a difficult fight against itself to delve into what has been repressed and try to find their source. Would it not?"

"Sure."

"After a while wouldn't even a courageous person be halted by pain and the mind's powerful repressive strength?"

"I would think so."

"But, what if the source of the pain could be diminished?"

"Where? In what? You mean painful things that happened in the past?"

"Yes, primarily. But also what will happen."

"Well no, not in the past. The damage has been done, permanently."

"If you came upon a lion without protection, you would be terrified, right?"

"Of course. Who wouldn't be afraid?"

"Later, if you came across that lion again and you were armed or in a car with the doors locked, or if the lion had been tamed, you would not be as afraid. Would you?"

"No."

"In a likewise manner, what if it could be done that what was painful was not only less so, but you experienced it from a stronger position?"

"Well, it would be easier to experience, and, well, there would be less of a need to repress it. But, Iris, what happened happened. The past cannot be changed!"

"In the sense that the past is something that happened, no, it cannot be changed. Although, the way in which the past is remembered—that can be changed. Say, well, imagine again the waves of time bringing in the future and along with it dredging things off the bottom of the memory into the present. And what they bring in, as I mentioned before, represent our distance and closeness to being. So somehow if we were able to move closer to being, then what the waves of time brought into the present, whether it be from the memory or the future, would represent that closeness and make one stronger; therefore repressed memories, lifted into consciousness, would not be as threatening."

"So the past would not be changed, only the memory of it?"

"I would say that the past is changed because the past only exists in the memory."

"Okay. I can look at the past in that way."

"In getting closer to being by tracing back the good and pleasant experiences for which it was and is responsible, don't you think that would be much easier than tracing back painful experiences?"

"Yes. I see what you're getting at. By becoming more a part of being, what has been unconscious can be made conscious without having to experience the pain beneath it.

"You know, Aunt Iris, I've been listening to you as though I were being led along a trail. How do I know what you've been showing me is true? How do I know your ideas about time and being and our relationship to it really exist? People ease their minds with all sorts of beliefs. How do I know what you are telling me is not just in your imagination?"

"Yes, imagination is a powerful creator of endless worlds, some real some not, and these worlds can play tricks in the mind, especially an isolated, anxious mind; but it can also be a long reach beyond itself into a living tree laden with fruit. I agree with you that it is hard to know whether what is imagined is real or not. I believe what I've told you is true because it makes logical sense, is consistent with my own experiences, and I have, I really don't think I've fooled myself, become happier and have regained lost parts of myself. My intention is not to convince you of my beliefs. I'm only trying to answer your questions. Although, I love you and hope that you will find some comfort in this."

"You have already comforted me." I took her hand and held it.

"Would you like me to describe some of my experiences to you?"

"Of course."

"Years ago I sincerely started to trace back my strengths and pleasant experiences. Not just pleasant experiences with others such as being loved, loving another, acts of kindness or friendly conversation, but also exhilarating experiences in the natural world, like a beautiful sunrise or a clear, blue day at the ocean or the beauty of the mountains— any experience that really made me feel alive and made me feel, oh, a love for life. I would try to concentrate on the experiences, feelings, and emotions they aroused in me, meditate on them, and try to find their source. I found that all these varied pleasant experiences would produce in me the same fundamental feeling, and its source was being or life or the essence of life or whatever you want to call it.

"Slowly an avenue opened up to my inner life. I looked down that avenue and yearned to be at that distant place. I felt that if I were there I would always be secure no matter where I went, that it was the source of everything good and beautiful, that it was the rich ground out of which grew hope and meaning, was a place where guilt, anger and resentment never dwelt, that it was a pool of love in which I could soak, and was a place where I would always feel at home.

"Even though I felt I had this increased awareness, I didn't feel that I had actually moved closer. I still felt the distance.

"Well, more so really because I was more aware of it. What was holding me away, I realized after some time, was that I didn't want to consciously experience the ways of my separation. In wanting to be closer to a fire's warmth you not only have to feel its warmth but also the cold from its distance, in a similar way, to know you have to move closer to being you have to consciously experience its distance. So, from a new position of strength, I began to bring painful memories into the present, and whenever I would feel anxious, usually when alone and restless or in an anxiety causing situation, such as being criticized, I would try to experience it and find what was behind it instead of arguing or leaving. It's important to do this from a place of strength because these things are painfully strong and can, without a sure footing, knock one off balance.

"After that I concentrated on, well, I went back to the avenue and felt that I had moved closer to my essence. I remember how excited I was the first time this happened. I really felt that I had moved closer. I felt more secure and confident. Nature was more beautiful. I became more interested in painting and music. Some painful memories were not as painful. I didn't feel I had to be busy all the time, and criticism didn't hurt as much, and what people thought of me wasn't much of a concern. I felt lighter, freer, and more alive. Nothing concerned me much except this new adventure I was on. For a while I bathed in this increased closeness, tried to understand it better, and make it more solid. From this new position of strength, I once again delved into experiences of separation, passed through a wall, came out of it, felt closer and stronger, and felt things evaporate as lost parts of myself returned. Gradually, I gained more of an understanding of what would move my life forward and what would not. Along with this movement, I've developed a vision of what I could become, a likeness of my future self, and I've held this in my mind and from her I draw strength. One day I hope she is what I will become.

"For a long time it was a struggle; I had many setbacks. I hit a turning point when I felt the desire to end my defensive system grow past the desire to maintain one, so now in contrast to fighting it as I did in the beginning, my old defensive system is becoming undone by itself. The power beneath is weakening. Now, I rarely try to make feelings and experiences of separation conscious. Mostly, I've been moving forward by digging my roots deeper into being.

"Now, since I've been doing this for so long, it's hard to imagine not being in this process. As I move closer to my inner life, I also feel closer to life in the outside world. This division between my own inwardness and the inwardness of other things is melting, so now I pretty much have the experience of moving closer to life itself.

"One of the best things about this adventure is that it has enabled me to love you the way I have."

"I'm glad you went on it then," I said.

"Well, I think I understand most of what you've said, Iris, but what about what happened in the past? They can't be undone or can they? I don't understand that yet. I mean, what I suffered with the loss of my parents and what happened afterward and the big section of my life that is missing, I'll always have that with me, won't I?"

"You may or may not, all depending on what you do," she said.

"The tragic death of your parents and what happened to you afterward cannot be changed. You're right—that was something that happened to you. Loss suffered here on earth is, as I said before, a way in which separation from being is experienced. By becoming more absorbed, all the ways in which separation is experienced will go down and those of uniting more with life will go up. You cannot get your parents back, but you can have the scars of their loss healed and the emptiness you feel filled. And if you venture in this direction, you should be able to remember them without having your security shaken.

"I can remember many things now that I never could before. I think of them as past in the sense that they do not upset me. Does that make sense?"

"We'll, yeah, I'll think about that."

"You know when I was much younger," she laughed, "I had many of the same worries and questions as you do now. I think most people do. But all those questions like what is life all about, what is the meaning to life, why am I here — all those questions disappeared when I felt my self move closer. It just makes sense. We are in life; life is to be experienced, and by experiencing it more and feeling more a part of it as time goes by; I mean, why would those questions remain? Questions like that fade when life becomes more enjoyable. That's not to say that you can't have your share of happiness now. Asking questions and pursuing their answers is a healthy sign."

She stretched and raised her hands toward the sky. "Well, Bobby, that's my little philosophy of life. The way, as you say, I've been able to stay sane in this sea of insanity."

"Still Aunt Iris, even though you have found your way and are happy with it, doesn't the destruction of nature and human cruelty upset you? You're not insulated from all this, are you?"

"No, I'm not immune to it. You know as well as I do that I care; you know what I've done to help. Maybe I am too concerned about my own self; I'm not sure. Those things do sadden me, but they don't depress me as they once did. The world is the way it is. I can't save the world. And I don't know if I would if I could. I believe there would have to be a change in a fundamental law of nature, which, besides being impossible, would do more harm than good.

"Life is much bigger and wiser that I am. It is playing itself out on earth. Many have found enjoyment in life. Those who haven't, well, they have each other to put up with. Perhaps one day they will find their own source of lasting happiness. I don't know. The human race is like a big, muddy, tangled web in transformation. And perhaps, to be optimistic, those who shine like specks of gold in mud will venture forward and shine through this tangled web and spread their movement to their children and others, and with time this movement will spread and smooth out all the tangles until a golden, mandalic web of perfect harmony and beauty will shine throughout the solar system.

"Who knows, maybe this will happen. But I doubt it." She laughed.

She became serious again. "Bobby, even though there's a lot of death and destruction, it doesn't mean you can't have a good life. I've had a good life. No matter what happens to the world, no matter what other people do, the potential to become more a part of life will always exist. There may not be much hope in the world, but there is hope in us. Life will go on and take joy in its own existence no matter what the human creature does. And we can always share in life's joy and exuberance. A person can kill the life within himself, he can destroy the world around him, but he cannot kill life. You can be happy and find meaning even though unhappiness and meaninglessness surround you.

115

"So Bobby, now that I'm older, I feel that I've made peace with the world, and that has given me another kind of happiness. It was a goal of mine when I was younger, and now that I can honestly say that I have successfully achieved that goal, I can leave this place with few regrets. I can say to myself, 'Yes Iris, that was life all right. It was an experience worth living for.'" She laughed and pushed me.

"Anyway," she continued, "you can come and ask me anything you want, and if you decide to go on this adventure that I've been trying to explain to you, I will help you in any way I can. Your Aunt Marty could also help you. She seems to be moving closer. But your Uncle John, I don't know about him. He's tightly wrapped in words.

"Has what I've said helped you, Bobby."

"Yes. Very much. You've given me a lot of ideas to play with. Thank you."

She stood up, reached to me, and said, "Here, take my hand. Let's go home."

With a heart full of affection, I held her hand as we walked out of the low surf onto the warm, evening sand.

In the evening twilight, I was sitting next to Iris on the back porch gazing at her garden. Raspberry, gooseberry, and blackberry bushes and other species of shrubs growing under huge oak trees had frail, broad leaves and long stems that bent outward toward the sun. The center of her garden, which received the full light of the sun, was thick with lush tomato plants, corn, rose bushes, massive broccoli plants that looked like bushes, and tall beet stalks. Underneath this thick vegetation, were some small, pale, distorted plants trying to weave their way into the sunlight. Over to the right beneath a row of lilac bushes were many thin, dwarfed plants: dandelions, Swiss chard, carrots, poppies, to name a few, trying to survive in the shade. Many of their cousins lay dead on the ground. I stood, turned to go into the house, turned back around, and glanced over her garden. All in all it was growing very well.

Chapter 11

As Aunt Iris grew older, she spent more and more time alone in her garden. We took fewer trips. She saw her friends less often. She told me fewer stories. Her movements became slower, but her alertness didn't seem to wane. Someone who did not know her probably would have thought that she was not very alert, for she seemed to be in a trance quite often. She was alert though, very alert to things she was concerned about.

The day she told me she was nearing death is as clear as this present moment. She was sitting at a table in her garden near the bird bath, arranging flowers in a vase. I was sitting next to her watching.

She had her usual expression while arranging flowers—a slight smile, sleepy eyes, a content relaxed face. She pulled out flowers, stared at the arrangement, placed them in a different location, then moved the vase around, and rearranged some more. I think a bomb could have blown up next to her without her noticing. I didn't think she was aware of me until she spoke.

"How do you like the flowers, Bobby?"

"They're very pretty."

"You know, I'm old. I feel lately—I feel it very strongly—that I may die soon. I want to talk to you about it."

I was silent. She placed her hands softly on my cheeks and kissed me on the forehead. Then she turned toward me.

"I'm the only person you have. I'm concerned about what will happen to you after I'm gone."

"I'll be all right." I had to force the rest of my words. "Let's not talk about this. You can't die. I don't want you to die." Pressure was building up across my forehead and making my head ache.

"I know you don't. For your sake, I don't want to either. But we all die. Everything dies."

"I know, I know, but Aunt Iris that means I'll never see you again. I'll never be able to talk to you again. What'll I do without you?"

My whole body tensed up, and my head throbbed. She touched me, and I immediately hugged her as hard as I could. We sat there holding each other for a long while. She then leaned back and looked at me.

Tears were in her eyes.

"Let yourself cry, Bobby. Don't be afraid. It'll ease the pain.

"Crying is only the other side of laughter. And you know how we feel about that." She forced her ornery grin past her sad, teary face.

"Sometimes the only thing you can do is cry."

I held onto her and cried. After my crying subsided, I said, "When do you think you're going to die? How soon?"

"I don't know."

"A week, a month, a year?"

"It's hard to say. I just feel it coming. What I wanted to talk to you about was you. Do you have any plans on what you intend to do?"

"Well, yeah. I'd like to try to move my life forward as you have."

"Yes, I know. But, how do you plan on making a living?"

"I don't know. I haven't given it much thought. Human beings weren't made to do one thing for their entire lives. I won't get crammed into that box. I'll be me and follow my interests and hopefully make enough money to live comfortably. Maybe I'll try writing."

"Yes. You always have liked writing stories. John would help you if you wanted."

"Don't worry about me. I'll be all right."

"I'm more worried about you being alone and becoming lonely. You have your friends, but still you keep to yourself."

"I'm not worried about becoming lonely. I get along with a lot of different types. I'd rather be alone than with someone just to have someone around. I don't need someone talking to me about things I could care less about. Anyway, Aunt Iris, I don't get very lonely when I'm alone."

"That's true."

She looked at me for a while. "You know, Bobby, I think I'm just worried because I won't be here to look after you. Sometimes, you seem so fragile, as on the first day you came to live with me. You looked like you needed someone to mother you. Now, don't get mad at me, but you still look like that sometimes. You're still such a little boy. And yet, at other times, you are so independent. You always have been. You'll be all right. I can tell by looking at you now. If I believed in angels, I'd say you had a guardian angel."

"I'll miss you Aunt Iris. Please don't die soon."

"I'm afraid I may."

For the rest of the day and until she died, we were always together.

Her movements continued to slow; she did less and less, and even her alertness slowly faded. She spent most of her time in her garden. One morning while I was eating breakfast, I sensed that she was not going to get up. Many times she did not get up in the morning because she had been up all night, but this time I had a different feeling. After eating, I made her breakfast and took it into her room.

The door to her bedroom was off to the left of the kitchen facing the back of the house. Both rooms had doors opening onto the back porch. I liked her room; it was light and cheerful. The wall between her room and the porch faced south and was solid windows. Many times while sitting in the kitchen, I would watch the rays of light glide through her room and give life to the floating dust particles, and I would imagine myself as one of those particles coming alive in a ray of light and then, in an instant, disappearing into the shadows.

As you entered her room, if the sunshine didn't overwhelm your senses, her walls, covered with the paintings she had done of flowers and plants, did. She continually changed the paintings from a stack of them she had done. Most of her paintings were of flowers in a vase.

Each painting evoked a different feeling in me, and as I looked at them, I felt they were characterizing various stages in a person's life or the different faces people cover themselves with. This day, her walls were lined with my favorite paintings.

The lightness of her furniture added to the lightness of her room. To the right, against the wall as you entered, was a birdseye maple dresser and next to it a small dressing table. In the back of her room, facing the windows, was her matching bed. There were chairs scattered around the room. A rocker beside the bed faced the garden. In front of the windows was a long, oak library table covered with books, magazines, newspapers, bills, sketches, and other papers.

Under all this was an Oriental rug dominated by light blue. Noticing she was asleep, I gently placed her breakfast on her dresser and sat in the rocker beside her bed.

Out of the covers, which rested neatly around her face, lay her arms, one hand on top of the other. She looked peaceful. She still didn't have many wrinkles, and with her white hair flowing around the child in her features, I felt she was eternal. As I stared at her, she seemed to glow. Random memories began crossing through my mind, and I began to dwell on when I first saw her sleeping on the ground, to sitting on her lap, to that night when she put me to bed and told me a story. Boy, could she tell a story!

I've often wondered what kind of person I would have become if it had not been for her. She had a powerful impact on me, to say the least. If I hadn't lived with her, I wonder, would I still laugh at the world, would I still feel secure in most places, would I look at things the way I do, would I have loved someone else as much as I loved her? That was the greatest thing she ever did for me. She was loveable; she brought it out in me. There is nothing like being loved, but, oh, knowing someone you are able to love—there's nothing like that either. Many times I feel they are the same. I would not have loved Aunt Iris if she had not loved me.

She rolled over toward me, opened her eyes, and let her arm dangle over the side of the bed. I could tell she was still asleep.

Everything around her was soft: the blankets, her down pillow, the color of her bed, the light slipping through the shades, the feel of the rug on my feet. Her face was soft and gentle as always. Looking at her reassured me. This was not one of a few times I watched her sleep; I watched her sleep often. I used to do a lot of thinking and daydreaming while watching her sleep.

She slowly opened her eyes, focused on me, lifted her arm onto my lap, and said, "How long have you been here?"

"Oh, a few minutes. I made breakfast for you."

"You look watery eyed. What's wrong? Have you been crying?"

I touched my cheeks. They were wet.

"Oh, I guess so I've been thinking about you and me, about what you've done for me, about how much I love you."

This time I felt tears slide down my cheeks.

"I sure love you, Aunt Iris."

"Thank you, Bobby. You never cease to surprise me."

"Here," I moved the tray toward her, "do you want something to eat?"

"No. Thank you though. That was thoughtful of you. I'm not hungry.

"Would you open the blinds for me?" Light filled the room. She sat up. "What a sunny day. What time is it?"

"Around noon. What are you going to do today?"

She seemed to fall into a trance after I asked her that simple question.

"Aunt Iris?"

Her voice was faint and distant when she replied, "What?"

"Aunt Iris, are you all right? You're not getting out of bed today, are you?"

"I don't think so. How do you know?"

"I just felt it. That's why I brought you breakfast. You know, it's not like me to bring you breakfast."

I laughed. She smiled.

She looked at me as though she weren't going to see me again. She touched my hands, then softly ran her fingers down each side of my face, examining it closely; her hands stopped at my shoulders, while gazing kindly into my eyes, hers began to water, and then she drew me close to her. In a soft whisper, she said, "I'm going to miss you."

I leaned back and held her hands in mine.

"I don't want you to die. I don't. I want to always see you."

"I know, Bobby. You're the only reason I don't want to leave. But Bobby, no matter how much you love someone or need them, they are going to die, or you are going to die leaving them behind. For you to wake in the morning, you have to first fall asleep at night, and for you to sleep in the evening, you have to be awake all day. Life and death are the same way. They follow each other round and round. Sleep restores our energy for another day, death for another life. That's why kids have so much energy." She laughed. "Seriously though, I'm tired, Bobby. I've been awake all my life. I could use a long, deep sleep."

She closed her eyes for a while, opened them, and began to think out loud. "I just don't know how people seem to forget that they were once not here. We think of death as robbing us of our immortality, as though we were once not dead. Where was everyone before they were born? I don't know what others see, but when I look back into the past and out into the future, I see the same thing. Death returns us to the place from which we came, takes us back home after we have ventured out into life for a while."

Quietly she said to herself, "Death breaks the continuity of awareness." She paused. Then her face lit up and she said, "Imagine this, Bobby! Think of this! The idea of existing before or after this life is always presented in linear time, as the kind of time we experience here on earth, which is only one kind of time. In particles, with their great speed, reactions often happen in the future before they occur in the past, and, do you remember one time when I was talking to you about supraliminal communication, about how particles can communicate instantly, faster than the speed of light?"

I was awed by the activity in her mind so close to death.

Absentmindedly I said, "Yeah. Some physicist thinks there is an underlying wholeness to everything. How an action in one part of the universe has an immediate reaction in another."

"Well, who knows what the realm is like after death? There could be instantaneous traveling in time, instantaneous awareness forward or backward, so that you and I could be here in the same place at different times as the same person. I could be seeing myself, somewhere, either in the future or past, as a young man seeing himself as an old woman nearing death. Arriving and leaving, passing back and forth, we get to see ourselves in different ways, just as we feel different aspects of ourselves pass back and forth inside. Great love people have for each other could be those parts of the person that have great affinity for each other, whereas hatred between people could be those aspects of the person that are divided and separate.

"All the different types of people in the world could be all the different aspects of one person. Maybe there are just a few people living on the earth right now. They are just living here at many different times."

"But, Iris, there are so many people."

"Yes. I know. And there is also so much time. It was just a thought. Fascinating, though."

She looked through me and said, "Please don't be afraid for me. I'm not afraid of dying. I have felt for a long time since I got into the process of becoming closer to life that it doesn't matter whether or not I know what will happen after I die. My life, as it continues through death, which I believe everyone's does, will continue with the same direction and momentum I have given it in this life. In this way, even though we are blind, we can control our life as it is metamorphosed by death. Maybe death is just a break, a pause in the continuity of life, an eternal moment in reflection."

"Once again, absentmindedly I said, "Yeah, death takes us on an adventure we can't remember.".

"I wonder. I wonder if it'll be as in a dream. If I'll dream and then fall asleep again and then wake up in another dream and go from one dream to another. Or maybe the dreams will be real. I'll be in dreams just as I'm here now. I've never told you this before, but sometimes I think this physical world is a veil, and death is a door into the real, substantial world. So many times this life has seemed like a dream.

"I'm grateful to have lived. Very grateful. To have missed it, to have never woken up into it, would have been, oh, now that I know, how can I know the experience of not knowing? Yet, there must have been a time when I did not know, when there was no knowing at all. I'm satisfied, truly happy that I have experienced life. It's been a miracle to me. It has taken billions and billions of years for life to reveal itself in the forms we see around us; in everything it shows itself and speaks to us. Together we are here to breathe it in the fresh air, to see it in the beautiful flowers, to feel it in the warmth of the sun on my blankets, and to love it in our love for each other. What a miracle for us to meet on this tiny planet in this particular place and time." She spread her arms. "In all this vastness we met. If this moment had been my whole life, which it may very well have been, I would still be grateful."

She stared out the window for a long time before speaking again.

"But no, our meeting has not been a miracle. There is much more going on than what we realize. You have often said to me that I saved you. When you're young, when you can't conceptualize on a large scale, it does appear that someone has come into your life, whether it be for good or bad. But, it is not that simple. We did not meet by accident.

"The touching of our movements is what brought us together; it is our togetherness. We are parts of each other. Our desire to move forward has brought us together. It wasn't John and Marty who brought you to me. Now, Bobby, now that you're older, you can realize this and won't need me any more. You can move forward on your own. You can. Believe me. You're an adventurer, Bobby. In the truest sense of the word, you're an adventurer. The adventurer in you won't let you rest until you find a home."

She sank back as if that had taken her last bit of energy. Her eyes closed slowly. She lay motionless. Her breathing slowed and became shallow. I continued to hold her warm hands. After a few minutes, she opened her eyes and said, "When you first came to live with me, I never imagined what you would bring into my life. My brothers and sisters didn't know what they were losing." She gripped my hands tightly, and with a sincerity I had never seen before, she continued, "Thank you for letting me love you. You don't know what you've meant to me. You're life has brought so much into mine. I want to tell you something before I leave. You know, the old advice before you die trick."

Her ornery grin spread across her face, and just as quickly, sincerity returned.

"For all I've tried to teach you, just remember, believe what you see. Believe it no matter what; even if it hurts, or doesn't seem right, or if you think it should not be, or if others say you're wrong, believe it anyway. Even if you're the only one in the world who sees something and all others say it's something else, stick with what you saw and then you can decide for yourself whether it is real or not. That way, you can always rely on yourself. Believe in yourself, Bobby."

"I'll do that. Don't worry. I won't have any trouble with that."

We laughed.

She slid down into her bed. She would lie very still and look out the windows onto her garden then turn and stare at me for a while and close her eyes and rest. This went on for a few hours. Every so often I would feel her losing consciousness, and I'd call her name. She would look at me, smile, usually squeeze my hand; a few times we talked, but

I had a hard time understanding her because she seemed to be taking tremendous leaps in thought.

Her breathing gradually became shallower and farther apart. She turned toward me; we looked at each other with tenderness. Her breathing was sparse. She squeezed my hands and turned toward the windows with half opened eyes. With each breath I waited for another. I felt a strong movement in the room. Then everything was still. Her eyes were still open. She must have left with a lot of color. Her hands became cold and clammy. I folded them in front of her as she used to do herself. I remained with her and cried. I cried more for myself than for her. As throughout her life, Iris was where she wanted to be.

For months I could do nothing but think about and yearn for Aunt Iris. I felt she was somewhere, but I didn't know where. If I had only known where, I would have gone to see her. But, I didn't go anywhere.

All my time was spent in bed, on the porch, in her room, and in the garden. I hardly ate. I soon became restless. I paced around the house, in the yard, wiggled my legs whenever I sat down. I felt I had to go somewhere, see someone, but where this place was or who I had to see, I did not know. Feeling it to be nearby, I began looking out the windows, standing on the front porch looking up and down the street, and then I began going for walks which consumed more and more of my time. It wasn't long before I started spending my entire day walking up and down the streets of my home town. As I walked I would glance around to see if what I was looking for was there. Each day I failed to find something made me all the more anxious to get up early the next day for another excursion. But, it wasn't long before I succumbed to the emptiness of my home town. Wasn't much worthwhile there. I still took my walks, but they were aimless. I'd wander around without even knowing it. Before Aunt Iris died, I knew there was no future for me in my home town, but now that she was gone, I felt it to the center of my heart. If you had been born in my hometown, would you have felt you had a future?

The lack of a future began to separate itself from my hometown.

It was not long before I doubted I could have a future anywhere. I became convinced that no matter where I went, whom I saw, what town I visited, that I would not find anything to extend me into the future.

I tried to think on what Aunt Iris said about becoming more a part of life, but those thoughts kept on being driven away by feelings of loss and hopelessness. I shared in her beliefs, but not in the inner experiences from which those beliefs arose. My walks became more tiresome, and each morning it was harder for me to get out of bed.

It's hard to get out of bed without a future. Why bother? I probably wouldn't have if it hadn't been for my restlessness.

Something had to open up. My lack of a future was enclosing me and making me feel that time was no longer passing but had stopped. I tried to forget about it.

Part II

Chapter 12

One day, while aimlessly strolling the streets of my hometown, my aimlessness caught up with me. I was surprised it hadn't caught me before because I wasn't walking very fast. I felt that the only way I could get ahead of it again would be by aiming my feet in a definite direction. But I couldn't think of any reason to go anywhere. Then I asked, "Why do I have to have a reason?" Nobody else seemed to have a sensible reason for what they were doing. I'll just pick someplace and go there. I first thought of going to the corner store, but who wants to go there? You can always mosey on into the store. I did that every day anyway. It had to be on a bigger scale than that.

Then, I thought of going to the ocean, to the mountains, to the dump, and then I thought of going to see the President. That would take me in a definite direction, but I dismissed that when I realized I didn't want to head in the same direction he was going. My aim was better than that, if not my aim, then at least my eyesight. As I turned a corner, I tripped over something and crashed onto the pavement. Now, after all those aimless walks around town, I came to know the sidewalks weaving through my hometown better than the pattern on the linoleum in Iris's kitchen. If I would stumble and fall, it wouldn't be because of a lump, crack, or bump in the sidewalk; it would be because of an unfamiliar object. After examining my torn pants and cut knees, I turned around and found what had tripped me down. It was a book titled *From the Garden to the Hospital* by Edward L. Poppycock. It was torn, dirty and abused and looked like an old book. But to my amazement, it was copyrighted two thousand twenty one. This was only two thousand one. Very strange, I thought to myself. This strange occurrence warranted my full attention. I pondered the meaning of this for a long time. After about an hour on the sidewalk in a thoughtful trance (I guess it was an hour or so I'm not too sure), I was rudely yanked by the armpits out of my thoughtfulness.

I focused on the source of the yank and said, "What are you doing? What's the stretcher for?"

The man in white jumped back. "Well, gee, uumm, well." He stepped forward. "We were called that a man was paralyzed. Don't give me a hard time. We only came to help. What are you doing in the middle of the sidewalk anyway?"

"Look at this book! It's the future! And by some miracle it has been placed in my path. Don't worry. Soon you won't have to care for anyone because we are all going to evolve into robots."

"Yeah, right." He grinned at his friend in white. "Do you live here in town?"

"Why do you ask?"

"Just wondered, that's all."

"Well, yeah, I do."

He got a sad look on his face.

So I said, "But not for long."

He looked happy again. We went our separate ways.

I walked home clutching the book tightly in my hand. I was still deep in thought. After walking into a building, two trees, stepping on a cat, and getting lost about six times, I was struck by the meaning of the book while I was standing in a pile of, well, never mind, too much detail constipates the mind. A futuristic book! That was the only thing it could be.

The book was indeed futuristic. The thesis of the book was that vitamins, minerals, and proteins are unhealthy for us. The worst thing for you is to eat fresh fruit and vegetables out of the garden. That will put you into the hospital faster than taking vitamins in pill form. The logic follows this line. Our biological system has fallen far behind our intellectual and technological advancements. We have evolved beyond our organic origins. By no longer being involved in the organic world by growing our own food, working the land, building our own shelter, walking on the bare earth with bare feet, playing in the dirt, etc., we have entered a new phase of existence. Our biological system needs a push to adapt to our new environment of plastic, steel, glass, and concrete dotted with dog shit. This has to be done in steps, just as evolution is a step-by-step process. The amoeba did not evolve into a grizzly bear overnight, did it? So, to make the change to eating plastic, steel, glass, and concrete dotted with dog shit, the brilliant author developed a step-by-step change in diet that would alter man's biological system into being a machine.

I'll not go into all the steps. If you're really interested you can find the book yourself. I loaned mine to an unenlightened friend who used it to light his woodstove.

Reading the book was an uplifting experience. Most of the ideas I had never seen before. That was unusual for me because I rarely read books, newspapers, magazines, or even watch TV. I read the world. Here are a few quotes that should impress you with the originality of the book.

Vitamins, especially A, B, C, D, and E, are responsible for the foul odor humans emit when exerting themselves in a physical manner. If we would stop consuming foods containing these vitamins and cease producing and popping vitamin pills, the human race would become a sweet smelling species.

After years of studying the excretion process, from both the practical and economical standpoint, it has been found that excretion is grossly outdated. Billions of dollars are wasted on disposing the God-awful, foul looking, smelling, disease-laden crap through complex networks of pipes and flushes. It's value as a fertilizer is outdated, for we have already proven that food grown from the earth is unhealthy to consume. Consequently, through our step-by-step process outlined here, we should evolve to the point where we crap useful nuts and bolts.

In the future, we can expect to see the absence of the need for clothes, except when man wishes to decorate himself. The need for clothes, being to protect us from shifts in temperature and exposure of embarrassing body parts which will evolve out of existence, will be eliminated as we grow beyond our organic ancestors into the realm of science and technology. Think of the great savings we will all enjoy!

It has been proven, without a doubt, that protein is a menace to the strivings of mankind. Not only does our false need for it cause the death of millions of animals, but it causes dumbness of the brain, dandruff, bull leggedness, itchy heels, and tooth decay. Probably the worst aspect of protein is that it keeps us in direct connection with the lower animals by having to feed, raise, keep, and harvest them.

The most innovative concept he proposed was the profound change that would occur in our mental makeup. I had a little trouble digesting this concept, but, I thought, I've tasted so many other theories that I may as well take a healthy bite out of this one. The author traced all our mental problems to our link with the organic world. The nature of the organic world, he argued, specifically the animal world, was one of bothering each other. Animals bother each other for attention, warmth, food, to itch each other's fleas, poke each other, wake each other up in the morning, look at each other— all those things that keep them together. These needs are only a source of agony for us, for when they are not met, which is most of the time, we cry, scream, feel unloved and lonely, are anxious and often become a real nuisance. The realistic author, probably an abandoned child, knew that these needs will never be filled, and therefore all our problems could be solved by eliminating them. That was fine with me. I was tired of seeing the earth occupied by an overabundance of sad, lonely, insecure, nervous humans. Although, I could not imagine people not feeling that they had to bother each other.

So, the step-by-step evolutionary approach of Dr. Poppycock's would propel us beyond the bothersome organic world, develop an irreversible separation between us and them, and insure our future of mental stability. The new culture of the future would be a highly stable, tough, separate, out-of-touch bunch of steel, plastic, glass and concrete dotted with dog shit automatons. A quote from his awe-inspiring book sums it all up, "The less we are involved in nature, from walking on the grass to studying it in the scientific arena, the better off we will be."

This really sent my mind a-reelin'. The opportunity was all mine. Sent from heaven. The book would not come out until two thousand twenty one. I had twenty year head start on the whole of mankind, except for the author. "But wait," I thought, "what if he hasn't even conceived of it yet? What if he hasn't begun to write it? I'll even get a head start on him." Sometimes, I must admit, I get carried away with myself.

So, I took the step-by-step evolutionary diet to heart. The first step was to all at once stop eating what I've been eating and replace that with six months of nothing but Doritos and Cracker Jacks.

That was easy. I love Doritos and Cracker Jacks. All day long, while walking around eating, I would dream of my future self. No longer was I an aimless stroller on the streets of the world, but I had a purpose, a goal, and I could move toward that goal while walking and munching Doritos and Cracker Jacks. It was a dream come true.

Strong, tough, evolutionarily superior, full of steely vibes, not caring for the rest of the inferior organic world, I would be the head, the first of a new culture, the leader of the ultra avant-garde of the new wave of human machines. The world would know me. The author and I would become intimate friends. My mind just went off into these daydreams for hours. I hardly knew where I was half the time. You can ask the shopkeepers downtown whose storefront windows I had to replace.

But before these dreams were to come true, I had to withstand the ridicule of my unenlightened friends and neighbors. They never ridiculed my overall plan. I was smart enough not to explain the whole thing to them in detail. Although, every once in a while I would lose control over my mouth and just have to spout off a few ideas about vitamins, minerals, machine men, evolution, and the like. They simply laughed and thought I'd gone off the deep end. They kept on bothering me about eating nothing but Doritos and Cracker Jacks. I know a few health enthusiasts. Boy, did they get on my case! They always preach about eating right—good heart, good liver, all those silly soon-to-be-obsolete body parts; but they sure forget about your health when they hassle you so much that you become nervous, agitated, stressed, and bright red with anger. For Christ's sake, they could have given me a heart attack with all their hankerings and carrying-ons.

Some of their concern was well intended, especially when I lost forty pounds and most of my hair fell out. You know, sometimes when you get an idea, an idea you put a lot of faith in toward changing your life, it is hard to dismiss even when to others the results are disastrous. I've seen a lot of people ruin themselves on a false hope. While they saw me lose weight and hair, I saw myself going through an evolutionary change of not needing any more haircuts, losing organic

131

bulk, not needing vitamins, and detaching myself from earth foods by eating only processed foods. I was happy with my new appearance. Although, now as I look back, I felt like a flat tire. I couldn't do anything, couldn't think straight, didn't have any energy, and had to crawl back to Aunt Iris's after only walking down to the corner. I was waiting to burst out of my dilapidated state into a new dimension.

The only thing I burst into was the hospital. It is very hard to picture oneself as a deluded fool. How could I admit to myself that the Doritos and Cracker Jack diet was the cause of my pitiful state, especially when I had a closet full waiting to be eaten. I therefore conjured up the idea that I had leukemia. Depression set in deep and hard. I figured that if I hadn't contracted leukemia I would have made it to the author's vision. My skin was ghostly white. Five feet ten inches tall, ninety pounds. Most of my hair all over my body was gone, some of my teeth fell out, my fingernails were cracked, in many places on my body I had sores and cracked, bleeding skin; deep dark circles surrounded my eyes, and I could barely move. I don't know how, but I still believed in what I was doing. After a couple weeks in the hospital, threatened by doctors to put me in an insane asylum (threaten me with that and I'll do just about anything), I reluctantly agreed to consume something other than Doritos and Cracker Jacks. The process reversed itself, as did my thinking; I left the hospital after a five week stay.

Too bad the scheme didn't work. The plans I had were fantastic.

Besides that I could have proven others wrong. Never have I been called so many names, lectured so many times, endured so many dirty looks and snide remarks, and criticized so extensively, even about things that didn't relate to what I was doing (you know how some people like to bring things up from the past when they get a chance).

You would have thought that I burned down my own house, gave all my money to a rich man, tried to drink water by pouring it on my toes, stayed out all night without my clothes, or something foolish like that.

I don't know what people expect. All day long I see them dress up to show off to each other, brag to each other as to how much they have (as if what you have is more important than what you are), fight, cheat, lie, step upon each other on their climb for the mirage of social status dance the ego tangle, lose themselves in groups, and go through all those other antics in the same vein.

I was just doing the same thing. Would have been a leading figure in a new culture. I don't think my scheme was any more bizarre than a lot of others I've seen. All I wanted was a little attention on a large scale. My cousin is bad just so he'll get scolded by my aunt. He just sits there with a big grin on his face after doing something wrong. It's the only attention he gets. And he's sixty years old. I've never seen him suffer the ridicule I did!

I just don't understand people. I don't even understand myself.

Just as well. How boring it would be to understand yourself. I like a surprise every now and then.

Now, when I think back, I don't remember stumbling over that book. I don't even remember reading it.

Strange, very strange. Oh well, I guess we all have our moments.

Chapter 13

When I left the hospital I thought I was fully recovered, but after a few days I started having some thoughts that made me realize that I'd better watch out before I suffered a relapse. What first clued me in was the thought that I didn't have to have a future. My thinking was: "So what if I don't have a future? Big deal. Many people go through life without a future. You can't have everything, can you?" But, it wasn't long after thinking this way that a little battle flared between these thoughts and my painful feelings of not having a future. Once again, my feelings quickly overran my thinking.

To appease my feelings, I decided if I couldn't find a future, I'd invent one. Now that I look back, I can't believe how dangerously close I was to getting sick again. An invented future? What was believing that I was a leader of a new culture of human automatons other than an invented future? Where do invented futures go? Where do they come from? They go to the same place from which they come—nowhere: from nowhere to nowhere, from obscurity to fame, from poverty to wealth, from room to room, from lover to lover, from bottle to bottle, from needle to needle, from isolation to full-blown fantasy, and from silence to a megaphone.

I decided that it wasn't Aunt Iris's death or my disillusionment with the way of life in my hometown that had created my feelings of not having a future, but a simple fact that I had stopped growing.

When I was young, even when I was being tossed around from one relative to one another, I still felt I had a future. It wasn't until my late teens that I began to feel my future slowly recede into the past. And so, to regain a future, I decided that I'd have to keep on growing by either becoming a snake or a tree. I bought books on genetics, set up a little lab, and started brewing some genetic potions. I must admit I did get sick. Although this time I didn't land in the hospital; I landed on the bathroom floor where I puked my guts out into the toilet.

Then I really feared having a relapse when I started thinking that I should face the fact that I was an adult and should act like one and become a lawyer, buy a big house, furnish it with a showcase wife, become a conforming, respectable member of the community, have kids and a dog, but then, I remembered, which made me feel that I was healthier than I had thought, that I wanted to live an honest life.

After that I went to bed. What can you do in futureless time other than go to bed, especially with a friend who likes it as much as you do. Although this time I was alone rolling from side to side, staring at the ceiling, lying still for long periods of time with my eyes closed watching random thoughts go by and wondering how I would ever have a future if I couldn't prevent myself from being pulled out of the present by the past. I began to notice reoccurring thoughts about how if my hometown would change to the way I wanted it to be, then I'd have a future. Somehow, by my hometown changing, I would change.

I started thinking of ways my hometown could change to sustain everyone and quickly came to the idea that for that to happen individuals would have to be self-sustaining and not drain each other.

Thoughts about how this could be accomplished slowly materialized into imaginings of what such a town and its inhabitants would be like. My imaginings became more vivid and complex. Wasn't long before I began to believe that this place was not only in my imagination but somewhere in the world, and when I found it, I would find myself self-sustaining. That was when the adventuresome spirit possessed me. At the time, I was sitting on the swing in the gazebo reading an anthropology book on vanishing primitive cultures that were far more advanced than the culture suffocating me.

I stopped reading and said out loud as though speaking to Aunt Iris, "I'm never going to find a future sitting in this town, surrounded by folks without a future, and reading a book, probably written by one of them, that crowds my memory with impressions of someone else's experiences and ideas. I could read everything, memorize everything about different ways of living, and what good would it do me? I would still be the same. I wouldn't have found a home in the future. All I'd have is an overstuffed memory. What would I do with it? Impress others with my vast knowledge? I've got better ways to waste my time, not to mention ways to enjoy it. No, these books aren't for me."

I stood up, threw the book on the ground, kicked it, walked through the garden, in the back door, out the front door, and as I stood on the front porch watching people drive by while staying in the same place, I again talked out loud to myself, "And how am I ever going to find a home in the future by staying in this town where everyone is stuck in the past. They think they have a future. They think they have a home. They think they're found when they're lost and when you give them directions on how to get found, they think it is the way to get lost. I believe what I see, but I don't believe in it. This is not my home. This was Aunt Iris's. I never chose this place. I don't belong here. I've got to find my own home in the future. I've got to get out of here before it costs me my life to live here. Once I didn't have a life and now I do. I don't have a future, but soon I will."

While packing my bag, I felt I owed my hometown and the folks who somehow managed to survive in it something for teaching me what I did not want my life to become. Sometimes, if you know what you don't want it makes it easier to find what you do want. As I was peering through my binoculars, the idea of donating a building loaded with junk and decorated in the front by a statue of myself tickled my brain and wouldn't stop. I wished it could have been done the instant I thought of it. I couldn't remember when I was so pleased with myself. The idea was almost as good as having a future.

In a way it gave me a future for the rest of my days in my hometown.

Day and night I felt a tickling inside my head. It wasn't one of those tickles that just about drives you crazy; it was a gentle, pleasant tickle that bordered on an itch, and when it did itch, I'd send ripples toward it by rubbing my head. As my plan progressed, so did the tickles. I spent much of my time rubbing my head and poking Q-tips in my ears.

For my memento, I leased an old warehouse surrounded by other warehouses that were being converted into condos. It was four stories with about 4,000 square feet per floor. Some new items were put in the warehouse, but most of the stuff came from the junkyard, dump, and dumpsters behind second hand stores. The first floor was loaded with cars, a couple of RVs, motorcycles, snowmobiles, dishwashers, garbage compactors, backhoes, bulldozers, a few tanks and fighter planes, one small bomber, and other large goodies. Second floor: plastic furniture, computers, copiers, copiers that make copies of copiers, awnings, hair dryers, and other assorted junk. Third floor: toasters, electric popcorn machines, boom boxes, pinball machines, video machines, etc. Fourth floor: clothes, petro products, Barbie dolls, GI Joes, drugs, garbage bags, trash, etc.

From the inset of the outset, there were rumors as to why I, a young man known for his lack of ambition, was undertaking such an ambitious project. You see, as I was realizing that the road to the top really led downward, my motivation to get involved in my hometown slowly and steadily descended until it fell completely out of sight. I was happy for myself. Needless to say, friends and relatives (except for Uncle John) thought otherwise of me. They thought something was wrong with me. I had no drive, lacked the competitive spirit (that was almost as bad as being a murderer), had no future plans, didn't desire anything; was, according to them, on the road to becoming a bum. It was hard for me to understand what they really wanted me to do. I wasn't really too interested in knowing, although it did nudge my curiosity. It all sounded so vague.

"Don't you want to be somebody? You should do something with your life. Success is yours only if you try. It's time you develop some realistic goals in life." Somebody, something, success, goals — they all mashed together in my head and slid out my ear. Others didn't care about me; they were just annoyed that I wasn't like them. They'd say things to me like, "What are you wasting away for? Your dad would be real proud of the way you've become a lazy ass. Don't you want to be like the other boys?" Or, this I'll never forget. One day Uncle Wilfred asked me, "Ain't you got nothin' in between them there ears?"

What do you say when someone says something like that to you? I felt sorry for him.

Work didn't have any value to me; if anything, the value was a minus, for whenever I worked, I felt that someone was stealing a section of my life and that I was helping do harm to something or someone somewhere. I don't mind working on satisfying my needs — sometimes that can produce pleasure beyond belief — but helping someone get rich by producing junk nobody needed was something I hardly believed in. I don't want to look back through my life on my dying day and see it wasted away on that. All too often pursuits intended to bring meaning do not, so why waste time doing things you know, without a doubt, are absolutely meaningless. Work certainly wasn't enough to get me out of bed in the morning, and I hope that wasn't what got my parents into bed to get me here. Work was like digging your own grave, puking after you eat, lying in the basement trying to get a suntan, drinking poison to cure an illness, or packing a wound with dirt. Boy, did I get called a lot of names when I said stuff like that. A good man was a hard working man. Hard work made you proud and satisfied with yourself; kept you out of trouble and your mind off itself.

Whenever I thought about work, which was not very often, I'd always fall into a reverie about the story Aunt Iris once told me; she used to tell me a lot of stories. Once she told me a story about how human beings came to an end. After one of mankind's nuclear wars, a number of species of reptiles had their genes altered in such a way that they were returned to being dinosaurs. The dinosaurs ate the remaining humans. They were barely human, a peculiar shape and form, but quite tasty, little, radiated morsels. And that was the end of the human race. Anyway, once there was a mad Tibetan guru who was teaching his disciples the value of no possessions. One day he told his followers to carve tiny elephants out of water, then he left to eat fruit. Many years later he returned to find his disciples seated lotus style in a circle holding their carvings in the palm of their hands and meditating on fruit. The guru spoke thus saying:

"In the morning the sun rises.

In the evening the sun sets.

No ice in the desert.

There is fruit to eat.

"Oh beloved followers of the path, you have proven your worthiness to learn the way of non-materialism. Place your carvings in the center of your circle, and I will show you the way."

The disciples, having realized in their meditations that their guru was going to teach them the way by reducing years of patient work to rubble in a matter of seconds by jumping on their carvings, carefully placed their carvings in the corner and carelessly put their guru on the spot in the center and jumped him to a pulp.

I could hardly go anywhere or see anyone without being lectured and reprimanded for what I was doing to myself. I avoided over-achievers as though they carried a contagious disease. No matter what

I said or how hard I tried to explain how I felt, it didn't seem to do any good. They'd just keep on ejecting like a computer readout.

Finally, I resolved this problem by wearing a sign which read, "DON'T BOTHER ME, I'M BUSY," every time I went out for a walk. After I started wearing my sign, people acted as if I were the one with a contagious disease.

On the day of my release, I surprised myself by being up before the sun. The tickling itch, knowing what was going to happen, became so excited that I felt as though my brain was going to squirm out my ears. After sneaking up to the warehouse, I was shocked to see a crowd already pressing up against the ten foot high chain-link fence surrounding the building. The place looked more like a weekend rock concert than anything else. Tents, sleeping bags, people roaming about, police, dogs; I guess the only thing that was missing was music and rain. It was a clear, sunny day; a great day for romping off into adventures.

I finished my own personal touches on the building just in time to start the ceremony. From the platform inside the front gate, I had a king's view of my hometown folks shoving, punching, kicking, squishing those in front against the fence, yelling, screaming — acting as though they had all won the grand prize on a game show.

They looked like an army of ants being held from a jelly bean melting in the sun, only more disorganized. Ants are professional organizers. We probably could learn as much, if not more, from an ant as from a cow.

As I turned on the microphone, the tickling itch started sending long, slow, faint waves down my body. I was hoping I would be able to last to the beginning. Voice quivering I started, "Hello, hello, hello. Welcome to the big day, for both you and me. I am so happy you could make it. Is everybody happy?"

Shouts and screams followed that only tightened the waves and heightened my tension.

"As you already know, I'm leaving town; don't applaud too loudly, and leaving this," I pointed to the warehouse, "for you to remember me by. And so you won't forget who had the generous heart, a statue of myself has been placed at the main entrance. Wait till you see this beauty."

Taking short calculated steps in trying to control the rapid tingling waves from sending me wiggling and giggling to the ground, I managed to reach the statue, which was about five feet high and twenty feet long, and pull off the paint splattered drop cloth. My whole body began to shake visibly when I saw my concrete clone lying on its side with its legs crossed and head propped up on one arm. As I read the old familiar words, "DON'T BOTHER ME, I'M BUSY," on the sign leaning up against my likeness, a dozen title waves shook me from head to toe. I staggered back and forth, fell back against the statue, shook there for a while, and finally, with the help of a couple of security guards, stumbled back up to the podium. The guards had a worried look on their faces, asked me if I was all right, and when I replied that I was feeling fantastic and wished I could do this more often, they quickly let go of me and left.

I leaned forward to grab the microphone, missed, knocked it over, and almost flipped head first over the podium. Every movement of my body seemed to tighten and speed up the tingling, tickling waves that were racing up and down under my skin. An exciting chill bubbled up as the tingling raced down my skin, and as it bounced back up, a pleasurable, warm sweat followed in its wake. I couldn't decide whether I should continue with the dedication or jump up and down to further excite myself. And then, I felt, why should I be the only one having so much fun? I grabbed the microphone, raised it back up, and jumping up and down, screamed, "Well, let's go, I'm ready. Are you?"

At first, they stood there frozen and stared at me as if I were some kind of spastic maniac. "Well, what are we waiting for? What are you waiting for? I'm not waiting for a damn thing. Because everything is going to you. With the way I feel this could last forever. Don't just stare at me as though I'm some kind of raving lunatic. Come on. So what if I am? Just remember, this dedication is for you. Because after I leave, I will never return. Hope you enjoy it. Come on, tell me. Is everybody happy?"

That did it. They had become a bunch of screaming maniacs like myself. I was overjoyed. The sounds of their voices pressed inward and somehow caused the tingling, ever tightening waves to change from racing up and down to racing outward against my skin where they exploded into vibrating particles. The sequence became smaller and

141

tighter, and before I knew it, waves were following waves, overlapping and flowing under each other, and each time they burst into particles against my skin they jumped to a higher energy level, then dropped back a bit, jumped higher, dropped down and higher and higher as I sailed across the threshold of pleasure. I loved it. The waves and the explosions then blended together. All I could feel were millions of electrifying particles doing their reckless heebie-jeebie dance under my skin. And that wasn't all. No, I must have passed a second threshold of pleasure when the high energy, chaotic particles added a rhythm to their wild dance. Fearing I might suddenly transform into a bolt of lightning and shoot into the puffball clouds, I decided to concentrate my energies on the task ahead of me. I grabbed the scissors with quivering hands, headed toward the ribbon stretched in front of the gate, tumbled down the stairs, thoroughly enjoying every bump, and with determined wobbly steps, which reminded me of the way I walked for a short time when I was deluded that it would be best for me to walk the straight and narrow, headed toward the ribbon as one who was possessed. Partway there I was almost reduced to a giggling, squirming idiot on the grass as ten million electrified, dancing, pleasurable particles exploded under my skin.

I almost succumbed, but my future carried me forward. I raced toward the ribbon with rubbery legs, lunged with arms outstretched, completely missed with my scissors, but luckily, I was far enough so that my body broke the ribbon. There was a tremendous blast as the building inhaled and collapsed with a sigh into a pile of rubble. The millions of charged particles, instantaneously aligning themselves with the spaces between the atoms in my skin, shot out and enhanced my already glorious state by encircling me with a silver aura. I moaned and groaned and rolled around in the grass oblivious to everything. I felt like remaining on the soft grass in my pool of pleasure, but the thought of where I was and what I had just done and had yet to do snuck in somehow and lifted my head to see what was going on around me.

Most everyone was crouched down or lying flat on the ground, but those who had recovered were looking around in disbelief. I thought I'd better leave before they realized the joke was on them. I stood up, looked back at the warehouse, and fell in laughter. Where once was a warehouse was now a mangled and twisted steel frame with blown up junk scattered all around, and presenting this to everyone was the untouched statue of myself. Still laughing uncontrollably, I found my feet, slipped through the crowd, and staggered out of town.

I walked through the streets where everything looked the same and into the town park. An old couple sitting together on a park bench seemed worlds apart. Other people were sitting on benches scattered around the park. I wanted to get one last look at the fountain in the park before I left. It was one of the most beautiful things in my hometown. It was circular, made of crystal, and that day was spraying a fine mist up into the clouds. As I walked toward it, I felt my attention being drawn to a young, blond woman. I had seen her before but did not know her. She was sitting on a bench across from the fountain. I stopped near her so that I could see both her and the fountain. She was dressed in a short, black skirt and a red sweater with a black C on the front, and held a blue pom pom in her hand. She looked at me and blushed.

I said, "Hi. I'm Bobby. How are you?"

"Oh, I'm alive. Do you know what that loud noise was?"

I told her.

"You can't be serious. Oh, you are!"

"Yes, I am. And I will become more after I leave this place.

"Would you like to go adventuring with me. I'm on my way to go searching for a home."

"Really!?"

"Yes."

"But I don't know you."

"We can get to know each other while adventuring. It could be a whole adventure in itself."

"Well, I don't know. When are you leaving?"

"Now."

"You want me to go with you right now?!"

"Yes."

"I'm sorry. I can't. You seem very nice, and I've noticed you before, and I'd like to get to know you, but this is too sudden. I'm not that spontaneous. Anyway", she looked at her watch, "I have an appointment with someone who needs cheering up." She paused and stared at the ground and said softly, "I'm afraid to leave."

"That's a reason why you should leave instead of staying here."

"Yeah, I know. Still, I can't. Thank you for the invitation."

She stood up.

I took her hand in mine and said, "I have the feeling I'll be seeing you somewhere in the future."

"I hope so." She freed her hand, turned and walked away.

I looked at the fountain for awhile then walked out of town to the place where I had hid my bag, canteen and binoculars. As I was slipping the strap of the canteen around my neck, I saw a dead yippie yuppin' over hill and through dale. I started running, but decided that was no way to start my adventures. I wasn't going to run away.

I wasn't running away, I was going toward. I decided to leave; had made the choice of when, where and how, and was going to travel as I pleased. I stopped running and strolled along as though the world were mine.

But no sooner did I take a few steps than the triathlon man jumped in front of me and started screaming, "Where do you think you're going, you irresponsible little shit? You act as if nothing has happened. What the hell did you do that for? Do you know how much all that stuff was worth?"

"Of course. Who do you think paid for everything?"

"What a waste," he screamed. "Have you no values?"

I stepped back. "What are you getting yourself all worked up about? I've done nothing new, nothing different. I've only done the same thing that's done everyday except that I did it faster. Why waste time, huh? Just think of all the jobs I just created. Anyway, you should be thankful I didn't try to start a war to create jobs. I'm not nearly as crazy as everyone else around here."

"Just who do you think you are? Doing the same thing! You don't see people buy things and then blow them up. You're crazy. You really are. You know, you're lucky you didn't kill somebody. You're dangerous."

The veins in his neck were bulging, his eyes were popping out of the sockets, his face was red, and by the rest of his appearance I thought he might work himself into a total body spasm.

I started to laugh uncontrollably, but was jolted out of it when he locked his no pain no gain, muscle-bound arm around my neck and started dragging me backwards.

"You'll pay for this! The only place you're going is to jail! You won't get away with this!"

Heard barking dogs and saw a group of my hometown folks armed with guns heading toward us. I panicked. My search for a home was going to end before it began. Images of sitting in jail flashed through my mind. Neither am I big nor strong, but I am a wiry, little guy. I spotted a ditch coming up, and as he tried to drag me over it, I wiggled and twisted and tripped him into the muddy water and ran after my life. So, I really did end up running away from my hometown. They wanted me, but I didn't want them.

I thought for sure that they would catch me. But I only ran for a half hour or so before I no longer heard the barking dogs or saw heads bobbing over hills. I guess those dogs are meant to track dangerous criminals, not good-natured adventurers. Anyway, it would be hard for a dog to follow my scent. I walk lightly. Sometimes when adventuring, I don't even feel my feet touch the ground.

Chapter 14

Once behind time in a vast plain, I smelled such a rotten smell that I thought the earth had started to decay. I tried to escape from it, but as with most things rotten, I couldn't get away. Walked for miles in every direction in vain. Even looked at the bottom of my shoes. The smell was so overpowering that I lost my sense of direction. Finally, I wandered into mountains of garbage. As far as mine eye could see, from yonder pile to yonder pile, there was garbage. At first I thought I'd wandered into the hometown dump, but I knew from previous visits that our dump was not as magnificent. And so, my curiosity being awakened, I began to venture across that great expanse of trash. For half a day I tripped over empty cans, stumbled over broken down refrigerators, sunk knee deep in slushy slime, and tried to make friends with cat-eating rats. I spotted some buildings half buried in garbage. I quickened my pace, tumbled down a few hills of trash, then down one large pile to our dear mother earth.

How badly we abuse her. There she sits, bothering no one, sustaining everyone, and yet taken so for granted that people spoil her beautiful face with garbage. It felt good to touch her again. I ran my eyes along her lines for only a short distance before running into more piles of garbage. Across the clearing, narrow alleyways led toward the buildings. Running between the buildings were high chain link fences. Piled to the top of these fences was, yeah you guessed it, garbage.

To my right out walked a man dressed in a gray, pinstriped suit with a clothespin on his nose. He was of medium height and build, wore his hair executive style, had a handsome chiseled face and walked to the point. Then a man to my left popped out of an alley as though it had just given birth to him. He had a rough beard, torn dirty clothes, a soft, gentle face and an 'I've got all day' walk. He picked through the garbage as he strolled in my direction.

The man from the right was quickly upon me. He extended his clean, manicured hand and said, "Hello, Mr. Knowitall. I am Ed Wilson. We have been anxiously awaiting your arrival. It is very good to meet you." He gave me a hearty racquetball shake.

"Sorry to disappoint you, but I don't know that much. If I knew it all, I wouldn't be adventuring to find a home. I'm not who you think I am."

"You mean, oh no, you mean you are not the mediator?"

"Mediator? No, sorry I'm not. Although for you and your nose's sake I wish I were."

"Then what are you doing here?"

"The same thing you're doing here—looking at garbage."

"Really? So that's what I've been looking at all this time. I'm so glad you've come to tell me that. Cut the crap. Why are you here?"

"I'm curious about all this garbage. Don't you have a match?"

"Are you nuts? Don't you think we'd all get blown to pieces. Can't you smell the methane?"

"Oh, so that's what you call that rotten smell. Hey, if you lit it, you might be doing the world a favor by rocketing mankind into a new orbit, a higher plane of awareness. Oops, don't get mad. Just kidding. Sorry I'm not your mediator, but if you want me to be one I will. I'm an adventurer, I'll try anything."

"I bet you will."

By this time the man from the left was standing with us on our tiny island in the sea of garbage. He had a smooth, plump, distracted face. Out of his right jean pocket hung three pairs of headphones. From his spongy ears dangled at least twenty earrings. His pockets bulged. Two sets of false teeth crammed in his mouth made him talk with an echo.

Ed yelled at him, "Fred, this isn't the mediator. Where the hell is he? I haven't got time to waste waiting for him!"

"No, but you've got the time to waste everything else."

There was some rustling in the garbage. None of us paid any attention to it. I turned toward Fred, extended my hand, and said, "Hi, I'm Bobby."

While giving me a half-hearted shake, he returned, "Good to meet you. I'm Fred Hunter. Do you think we have enough garbage around here?" He laughed.

"Doesn't it bother you?"

"Of course it does. Wouldn't it you if you lived here?"

"Yes, but you don't seem much bothered by it all."

"Well, I don't want it here—that's for certain. But, at the same time, I can't do much about it. So why get all worked up over something I can't do anything about. Too many people worry themselves sick over things beyond their control."

"That's what makes it a worry. Why can't something be done about all this trash?"

Increased thrashing in the trash interrupted us. Suddenly, a long, drawn face circled by long gray hair and beard rose out of the garbage. A television cabinet adorned his head. Fred and I rushed over to help uncover the emergence. As we lifted him up, his thin body seemed to keep on going and going. All three of us, who were of average height, had to tilt our heads back to see his shrouded face.

Ed extended his hand and said, "Hello, I'm Ed Wilson. You're our mediator? I sure as hell hope not!" They shook hands.

Fred drooped his hand forward. "Hi. I'm Fred. Are you all right?"

"Yes. I think so. Nice to meet you. I must have been dumped on during the night. Never did I imagine when you wrote me that your garbage problem was so extensive. This will take some doing to undo, and of course, involve more than what I had anticipated."

"Involve more? Don't you think we have enough?" Fred laughed.

"Involve more giving from me. To restore my inner balance and harmony that will be disrupted by my great outpouring of energy, I will need to receive an equal amount of energy flowing inward. This, of course, will have to take the form of a quantity of money much larger than what we had agreed upon earlier."

"How much?" Ed snapped.

"Double."

"What?"

"Trash on the outside first needs to be removed on the inside. To be blunt, my dear man, I've double the work because I have to remove the clutter in your mind that has cluttered up your world."

"We haven't hired you to insult us," barked Ed.

"I only speak the truth, which is more often than not pointed and painful."

"What do you think, Fred?"

"He's got a point. It's worth it to me to get rid of this garbage. We can afford it."

Ed twitched from head to foot. "Well, I guess."

"I need to be paid in advance."

Ed roared, "In advance! I'll advance on you right now!" He stepped toward Knowitall with clenched fists.

Fred intervened, "Half now and half when you succeed. Take it or leave."

"That sounds fair."

Ed opened his brown leather attaché case, lifted out a wad of cash, and flopped it into the mediator's hand.

"Thank you, my good sir."

Ed said nothing.

"We may as well begin," said Knowitall.

"Yes, we may as well. The sooner you solve our problem the better," quipped Ed.

"That's the problem. I cannot solve your problem for you. Only you can do that. I can only help you find the answers within yourselves."

"I'd better get more than that for my twenty thousand." Ed took another step toward him.

"Calm yourself, my dear man. I would not have taken it upon myself to respond to your call for help if I felt that I could not unlock your inner doors that keep you barred from your own truth. No one has a monopoly on truth. All share in truth as we share the air we breathe. A breath of air gives life to our physical body, a breath of truth gives life to our spiritual self.

"On the surface it may appear that your problem is entirely of a physical nature. But, just as the physical world has emanated from the spiritual world, problems on this physical plane have their origin in the spiritual plane. The peculiar disharmony in your spiritual lives has manifested itself in all this garbage. These mountains of rotten trash represent the waste in your stagnant souls. By bringing your meager, tormented souls in harmony with the Divine Being, all trash shall disappear. To aid us in seeing your spiritual difficulties we will need the help of one whose eyes gaze upon the spiritual world.

"I cannot see into your soul so, therefore, I will beseech the help of one who can."

150

"Where is this one? Who is he? I don't see anyone to help you," Ed said sarcastically.

With an airy, distant voice, Knowitall responded, " 'Who is this one?' he asks. Why, one is a spiritual being. 'And where may we find this one?' he demands to know. We will find one's gentle soul in the spiritual world." He cocked his head back, puffed out his chest, and sighed, "I am a channel."

"Channel two or four?" I twisted the channel knob on the television cabinet.

"Ignorance betrays itself by mocking wisdom. Get behind me, fool. I am a channel to the other world. There we will find help in the wisdom of the Ancient Ones."

"(To the other world? Is that a soap opera or what?...) What channel do I find that on?" I twirled the channel knob again.

"Much spoken, nothing said. Listen to the silence. Therein will you hear the word of God."

He eased his rear onto a pile of ravaged books. A vacant look drew the life out of his face as he arranged his body into the lotus position. Ed grabbed the money in his hand, tugged, pulled, leaned back, and jerked the old man off the books onto a fresh cow pie.

Fred echoed, "Come on, you cheap bastard. Let go. Give this guy a chance."

"I've given him all the chances he deserves. I'm not giving some schizophrenic twenty grand for displaying to me the other half of his insane mind."

"Maybe it takes an insane mind to understand our own insanity. I don't think we can call ourselves sane with all this garbage around here. Do you?"

"Insane minds only make each other more insane. I was never this nuts before I met you."

"Yeah, I seem to be losing my marbles faster now than ever," Fred laughed.

Knowitall spoke with a sensuous voice. "Hello, boys. I'm Pom Pom. In my former life I was a cheerleader. I used to urge the boys on. Do you boys need a little urging?"

He stood up, gently placed his hands on his hips, and rotated them a few times. All of us stopped what we were doing and stared at the channel.

"Got a problem only a woman with many lives of experience can solve?"

He threw in a couple high kicks with his overactive hip gyrations.

Partway through his movements, he slid off the cowshit onto a worn out king size bed.

"You don't have to answer. Having the answers is my job. But, you know, the old man here is getting down to the end of the line, so I can say what I have felt all along. I don't care! I don't care about the problems you people have down there. Not many of us really care. We didn't care much when we were alive on earth, so why should we care while floating in the ether? All we care about is getting physical!"

Knowitall went through a few more smooth, pelvic gyrations. His voice became more sensuous.

"Why do you think we dead souls have insight into your problems? You expect us to have the answers to questions about the future of mankind, the nature of his past, the whereabouts of lost continents, the intricate working of the human psyche, the enormous problems you have piled upon yourselves. We're supposed to be experts on love, life, death and the way to achieve physical, psychological and spiritual wholeness. What do you think, death turns us instantly into gurus and psychotherapists, that death gives us the insights and intelligence that we so dearly desired when we were alive? We aren't enlightened, we're dead. We are not much different from what we were when alive on earth. The only difference is that we are now ephemeral — floating bits of nothing in this vast expanse of nothingness."

Pom Pom started jumping up and down on the bed. "We have nothing to distract us! I can't take it anymore! We never sleep, can't escape into worldly pleasures, we can't even lose ourselves in a sweet melody. All we have is the same mental activity repeating itself over and over again like a broken record."

Knowitall grabbed his head and swayed from side to side.

"We can't stop it, can't turn it off. The movie of our lives just keeps on running all by itself. We see everything: our successes, mistakes, regrets, pains and pleasures, our zigzagging life as it has traveled on earth and other planets. All it does is tease us. I want to get physical. I want to get distracted in worldly pleasures. I want a real live flesh and blood brain so I can repress away all my pains and only be aware of my pleasures. I want to lie in the grass, gaze into the eyes of my lover, feed each other, feel each other, have him inside me. Ooh, how I want to get distracted, how I need to get physical.

"Do I get in line behind some guy who gets run over by a truck when he's young? No! I get behind some old fart that wants to live forever."

Knowitall slid his hands upward from his hips and gently rubbed his chest, and as he did, he drew in his hips, bent his knees, slid his hands down behind his rear, and smoothly raised up while thrusting his pelvis and leaning his head back to the sky. He continued to move with such beauty and grace that I began to get warm and wished that Pom Pom would get born and grow up in a hurry.

He spoke again with more sensuousness in his voice than before, which made me want Pom Pom even more.

"Sorry to get so carried away, but I just can't help it. From float to float, all I can think of is getting physical. To return to where I left off or rather to where I wanted to get turned on, which is anywhere but here, I'll answer the question I posed to you about why you believe that we dead souls have insight into your problems.

"Although, I shouldn't have to answer. You should know just by looking at all the trash around you. You people down there are desperate for answers to your problems. Your problems hang over you like dark clouds. They're an eternal plague; they suffocate you with their foul odor. No matter where you go, you can smell your wretched, oppressive stench. You can't help but wallow in your own waste. You'll believe anything, follow anyone, give away everything, even your own life, to get rid of them. But what happens? Do you get rid of them? No! Death doesn't change much. The more you try the more foul and powerful your problems become. You people down there are such easy prey. You are desperate.

"I'd rather be desperate than what I am now. At least I could feel desperate; I'd get passionately desperate and have a ball. Listen, I'll let you in on a little secret. While Knowitall and I were standing in line to be born, we got to talking about how easy it would be to make a fortune as a channel. Both of us in our previous lives had a hard time of it. Knowitall starved to death. I was a slave. Knowitall was ahead of me in getting born, so we agreed that I'd be his channel if he'd leave his wealth to me. There are ways to arrange those things up here. Knowitall's only son in a short while will become a father to a baby girl. And can you guess what they'll name her, in spite of everyone's objections? Oh, why yes, you guessed it, Pom Pom.

"Oh, I can't wait to feel physical again. Enjoy your life, boys. Treasure every moment. You'll know what you've missed after you die.   :

"Treasure a breath of fresh air, a leaf of grass, the clear blue sea, the joy of falling asleep and waking up, laughter, the pleasure in friendly conversation, and, last but not least, the joy of sex. You're missing out by being consumed by your own garbage. Try to enjoy being alive now, because once you die, it'll seem like an eternity before you get born again. Take my word for it. I've been waiting in line forever.

"Ooh, how I'm looking forward to it all. I've been looking forward to it much too long. Come on, Knowitall, I've been waiting in line long enough. I've been boxed out of the physical plane for too long. How I'd love to have a box to bang. Come on, you selfish, old fart, time to give up what I want. Give someone else a taste of real physical life, someone like me. Here, this should help bring about a much needed transition."

Knowitall leapt off the bed onto the ground. The television cabinet flew off his head as he landed on some diaper boxes. Pom Pom kicked and cheered:

"Come in high, come in low, come on boys, go, go, go."

He then raced across our island, turned around, cartwheeled back to us — a front flip, back flip, a few more back and forth; he jumped, landed in the splits, which made my groin hurt, then leapt to his feet and pelvic thrusted from head to toe for a few minutes. He groaned, "Oh, I can't breathe, aaah my chest." He grasped his chest. Pom Pom yelled out, "Now we're getting somewhere. No more waiting in line. Hey you with the bag in your hand, yeah you, you with the cute little buns, come over here."

I strolled next to Knowitall. He placed his hand on my ass. I stepped away and said, "What do you want."

Pom Pom said sensuously, "You."

"I'd like to have you too. Maybe we'll meet when you come of age."

"I hope so. I'm going to be born in a place called The Land of Boxes. Why don't you look me up in about sixteen years?"

"Maybe I will. Who knows where I'll be in sixteen years. Perhaps I'll be where you are now."

"I hope not."

"Me too." I stepped next to Knowitall and whispered, "Pom Pom, can't you help these guys out. You must have seen similar situations before. They really need some guidance.

"But, before them, how about me? Do you have some advice for me?"

"What do you need advice for?"

"I'm searching for a home." I told her some of my past.

"Well, I wish I could help, but I'm looking for a home too. Do you think I've found one up here in the endless nothingness? You don't have to answer that.

"So now, about this garbage problem, yeah, I guess I'll try to help. One last phony advice-giving session before I go where I'll need advice." She snuck in a little ass rub and said, "I hope I get some penetrating advice from you."

"I'm sure you'll get plenty of advice that will hit home."

Pom Pom yelled, "Hey boys, what seems to be your problem? Why can't you get rid of your garbage?"

Ed snapped, "What do you care?"

"Just thought I'd help while I was here. Don't you think you need some help?"

"No, I don't. But he does," Ed pointed to Fred.

"Well, Mister," Knowitall turned to Fred, "so all this is your fault?"

Fred said, "It all depends on who you talk to. Some say it's mine, some say it's his, some say it's both of ours."

"You seem much more congenial than that one over there."

Knowitall pointed to Ed. "Why don't you fill me in as to how you two have amassed so much trash."

"It's quite simple, really. Where Ed lives they throw away a lot of good stuff. Just about everything has something worthwhile in it. To us it's a crime to be so wasteful. We save and pretty much live off of what they throw away."

"But do you really need everything?" she asked. "Some of this stuff is really garbage."

Fred said, "You've been around. You should know that what you throw out today you'll need tomorrow. These mountains of trash are our unnatural resources."

"Well," she paused, "there seems to be no stopping you. Say, Eddie baby, can't you guys stop being wasteful? Can't you maybe separate the good from the bad and throw out the bad before this fat, little pack rat hoards it?"

"It's not profitable. It's a waste of time."

"How can it be profitable for Fred's townsfolk but not for yours?"

"We can't get out of it more than what we put into it. I don't know how it is profitable to them. I have as little to do with them as possible. One thing I know is, they don't compete with us. They look after themselves, that's for sure."

Fred responded, "We stopped competing some time ago. There is more harm than good in that game, so we got out of it, and now, it's funny; now that the pressure is off and we look at things differently we're more efficient than we were before. Ed, I wouldn't complain about our not competing if I were you. You'd be in a world of shit, literally, if we set out against you."

"Get lost! We'd put you so far in debt that you'd never again see the light of day. You'd turn your back on your ideals and start wasting everything just to pay the interest, and in the end, you'd come begging to us to take you over."

"What is this — joke time?"

I got between them and asked Fred, "What do you do when others try to compete with you, when they sell their products cheaper than you?"

"We buy some stuff, if it's good and lasts. But, we really don't import much. Some things we import just to see how it's made and then we make it. Most everything we need we make ourselves. We don't need much. We aren't big consumers.

"The price of a product is often more than what it sells for. Sometimes, all depending, besides giving money for a product you can also give away honesty, friendship, values, your conscience, loyalty, security — a whole way of life. You have to be careful. We watch very carefully what is imported and how and who makes the stuff. If we don't like the way they do things or what they do with our money, we won't buy from them. Sometimes, the real price tag is so high that it will kill you.

"It's a crime to waste nature to satisfy greedy, selfish desires. The earth's resources are a gift, not something to be taken for granted and spoiled. The profit we realize is in our feelings of love toward the earth and each other. We don't abuse and exploit each other or the earth for empty personal gain. We take care of each other, and if our economy veers off in a way counter to that, then we figure out a way to correct it and still survive."

Ed gritted his teeth. "Selfish desires! Empty, personal gain! You make me mad with how you misunderstand our way of life and mislabel healthy, individual ambition. It is individual ambition that has lifted our people out of the pain and despair of want and poverty. Individual ambition, the desire to realize one's full potential and rise above the slovenly crowd, that is what has moved mankind forward and is what drives our economy. The fortunes they have made and the well deserved recognition they receive are their just rewards for making a better way of life for everyone. These individuals are the dreamers, the producers, the makers, and the builders in our town, and for them to continue to give us the way of life we all enjoy, we let them do as they see fit. If we didn't, if we tried to regulate or contain their drive, then they'd lose interest, and everything would return to the impoverished life our ancestors suffered through. So if some good things get thrown away or if we throw away things to make room for a new product line, so what, who cares? Better to waste a little than to let the economy slow down by not wasting at all. Fred, do you think our body digests all the food you eat? Haven't you ever seen a few

157

kernels of corn in your shit? I suppose you pick out the kernels and eat them.

"Death and waste control nature's exuberance. Without them nature would outgrow herself and die before her time. Our way of life simply follows nature's. We are in harmony with her."

Fred rolled his eyes and said, "Talk about mislabeling! I still can't believe you try to justify your greedy, cold-hearted, wasteful lifestyle by trying to compare it to the way nature operates. Your way of life is in harmony with nature as bitter is in harmony with sweetness, as chemical waste is in harmony with pure water, as war is in harmony with peace, as ugliness is in harmony with beauty, as chaos is in harmony with order, as destruction is in harmony with creation, and as hate is in harmony with love. Where does nature waste? Where is nature's dump? Death in nature is movement in the food chain. Those things that die today sustain tomorrow. As for the corn in my shit, no I don't eat it, but it makes its way through the food chain onto your plate.

"I've seen how your ambitious individuals operate. They are ruthless. They care for no one but themselves. They use everything and everyone for their own gain. They are the cause of the disintegration of your way of life. They manipulate others with fear, for they are afraid. Fear fuels hatred, and that hatred is turning back on you and yours.

"It's fear, not any individual's vision of a better future, that drives your economy. Why are these piles of garbage here? Why are you so wasteful? Yeah, go ahead, justify it all, rattle on and on, pile up your words into mountains of books that will one day end up in the trash. You don't justify anything. You don't talk; fear does. You don't change your way of life because fear controls you. Fear is devouring your people. Where it is taking you is far worse than where you are now. Why do you think so many have left your town?"

"Those who have left were losers and weaklings. They couldn't keep up."

Ed grinned, "You make me laugh by calling us afraid. Fear does not control us. We use fear to separate the strong from the weak. We don't want nor do we need anyone who cannot stand up to the demands and pressures of the future.

"We are not afraid. We are free. Everyone is free to pursue life, liberty and happiness. What a man becomes is up to him. Take away his freedom, take away the challenges in life, tell him what to do and become, and what do you get? You don't get a man. You get a slave with no sense of pride and accomplishment. Freedom gives us the opportunity to learn from our mistakes. Maybe we have made a few mistakes, but by allowing everyone to participate in the government, solutions will be found. Freedom is the cornerstone of our way of life, not fear. Those in fear have not used their freedom wisely."

"Yeah, right! You're free to speak your mind, what's left of it anyway. How free is anyone when he has to use others to be financially secure? I suppose those being used are free. If they were free, they wouldn't be getting used. I suppose their freedom to be used fills them with dignity and self respect. Tell me Ed, I want to know, how free are people to own property when that right is used to prevent others from owning property? How free are people when they have to sell their future in order to exist in the present, and when that existence is dependent on the existence of companies and corporations that are dependent on an economic system that is out of control? How free is someone to pursue life when that system takes away the means to support himself and everything else he has worked his life away for? How free when boxed into a life you don't want? How free are people to pursue liberty when, in order to live, they are forced to make things they don't care about, consume things they don't need, and in doing that, contribute to a system that they not only don't believe in but is doing deadly harm to them and other living things? And tell me, you right-winger flying around dropping your rightness right in everyone's eyes, tell me how free was that woman and child I found last winter frozen to death in a shopping cart behind one of your fine gourmet restaurants? Tell me, how free was she to pursue life, liberty and happiness?"

"That is an unfortunate price paid for freedom. We are free to create our own freedom. Those not strong enough fall by the wayside, and seeing this, others learn how not to let that happen to them. Deer would never have learned to run fast and jump high if they were not chased by wolves. Part of our freedom, if you would look closer and not be so obnoxiously self-righteous and critical of everything we do, is the freedom to be exposed to threats. Without challenge, the will to live never comes alive. Those who get run over are not strong enough, and therefore do not deserve to live anyway. It's just, as I said before, a fact of nature. Where would evolution be if everything were protected from death? It would be like a bowl of mush."

Fred sneered. "Yes, yes, you are so right. It is in the cause of freedom that everyone is pitted against each other in struggling to survive. It has nothing to do with selfishness. All the other species in nature, they compete and fight amongst themselves to survive, don't they? Gorillas fight with each other all day long, don't they? I get sick when I hear you use the word nature. You separate events from nature to support your cruelty. Nature cooperates more than anything.

"Fear keeps your people from joining together to overcome life's dangers. How can life be enjoyed when danger is hung on a thread over everyone's head? That sure makes a person feel free, especially free from the threat of others trying to steal what he's got. How's the crime rate, anyway? I heard a lot of people are afraid to go out at night. Pretty free, aren't they?"

Fred sighed, "Well, we're not getting anywhere. I think Pom Pom should by now understand the cause of our problems. What do you think, Pom Pom, or do you even care?"

"Yes, I care. I have a couple of thoughts. Whether you'll be able to use them or not, I don't know. One thought is that both of you are too serious. Try to laugh a little bit more. If you laughed more, you could probably laugh away most of your garbage, both in and outside your minds. My other thought is that you should wake up every morning with the word compromise on your lips. Neither of you has a way of life that doesn't need improvement. Compromise. Do you know what that means or have both of you forgotten? It means blending, combining, bringing together some elements, leaving other elements behind. From my viewpoint out here, creation is one big compromise.

"Matter has compromised with space to create different densities of forms. The beautiful, misty blue orb on which you are trashing about is a miraculous compromise of millions of things. Just take two for example. The blending of earth and water. What would be, what could live, if the two had remained separate, stayed on each side of their fences and yelled back and forth at each other: 'No. Get away. I

160

won't have anything to do with you.' You wouldn't be here, that's for sure. And I wouldn't be able to visit the place. But they have combined so lovely plants can grow. Beautiful fish glide along the bottoms of lakes and streams. Animals play on the water cushioned ground.

"Things combine into new forms to meet changes and challenges. My advice to you is to combine some of your ways while ending others. Bring together your efficiency of production, your appreciation for the earth, your sharing, your cleanliness, your desire to want others to be as well off as you want to be, your concern for yourself, and your ability to build and create things that last for a long time, and, of course, if I land anywhere around there, bring together the sexes.

"Do I have to say what you should leave behind? Yes, I guess I should. Greedy Ed probably won't feel he's getting his money's worth if I don't. Dump your greediness, your fear of caring for each other, your selfishness, and that means you too, Fred. You're being selfish by stockpiling all this garbage. I very much doubt your sincerity about preserving the earth's beauty with all the garbage you have piled on her beautiful face. Like most men, you seem to be more talk than action. Your garbage stinks and smells and is a breeding ground for disease. It fills your streets. Separate the good from the bad and get rid of it.

"Dump your wasteful ways, your obsession with time. You're wasting time anyway by being wasteful. Dump your cruelty, your cold heartedness, your dead ideas about the earth, for the earth is alive and an intelligence beyond your comprehension; dump your polluting, and, most of all, dump justifying the existence of those things you should dump.

"Most of all, boys, in all sincerity, for I do care, it's just hard for me to care now that I'm so close to getting physical, but most of all think about what you want in life. Do you want all this garbage? Do you want to live apart? Do you want to waste your life by wasting? Don't you want to feel close? Don't you want to be in love? Wouldn't you rather give your affection to another human being than a dog? You're in the middle of life, and yet you haven't thought about it. Start thinking about life, start loving life. That's all you've got. I'll tell you, believe me, the more you waste the longer you'll be dead. And, you'll

161

hate being dead. You'll want to get physical as fast as you can. Believe me, I've had the itch before, but I've never, no never, itched this long.

"Well, boys, that's it. Take it or leave it, but please don't waste it.

"Oh yes, one more thing: give your best to your children because soon I will become a child."

Knowitall slowly lowered himself on the ground and lay down. His skin turned pale white, his face withered and darkness pressed in under his eyes. He looked as though the channeling session had taken the last bit of life out of him. Suddenly, he jumped to his feet and Pom Pom's voice yelled out, "Oh no you don't, old man. Don't try to regain your strength. As I said before, I've been waiting in line long enough."

He then cartwheeled around our island a few times. Stopped in front of us. High kicks, front flips, back flips, more high kicks, pelvic thrusts, more high kicks, then he sprinted back and forth across the island many times and topped it all off by returning with high arching cartwheels. He collapsed in front of us and moaned, "Oh, no, I can't breathe. I can't breathe. I can't catch my breath. Oh, oh, my chest. Help me, help me. My chest is killing me."

I rushed over to him. As I bent down, he jumped up, hit me in the head with his shoulder, and knocked me on my back.

Pom Pom yelled, "Don't, don't you help him. I'm finally getting somewhere. I can see him floating toward me. Come on Knowitall, you can make it, honey."

He did some half hearted, high kicks, slowly bent downward for a pelvic thrust, raised up slightly, groaned, and fell dead on the ground. I placed the television cabinet back on his head. Ed yanked the twenty grand out of his hand and kicked garbage on top of him.

I turned to Ed and asked, "Do you plan to take Pom Pom's advice?"

He laughed. "Are you crazy? She was lucky I stayed long enough to hear her garbage. She doesn't know anything about business, not to mention her naive view of human nature. What am I saying? She? She who? Knowitall was a masochistic schizophrenic bent on self — destruction. Caring! Sharing! This is the real world. Those who care fall by the wayside. You have to look out for yourself, no one else will. Screw them before they screw you. If you help others, when the time comes for them to return the favor, they are nowhere to be found or have forgotten who you are.

"Besides that, Fred can't be trusted. Once I had everything set. I made an agreement with Fred and the trash service to remove all the trash, which wasn't much compared to what we have now. You know what Fred did? Behind my back, on the day they were supposed to begin to remove all the garbage, he paid them not to come. So, in effect, he bought all this garbage. Isn't that cost effective? How could I ever compromise with that sleazy liar."

Fred got raised. "I wonder, Ed, were you born an idiot or do you practice at being one? Look at him, Bobby, look at that nervous, angry, greedy fool. He'll never change. Pom Pom was right, compromising does bring about new things, but you have to have something to compromise with. There's nothing, I mean absolutely nothing in Ed's way of life that I'd want in mine. I don't want any of his time saving, efficient, wasteful machines and managers in my town. We do just fine without them. A compromise with him would only poison what we have. I'll just sit around and watch his way of life rot into the ground.

"We'll see who gets buried, you passive, little, fat ass. Watch out! One of these days we might just get rid of you and yours and all this garbage all at once. I've had it with the likes of you. This was one big waste of time. I should have known better. Anything with you is a waste." Ed stormed off to the right.

Fred extended his hand to me. "Nice to have met you, Bobby." He turned and moseyed off to the left, picking through the garbage as he tried to find his way.

I wandered as they stayed behind time in garbage. I was glad they didn't have any nuclear weapons.

Chapter 15

For days I walked across an arid, dusty region that must have been the place where God discarded the first two unacceptable human beings. He probably had planned on their dying and that being the end of the human race. But, as fate would have it, they survived. I was wondering if I would survive. Finally, at the end of my seventh day in that miserable place, I came upon a small village nestled in a moist, fertile valley. The area reminded me of Aunt Iris's garden. I recognized many plants that had been favorites of mine in her garden. That was reassuring. At least I hadn't walked off the planet; although, I thought to myself, maybe I would have been better off if I had.

My feet were sore, so I decided for the first time in my life to buy a car. The relatives I stayed with before Aunt Iris had cars.

Aunt Iris never owned one. She thought they were the most useless, ridiculous, addictive, monstrous, deadly things man had ever made outside of missiles and tanks. Like most of her opinions, I shared that one with her too. But, as my hot feet took priority in my seething brain, I decided to buy a car.

The only thing I was concerned with was buying something that moved while I sat and wiggled my feet. The size, shape, color, and style never crossed my mind as something to consider. Upon walking into the first car dealership in my path, I was met with a gruff greeting from a manufactured salesman.

"Do you want something?"

"Well, I haven't come in here because I want nothing."

There was a long pause as he fondled his colorful tie.

"Are you sure you're in the right place?"

He eyed me up and down. I was dirty, had a torn bag in my hand, a canteen around my neck, looked homeless, which of course, like most everyone (even those with homes), I was. After walking over to the nearest car, I said, "Does this car run?"

"Of course it runs!"

"I'll buy it. How much is it?"

"Thirty-two thousand."

"Are you out of your mind? That much money for something that could kill me?"

"No, I haven't lost my mind, but you seem to have lost yours."

"Would you show me the cheapest thing you've got that moves?"

"Do you have any money?"

"Do you think I'd come to buy something without money?"

"I don't know. I just don't want to waste my time."

I pulled a wad of cash out of my bag. His manner changed in an expected fashion.

"Yes, sir!"

He took me by the arm. "We have a real nice clean selection of used cars. Right this way. I believe we have something that will fit your needs perfectly. Here, this one here, isn't it a beauty. Starts every time. An old lady kept it in her garage. Rarely drove it.

"It's over twenty years old. Looks new, doesn't it? Look at the odometer, sir. Only reads thirty-five thousand. This car is a great deal, sir." And on and on, making me wish that he spoke a language I couldn't understand.

Finally, after enough gibberish, I pointed to a beat up old car and said, "How much is that car?"

"You don't want that car, sir. It won't last."

"How much is it?"

"It's been sitting here a long time. Really, sir, I don't recommend it at all. Now here, look at this shiny ..."

I screamed, "How much is it?"

"...this shiny red car. Look at the interior. Just like new. Slide onto the seats. Here ..."

I grabbed him by the arm, jerked him toward me, and yelled, "How much is it? Can you hear me? How much does that junker cost?"

"Okay, all right. You don't have to blow out my eardrums. It's five hundred dollars. As is."

"I'll buy it. And would you please hurry up before I get sick?"

"The sooner you leave the happier I'll be," said the gentle salesman.

After sliding onto the soft seat, caressed from behind and below, I almost fell asleep. My foremost desire, well, that's always hard to decide upon; there's always a few competing at the top. Sometimes, one wins momentarily, carries me away and then leaves without telling me what to do next. Anyway, I was pretty sure my foremost desire was to find a place to wash up and sleep.

It had been a long time since I'd been in a car. They sure didn't look the same. The ones I had been in long ago looked simple. This one had a surplus of dials, switches, and buttons, all of which were a source of wonderment. That was fine with me. If I didn't know their purpose, then I didn't have to bother with them. I tried to remember what my aunts and uncles did when they drove. It couldn't have been that hard. I remembered that they shuffled their feet around on the floor while moving a few levers near the wheel. There weren't any levers by the wheel on this car. For a brief moment, I thought of asking a policeman how to drive, but decided against it when I realized that he'd probably demand to see my driver's license. The odds, I thought, were in my favor of not being stopped, so why bother to get a license? I might not even enjoy driving. After a few jerks, stalls, quick starts, sudden stops, burning tires, driving up on the curb a few times and almost hitting a crossing guard, I made it outside of town on a hill overlooking the valley and glided into a place that rented cabins.

There were a number of cabins forming a U shape, and in the center was a telephone booth, cans, weeds, and an empty swimming pool filled with trash. The owner of the place was an older man — thin of hair, sharp, pointy nose out of which curled wiry hair, thin parched lips, bloodshot eyes with whitish gray surrounding the pupils, a potted, worn face, and a Headweiser cap teetering on top of his head.

He looked as though someone had just hit him in the head with a baseball bat. He stared blankly at me. As I filled out the card, I could feel him watching me, but, at the same time, I felt as though no one was watching me. His movements were slow, without expression, and his speech was pure monotone.

After I paid him, he said, "No young feller. I know alls about ya young guys. Don't ya think ya can fool me. I's an ole timer but quick as a whip. Ya young studs are all the same. Ya rent ma little ole cabin all by yaself. Then all yas friends come ova, girls too. Buy lots of beer and raise hell and leave my little ol' cabin a goddamn mess. I wouldn't a mind it so much if ya'd invite me ova once in a while."

He grinned as a baby who had just wet himself.

"Now, listen here. See this here paper. It says I rented just to ya. If I's sees a bunch around or hear hell raisin', out ya go. O.K. Do you folla?

"Now don't ya think I'm ..."

I felt as though years had passed during his few words. His words oozed out of his mouth like cold honey from a jar, dripped on top of my feet, and weighed me down. He was still talking as I walked out the door.

That evening after a nap and a hearty meal, I decided to gaze at the stars. Stargazing was and still is one of my favorite occupations.

There's a lot to see up above. I've tried to imagine a world without a starlit sky. It becomes so depressing that I have to curb my imagination, which can sometimes be a near impossibility.

In that arid area the stars shone bright, sparkling as though they were trying to say something to me, and seemingly within arms' reach. They were especially distinct and clear due to the new moon.

As I gazed up into the sky, its vastness overwhelmed me. My eyes saw the arch of the Milky Way and its dusty stars. Beyond our modest galaxy were billions of galaxies. Some I could see as specks in the sky, but most were beyond my vision. They were all moving so fast that the light from them would not reach us for billions of light years, and beyond them was infinite space, and in that empty vastness I imagined other universes like our own, expanding outward, and someday, the galaxies from them would cross over our galaxies as concentric ripples overlap as they move outward from stones thrown into the water. These galaxies were filled with billions of stars, surrounded by billions of planets, which were covered with zillions of life forms; and it all seemed so vast, so awesome, so wonderful and important that I began to feel I was only a tiny, insignificant atom in the magnificent scheme of things; a little nothing whose existence meant less than that, whose life span was just a wink of the cosmic eye; as far as the universe was concerned, my speck of a life meant nothing. The sky was engulfing me; in its vastness I was becoming lost. The ground on which I stood was moving away. I felt I would disappear into black space. I touched the ground but hardly felt anything. I tried to feel my face to see if it was still there, but could not find it. In a panic, I ran through the screen door of my little cabin, attacked the refrigerator, and devoured its contents. Slowly, the world returned. I began to feel heavy; sensations of gas bubbled inside me. I felt the smooth, cold sides of the fridge. The room returned to surround and hold me. I slumped to the floor satisfied that I was still here.

My stomach began to feel like a methane generator. It churned, rolled around, shot gas out both ends, bubbled furiously, and was painfully expanding. Usually, like everyone else, I avoid pain. But, at that time, pain was a welcomed reassurance that I still existed.

Glanced around. Spotted an empty bottle of ketchup, empty herring jar, empty package of bologna, an empty bag of Doritos, empty dill pickle jar, a half eaten loaf of bread, two empty cans of pork and beans, three mutilated banana skins, orange rinds scattered all over the place, empty package of cheese, an empty quart of soda, and an empty half gallon of milk. The worst thing was that I didn't taste any of it, not even the Doritos. My poor stomach was wishing it belonged to someone with a more sensible diet. It looked like a big fat, jolly Buddha belly.

Holding and rubbing my stomach, I returned to gaze at the stars.

I lay on the soft grass, my entire body happily in contact with the earth, and let my eyes and mind wander in space.

Again, the magnificence of the universe overwhelmed me but in a different way. As I gazed at it, I thought of the things we knew about it. Behind all that immensity and complexity were a few simple forces that moved the universe and held it together. It was possible that these forces had their origin in one force, and this one force had its origin in nothing. It all just seemed to lie there in space, moving to the tune of a silent song just as I, at times, am moved by silence.

We know so much about our universe: that it exploded outward and is still expanding, the time period of all this, what the universe is made of, the birth and death of stars, the evolution of matter and life itself, the intricate workings of the laws of nature, the composition of all sorts of molecules and how they interact. And what fell on me like a meteorite was that I was a member of the species, the only species on earth, that was able to comprehend this, and that I, Bobby, could also understand and share in what others had found.

Usually I don't feel fortunate being a member of our species, but during moments like those, I do. I guess there are some worthwhile human attributes.

Very unexpectedly the question, what is the purpose of all this?, drifted into my mind. The answer that emerged was — there was no purpose to it all. Life lives for itself. Why does life have to have a purpose? It has nothing to prove. And to whom would it prove it, anyway? God? God could care less. If there's anything in the universe that has no purpose at all or is concerned about a purpose for being, it's God. What does he have to worry about? He's sufficiently self-sufficient. I doubt the stars ask themselves why they are there or why they are the ones that radiate in darkness. They just float around and shine and shine and shine. I envy them. I wouldn't mind floating around and shining all the time. Our own sun doesn't wonder why it's the one who shines kindly on our planet and gives us life; nor does it wonder what the purpose is of the life it provides. It's happy just being what it is. Even the animals don't seem to be aware of the question. I've never seen one scratch its head with a perplexed look, withdraw from activity in deep, dark depression, or pace around when it wasn't looking for something; but then again, I've never seen them do a lot of things we do. They just live and die like stars.

My eyes then focused on the constellations. I quickly spotted the little and big dippers. That was it for the standard constellations.

I never have been able to picture any other ones. Then other things began to form before my eyes. I saw a line of stars curve across the universe, a comic strip called Cosmic Comics in which God lost the universe and was running into many mishaps in trying to find it, a bathtub, a 1968 Buick Skylark with am fm radio and snow tires, 2001 Playmate of the Century, a hot fudge sundae, a cabin in the woods, an endless extension ladder... and then, lo and behold, mine eyes beheld vast corridors stretching from star to star. The corridors were held by white threads at each of the four corners. Between the bottom threads spanned a milky white floor. The sides were clear. In these corridors human souls were traveling from one star to another.

Some were skipping happily along, a few were running, others were strolling, some were taking a few steps, stopping for a while, gazing out into the vastness, and then taking a few more steps; many looked as though they were being dragged along, some seemed to be shoved along by the scruff of their necks, others seemed to be pulled along by the nose, and still others looked as though they were fighting someone all the way along as the invisible person yanked them to their new home. I felt my gaze being drawn to a particular corridor. It came down toward me and curved out to the outer galaxies. The words "Bobby's Corridor" suddenly appeared on its side. I jumped to my feet. I knew it! I had always known I didn't belong here. No wonder life didn't make any sense to me.

The corridor mesmerized me. It began to move toward me until it was only a few feet away. A crack appeared in the curve. A blond angel, looking a lot like the woman in the park I invited to go adventuring, appeared at the crack, and said, "Bobby, come on. You fell out. Take my hand. You're on the wrong planet."

She stretched her hand toward me and said, "Jump. Jump up and grab my hand."

Starry-eyed, I jumped and jumped, but my hand stopped short.

After climbing up on something, I was sure to grasp her hand, but no matter how high I jumped, I couldn't reach it. Then the corridors disappeared.

Discouraged and disappointed I sat down and held my head in my hands. Why didn't I make it? Would I ever get another chance? In vain I was traveling over this earth searching for a place where I felt at home. And now, in the middle of the night in an unlikely place, I had a chance to leave this planet and travel in my own corridor to the planet on which I rightly belonged. Why, oh why, didn't I make it back to my corridor? What was there left for me now that I was misplaced in space and probably in time?

While I was pondering my troublesome predicament, I felt sharp pointy edges pricking my rear. After feeling the surface upon which I sat, I discovered that I was on top of the roof of my car. Maybe I was trying to tell myself something about my purchase. The edges and points of the dents reflected light from the sky. The light began to twinkle. The twinkling became more pronounced; the darkness took on a deep dimension, and before I knew it, I was gazing into another universe. How could that be? I'd never looked down at the sky before. I looked up — stars shone from above; gazed down — stars twinkled from below. I was between two universes! A black hole! Falling through a black hole from the universe into which I was born to another altogether different universe. Renewed hope filled my soul. No, I hadn't missed my home.

Another planet in this universe was not my destiny. This universe was not for me. Not only did I belong on a different planet but in a different universe. And all along I thought I shared in the typical existential dilemma of modern man; trapped in an absurd existence from which I could not escape. Just trudging along, alone, feeling separate and different from others, a solitary human being in pursuit of who knows what, driven by mysterious desires, bounded on all sides by nothingness, just like a star in the void.

My existential predicament ran deeper than I had expected. I did not belong in this existence at all; existence in this universe could only be nothing but foreign to me. I belonged in a different kind of existence in a different kind of universe. Perhaps, this universe was the inside out, the reverse of where I should have been. That would explain why everything appeared backwards to me. Instead of traveling in time to different spaces, maybe, I was supposed to be traveling in space to different times.

Sheer excitement ran through me as I tumbled and fell from one universe to the other, but was abruptly shaken when I landed flat on my back, had the wind knocked out of me, and upon looking up, realized I had landed in the wrong universe when I saw a young man standing over me, belly hanging out of his tee shirt over his belt, a tin cap protecting his brain, beer in hand, and a disgusted expression giving a little life to his bloated face.

"What the hell are you doing jumping on top of your car?"

Gasping for breath, sorely disappointed and irritated at where I found myself, I said, "I'm breaking it in. What does it look like I'm doing."

He staggered away mumbling to himself.

After regaining my breath, I stumbled into the cabin, lay gently on the bed, and fell into a deep sleep.

That night, I dreamed I was the creator of the universe. I was standing in the center of the universe, reaching out into it, and after gathering up stars as though they were snowflakes, packed them tightly

172

into a ball. After packing all the matter in the universe into a ball the size of a soccer ball, I set it down in front of me. Taking seven steps backward, I approached the ball with an easy rhythmic stride and kicked off the universe. It exploded as if it were made of sand. Tiny stars spun out into space in all directions. I sat back to admire my creation. Never had I made a bad kick. The ball always exploded in a smooth, even manner. What I enjoyed most was watching the planets that pulsated with life. They were jewels in the sky. I had the ability to be anywhere and everywhere in the same time. Traveling from one place to another, I shared in my creation. I visited the earth when man first appeared. The life span of a man was shorter than the blink of an eye. As soon as I saw him, I knew what he would do to himself and to one of my favorite jewels. After leaving the earth, I forgot it existed. As the galaxies began to slow in their outward expansion, I gathered them up again into a ball and gave the universe a new birth. This ritual of gathering it up and kicking it off I repeated forever, not only with the universe from which I dreamed but with all my universes. Doing it once was doing it forever, and doing it forever was doing it once.

The next morning I woke with a renewed interest in adventuring. I felt I had seen enough in that area, although I had only been there one day and spent most of it at the cabin. But still, I was anxious to move on.

After packing my dented car with my binoculars, torn bag and canteen; I climbed inside. Once again, there I was faced with a steering wheel, radio, windshield, and an array of gauges. I got out of the car. Walked around it a few times; wasn't sure if I wanted to take that thing with me or not.

The whole purpose of my trip was to see, and hopefully in seeing, find a home. But shielded from the world in a steel box, I was afraid I wouldn't be able to see much. And what would I do if I became addicted to the box? It had happened to so many; I feared it would happen to me, and before I knew it I'd be traveling from one place to another, getting out, looking around, snapping a few pictures, and hopping back in to another place. Or worse yet, I could fall into the total box syndrome where I would wake from my box bed, leave my box house, drag myself into my box car, drive to a big box building where I'd spend the entire day in a cubicle staring at a rectangular

173

computer screen, return to my box car, drive to a bar to drink beer and eat a box of popcorn, return to my box house where I'd be greeted with a box on the ears for coming home half smashed, eat my TV dinner out of a box, sit in a chair and stare at the tube, climb back into my box bed where my wife and I would bang our boxes together, and in the end be buried in a box.

But, my feet were still sore. I decided to let the car take me.

I had my doubts when I first pulled onto the highway. I was used to seeing things up close. There I was coasting along, seeing from a great distance, at least it seemed great to me. To compensate for my removal from earthly objects, I steered from the passenger side. At least I had a closer look, but a closer view of trash along the side of the road was not what I had in mind. There were places I saw off in the distance that, had I been on foot, I would have traveled, some interesting hills and formations, but no roads cut across the fields toward them.

The next difficulty I encountered was horn-honking and people swearing at me as they raced by. I was only going ten miles an hour.

That was fast enough for me, but not for them. I couldn't see anything by going faster. As I drove along, I saw many beautiful plants and flowers, which needed closer attention. But, I quickly learned that in a car you keep on going, so I kept on going. The honking and swearing was getting on my nerves and distracting me so much that I couldn't enjoy what little I did see, so with a little movement of my toes, the car jumped to ninety miles an hour. It was amazing. I was racing along a country road, rolling and bouncing along, not seeing much of anything, but actually being thrilled to life by high speed.

So, I thought to myself, this is what it must be like for those who always have to be busy doing something.

Up ahead to the right, a vine hanging all over a huge weeping willow reminded me of eternity hanging in time. It captured my interest completely. As I whizzed past it, I turned around so I could still see it, and at the same time, heard a loud crash, and the car seemed as though a giant Martian were trying to shake it apart. My precious box on wheels had departed from the road, smashed through a farmer's fence, and was bouncing across his field. Ahead was a ditch for which the car seemed destined. Not knowing what to do, I figured the car had better jump the ditch, or it would crash into the side of it. I floored the car. It made a howling noise that sounded as though it were going to explode, took off like a bullet, flew over the ditch, tipped its nose downward, caught the top edge of the bank, flipped end over end, bounced off the rear, flew in the air, and squished into the top of a majestic pile of manure up to the bottom of the windows.

What a view I had from the top of that pile of crap. The hills rolled endlessly. I could even see the town. I wondered what the stars would look like from that spectacular perch and was considering staying there until dark when I noticed a farmer, with a pitch fork in one hand and a computer in the other, shouting at me. After grabbing my bag, binoculars, and canteen, I crawled out the window and slid down the slick shit.

Blue jean overalls draped his lean body. A few days growth of beard rounded the angularity of his face and darkened his already dark eyes. He stuck his pitch fork in the ground and shouted, "What the san hill you think you doin' tearin' up ma field and busin' up ma fence. If I hadin a bin out, all ma cows would be loose on the ha'way. You young people always gotta be drivin' so dang fast. Where you think you a goin' so fast? You gotta girl you pluggin ore yonder?"

He took off his cap and scratched his bald head.

"I hope yous gotta enough money to fix all this here damage."

Standing back and gazing at the crap crowned with my car, I said, "Don't they look like they belong together? That car just fits in there perfectly. You know, I don't think I could have planned a more suitable place for it."

"Well, gall daingit. That's my ole car. I regretted ever gettin' rid of that thing."

"Well, looks like it has come back home to roost.

"Hey, I'll make you a deal. You fix the fence and I'll give you the car. What do you say?"

He scratched his head for a moment. "Yeah. She alwayz waz a good farm veehicle."

"That's great! What's your name?"

"Elmer Fusster."

I signed the car over to him. I picked up my belongings and headed out across the field through the hole in his fence. As I looked back, Elmer was still standing there scratching his head and staring at the car.

I probably would have kept it if it could have taken me to the stars. But, if I had as much control over a space vehicle as I did with my car, I might find myself way off in some region of space opposite to the way I wanted to go. What difference would that make though? A space is a space no matter where it is. It just depends on what you want to do while you're in it or what you may want to put in it. Anyway, I can think of easier ways to visit the stars. All you have to do is make friends with them, and they'll invite you up for a visit any time you like.

Chapter 16

While I was wandering over hills and through dales, I came upon on a sign that read: "This way to the Society for the Prevention of Cruelty to Humans. There was nothing pulling me in any direction, one hill was as good as the other, so the curiosity that was instilled in me by this sign was enough to tug me in that direction. My curiosity quickly became transformed into excitement and hopefulness, for as I was clicking along on top of that well-beaten path, I began thinking about how nice it would be to find a place where others felt about things similar to the way I did. Now, don't get me wrong. I'm not the type who wants to dominate others into being a certain way; I'm no Christian. I just wanted to find a place where others genuinely cared about each other and cherished life. As is the case with me, one thing led to another, each bud flowered, my click turned into a skip, inward thoughts transformed into happy songs, and by the time I reached the city, I had imagined everything to be brightly painted, the inhabitants peaceful and smiling, clean city streets, no junk, no pollution, people living from moment to moment, huge parks filled with flowers, lovers strolling happily along unaware of time and the rest of the world, dogs loving cats, cats loving birds, and everyone being content with who they were.

I was so absorbed in my thoughts that it wasn't until I entered the city and noticed the sign, "Home of the Society for the Prevention of Cruelty to Humans," shot full of holes and dangling on a post, before it occurred to me that maybe this place wasn't as I had imagined. I stopped. Looked around. Cracked weathered siding was falling off the buildings, windows were broken, doors were dangling off hinges, roof shingles were blown off, weeds had taken over, vines were growing over the roofs, and small trees grew out of the gutters.

The people were just sitting on their porches and lying beside the road. Their clothes were torn and dirty, their children thin and sickly. My song died in mid-air; legs became heavy along with my heart. Hope vanished. I trudged into town hoping that what I saw was not what it was.

After two blocks of seeing as much as I wanted, I stopped in front of a house where a young skinny man with a scraggly beard dripping off his face and a woman whose hair looked as though it was matted with mud were slouched on an old, stained, torn couch on the front porch. Dark circles hung under both their sunken eyes. Their chins were glued to their chests. Frowns sagged to their knees. As I spoke, I wondered whether they would be able to respond or just sink farther down.

"Excuse me. Hate to bother you at a moment like this. Sorry if I am interrupting anything, but could you tell me where the Society for the Prevention of Cruelty to Humans is?"

Without looking up the woman replied, "What do you want to go there for?"

I thought to myself, "Come on, just tell me. You don't care, and I don't want to explain myself." Then I said to them, "Don't tell anyone this, but a few months ago I met a man who was dying, and before he died he told me that a long time ago he robbed a bank and buried the money behind the Society for the Prevention of Cruelty to Humans. So, if you please?"

Chins still glued, they responded in unison, "Oh, yeah? I bet he did."

Raising his head and assuming to muster up all his strength and resources, the man stared vacantly and said, "Keep on going for three blocks, turn right, keep on going." He waved his hand forward and fell back.

"Thanks."

I started to walk away, then stopped, stood there for a moment, walked back, and said, "Do you people always live like this?"

That unglued both their heads. She replied, "What do you mean? What's wrong with the way we live?"

"Things are falling apart and you just sit there."

"What else? What can be done? Things follow their course no matter what you do. Ever heard of entropy?"

At that moment, the gutter hanging on a few rusty nails fell off, landed in a mud puddle, and splashed muddy water on the two victims.

He mumbled to her, "Bound to happen sooner than later."

With a burdened voice, she mumbled back, "Yeah, it's karma."

I said, "Take it easy."

They replied, "Wish we could."

I waved. They waved.

The movement of their arms put them in forward motion. They slid off the couch and knocked the two remaining balusters out from under the rail. It fell across their legs and pinned them to the floor.

Through it all, they kept on waving as though nothing had happened. I just walked away.

On my way to the Society, I saw the same kind of things, although I did see a puppy and kitten playing together on what looked like soft grass. I almost walked past the Society. If it hadn't been for people hanging out of the windows, cramming in at the doors, and legs sticking out of the roof vents; I would have passed it by and, lacking interest to retrace my steps in order to find it, would have walked right out of town into another adventure. But, the odd behavior stopped me in front of the moldy, green colored, block building. A decayed wooden entry way was tilting away from the front of the building. Above the pink door, in faded red chipped letters, was the sign: "Welcome to the Society for the Prevention of Cruelty to Humans — Our Home is Yours. I was hoping it wasn't true.

As I approached the doorway, I heard screams and cries coming from inside. The door was locked, so I walked around to the side and stopped by a window where a couple of people were trying to climb in off the top of garbage cans.

"Hey, can I look in there for a minute? What's going on in there? Hey, come on. Hey, can't you hear me?"

They acted as though I were a piece of air.

I yelled at the top of my lungs, "Do your ears work or are they just there for decoration?"

I started yanking on the pant leg of a short stocky man. Without looking down, he furiously kicked his leg as though he were trying to shake mud off his boots. One kick hit me in the head and knocked me down. It's not like me to do what I did, maybe the behavior around the place rubbed off on me extra fast, but I jumped up and with unusual vigor, kicked the garbage can out from under his feet. He dangled there a few minutes before falling to the ground.

He jumped up and turned at me. His appearance made me cringe. Wild, knotted hair stuck up straight, sweat poured down his face, and his eyes gleamed and bulged out past his nose. He ground his teeth, curled his shoulders like a lion, and screamed, "You sonufabitchin' cocksucker. Take this you bastard." He reached down and picked up a stick.

"Calm down. Come on, all I want is to…"

I picked up a garbage can. We danced around the parking lot to the tune of the swinging stick, garbage can cha-cha.

"… look in the window. Can't we talk about this? For Christ's sake, you're going to hurt somebody with that stick. Not so hard. I thought this was a place where people were kind to each other. Oh, holy shit, look at that, your friend just got in."

He turned toward the window. I jammed the garbage can over his head, jumped on top, and start beating the can all around with his stick. After a few minutes, I lifted off the can. The madman stood up, fell back down, got up, and staggered around the parking lot as I raced over with the can, jumped up, and looked inside.

I couldn't believe it! I started to quiver. You would have thought that those inside would be soothing each other, patting each other, making things better for each other, saying to each other that everything would be all right, but no, it was a tangle of cruelty.

Below me a big, fat, sweaty guy had a thin man by the ears and was rubbing his face up and down his sweaty belly and then every so often would cram the thin guy's face into his arm pit and almost suffocate him. With one hand, the thin guy was pinching the fat guy with pliers, causing bleeding and red swollen marks, and with his other hand, he was grabbing a woman who was pinned against the wall and being raped by a man with one arm and one leg. The woman was digging her pointed high heels into an unconscious old woman lying beneath her. All the while, the fat guy was laughing, "Here you go thin man. Have some sweat. You act like you never do it." The thin guy was screaming, "How's this feel, you fat ugly slob." The one-armed, one-legged man was pleading, "What's wrong with me? Look at me, look at me, I'm you're lover." She was yelling, "Get out of here. Leave me alone, leave me alone. Fuck that old woman on the floor." Behind the one-legged, one-armed man a scrawny, teenage boy was swinging an ax at a stake chained to his leg. A circle of people of all ages were screaming, "Stupid boy, good for nothing, abandoned child. Ever feel loved? Who would love you? A hopeless, dumb bastard like yourself."

A young woman was preparing to light some gas she had just poured around the outside of the circle. But before she did, someone lit her; she fell into the others, and up they went. They put themselves out, blamed the boy, and started beating him. This caught like wildfire.

Those around started beating on the group that was beating the boy, others started to beat them, and this spread until everyone was beating and being beat except for a few huddled in the corners, some wild-eyed maniacs screaming at the ceiling about the coming of evil incarnate, a couple of human stone statues, the many oblivious pacers, the walking hallucinating madman who was exclaiming that good and evil were in the palm of his hands, and the strolling, gentle souls pledging not to harm anyone while they burned themselves with matches.

As karma would have it, my quivering shot into violent quaking. I lost all control and crashed to the ground. The madman came to, picked up his stick, started beating me, and yelling, "Think you're smart? Take this and this and this." More than anything, the smacks knocked me out of my quaking. I grabbed the stick out of his hand and yelled, "Okay. Okay. We're even. I got you, you got me, and, damn, at least I didn't hurt you." I rubbed my legs. "Okay?"

"All right. Now get lost."

He quickly turned. I grabbed him by the shirt and said, "Wait a minute."

Before I knew it, he wrestled me to the ground and started pounding on my back.

I yelled, "No. No. Goddamnit. I don't want to look in there again. Calm down."

He stopped.

"You people really get carried away. Stop it. Let me up. Believe me, I've seen enough. All I want to do is leave."

"Yeah, sure."

"Get off."

"You even go toward that window, and I'll punch your face in."

I rocked him off and wiggled free.

"See, I'm leaving." I stepped back. "But, here, wait. Doesn't anyone work here? It's a cruel circus in there. Those people need help. They're going to kill each other."

"What do you mean? Didn't you look inside. Everyone is working themselves to death." He tilted his head back, rolled his eyes up inside his head, and squealed with laughter.

"You're all crazy! What the hell is going on there? This is supposed to be the Society for the Prevention of Cruelty to Humans. Prevention, not invention."

He suddenly became calm, gently placed his hand on my shoulder, and with a soft tender voice said, "I'm sorry you are upset. I really am. I used to work here. So did many others inside. We once prevented cruelty here." He erupted in wild laughter, gripped his face with his fingers, and pulled downward. He quickly regained his composure. "Believe it or not, I was once a nice guy. So were the people inside. Time spoils everything. Whoever said time was a healer of wounds probably caused his mother's death while he was being born. Time is a growing wound. It decays and rots everything good and decent. Look at me. I'm living proof."

He dropped all expressions as he let his arms fall to his side.

His eyes were scared and empty. The skin on his face sagged with weariness. I looked closely in his eyes, then turned away in fear of what I saw. I talked to clothe the naked silence.

"I don't understand. What do you mean? Everything good turns to bad? There is no use in trying to be good? Will I only lose what I hope to gain?"

"Yes. There is no hope in the world. Why, why," he screamed, "why do human beings think they are exempt from entropy?

"We're the most pitiful creatures on earth, and why, why do we think we can be good and stay good and one day die and go to heaven where there is no decay? I'll tell you why. I'll tell you." By now he was shaking violently. "Because we can't face the fact that we are the scum of the earth. Oh, the human race, the center of the universe, the exalted species blessed with divine love, made in God's image! It's all a bunch of horseshit. We are the most disgusting species ever to set foot on this planet. We are lower than that measly bug." He ground a potato bug into the dirt with his foot. "Just look around at the trail of destruction we have left behind. We are worms. We crawl in darkness then turn around and crawl back through our own shit. Don't we? We breathe, drink, and eat our own waste. The earth was a beautiful place until we came along. Wasn't it? We are like the drunken bum lying in the gutter who has beaten his wife half to death and abandoned his kids. The pathetic hopeless creature! Does he believe he's a drunken, worthless slob lying in the gutter? Hell no! He's lying in a cesspool of delusions of grandeur. He's loaded with money, a blonde on each arm, a big shot in the city. Everyone is stopping to ask his advice. The human race is in the gutter. Deep in our hearts we know we are trash. But we can't face it. We can't believe the truth. So we invent God and heaven and all that other bullshit and set ourselves up as the most blessed creatures on earth whom God loves and cares about the most. And if we're good during our short, pathetic lives, we get to join him in heaven for an eternity of bliss. Without us, there would be no reason for creation. All this was created for us to own." He spread his arms far and wide. "Or no, we don't get one chance, fuck no, we get all the chances we want. God loves us so much that we get reborn and reborn over and over again on this wretched planet until we have learned all our lessons and then deserve to enter nirvana or heaven or whatever else you want to call that place that only exists in our insane minds. Isn't that right? Isn't that what we putrid creatures think? There is no God. There is no salvation. All that crap is just fantastic delusions to cover up the fact that we are a bunch of worthless, rotten, scum bags. We are mad. I am mad, and I'll tell you, madmen see the truth. It is no lie that geniuses are a hair away from insanity. When you're mad, and I can tell you because I am going mad, your mind falls apart, the inside comes out, and you have no more reason to lie to yourself or anyone because you know you are losing the only worthwhile thing you've got. The truth comes pouring out on its own. What is personality? Personality — I've had some education — personality comes from the word persona, which means mask. My mask is being torn off. And it feels good. I'm sick to death of having myself inside a phony box. I'll say what I want, I'll do what I want, I'll be cruel if I want, I'll be good if I want, but most of all, I'll tell the truth. And this place here — this madhouse, the Society for the Prevention of Cruelty to Humans, this is the truth. This is what man's organized efforts to be kind lead to. To cruelty. You know why? Because their intention in the beginning was not to be kind, but to be cruel. Oh, they used to put on the phony smile and phony concern, but in reality, behind their mask, all they wanted was control and power, at any cost, so they could put our mask back on ánd force us to live a phony life in a phony society. We have passed that stage. We are passed ever wearing a mask again. But no, convince them of that. Never. There is hope. There is trust. Trust me, and I'll make you a phony again. But it didn't work. It can't work. We are too far undone. But they couldn't see it, so they turned to their cruel methods, tried to shove our reality back inside, and jam our masks back on. It was so much justified by their textbooks and highbrow intellectual gibberish. This place is not kind, this place is becoming undone. All ends in decay. Everything. If there is a God, then God is decay. He is decaying. He has already decayed. He's as mad as I am, as mad as we all are. We're made in his image, so what else can he be? We are all boiling inside with evilness. We sneak around, let a little out here and there when no one is looking, when everyone says it's okay. But is it really so bad? Calling it bad only makes it worse. Why can't we be forgiven? Why can't God forgive us? Why can't he? I'll tell you why! Because the sonufabitch doesn't want to, because he can't. Oh yes, tell me, go ahead tell me like a good Christian that God possesses divine love and infinite mercy. If he does, then how can he send us to hell for doing things he doesn't like, things that aren't too bad to begin with, especially when it feels so good?" He rubbed his crotch. "Nice guy, isn't he. I've kicked ass when pissed off, but I'd never burn someone for an eternity. I'd never do something like that. Oh, but here it is; I can read your mind — God doesn't do it, the Devil does. The Devil is the evil one. Who created the Devil? Where did he come from? Why is it that God doesn't punish us when we disobey him? He sits in judgement and, of course, finds us all guilty of one delightful sin or another, and then, with a heart full of sorrow and regret, sends us over to the Devil to be punished, just as heads of governments who hire others to do their dirty work. Then the Devil is supposed to enjoy punishing us when it wasn't him we've disobeyed but God. Why should he enjoy it? Why should he even care? God should be the one taking pleasure in torturing us in hell. But he can't let himself. He can't admit that to himself. He's too goddamn good! So he invented the Devil and said it's all the Devil's doing, but it was God all along. The Devil is God's creation, a figment of his imagination. God is schizoid. Dr. Jekyll and Mr. Hyde. God has lost control over the Devil. The

Devil has separated himself from God and now has his own existence, just as my desires have separated from me and do whatever they want. The Devil is now everywhere, in everything, in you and me. He's the power of undoing. Everything is becoming undone, everything!" He let out a short hysterical laugh. "Look around you. Go ahead. Look!"

He gripped me by the shoulders and spun me around. "Do you see anything: the trees, the grass, the sun, the universe, yes, the whole damn universe; is there anything, once it is fully created, complete, perfect, blooming full of life, that does not, from that moment on, begin to become undone? Yes, I am mad. Everyone is going mad. Madness is entropy of the mind. The mind, just like everything else in the universe, runs out of energy."

He quickly regained himself again, wrapped his arms around me, and whispered in my ear, "I really was once a nice guy. I was. I strove to do and be my beast, I mean my best. I was being human. I cared for others. I felt I was going somewhere with my life. I used to be successful"

"At what?"

"Marketing sneeze catchers."

"What are those?"

"It's a little plastic arm that hooks under a shirt collar. It has a biorhythm sensor that senses sneezes. When you sneeze, the arm flies out, catches the snot, retracts, and waits for another episode. That way you can continue talking right through a sneeze. They are great for conferences. Ours have a little mirror on them, so you can get a quick look at yourself."

He began to quiver. "Inside I felt, oh, it's hard to explain; I felt something stop and things, myself, whatever, just begin to fall back beyond my control. I have tried to regain control of myself. I have. That's why I came here." He began to cry. "But it only got worse. I can't control myself. I can't. My mind is running out of steam. Believe me, young man, do what you want to do now, for you never know when it will begin. And believe me, it will, it will!"

"I'm doomed. I know it. I realized in past life therapy that a few lives ago I attained perfection. I have reached the zenith, now it's just a long road into the depths of hell."

185

He jumped back, raised his shaking hands up to the sky, and stared wide-eyed upward. "It's okay. It's fine. I'll be all right. It's just the natural order of things. Look at those dead leaves on the ground." He snatched a bunch of leaves and crammed them in his mouth.

"They will disintegrate. All the microscopic pieces will continue on their way into something else, something larger, something greater than themselves: trees, cows, mountains. My mind is like a dead leaf. The pieces of my mind are drifting apart in inner space to become raw material for other minds that will go mad, or, yes, become divine minds, yes sublime minds. It's fine. Give me a dime. Death is time. I'll be a part of God.

"It's great; why fight it? It's the natural order of things." He jumped up and down and waved his arms and started laughing. "Help it along! May as well have some fun while I know what fun is. Yes, yes. You cannot fight it. It's the destiny of all things to become undone. Rejoice. Rejoice. We are part of the grand plan. Isn't life great?"

I placed my hand on his shoulder and said, "Come on, come with me. I'm an adventurer. I'm trying to find a home. There is more in life than decay. Come on, move onward or else you really will become undone."

"You stupid, naive bag of shit. Move onward! You move onward! You don't care about me, and I sure as hell don't give a shit about you! Nobody gives a fuck about anybody."

He ran and jumped onto a garbage can, smashing himself against the building. He started yelling, "Let me in! Move over you big, fat piece of shit. Move your fat ass before I jump inside and kick it in."

A large, fat hand rose up, grabbed him by the hair, and rocketed him inside.

I walked to the front of the building and found the office. It had a rusted steel door with a window. On the window was a sign: Help Wanted — A Being Human. I yanked the sign off the window, threw it on the ground and looked inside. Cobwebs networked everything together, including the mouse turds covering the floor. Posters of nurses and doctors dangled from the walls. A couple of broken chairs were lying on the floor. A gray metal desk, tipped over, was rusted from a leak in the roof. The walls were a puke green. I could smell the lingering stench of dead souls drifting up from under the battered door.

I sat my weary self and aching body on a partly decayed wooden bench to the right of the door. I leaned against the building. The thuds from inside vibrated through my back.

A being human? What did that mean? Usually when a person is being human, you think he's being kind. Why attribute that characteristic to being human? It's the one you see less often. It's as though other animals cannot be kind. One summer Aunt Iris and I lived with cows. They were much kinder to us than human beings.

Although, a large one stepped on my foot and didn't seem to give a damn. Human beings have many characteristics: kind, cruel, intelligent, stupid, funny, sad, imaginative, creative, destructive and on and on, but which one stands out the most? Destructive is what stood out in my mind. Yet it was something to overcome, to rise above, and when you did, others generally thought you were being human. I thought of Aunt Iris, of how human she was. I remembered her saying that being human was moving forward, developing our finer characteristics. Many times she said that what made us human was the ability to become what we really are, and when we do, we become less afraid and more kind.

But yet, we are not the only ones moving forward, life moves forward, a baby calf moves forward. Even a tiny bacterial spore moves forward when it sends out little packets of genetic material to find a better home. Moving forward is what separates life from what it is not. We have to move forward to live. But, what if the madman was right?

What if we just, no matter how hard we try, run out of cohesive energy and fall apart? Although mad, he was right in saying that everything becomes undone.

I didn't want to think about that being true. Are we the objects of some sick, cosmic joke? "Try to be good. Don't try, give up and turn back. It makes no difference fools, you will spoil in the end." Maybe it was true. Maybe we all become undone in the end. Or maybe there is no end. We just keep on going round and round. Little pieces come together to form a whole; the whole takes on a feeling of being, moves forward, develops to its fullness, then the pieces drift apart as the feeling of being is lost, and then when everything is in complete chaos, the pieces begin to reform. But then, I thought, maybe, when you rose to the top you could step off before going down, and like the Buddha, become forever free from going round and round. Perhaps, that is what being human meant.

But if we could not step off the top, just kept going round and round, then why even try to move forward if it only led to going back?

Why bother to find a home if I would only lose it? If by trying you moved forward through the cycle, then by not trying you'd probably move in reverse. So, what would be the difference? You'd move through the cycle whether you tried to enhance your life or not. Why bother to try at all? Why not decompose on a couch and blame your pathetic state on entropy?

I had to get out of there. It was too much like my hometown. Just another human endeavor that turned into its opposite. It reminded me of school. Instead of feeding my love for learning, my school began to starve it.

I stood up. My spirits ached more than my back. Bleakness covered me like a black cloud. I looked through the window at the decay, turned, and trudged away alone, my head buried. I could barely lift my legs against gravity, which somehow increased tenfold. I yearned for Aunt Iris. I yearned to be held softly in her arms, to have my aching head caressed, and to have these words whispered in my ear, "Bobby, it will be all right. Everything will be fine. Your efforts aren't for nothing." I wanted my parents. I didn't want to try. I wanted to be taken care of. I wanted to be free from the world's insanity, never again feel my feet touch the earth's hard, cruel surface. I wanted peace, security, tenderness; I wanted a home.

I imagined that somewhere long, long ago I was asked whether I wanted to live or watch life from a distance like a cloud. I wished I had said I wanted to be like a cloud.

Chapter 17

I walked away from the Society right into a lush, narrow valley.

Maybe, I thought, if I don't find a home soon, I'll give up adventuring and find a nice herd of cows to live with.

Iris and I liked to watch cows. The first time she took me to watch some cows was shortly after our first sailing adventure. It was in the meadow behind her house. Her neighbor sometimes grazed his cows there. Was a clear, peaceful day. The grass was a bright green, laden with dew and flavored with wild flowers. The cows would munch on some grass for a while, rub up against each other, say hello, rub each others' noses, then lie down in the warm sun and daydream. Then they'd get hungry again, eat more grass, wander around the meadow and please themselves by lying back down in the cool grass and floating with the clouds. Then, in the evening, they would stroll into the barn for a tit massage. They knew how to live the good life.

Gradually some of them circled around us and stared. A young, dumb-looking cow stepped right up to us and started sniffing. Iris scratched her between the eyes. She got a dreamy look on her face.

"You know, Bobby," she said, "if you look closely into the eyes of a cow, you'll see her intelligence. They have that absentminded, not-all-there look. That is really the look of intelligence. You can see that same look in the pictures of geniuses: Freud, Einstein, Mozart, Shakespeare, Thoreau. They all have it."

"Yeah, I know what you mean! I've seen that same look on pictures of Alfred E. Neuman. He's a genius, isn't he?"

She laughed. "To some he is.

"Anyway, it's a disguise with cows. They act and look stupid because they know that if we ever found out how intelligent they are, we'd torture them in laboratories to find out how smart they are. We don't want any other species to be smarter than we. Perhaps we are the most intelligent species on earth, but that's not much to brag about when we're also the most cruel and destructive. But I have my doubts about our being the most intelligent. Cows have it over us. You'll never see a cow work herself to death for something she doesn't need." She laughed.

"What I love most about them is their simple lives. I've tried to live like them," she said.

"Maybe I will try to live like them, too."

What impressed me most was how much cows were loved by the rest of nature. When a cow serves nature one of her pies, it's time for a celebration. If you could understand plant language, you would hear them say, "Get ready everybody; here comes dessert." The grass grows taller and becomes greener, birds sing, worms squirm excitedly in the dirt, and flowers bloom. When we dump on Mother Nature, she prepares for a wake. Everything turns black, the grass scrivels up, worms slowly descend into the earth (if they can), birds die, and the earth cries and puts into motion her revenge. For a while I fancied becoming a cow when I grew up. But, as I later realized, some things that are possible when you're a child are, for some reason, not possible when you're an adult.

I lifted up my head and was comforted by soft, white puffball clouds floating across the valley. Between the clouds, the sky was a clear, deep blue. My perception kept on changing back and forth from watching the clouds drift through the blue to watching the blue drift through the clouds. Peaceful clouds, sustaining life below with moisture and nutrients from the sea, slowly drifted, combined, then broke apart and recombined in myriad, soft shapes of beauty. In this upper sea of softness, a huge towering cloud scraped over the ridge to my right and slid into the valley. A huge puffball billowed out of the top, then another puffed out, and another and another, and outward and upward the cloud expanded, reflecting back to earth her own beauty. The entire silky mass sank deep into the valley. So deep that I felt I could touch her. Drifting peacefully along, showering her pure white softness on the hard world below, she sank closer and closer toward me. Slowly, silently drifting away, I lay on my stomach with my head over the edge, and without a care on the world, watched the earth float by. How beautiful she was! How soft and green! How trivial were human concerns.

Down from the snowy, red mountain tops streams tumbled through the dark green, conifer forest. I imagined the water sinking into the dark earth, surrounding the roots of those magnificent giants, and joining the trees to the rest of life as it flowed up through them into the clouds. The streams joined together in the valley before flowing into a small lake. From the other side of the lake, the stream slid through a slit in a canyon wall and fell a long way beside a cliff until it hit a protruding rock and showered into a pool.

The dark green blanket on the mountain sides formed a ragged line where it met the light green meadow sprinkled with wild flowers. A gentle breeze blew. Shades of green speckled with dancing colors waved across the surface. The meadow looked so soft and inviting that I almost jumped off my cloud. A small herd of deer strolled out of the forest into the meadow. They began to be fed by the grass. The grass showed its happiness in feeding the deer by waving more brightly in the breeze, and the deer returned the gesture by wagging their tails and feeding the grass in their regular way.

Everything below teemed with life. Life seemed to be in an electric frenzy, trying to break out of the forms which contained it. I backed onto my cloud in fear that life might explode below and send me downward. The earth was a place where life was happy to be.

I let my gaze wander far and wide over the colorful, earthly forms floating below me. I didn't see any scars on the earth's face, trees blown apart, blood flowing in the streams, dead bodies scattered on the ground, piles of extinct species sustaining the marketplace, men raping and killing women and children; but then again, I didn't see any beings human trying to live together.

I felt I was stretching out, becoming thinner, lighter, and drifting apart. I feared I might diffuse into a long, thin cloud and never be able to gather myself up again. But, what difference would it make if I did? Won't I scatter apart someday anyway and reform in another place and time, just as clouds endlessly scatter and reform?

Without concern for what I would or would not become, I let my eyes drift across the sea of puffball clouds. Toward the top of a large cloud in front of me, a large section turned down and stretched out into a giant wing. On the other side another wing appeared. Between the wings a figure began to form. I kept my eyes on it and was overjoyed when I recognized the angel I met while stargazing. She flapped her wings, dispersing all the clouds around her. Standing alone in the blue, she motioned for me to come. I tried to stand, but sank up to my neck. I looked below the surface, as though looking underwater, for something hard to stand on, and when I finally climbed to the surface, she was being absorbed by clouds enclosing her from behind. Disappointed, I dropped below the surface.

Bobbing around in there awhile and finally crawling back up at an angle, I again let my eyes wander across the clouds. I let them coast back and forth, back and forth. I don't know if I failed to see her or if she just appeared in an instant, but while my eyes were returning back after going forth, I saw Aunt Iris standing in the clouds with her usual content smile. A chill shot through me; tears formed in my eyes. This time I wasn't going to look away. Part swimming, part crawling, part doing whatever I could to stand on that soft sea, I was almost on my knees ready to stand when a slight breeze stretched her upward, blended her features together, and slowly leaned her back, outward and long until she was transformed into a smooth flat path that curved around to the right of the cloud that had engulfed my sweet, hopeful angel.

I don't know of any two things that attract each other more than a path and an adventurer. If the adventurer doesn't get on the path, the path will surely get under the adventurer. Not giving a thought as to whether I would sink or stand, I stood up and got on the path.

As I walked along the path, I thought of Aunt Iris, her enthusiasm, her happiness, her love for life, her devotion to becoming more a part of being; and I wondered, How can everything become undone?

How can life become undone? To appear in all things, to glow through everything, to sustain everything; how could it eventually become undone? Even if, eons away, the universe becomes undone, will life itself disappear? Is the universe life? I didn't feel so. I still don't feel it. From the atom to the rock to the bug crawling on the rock to the entire universe, I felt that life was what formed those things, made them a part of itself, and that when life left they then became undone. The leaf decays not because it is separated from the tree, but because it is separated from life of which the tree is still a part. And I felt that if I just kept on trying to move forward, actively pursued becoming more a part of life, then I would always be a part of it. I didn't care about the possibility of eventually becoming undone. It didn't matter. From what I saw Aunt Iris do to herself by moving forward and the unhappiness others brought upon themselves by letting themselves fall back, I was all the more convinced that I had to try to move forward. Besides that, I didn't want to go backward and become cruel. I wasn't going to let that happen through my own lack of effort. If some day nature took me into a downward course, then that would happen, and I would have no control, but until that time, I wasn't going to let myself decay and become mean just because some lunatic said that that would happen to me someday anyway. I wasn't going to fall into the trap of rationalizing my own cruelty because I didn't want to make the effort to be kind. I was so excited and happy to be feeling that way that I knew I had to stop thinking. Sometimes, thinking can push out a good feeling. So, I stopped thinking, relished in the feeling, took another step forward, and rounded the cloud.

I came upon rolly-polly, cloud people, like snowmen with legs, dancing, singing, and strolling about in a cloudy marketplace. The shops in the marketplace circled a park. Aunt Iris's path led directly into the park. Scattered throughout the park were rounded benches and tall wispy trees. In the center, a cloud fountain was spouting tiny clouds. I gazed at the scene and felt my happiness at finding such a happy, peaceful place. What a relief the cloud town was from the Society.

As I drifted toward the cloud fountain, an old woman, coming out of an ice crystal shop, slipped off the icy top stair into a middle-aged man who tried to catch her with his short puffy arms. They giggled down the steps, bumped over a family walking up the walk, and with infantile grins on their faces, they rolled over each other into the cobble, clouded street. Seeming to enjoy the move from vertical to horizontal, they lay in the street laughing, talking, getting acquainted with each other; and then the old woman began telling a young boy and girl about the time when, long, long ago, there were many wars and clouds were made of fire. Hand in hand they strolled over to a bench in the park where she continued her tale. The others, still engaged in lively conversations, waltzed into a snow cone shop.

I sauntered toward the fountain. The walls of the fountain rose straight up about three feet, curved over the top about a foot, then flowed straight down the other side. The fountain was about fifteen feet across. Large snow crystals, about the size of sand dollars, formed the circular fountain. The crystals were randomly layered over each other. As I looked at the surface crystals, my eyes were led to the ones beneath them to the ones beneath those and deeper and deeper until I became lost in their depth and beauty. The sunlight made the fountain dance in endless, rainbow colors. The colors reflected and re-reflected through the fountain, creating the illusion of infinite depth. I felt that in a similar way the moment reflected off itself, and in that way, time and its seeming endlessness were created. The fountain was the most beautiful thing I had ever seen.

The inside of the fountain bubbled as dry ice does in water, but instead of the mist drifting downward, round marble size puffballs rose off the surface. The rainbow colors, as they streamed through the cloud fountain, turned pastel in the tiny clouds and added a mysteriousness to the fountain. As the tiny clouds rose above the fountain, they freed themselves of color. Slowly upward the puffy molecules rose, combined, recombined, and formed larger and larger clouds until they drifted off together as a fully formed cloud, another world.

Suddenly, a strong wind blew. The marketplace stretched into long, wispy clouds, which vaporized high in the air. Happy cloud people, a little too fat and low to the clouds to be blown upward, were rolled into smiling balls as they rolled up a cloud and stuck in the side with their smiles facing me. The entire side of the cloud was a mosaic of silly face balls. The faces slowly blended into the cloud.

I wanted to follow them. I wanted to blend into a cloud. But they were gone, and for all I knew, they could have reappeared in another cloud halfway around the world. Nevertheless, undaunted in spirit as all true adventurers, I began to climb the cloud in hopes of finding the happy, cloud people.

Have you ever tried climbing a cloud? It is similar to walking on crusty snow. Walk softly and gently and you may stay on top, but get a little rambunctious and down you go. After placing my right foot gently on a cloud, I pushed slowly while concentrating on the smooth sensations. Did the same thing with my left leg, then my right again, and on and on, slowly marching across the clouds. But, it wasn't enough. I wanted more. So, after finding a dense firm spot, I took off my clothes, jumped up, pointed my toes downward, and slid through.

The cloud felt like thin, soft water. I flipped backwards, then forward, and leaned back again as I slowly sank in softness with my legs and arms spread. Slowly gently still sinking in soft pleasure, I was unable to separate my feelings from the kind cloud. What a gentle cushion it was compared to the hard unfeeling world.

Slowly I drifted into stillness. Everything was quiet. I was surrounded in a numbing pool of softness. All the jagged edges of my body, fingers, legs, nose, etc., became rounded and turned inward. I became an oval. That's all I felt myself to be. Time reflected back through itself into the moment.

I began moving upward, slowly at first, then accelerating rapidly. Through the top layer of the clouds I soared. All around worlds of clouds were exploding out of nothing. I was watching the mystery of creation.

A long plateau slid outward below me. Hills rose out of it. Some kept on rising into mountains. The cloud I was on floated upward, rolling me off to the left side onto the top of another rising puffball. I leapt to my feet and began climbing the cloud as it grew. It was as if, all of a sudden, I had become an expert cloud climber. I jumped off my cloud onto one that was racing past. Its round top shifted downward as a cliff jutted upward, connecting my cloud with a mass of rising giant puffballs. I dug my feet into the side of the cliff and scaled it with ease. Got up to the top, jumped across a ravine onto another rising puffball, slipped on the side, and bounced and giggled downward from one puffy cushion to another. Jumped to my feet onto another rising puffball and onward and upward I climbed over hill and through dale. Their rise slowed as I climbed, and just as I stepped onto the top cloud, its ascent softly stopped.

All around me the new wondrous world spread to the horizon. The pure white surface sparkled with delicate colors. I wanted this to be my home where I could float forever far above the cruelty below, far above meager human concerns, forever free from entropy. I could stay away, watch life from a distance, and drop a little dew on those below when nature called. Never again did I want to step upon the hard cruel world.

As I gazed miles downward over the sea of puffball clouds, I thought what immense pleasure could be soaked up by jumping and sinking for hours through their softness. Wanted to return to an oval surrounded by soft oblivion. I stepped to the edge, leaned forward, bent my knees, spread my arms, and just as I was about to leap into fluffy euphoria, I tripped over a rock and landed on a giant puffball.

As I lay there on that flattened mushroom still somewhat cushioned from the hard world, I watched the clouds float by and yearned to be with them again. And then, as though watching a movie, my adventures began going past. I laughed while I watched them, but as they came to an end, I began to think of Aunt Iris, of my longing for her and her love for me, and I became sad.

Out of the clear blue, like a cloud, a memory of her asking me how I felt about my friend Timmy moving away floated into my mind. We were leaning on a fence watching cows graze in a field. All the cows strolled away to the other side of the field except for one consumed with eating. She lifted her head, saw that the others had left and ran to them.

Iris looked at me with her wise, this day sad eyes, and said, "Do you miss your friend Timmy?"

"Oh, I guess a little." I blushed.

"Just a little!? Wasn't he your best friend?" She gave me a penetrating look.

"Well, maybe he was. What does it matter, though. I've got other friends."

"Hmmm, why then if you don't miss him that much have you been dressing like him ever since he left?"

I looked at my clothes. "I always dress like this." I blushed again.

I had lied to her and myself and was still lying to myself.

What was trying to be a leader of a new culture, blowing up a building filled with junk, waiting for advice from a horny spirit, pretending that I belonged on another planet in another universe, expecting to find a place of kindness, and when disappointed, escaping into the clouds; other than lying to myself that my flights would eradicate my past experiences of loss and rejection that not only were gripped in my memory but were driving the direction of my life. By lying, I felt I had betrayed Iris's love and concern for me. All the times she comforted me out of nightmares, the times she nursed me through sickness, the times she took me hiking and sailing and adventuring to distant places, all the times she spent caring for and educating me after rescuing me from school and trying to protect me from the world's cruelty, and all the many ways, both direct and subtle, she warned me of the dangers of fleeing from painful memories and experiences; how was I thanking her for all that time and love? By fleeing! I wasn't just escaping from loss but from her, for my life was traveling away from hers, away from a future, away from a home, away from happiness, away from being. Didn't I leave her home to find my own home, to find a way of life that made sense to me, to try to move closer to being? How can a light be found by putting on a blindfold?

I decided right then that I was going to stop fleeing, accept what my adventures had to offer, and try to learn from them what I had to do to find a home on this, yes this, planet. I jumped up, blew a kiss goodbye to the clouds, and went looking for adventure.

Part III

Chapter 18

Once upon a travel I became tangled in oak brush. Every step I took, every turn I made, the branches wrapped and locked themselves around my arms and legs. I tore them apart, climbed over, crawled under until I broke through into a sunburnt, expansive meadow.

In that wide open meadow was an immense stone wall surrounding a city. I immediately became entranced with its beauty and excited about the possibility that this might be the home I was venturing to find. After my disappointing visit to the Society, I was vulnerable to any sign of a home.

Aunt Iris and I used to enjoy a great deal of time looking at stone walls. We would sometimes spend days bicycling from one stone wall to another, comparing them, deciding what we did and did not like about them and why. We even built a few small walls in the garden. So, when I saw this mammoth stone wall off in the distance, I ran up to it as fast as I could, which wasn't very fast after my battle with the oak brush.

I stopped within a few feet of the wall. Without a doubt, it was superior to every wall I had ever seen. The blue-gray granite stones were cut and placed so that each stone supported those above. All the vertical joint lines were staggered. The mortar joints, all one quarter inch wide, had been compacted to a glass-like finish. The intricate patterns created by the stones mesmerized me. I felt I was being hypnotized by the beauty of this magnificent visual symphony. In my daze, I began to feel there was something unreal about the wall. I staggered back, looked the wall up and down, back and forth, traced the outline of the stones, the exactness of the mortar joints. Tried to find an imperfection, a flaw, a sign of the human touch, but didn't see any. The wall was too perfect, and in being perfect, it lost some of its beauty. I became suspicious and lost enthusiasm about this place becoming my home. Perfection often hides deep imperfections.

I walked along the wall, stopped, examined the new area, and continued along in this way. I came to a corner; rounded it. I didn't know it then, but later learned that the wall made a perfect square. After walking next to the wall for a couple of miles, unable to find any imperfections, I came upon workmen scrubbing and cleaning the wall, polishing the stones, redoing the mortar joints, in short, wasting their time in useless busy work. How can perfection become more perfect? Well, I guess it can when inner imperfections infect perceptions.

When I got close enough for them to hear me, I woke my voice, for it had been many days since I had spoken to anyone, and yelled, "Hello. Nice day, isn't it? It sure is good to see you people."

They stopped their doings and stared at me as though they had never seen anyone before. My first thought was: what have I come upon — a bunch of workaholics with no social skills? But then, about ten feet away I stopped and stared back at them.

From afar, I noticed that each of them had a box around their stomach. I was concentrating on the wall so much that I didn't give it any thought; just assumed the boxes were part of their spiffy, blue overalls. But now up close, the boxes tore my attention off the wall and onto them. The transparent boxes went from the bottom of their rib cages to their waists. About a third of the way from the bottom was a stage that spanned across the entire box. Behind the main stage were many smaller stages above and below the main stage and at different depths within the box. The box seemed to have great depth, much more depth than the depth of a human body, with small stages fading into deep darkness. I got the feeling that the stages went on forever in both space and time. The stages were webbed together with stairs that went in all directions. Narrow stairs to the right and left, and a wide staircase in the middle led down to the main stage.

I closed my eyes, rubbed them while thinking that maybe all my time alone was causing me to see things, but when I opened them the box people were still box people.

"How odd," I thought to myself. But, as it turned out, I was the odd man in the Land of Boxes.

My attention was taken away by a man dressed in a sparkling, white overall with a white hard hat. He extended and said, "Hello, sir. How do you do? What brings you to our fine city? Can I be of any assistance?"

The scene in which we were standing appeared on the main stage of his box. The only difference was that he had a box in his hands. He raised the box over my head and crammed it on me. He then grabbed me by the hand, swung me around his head, and hurled me into the oak brush.

Leery that activities on the inside may switch to the outside, I said, "I'm not sure if you can help me or not. You see, fine sir, I am venturing to find a home. I'm doing fine and don't seem to need any help. Although, now that I think about it, I would like to see the magnificent city that lies behind this beautiful, stone wall." I spread my arms far and wide.

"You are more than welcome to visit our city. We welcome all foreign travelers with open arms." In his box, I was entering the city's golden gates. Just as I was about to step inside, he appeared and slammed the gates, knocking me about twenty feet in the air. I smashed to the ground where I lay motionless.

I said, "Thank you for your hospitality. Where may I find the entrance?"

"Just keep walking in the same direction, my dear sir. It is not far." In his box, he pushed me in the opposite direction.

Just then a worker on the top scaffold dropped a trowel into a bucket of mortar next to us. Mortar splashed on the man's white uniform. He screamed at the workman, "You clumsy, stupid shit. Watch what the hell you're doing before you hurt someone. Another trick like that, and I'll have you carrying hod until your back breaks. Stop staring down here, get to work."

On a smaller stage in his box, he was holding the man's head in the bucket of mortar, and when the man stopped wiggling, he yanked him out and threw his lifeless body against the wall. On a recessed small stage midway in his box, a woman tore dirty clothes off a small boy, jerked him on to her lap and beat his raw bottom with a stick.

I looked up at the man on the scaffolding to see if there were any revealing events taking place in his box, and of course, there were.

He turned into an eagle, flew into the air, and the higher be flew the larger he became until he was the size of a small airplane. The eagle dropped a turd about the size of a cow that crushed the clean white supervisor into the ground.

I said, "Thank you for your help. You have been most kind. But, before I go, may I ask you a question?"

"Yes. Ask me anything you like. I am an open book."

"Does everyone here have a box?"

"I do not know what you mean. I hope you are not being obscene."

"No. No, kind sir. I'm sorry if you took that the wrong way. What I mean is the box around everyone's stomach."

He stared back at me with a dumbfounded expression. In his box, he was cramming a box down around me.

"You know, the box with the stages and ..." I began to explain what I saw, but the more I spoke the redder he got until he started trembling and grinding his teeth. I stepped back.

Forcing his words, he said, "I do not know what you are talking about. I believe you have been in the sun too long. You had better visit our city before we close the gates. Then, I strongly suggest you look elsewhere for a home. Good day, sir."

"Yes, I agree; it is a good day. Sorry to have walked on virgin territory. Goodbye."

In his secret box, he grabbed me by the shirt, dragged me over to the wall, shoved me down, and yelled, "You're no different than anyone else. What makes you think you're so good. Here," he kicked a bucket of water in my face, "scrub these walls until you can see your ugly face in them. Don't get up until you're done."

I continued walking along the wall, watching the workmen point and polish. As I passed they stopped and stared as though they had never seen a foreigner. From what I was seeing in their interiors, I was wondering whether or not I wanted to see the interior of the city.

Soon I was upon the gates of the Land of Boxes.

I stopped in awe of their beauty. The gates were about twenty feet tall, fifteen feet wide, and made of gold. Vertical, two-inch round bars six inches apart started a few inches off the ground and rose to the top. The same bars ran horizontally. Where the bars joined each other, a four-inch circle was formed, and on the face of it were three raised concentric circles about a half inch apart. Inside the inner circle, about two inches in diameter, was a raised star. Golden vines, leaves, and flowers climbed all over the gate. About four feet off the ground was a massive lock about two feet high and one foot wide, which looked as if it were designed to keep out King Kong. The same vines, flowers and leaves were engraved into this lock on a smaller scale. I sat down and fancied that it was the gate leading into heaven.

I strolled through the heavenly, golden gates into hell. You would have thought the stonework to be, like a beautiful woman, more lovely on the inside. But it was falling apart. Stones were lying on the ground. Many others were loose and about to fall. Large sections of mortar had tumbled to the ground. Moss, weeds, and small trees had taken root. Nests, cobwebs, turds and dirt covered the walls. Rats were scurrying along the ledges.

From the inside, it looked as though a well directed sneeze would reduce the wall to a pile of rubble. I walked next to it, poked it a little, felt the stones, and then stepped back and wondered if, somehow, when I walked through the gate, I had a lapse in memory or somehow walked through a passage in space and time and was really somewhere else. After walking out the gate and back inside, I was assured that my brain hadn't skipped or some other odd event hadn't happened. Still, it was hard to believe, but not as hard as some other things I've seen.

A courtyard a few hundred yards wide between the wall and the city was covered with trash. Upon reaching the city, everything was clean again. Clean, well-dressed box people were scrubbing the streets, washing the tall, red brick buildings, cleaning the rectangular windows, painting the trim white, and like the useless work on the exterior of the walls, everything they were cleaning was already clean. And like the workmen on the outside, the inside workers stopped and stared at my boxless body, and in their boxes, jammed a box on me.

Feeling I needed to fill my interior, I walked toward a food store. Past an iron gate on my way up the steps to the store, I stopped and said to a neat, older man cleaning the windows, "Hi. Nice day, isn't it?"

"Yes. It sure is, young man. Welcome to our store. I'm sure you'll find what you need."

"Thank you. I'm sure I will."

I walked in the store and wondered whether he had ever been inside. And once again I wondered if my brain had skipped. I walked back outside. He was still scrubbing. Walked back inside; it was still the same. The place smelled of mildew and mold and looked as though it had just been looted. An old, wrinkled, dirty woman dressed in rags crawled out into the aisle at the end of a counter, looked at me, and crawled back. Feeling faint, I turned and walked out into the stale air.

The old man, with an unfocused stare, pretended to look at me and said, "Thank you for your business. I hope you got what you wanted."

"What?"

He repeated himself word for word. Time stalled. I said, "Have you ever been inside?"

"Why yes. It is a beautiful store, isn't it? Nicer on the inside than on the outside?"

"You can't be serious. That place is trashed. Look in the window!"

"Yes. I see. Oh, there is my lovely wife. Hi sugarbuns." He knocked on the window and waved.

I was weary. It was obvious that I would feel at home in this town as little as I felt at home in my hometown.

I turned away without saying goodbye. That was not like me. I already had no respect for the people in the Land of Boxes. I walked out into the street, and after looking up and down and seeing a park a few blocks away, walked toward the park. Everything seemed to be becoming more and more unreal. I needed to regain myself before going any further.

Near the park, I turned around, and along the street, box people were staring at me. I shivered. At the entrance to the park, I paused for a moment, trying to decide whether I should risk a stay or leave before something happened to me. The last thing I wanted was to be boxed in the Land of Boxes. But, needing a rest and feeling confident that I could not be contained, I strolled into the rectangular park.

The park was one of those tidy parks where nature is denaturalized by hedge shears. All the trees, shrubs, and bushes had been cut into triangles, rectangles, and squares. The park needed a small herd of elephants to take up residence.

In the middle of the park was a round fountain that seemed to be spraying a fine mist up into the clouds. I immediately fell into a reverie about my sojourn in the clouds as I floated toward the fountain. Near the fountain sat an old couple side by side on a bench.

He was reading a paper, or more correctly, the paper was reading him, and she was staring at her shoes. I was stopped by the contrast between their retired exteriors and their lively interiors. In his box, they were sitting together on lounge chairs at the beach. He turned young, jumped up, grabbed her by the sides, whereupon she flattened into a surf board, and running with his new surf board into the surf, hopped on her and paddled over the waves. He surfed for a while, ran back onto the beach, and jammed the board down into the sand. Around him naked girls with large breasts appeared playing volleyball. It was his turn to serve. They rotated. He served low beeline balls to the girls on the other side. I glanced over in her box. They were young, strolling hand in hand beside a lake, stopping, kissing, strolling some more; he stopped and whispered something in her ear and held her under the soft, clear moonlight. On an upper stage she was nursing a baby. Below on another stage, she was sitting pregnant in a soft chair with a sweet smile upon her face. Then her main stage changed to her and her husband, young and excited, lying on a soft blue rug in front of a fireplace. I glanced over at his box.

He had already finished serving the girls on the other team and was now serving the girls on his own team. I laughed and then felt sad.

The red brick path on which I was walking separated and widened as it curved around the fountain. The outside of the walkway was lined with benches. A few people recognized them as places to sit, but most saw them as something to clean. They all stopped what they were doing and stared at me. As I turned to leave, I felt someone's eyes on me.

I turned around. On the other side of the fountain, a young woman with long blonde hair and sparkling blue eyes smiled and tilted her head to one side. She wore a black short skirt and a red sweater with a black C on the front and held a purple pom pom in her folded hands.

Her box was lovely, and the closer I came the more she attracted me.

Others' boxes were much like the other interiors — dark, dingy and broken down. But her box was clear, clean, delicate yet strong, and what was most attractive about her box and made me feel, at first glance, that I could fall in love with her was that on a large stage behind the main stage she was struggling to remove her box. In no one else's box had I seen that.

"How are you? I'm Bobby. Would you like some company?"

"What kind of company are you?"

"I'm good company to keep." I sat next to her.

"Good. I'd like to keep you. Well, I'm okay. I guess. I just came back from the doctor." She sighed. Her right ankle was bandaged.

"A doctor?" I said. "Where I come from going to the doctor is like being cornered in an alley by a robber with a knife. You either cough up or suffer. Have you ever heard how doctors came to be?"

"No."

"A long time ago bloodsuckers were put on people to make them better. People, that is. The ways of the bloodsucker were then studied, schools were opened for just that purpose, and those who excelled at learning the ways of the bloodsucker were named doctors."

"Yeah, I know what you mean. One of my neighbors had a heart attack but no insurance. They fixed him up all right. They fixed him good, real good, so good that the bills drove him into bankruptcy. He lost everything. He died shortly afterward. He didn't even bother going back to the doctor.

"But, you know," she said, "that's not all they're after. Get this. I go to the doctor, right? Look at my ankle. It's swollen, right?"

"Yeah."

"Look at this." She raised her legs. "I've got a short skirt on, right? The only thing that has to be taken off to examine my ankle is my sneaker."

"Yeah. Your skirt fits your figure very nicely."

"Thank you. So, I go to the doctor, tell him my ankle hurts, and get this, he tells me, yeah, doesn't ask, just tells me to take off my clothes for an examination."

"Did you?"

"No. I may have if he had had some passion in his eyes, but, no, he was a squirrelly, bug-eyed, creepy little; oh, I just get the creeps thinking about him."

"How did you hurt your ankle?"

"Cheerleading."

"Cheerleading!?"

"Yes. You look like you've never heard of cheerleading before."

"What is your name?"

"Pom Pom."

"Pom Pom!?"

"Where have you come from? Haven't you heard of anything? Pom Pom. Yes, that's my name." She stood up, limped forward a few steps, turned toward me, and teetering from one foot to the other, shook her purple pom pom around her box.

"Come here, Pom Pom. Sit next to me. Have I got something to tell you." I told her about my stumble through Garbageland.

While I talked, she kept her eyes on mine, and at moments, seemed to get lost in them. After I finished, she continued to gaze into my eyes for a long time before speaking.

"When I first saw you walking through the park, I thought to myself, he looks familiar. This is unbelievable, unreal! Cosmic! That's what it is — cosmic! I'm a Buddhist. I believe in all that reincarnation stuff. You know, I really do. I believe we have to have more than just this one little life. I just don't think we live and die and that's it. What would be the meaning of it all? I feel it. I felt it before. I know I have. It's got to be true. Because, you see, besides feeling that I have met you before, cheerleading has always come natural to me. I was cheerleading when I was two. I never took any lessons. And, I'm an only child. My parents inherited a fortune from my grandfather, and as you said, it will all go to me. Listen to this, this is no lie: he was found dead in a garbage dump. He was missing for a long time.

"My parents didn't know what had happened to him. They searched and searched and finally found him in a dump, and you know, there was a town being buried by that dump. And how could you know all that? I've never met you before. Can you believe it? This is unreal! No, it's real."

She jumped up, kicked her legs high, well, as high as her swollen ankle and short skirt would let her, and cheered:

"Cosmic, cosmic, here we go.

All part of the same show.

We are here now, we were here then.

Free me, free me, free me Zen."

While she cheered, I was captivated by her excitement more than her words. I watched her every movement: the way her full lips formed her words, the gesturing of her thick eyebrows, the cute way she tilted her head sideways. I looked at her with affection. Never did I think, after seeing the decay in others' boxes that I would find such beauty and liveliness inside the Land of Boxes. She didn't pause long before racing with her words.

"So, you're Bobby? What are you doing here? What were you doing in the dump, besides meeting me? I know, you're here because I'm here.

It's got to be! What else, tell me, why else are you here? What do you do? Oh, I'm so excited. I could love you to pieces!" She hugged me around the shoulders and gave me a quick kiss. In her box she was taking off my clothes.

"I'm looking for a home."

"Oh, poor thing. What happened to your home?"

I told her about losing my parents, Aunt Iris, and my hometown.

"Now I'm adventuring here and there, hoping to find a place where I feel at home. I thought at first when I saw the beautiful stone wall surrounding this city that, maybe, this place might become my home, but now that I have had a closer look, I don't think so. It's too much like my hometown — people pretending to be something they are not."

On a small stage in the recesses of her box, she was sitting on a stiff arm chair staring at the ground with her head in her hands.

She stood slowly, trudged onto the main stage, kicked two lovers over the side, and walked through the front of her box. Pom Pom on the outside slumped downward, hung her head, and sighed, "Yeah, I know what you mean. I'm not what I appear to be."

"What do you mean?"

"I am cheerless, without hope and happiness. But no, I can't be that way." She perked her head up, smiled, and waved her hands back and forth in the air. The sullen Pom Pom appeared on a stiff chair in the center of her main stage. On the outside, she cheered:

"I can be anything.

I can shine.

If only I could sing.

And my own mind were mine.

"Oh yes, oh yes, I am a ray of sunshine, a source of good cheer, the woman filled with hope and happiness who can lift anyone out of their despair."

Her smile withered, she sank down as sad Pom Pom on the stage, once again, disappeared through the front of her box.

"You see, my lifelong friend, I don't just cheer for players in ball games, I cheer for players in life. I cheer everyone on, everyone except myself. I even go out, when they get discouraged, and cheer for the men forever working on the outside wall. But I am not full of cheer. I am trapped inside myself, trapped inside these stone walls, trapped inside the definition others have placed on me.

"Yes, look at me. I am a cheerleader, right? I was born with a Pom Pom in my hand and a bright, cheery face. Isn't that what we are — what others have defined us. All these people I cheer up. Why do they need cheering up? It's because they've been defined as cheerless, losers, low life's unable to do anything right. They have not been loved and praised. They've been called names, rejected, humiliated, ignored, put down. I go in and try to reverse their definition. Do I succeed? Do I transform them into cheerful, hopeful winners? No. Oh, I do for a few minutes, a few hours, and sometimes if I'm lucky, a few days; but they always return to their definition. It's discouraging; makes me feel like a failure.

"Isn't everyone here so perfect, so clean and spiffy and varnished over? They make me sick. You know what perfection is, you know what it is?"

"What?"

Once again she raced with her words. "It's some half-baked notion about this something we should be that we got from our parents and they got from their parents and on and on back to the mischievous monkey. So we try to become this idea completely, perfectly, but we can't because no one really knows what it is anyway, so all we do is fail. Who doesn't fail against the impossible? Instead of perfection being a complete solution to a problem, it becomes a problem in itself that never gets solved and prevents us from really becoming perfect. Always expectations, demands, sweat and tears, trying to fulfill them, and what's the reward? — reprimands for not being perfect enough. I know. I cheer these people on all the time. They don't need cheers. They just need to realize that perfection is a process perfected by mistakes.

"Who really wants to be perfect? I don't, not anymore. I used to. Oh yes, I used to. Because I was loved for being a perfect cheerleader. But, you know, I'll tell you something. They didn't love me. They don't love me. I mean me. They love the plastic image I've created. They love that I pretend that everything is going to be all right, that I'm full of good cheer for them, that I can make them into winners. Oh, yes. I'm just so perfect. The perfect smile, the perfect cheer, the perfect body, and if you can get me into bed, the perfect lay. Isn't that right? Aren't cheerleaders perfect lays." She smiled as her eyes lit up.

"So I've been told."

"So you may find out. Tell me, Bobby, what is your pretension?"

"Oh, don't tell me. Naiveté. Right? You pretend to be naïve and innocent — a cute, little mama's boy all the girls want to care for and love. You need cuddled and caressed and protected from the cold, cruel world. So you've been told, huh? You don't fool me, Bobby. So you've been told, nonsense, so you know by going to bed with every cheerleader in town. Tell me the truth, cute stuff."

She ran her hand up the inside of my leg. I pushed it away and said, "Oh please, you're going to make me blush."

She laughed, then turned serious again.

"I don't want to pretend to be perfect anymore. I want to make mistakes. I want to stumble and fall. My whole life has been choreographed. Every moment, every step, every cheer is planned from beginning to end. Even my love-making is choreographed. I know what pleases. I know what lifts men up. I have it all planned beforehand. You told me how I was boxed out of this life in the spiritual plane and eager to get physical. Now I am physical, physical every day, but I'm still boxed out of life.

"Aha, you say to yourself, she knows about her box. The secret in this town everyone keeps. No one admits it! No one talks about it. Can you imagine carrying this thing around with you," she patted her box, "and denying that it exists. How can they? No matter what you do it gets in the way. I'm sick of it. I want rid of it."

On a stage behind the main stage, she tore off her box and ran downstairs to the central staircase. As she descended the stairs, two guards at the bottom ran up, grabbed her, and threw her up on the landing.

Pom Pom sighed, "I don't know. I'm a person in a box, a programmed robot."

She stood up, stiffened, and marched around like a soldier. She stopped in front of me, saluted, and with a voice as deep as a sexy blond's voice can get, began talking abrupt robot talk.

"How do you do?"

"I do as I do," I said.

"And how is that?"

"Not very good. I need to be cheered up."

"Well, sir, today is your lucky day. I am a cheerleading robot programmed with the latest space age cheers that will rocket your spirits into the stratosphere." She mechanically bent her arms at the elbows and pumped them up and down as though lifting weights:

"Come on boy, drop that frown.

You can stay up.

Don't have to fall down.

Come on, boy.

Life is a joy.

You can win, you can win.

Come on boy, let's see a grin."

I put on a goofy smile and laughed. She gave me a tender smile, returned to her fluid movements, and leaned against me as she sat back down. She looked directly into my eyes as she spoke.

"You know what I want? You know what I really want?"

"What?"

"You're really listening to me, aren't you? Oh, how nice to find someone who listens."

"Yeah. I am. I don't see anyone else. Who else would I be listening to?" I smiled.

She elbowed me and said, "Come on."

"Okay. I'm just having a little fun. No harm meant. Tell me, I want to know, what do you want?"

"I want to be passionate. That's what I want. Don't get me wrong, I don't want to have sex all the time. Well, now that I think about it, I wouldn't mind that either, especially with a passionate man." Again, she eased her hand up the inside of my thigh.

I said, "Would you please continue, with words, that is."

Leaving her hand on me, she smiled and raced. "I want to do everything with passion, with feeling. When I wake in the morning, see the sun rising, I want to get up not because it's morning and I'm supposed to get up or because I can't sleep anymore, but because I'm thrilled to be alive, because there is a brand new day to enjoy. And when I go out to cheer, I want to cheer because I feel for those I'm trying to uplift, because I care about them, because I, oh," she looked at her watch, "I've got to go."

She stood up. I grabbed her hand, pulled her down, and said, "Please stay! Just another minute. Okay?"

"Okay."

"I'm so happy to have finally met you on the physical plane." I smiled and ran my hand up her firm back.

"Me, too. Except I don't remember meeting you on any plane, not even an aeroplane."

After she said that, I knew I could be in love with her.

I said, "We should travel together. Besides traveling to find a home, I'm traveling to find someone like you. Someone who doesn't want to be boxed in. Although, now that I have met you and your box, I don't think boxes are all that bad. They can be intriguing. I seem to be developing a passionate interest in your box."

"You are, huh? Don't you think you're being a little bit bold, young man?" She turned toward me, tilted her head back to one side, eased a gorgeous smile, and slowly ran her right hand across the side of her face and through her hair.

I said, "I'm sorry if I'm being too up front. Perhaps you would find it more fitting if I approached your box from the rear?"

"Either way is fine with me."

"To be passionate is to be truthful, isn't it?" I asked.

"Yes, oh yes. Please, tell me the truth."

"The truth is I want to know your box."

"In what way do you want to know it?"

"In every way possible."

In her box, duplicates of us erupted in a heap of activities that made the *Kama Sutra* look like a beginner's manual. Some of us, in positions I knew I'd thoroughly enjoy, began moving toward the front of her box, and I thought, oh no, oh yes, will Pom Pom and I get passionate in the park? She slid her left hand around my neck as she softly glided her other hand up to my waist, and tenderly kissing my ear, whispered, "Meet me here at dusk. I'll go with you."

She drew away from me and spoke as though thinking out loud, "But I'm afraid. What will I do? What will I say once I leave? Everything is so well-arranged in here. I am very well-defined in here."

"You don't have to tell me."

In her box, her box was lying next to her at the top of the main stairs. She picked it up, threw it at the guards at the bottom of the stairs, and ran past them.

"But no, no. I have to leave. Fear is part of leaving. We all cut the cord at different times in our lives. Now it's my time.

"Sorry, Bobby, but I've got to go. I don't want to. I want to be with you, but I've got to keep an appointment to cheer up this big, fat hot dog vendor named Ignacius. He's got one of the biggest boxes around. I don't know why I bother. He's a hopeless case. He doesn't care, he just cares about blaming everybody else for his failures. Besides that, he's one of those guys so convinced he's a failure that whenever success comes near he does everything he can to drive it away. Still, I have a promise to keep and an even bigger promise to keep with you. Got to go. See you at dusk."

She gave me a long, warm kiss on the lips, then strolled away rhythmically swaying her hips to the beat of my heart.

I was thrilled to have finally met Pom Pom. What a relief to have found her after my disappointing visit to the Society. Meeting her on the physical plane was the turning point in my adventures. Together we could find a home. For a while, I sat on the bench imagining all the things we would do together, and with an imagination like mine, you can imagine some of the truly exquisite things I imagined.

Chapter 19

I couldn't sit there and wait for dusk. It was only a few hours away, yet it seemed like years. I stood up and decided to waste some time by venturing through the city streets. Although, it just wasn't a waste of time; I was still intrigued by the box people and their immaculate exteriors.

The path out of the park lead directly into a residential street.

The street had been swept clean. Weedless, crew cut lawns neatly edged, trimmed bushes, waxed plants, genetic diversity cut back, welcome mats everywhere, wrought iron fences and gates, barking dogs, clean and shiny houses without a speck of paint falling off; all these made me feel right at home. Although, instead of making me want to stay, they made me want to leave. All the houses and yards were different in their own way, and yet, everything looked the same.

As I was standing on the sidewalk admiring an elegant stone house, a van pulled up labeled "Sunny Acres." I thought, what does the van do — stretch and shine? Out stepped two men dressed in white and wrapped with solid boxes. Their thin lips were pursed together; a frown drained their faces. They marched up the long front walk and rang the bell. The door seemed to open by itself. They marched inside. The door closed.

The door opened. The two emerged from the interior carrying a man tied to an oak library chair. The one carrier held the chair by the legs while the other held the back of the chair. Each walked with firm, precise steps. Their mute facial expressions were set in plaster.

What a contrast they were to the man screaming and shaking in the chair. His dark eyes, wild with fire, instantly caught and held mine and reminded me of the madman at the Society. Messy hair, slept in clothes, dirty unshaven face: to me he looked like an old man trying to be a kid again.

They tied him, chair and all, to the wall of the van, closed up the back, and then turned their hard eyes on me. Chills ran through me as I saw the one man, in his box, throw me headlong into the van, while the other guy, in his box, dragged me into the street, pounded my head into the pavement, and while I was lying unconscious in the street, drove the van over me. They mechanically got in the van, put on their seat belts, and slowly drove away.

Concern making me brave when I really wasn't, I ran after the van a few blocks to the corner where it turned right. After four blocks the street turned into a driveway that went through a wrought iron gate. For a moment I stood at the corner and tried to decide whether or not to follow the fate of the man in the chair. I feared, after seeing the carriers' intentions, that I might possibly have the same fate as the chaired man, but, being the kind of adventurer I was, I kept on following.

Across the top of the gate, which was a miniature of the city's gates, in bold letters were the words "Sunny Acres." Inside, the landscape looked the same as in the park. The driveway went straight then curved in front of a rectangular, red brick building. The carriers were automatically loading the man into the building.

I stood at the gate and watched them until they entered. I was still hesitant. I knew I would not find a home inside; if anything I felt that by going inside I might be halted in my search.

Still, I wanted to know why the man had been taken away, what offense he had committed, and what was going to happen to him inside the building. Buildings often sanction people to do things to others that they would never do outside, especially to members of their own family.

As I entered, I was overwhelmed by the smell of dead and decaying souls. I staggered back against the door, opened it for fresh air, almost vomited, nearly left, but turned back to the inside.

I walked to the intersection of a long hall. To my right down at the end, the hall opened into a large room. Against the wall, facing me in the large room, was the chaired man, and he was still thrashing and screaming. Others were sitting near him, their boxes cracked and broken. Cautiously, I walked down the hall. Along the hall were doors leading into other rooms. Most doors were closed, and in those that were open, people were dusting, cleaning and doing paper work, except for one room which was filled with babies in boxes. Everyone's boxes looked weak and had fractures that looked as though they could develop into serious cracks. As with all box people I encountered during my invasion of the Land of Boxes, they immediately stopped what they were doing and stared at me. Some even came out into the hall and stared as I passed. I felt I was walking into a trap.

Near the end of the hall, I stopped unnoticed in a doorway and watched the beginning of a film titled "An Experiment in Empathy by Intellectuals." Students were sitting in a laboratory with notebooks on their laps. In front of them stood a professor in a long, white coat. He was bald in the front, had a long, pale face, drab eyes, and looked as full life of life as a mannequin. Next to him on a table were two monkeys in a cage. The one was grooming the other. They looked like life-long friends. The professor lured one monkey away from the other with a banana, grabbed him, and put him in a separate cage next to his friend. The professor connected electrical wires to the cage and began poking the monkey with a sharp stick. The monkey jumped and screamed, grabbed the bars of the cage, screamed, and fell back on the floor of the cage. The professor poked him in the side. Again the monkey screamed and leapt against the sides of the cage, and then started jumping all over the place and smashing himself into the electrified bars as the professor kept on jabbing him with the stick.

The monkey in the next cage was going berserk as if he were the one being tortured. Calmly, in a squeaky, high-pitched voice, the professor described the behavior of the two monkeys and conjectured about what they might be feeling and why. The students quietly took notes.

In the middle of the professor's inane remarks, I turned away and continued with deliberate steps. I felt drained and was quivering in a cold sweat.

The large open room was no more than twenty feet from me. To my left, a tall emaciated man was pacing along the wall. His head hung toward his feet. Every now and then he would glance from side to side with wary eyes. He swung his arms like a monkey. His box was cracked front and back. The left side, dangling downward, was held up by wires wrapped around his box. To the rhythm of his walk, he was chanting, "Intelligent — they'll make you into an idiot. Sensitive — they'll drive you out of your senses. Perceptive — they'll tell you you're hallucinating. Emotional — they'll rob you of them. Alert — they'll deaden your spirits. Proud — they'll make you ashamed to look in the mirror. Fighter — they'll turn you into a coward. Sane — they'll drown you in insanity."

Suddenly, he stopped, raised his arms and head toward the ceiling and screamed, "What have I done to deserve this treatment? I don't deserve to be treated this way! God, tell me, what have I done? I have hurt no one! I've committed no crime! Why am I imprisoned in this hell? It's not fair! Is there no justice? Oh, I'm guilty! I'm guilty without trial! I've done everything wrong! I'm just trying to be where being is impossible! An opening! Oh, my God, my God, my God! An opening! I need an opening." His head and arms dropped, and he continued his pacing and chanting.

Carefully, I began walking toward the chaired man. Before I reached the open door, a short, fat, slouchy man dragged himself out of the room. His hair was a mess. Dried food was smeared around his mouth, and he was staring vacantly downward; his box, thin and saggy, was laced with cracks and looked as though, at any moment, it would crumble to the floor.

In the center of his otherwise empty main stage was a white refrigerator. On a recessed upper stage, he was chained to a concrete wall. The chains crossed at his neck, stomach and knees. He was feverishly writing in a tablet. He stopped, stared at the refrigerator, then violently started rocking back and forth against the chains. The center chain burst. He lifted his legs, one by one, out of the lower chain, then grabbed the chain around his neck, tore it out of the wall, and hurled it against the right side of his box.

Cracks burst across his box as when a rock is dropped on thin ice. He jumped down to the main stage, opened the refrigerator door, and yanked himself out of the refrigerator. They merged together and cautiously walked toward the front of the box. All this happened in the time it took him to take a few steps. He stopped in front of me, hesitated, and with his empty eyes riveted to my chest, began to recite the moment he disappeared through the front of his box.

"Loneliness will force you to box yourself in cold isolation.

"Loneliness will make you not care about others and only be concerned about your own pitiful state.

"Loneliness will make you do things you don't want to do, go where you don't want to go, be with those you hate, and in reaction, hate yourself.

"Loneliness will make you do things to yourself that only your enemy would do.

"Loneliness breeds itself, and in so doing, sends us on pursuits that lead to more loneliness.

"Loneliness will make you do things to others that will make them avoid you.

"Loneliness will make you into someone you don't like.

"Loneliness will confuse sex with love.

"Loneliness will make you do things to your children that you hated being done to you as a child.

"Loneliness is our only companion.

"Loneliness will make you be a part of another's voyage into what you," he jabbed his fingers into my chest, "dread the most.

"Loneliness will make you feel that you'll always be unloved and alone."

He walked back into the empty refrigerator and slammed the door on himself. He, as a baby, crawled across the stage and began crying and hitting the refrigerator with his head. The refrigerator door flew open. The man, without expression, kicked the baby across the stage where it fell off the edge and disappeared in the bottom of his box. He laughed and slammed the door. I looked in the rear of his box, and there he was, once again, chained to the wall and writing like a madman. He turned away, still failing to look in my eyes, and slithered into the large room.

I followed him, but before I got to the large room, a husky, red-faced, male nurse trudged out of an office to my right pushing a cart full of pills and needles. The instant he saw me, he stopped, looked at me with fierce eyes and ordered, "Who are you? What are you doing here?" As with all those I encountered in the Land of Boxes, the activity on his main stage immediately switched to installing a box on my boxless body.

"I came to visit my friend over there." I pointed to the chaired man.

"Oh," he laughed, "the nut that thinks he's Freud."

"Yes. We are old friends."

"You are? He's not doing very well. I thought he'd be back. Why is it that I've never seen you visit him before?"

"I've been out of town."

"You have!?" He leaned toward me and whispered, "Why did you ever come back?"

I leaned toward him and whispered, "To help my old friend."

"Good luck! How can you help someone who thinks he doesn't need any help? That's what I'd like to know. He thinks he's got everything figured out. Poor Freud has serious delusions. Maybe you can help, maybe you know something. I hope you do. He's nothing but trouble. I'd like him out of here. Come, sign the guest book."

We went into the office. It was similar to the office at the Society, except this office was maintained. I signed in then walked out. He stopped me and said, "Visitors hours are about to end. You'll have to hurry."

I was feeling anxious and sick. I walked into the main room and shook from head to foot. If there were any people in the world who needed a home, they were those souls lining the walls. They were sitting in hard, gray plastic chairs. Some were shaking, while others hung limp in their chairs and, of course, all suffered with cracked and broken boxes. Most of their boxes were held together by gray duct tape. But some boxes, badly cracked and broken, were beyond repair and hung in pieces. There was much violence in their boxes, much changing of places, and sudden onslaughts onto the main stage. The characters were not able to keep their places for very long.

To my left, as I walked in, a man with a thin, partly broken box was staring at me. The moment I looked into his eyes, his eyes seemed to go out of focus, and he looked away; and at that same moment, the actors on the main stage fell down, and others on the upper levels fell and crashed onto the main stage. Everyone seemed to momentarily lose control.

Freud was becoming louder and more agitated by the moment. When I came up to him, he was yelling, "I am beyond all this. No one can help me. I don't need any help. I understand it all. I have analyzed the human mind. I am the king of psychoanalysis!"

On the main stage, Freud was sitting at a desk observing and recording the events on the stages above and beyond him. His hair was ruffled, his clothes unkempt. He looked as though he had been in a fight. On an upper stage, baby Freud was nursing on his mother's soft, warm breasts. His father appeared, pulled the baby off her and began making love to his wife who seemed to enjoy him more than her son. As young Freud watched, he grew until he was much larger and stronger than his father. He pulled his father off his mother and beat him to death. Freud then returned to being a baby, and after crawling up upon his mother's lap, expected to be nursed once again.

But his mother, with a look of fear and loathing, picked up her child and violently shook him and yelled, "I hate you. I hate you. You interfere with my pleasure." She threw baby Freud off her stage. He flipped through the air, crying and screaming, smashed onto Freud's writing table on the main stage, and sent Freud and his papers flying backwards. Chaired Freud covered his face with his hands and cried, "What have I done!? Never again will my mommy love me. Such foul thoughts and deeds have I committed. Never again. Never again. I'm bad, too bad to be loved."

Up on a stage to the right, six beautiful women were oiling his body, feeding him grapes, and massaging his penis into a terrific erection. The most beautiful woman with black, mysterious eyes, long black hair, and full voluptuous lips eased herself onto him.

Delirious joy distorted his face. Five more penises sprouted on his body. Five sensuous women got on for a ride. But soon, Freud looked bored. The beautiful, dark woman shoved a spoon of cocaine up his nose. Pleasure returned to his face but only for a moment. He threw the women off. Freud dove into a bath of warm chocolate that suddenly appeared. He quickly jumped out and yelled, "I'm not obtaining any pleasure in here. My desires can only be satisfied in the real world."

He raced down six flights of stairs and entered the main staircase, when two desire guards dressed in priest robes caught him in mid-air and threw him up on the landing. Freud, encouraged by the setback, jumped to his feet, dodged to the right, dodged to the left, and like a star running back, slipped through the guards' hands. The guards didn't seem to mind. They were busy licking the chocolate off their hands. He ran by Freud the writer, who was still gathering his scattered papers, and just as he passed through the front wall, chaired Freud rocked himself forward and bit a young, shapely student nurse, who at that moment was walking by, in the ass. She jumped, yelped, and wet herself. Freud, face down on the floor, tilted his head toward her, and with an infantile grin said, "The pleasure is all mine."

Magically, Freud was back on his pleasure stage, laughing and licking chocolate off himself.

From the bottom of this pleasure stage, a ladder led to a barren stage. On this stage, Freud was lying on his stomach and moaning, "I'm so unhappy. Everything is meaningless. All my pleasures are empty. All I want is to be loved. Love is the greatest happiness. Why, oh why, am I without it?"

Meanwhile, on a stage in the shadows on the lower left side, Freud and other men were lounging in chairs and enjoying lively conversation, while women were cleaning, preparing food, caring for children, keeping their mouths shut, in short, satisfying the men's every whim. Down off the front stairs to the next stage, women were staring goo-goo eyed at huge penises on display racks. They were petting them, stroking them, polishing them, hugging and kissing them and flying the larger ones around the inside of the box as though they were slow moving rockets. On the stage below, which was brightly lit, naked women with long, drawn faces were pacing and cursing their sex. Suddenly, a table of penises appeared — all colors, shapes, and sizes. Heads sprung up, juicy grins appeared, and the women rushed to the table, plugged penises into their vaginas, and started having sex with those women who failed to get one. Freud the writer stopped writing, stood up, held his head, and stared wide-eyed at the wild scene. He turned, ran through the front of his box, while chaired Freud, still looking up from the floor at the shapely student nurse, exclaimed, "I understand the cause of your discontent, of all women's discontent. You desire a penis. You hate yourselves for not having one. I'll tell you what, toots, you help me get out of here, and I'll give you mine for free."

Still rubbing her ass, she replied, "You scare me. She turned to the nurse and said, "I think I'll do my internship elsewhere." She then ran down the hall.

The nurse looked at me and said, "Your friend is quickly regressing. I better go get the head psychiatrist." He rushed down the hall to the room where the movie was being shown.

I lifted Freud upright. His wild eyes calmed slightly. He smiled and said, "Thank you, young man. Please help. You seem like a kind man. I do not deserve to be tied in a chair like a wild animal. Please untie me. Please!"

"Sure. I can't see any harm in that."

I began to untie Freud. He was smiling bashfully at me. In an upper recessed box, he was kissing me and taking off my clothes. When he was almost free, the nurse and doctor yelled in unison from behind, "Get away from him."

The nurse ran up, pushed me away, and retied Freud. The doctor, a thin, short man with his hands in a white jacket, stared at me and asked, "Who are you?"

"I'm a friend of Freud's."

The doctor scowled, "He needs restraint. We know what is best for him. Visiting hours are almost over."

On his main stage the good doctor was grafting a box to my body.

On a low stage behind his main stage, he placed his hand around Freud's head. Freud's head slowly shrank down to the size of a baseball then turned into a pile of money. The doctor smiled with glee. On a stage next—door, the good doctor did the same thing to me.

I said, "Goodbye. Take good care of my friend. I'll be back tomorrow."

"Good day."

Just as I turned to go, a springy man bounced in with a briefcase swinging in his hands. His clothes were colorful, his hair was matted to his head, and he had the extraordinary ability to talk rapidly without any facial expressions or gestures.

He speeded with his words.

"Good afternoon, Dr. Morgan. Lovely day, isn't it? Yes, yes, yes, lovely day."

He scanned the room.

"Well, well, well, I see everyone is doing fairly well in here.

"Thank God for modern medicine. Without it, do you remember, these people were all over the place screaming, yelling, pacing around, fighting, and being totally out of control. Now look at them after being helped by medicine. Yes, yes, yes, now look at them, they are under control and manageable. Soon, many will be able to return to being productive members of society. The scientists back in the laboratory feel so proud and get so much satisfaction by providing the much needed help to these poor, unfortunate souls. I tell them, yes I tell them, how much they are helping relieve the suffering of your patients. Such a medical breakthrough, yes, greatest medical breakthrough of the century was the discovery, such great geniuses at work, yes, yes, that mental problems are caused by chemical imbalances in the brain. No more need for painful, pointless, non-productive years of psychoanalysis. Just a few pills and within weeks, sometimes within a few days, vast improvements are seen. How often is there any improvement with psychoanalysis? Not very often, let me tell you, never!

"Any state of mind, any emotion we can produce and continue to reproduce with a drug. Yes, yes, yes, we can. Dear Dr. Morgan, what states of mind are you in need of today?"

During the drug salesman's spiel, Freud's face became more and more flushed, and in his box the drug salesman appeared next to Freud the writer. Writer jumped up, grabbed him by the hair and marched him across to the far right of the stage where he slammed his face into a closed door, opened it, then locked him inside. Freud, on the inside, looked to the outside, smiled, slipped through a crack in his box and started yelling, "Woe to you fools who deny the discoveries and advances of psychoanalysis. All you're looking for is a quick fix for your customer that will make you a great deal of money. Every psychological event has a corresponding physiological event. You are treating symptoms instead of causes with your drugs. The trauma of rejection and neglect sets into motion chemical processes that are quite different than love and acceptance. Your patients do not need drugs. They need to unearth those painful events in their past that torment them day and night. Only by lifting into consciousness those dark, terrible truths that they keep imprisoned in the depths of their unconscious minds will they be able to heal their emotional scars and make themselves whole. We have to find the root cause of their symptoms. Are you looking for the root cause? No. You know why?"

Freud's voice grew louder and louder until he broke out into an uncontrollable scream.

"Because you do not care about what is happening in the unconscious minds of your patients. If they show signs of sick, repressed normality, you think they are cured. If they can walk, talk, go to work, and come home without having a nervous collapse, you are satisfied. You could care less about what they are feeling on the inside. They could be dying inside, and you wouldn't care just as long as you can sell them your pills and make a fortune. Isn't that it? Turn your patients into zombies for a profit! You will all go to hell before you do that to me."

As he was talking, all of the Freuds in his box were getting increasingly excited. Toward the end of his talk, pleasure-loving Freud, patricidal Freud, and Freud in the lounge chair raced down the stairs and merged in a collision at the last landing. This combined Freud had a mean and hungry look. The guards at the bottom took one look at him and stepped aside. He ran into and combined with Freud the writer, who had just torn up his papers and thrown them to the floor, and threw himself against the front of the box. Freud's box burst wide open from top to bottom. At that same moment, Freud stopped talking, rose to his feet, and with tremendous strength, hurled himself backward against the brick wall and shattered the chair.

Freud ran toward the door. But before he even reached the hallway, the nurse tackled him and pinned him to the floor. Another nurse sat on Freud.

Dr. Morgan sighed, "These armchair psychologists are a real nuisance. Those psychoanalytical theories are so outdated. They are no longer valid.

"This couldn't have happened at a worse moment. Couldn't his timing have been any better? In a short while I have to be present at the closing of an apartment building I'm buying. What a deal I'm getting. A conglomerate is unloading some of its smaller holdings to raise capital for a takeover. This apartment house is always occupied. I'll make a fortune with it. And after the closing, I plan to meet some colleagues at the country club for a round of golf. Wait till I tell them about Freud. How amused they'll be."

"Oh well, I guess we had better treat Mr. Freud. His medication hasn't been very successful. Do you have anything new for his condition?"

The drug salesman asked, "What is his diagnosis?"

"Paranoid schizophrenia, manic depression, hysteria with aggressive tendencies accompanied with slight hallucinations and delusions of grandeur."

"Yes, yes, yes. We have a new drug just for that condition. It's called Sonic Cyclomind. Here, here, have a free sample."

The drug salesman popped open his briefcase to unfold a colorful assortment of pills, pulled out a bottle of red pills laced with tiny silver lighting bolts, and handed it to Dr. Morgan. He glanced at them, got a glass of water, then went over to Freud, and said, "Here, Mr. Freud. Be a good boy and take your medicine. It will make you feel much better."

He placed a pill in between Freud's lips. Freud spit it in Morgan's face. Morgan yelled, "Open his mouth, open it wide. I've got a meeting I can't miss."

The nurses pried Freud's mouth open. The good doctor poured half the bottle in Freud's mouth, dumped in water, and the nurses squeezed his mouth shut. Freud squirmed, turned blue, his eyes watered as his cheeks puffed out, but eventually he swallowed the pills.

For a moment Freud became calm. Then, suddenly, his eyes bulged out of his head, his hair stood on end, and in one quick movement, he sprang to his feet, throwing the two nurses off to the side.

Dr. Morgan sneered at the drug salesman. "What the hell did you give him?"

"Oh, no, no, no. I gave you the wrong bottle. Oh, no, no, no. I got confused in all the excitement. Sonic Cyclomind isn't a sedative; it's for severely depressed patients who barely have enough energy to move their baby finger. Sonic cyclomind is concentrated adrenaline combined with amphetamine."

"Why you idiot," Dr. Morgan screamed. "What the hell am I supposed to do now? Look at him."

Freud was tearing apart the rope that was bound around his body. He tore it off his legs, and sprinted down the hall toward the door.

Morgan yelled, "Get him, get him. Sound the alarm. Oh, for Christ's sake, this is all I need."

The two nurses were close behind him, and I was right behind them.

At the junction with the hall that lead to the outside, the nurses were ready to grab him, but just as they turned the corner, Freud slammed into a tall, metal file cabinet that movers were pushing around the corner, and bounced back dazed into the nurses' arms.

Dr. Morgan, who was strolling from behind, yelled, "Quick. Quick. Before he comes to, get him into the electro shock room."

Freud was trembling, semi-conscious. His eyes half-closed, a trickle of blood ran down the left side of his face.

Morgan screamed, "Hurry, hurry. Get him on the table. Come on. Come on. We haven't got all day. Tie him down. Get the electrodes on. Good. Good. Hold him down."

Morgan pushed the button. Freud shook and convulsed. In his box, people fell off the stages, down the stairs, rolled backwards out of sight, and some just plain disappeared. Morgan kept on hitting the button. He stopped. Freud lay motionless on the table. The interior of his box was in shambles.

Slowly, as though waking from a deep sleep, the inhabitants of Freud's box started getting up and trying to rearrange the mess. But they just wandered around in a daze not knowing where they were or where anything belonged. Many had fallen onto different stages, but instead of going back to their stage, they just sat staring into space. Even Freud the writer, sitting in a pile of papers, did not seem to know he was a writer.

Dr. Morgan rubbed his hands together and said, "Now that we have him here, I want to make sure we have no more trouble from Freud. Go get the anesthesiologist, Weber."

The nurse returned with the anesthesiologist. They put Freud under and cut out part of his brain. Everyone in Freud's box collapsed. Freud was cured.

Morgan sighed, "Good, very good. All's well that ends well." He glanced at his watch. "And I've even got enough time to make the closing. Things work out in the end. Where there's a will there's a way."

As the good doctor turned to leave, he ran into me.

He gritted his teeth. "What are you still doing here?"

"I'm looking after my friend."

"Your friend is fine. He is on the road to recovery. Didn't I tell you before that visiting hours are over!?"

I glanced around in the nurse's and doctor's boxes, and in each one on their main stage, they were doing to me what they had just done to Freud. I thought to myself, "Get the hell out of this town before your search for a home come to an end."

I said to Morgan, "Yes, I was just about to leave. I'll be back tomorrow to check on my friend. Goodbye."

"Goodbye. Do come by tomorrow. Freud will need the support of others to help and hasten his recovery. We will look forward to seeing you." He smiled the deceitful smile of the Land of Boxes.

I rushed out the door. Never was I more afraid as then, except in the long, dark room when Uncle Ed sat dead—like in a hard stiff chair. I didn't want a box around me and I didn't want to be seen as a problem that needed to be treated. I ran to the park hoping that Pom Pom had come early, but she hadn't. Others were there putting a box on me in their boxes. I became more afraid. I ran through the alleys to avoid box people on my way out of town. I ran into an open street.

Turned back into another alley that was overflowing with trash. My heart was racing, my legs burning. I was quickly losing my breath, but midway through the alley, I gained a second wind and picked up speed. At the end of the alley, hustling around a corner, I heard someone crying and rustling among some trash cans. I stopped, but then thought that these people's problems were not my problems. I started up again, but was halted by the familiarity of the cry. Goose pimples broke all over me. I shivered. I knew that voice. I knew that cry. I turned back, threw the garbage cans away, and there, hiding behind some rusty trash cans, was my cousin Eddie, his box cracked and broken.

He looked at me. Both shame and joy ran across his face. In a weak, helpless voice he cried, "Oh, Bobby, Bobby, help me, help me.

"I can't go on anymore." He grabbed a crack at the top of his box and started to pull his box apart. With a strong, deep urgent voice he said, "I don't want this anymore. I don't want to be boxed in. I want to be free." He stopped, pulled out some gray duct tape and began taping the cracks. He cried, "No. No. Be good. I need you, need you. My daddy says to keep you." As soon as he taped himself up, he tore the tape off and fell back in the trash. He looked up at me. His eyes were sunken, his skin pale and drawn. He looked as though he'd been locked in a dark cellar without food or water for days.

In a weak voice, he gasped, "Help me, Bobby. I'm hopeless, helpless. They're going to find me here. Don't let them get me. No. No. Leave. Leave me alone. I'm not worth it. Go. Run. Leave me alone before they come. Leave me. Save yourself."

In the deep, lower part of his box, Eddie was on his knees praying to a shadow. "I'm not asking you for much. Please, please, love me. Love me for who I am. That's all I ask. That's all. I need your love to live. Please do it for me. It's not too much to ask for, is it? Please? I'm begging you. That's all you have to do for me to live. Without your love, I will die."

Stairs dropped forward from that stage to another on which Eddie was staring motionless into a black box. Below this stage, not far above the main stage, Eddie shot himself in the head with a handgun.

He lay still for a moment, stood up and shot himself again. This scene continued to repeat itself. On the opposite side of his box from this stage about midway up, Eddie was nailing rafters onto the top plate of a cabin in a forest.

I heard some talking down at the end of the alley, looked and saw Eddie's father with the two carriers who had taken Freud out of his house. Ed spotted me and yelled, "There's Bobby. I bet he's got my son with him. I bet Bobby is telling him lies about me."

Ed yelled at me, "Get the hell away from my boy, you rotten sonufabitch." Then he turned to the two carriers. "Come on. Let's go. He's got my son!"

They started running at us.

I turned to Eddie and said, "Come on, Eddie, let's go. You've got to get out of here. Believe me, if you stay, they'll drug you to death. You don't need to get drugged into believing that you don't have a box."

Eddie looked up at me from the trash, which seemed to have a hold of him. His bloodshot eyes swelled as he said, "Help me! Help me! Don't let him near me. I can't take it anymore. Go. Go on, Bobby. Go tell them I'm not here."

Suicidal Eddie stopped his repetition, stared at the ever-widening crack in the front of the box, then with controlled steps walked down his stairs toward the main stairs. When he was in the middle of the last flight of stairs, two guards, hunched over like football linemen, charged Suicidal and pinned him to the stairs. Suicidal wiggled free and ran back up to the landing. The guards rushed him. Suicidal shot one in the leg. He fell down to the main stage. The other guard, undaunted by his comrade's wound, kept coming. Suicidal hit him in the face with his revolver, pushed him against the side of the stairs and quickly ran past him onto the main stage.

Eddie the carpenter, seeing Suicidal enter the main stage, jumped off the top plate of his cabin onto the main stage and tackled Suicidal. They wrestled until Suicidal got on top and began beating Carpenter in the head with his gun. Carpenter nailed Suicidal in the back of the head with his framing ax. Suicidal fell forward. They both lay there together moaning in pain. Slowly, Suicidal stood up and began walking toward the front of the box, but before he got there, Carpenter threw his framing ax deep into Suicidal's back.

Suicidal fell to the floor. Blood trickled from the base of the ax.

Suicidal raised up on his knees, reached behind him, and tore the ax out of his back. The trickle of blood burst into a stream. Both stood up together. Suicidal turned and shot Carpenter in the chest.

They fell to the floor. Suicidal pulled himself up and crawled, gun in hand, toward the crack in the front of Eddie's box.

Chapter 20

Ed and the two carriers were bearing down on us. Ed screamed at me, "What the hell have you done to my boy? Get the hell away from him. I kicked your ass when you were a kid, don't think I won't kick it now." He raised his fist and came at me.

Eddie cried, "I'm a loser, a loser; I don't deserve to live. Look at all the trouble I'm causing everyone. It's all my fault."

I leaned back and with my right hand grabbed a heavy steel garbage can filled with trash, against which Eddie was leaning, and just as I lifted it, Eddie raised a revolver up towards his head. I shoved the can against him. The gun went off, and I felt as if someone had pressed a red hot iron against my thigh. The sudden intense pain only sharpened my anger against Ed for hurting us when we were children, and so with delightful rage, I tightened my grip on the can, swung with all my might, and blasted Ed squarely on his box. He flew about five feet backward, and landed on the back of his box where he lay wiggling his arms and legs like a beetle on its back.

The front of his box was cracked open from top to bottom. Out of the crack, I heard a child whine, "Mommy, Mommy, Bobby hurt me. Get him, Mommy."

I swung around to Eddie. He was raising the gun toward his head. I grabbed his hand, twisted the gun out of it, and threw it in the trash. Grabbed him by the shoulders and said, "Come on Eddie, let's go. We've got to get out of here."

He was limp. He moved his mouth as though to speak but nothing came. I threw him over my shoulder while listening to Ed and the carriers. Ed: "Get them. Don't mess with me. Get them. Look Bobby's kidnapping him." Carriers: "Don't worry, sir. They can't get away. We'll get them. But first, we need to take care of you. Your box is badly cracked. We have to take you to Sunny Acres for repair.

"Those are our orders — to take anyone whose box is cracked." Ed: "Orders, smorders! Get them. You stupid bastards. Get your fucking hands off me." Then, once again, a child's voice as they carried him away, "Mommy! Mommy! Help me! Mommy!"

I ran to the end of the alley, turned right across the street into another alley, ran down to the end, and turned right again. The Sunny

Acres van drove past, stopped, backed up and turned into the alley. I stopped, turned back after taking a few steps, and noticed a warehouse steel door ajar. I ran inside down a dimly lit hallway lined with closed doors on each side. At the end of the hallway, I bounced in a long high arch, as though I had run onto the moon, into a dark expansive room. Time eased to a stop.

In this room there were white, flat circular disks, like spotlights focused on a dark stage, at all levels from below the floor to far above. On these platforms people were enjoying eternal pleasantries. A mother, dressed in a soft white robe, was nursing her baby. An old man was rocking a boy who looked very much like the old man. Both shone with content, dreamy faces. I gently landed on the floor, pushed off with my feet, and slowly sailed through the air. A young couple, he dark and angelic, she fair and tender, were having a picnic on a mandalic blanket. Below them another couple were making love. Farther down a mother was combing the hair of her daughter, and above them, a delicate child was handing a bouquet of flowers to her father. The father picked up both the bouquet and child and held them close. On many platforms, people of all ages and races were asleep together. As I bounced off the floor again, a woman was telling a story to a group of alert children sitting in a circle.

I hit the floor again and bounced out through a door into the courtyard. I raced toward the Golden Gate. The carriers appeared behind me and started yelling, "Close the gates! Close the gates! Hurry! Hurry! Close the gates. Don't let them escape."

The gates slowly began to close. I felt adrenaline dump into my system as I burst into high speed. The gates started closing faster.

The carriers were close behind. I passed through a narrow opening between the gates. The gates slammed shut on Eddie's box and tore it off. He screamed and collapsed on my shoulder.

Behind the gate the carriers yelled, "Stop them! Stop them! They can't get away! Stop them!"

The workmen on the scaffolding started throwing stones at us. As I turned to dodge a stone, another hit me in the side of the head. I stumbled forward, caught my balance; my vision blurred as blood and sweat burned into my eyes. The oak brush was still more than a hundred yards away. I felt that I had to make it into the brush, for if I fell in the open meadow, I feared that they would come out and drag us back to the Land of Boxes. Suddenly, Eddie's weight bore down on me, my leg burned, and I lost my strength. I staggered, fell on my knees, raised up, and stumbled into the brush. It was now dusk.

I looked back; no one was coming. The oak brush was a blur. In the blur I saw deer paths. I made it onto a path, stumbled along, but quickly veered off into the tangled brush and collapsed.

I dreamt I was walking through the woods hunting deer. A doe stood up in some ferns and looked directly into my eyes with her soft, innocent eyes. I shot her. I had part of her side skinned down to her belly. I turned to sharpen my knife, but when I turned back, the deer was walking away through the woods with her skin dangling and flesh exposed. She looked at me and said with her eyes, "What have you done to me." I ran after her, but no matter how fast I ran she kept in front of me and kept talking to me with her eyes. I covered my face with my hands, fell to the ground, and cried, "What have I done? God, what have I done? I can never repair the damage I have done. What have I done?"

I woke trembling in a cold sweat. Stood up, weaved, staggered, and felt the sharp oak brush scrape across my face. I tried to push it away, but only got more tangled and fell.

I dreamt I was skinning a fish. After I skinned the entire fish, I set my knife on the table next to the fish. The fish came alive and flipped off the edge of the table into the air. The air turned into light blue water. The fish swam slowly, as best it could, up away from me. I tried to reach it, but could not. As it swam away, it kept its sad, painful eyes on me, and with those eyes said, "Why did you do this to me? I will never be the same. I will never recover from what you've done to me. I will never be the same. No one will ever be able to help me. I will never be the same."

I held my head and cried, "I have done a terrible thing. I will never be forgiven. I have done a terrible thing."

I woke, stood up, and vaguely remembering where I was, grabbed hold of some branches and tried in vain to hold myself up. I fell on my knees.

When the sun was high in the sky, I woke thinking of Eddie as though I had been thinking of him all night. I pulled myself up by some branches, looked around; he was nowhere to be seen. My leg was still oozing, my left eye was sealed shut with blood, and I felt guilty for having taken Eddie from the Land of Boxes. I felt that the sudden loss of his box had been too much for him, that he would not be able to recover from such a traumatic shock. I figured that he must have returned. And what a terrible fate would await him there. Far worse than what would have happened if he had stayed. Although I had saved his life, I felt that now, upon his return, he would lose it.

Nearby, I heard the music of a stream. I limped over to it, sat down on a soft bed of moss, took off my clothes, and lay on my back.

The cool moss and the mist rising off the stream refreshed me and brought down my fever. My head and leg still hurt, but not as bad as I hurt for Eddie. Below me the stream formed a small pool. I slid down to it along the rocks, sat in the pool, and slowly washed off my wounds. Both wounds could have used stitches, but when you are an adventurer and have just invaded the nearest town, it's hard to find a doctor.

Fever will take you places you will never travel to on your feet. And as the fever leaves, it sometimes leaves you in a new place. As my fever was leaving, it was moving my thoughts from Eddie's weaknesses to his strengths, and I realized that Eddie was strong enough not to return. He had been brave by trying to rid himself of his box in the Land of Boxes and he would only become brave once free of the Land of Boxes. These thoughts sent chills splashing across my body. I stood up and yelled with all my voice, "Eddie, Eddie. It's me, Bobby. I'm here. I'm still here. Can you hear me? Eddie, Eddie, where are you?" I ran to my clothes, put them under my arm, and as I was walking around and yelling for him, I heard his faint voice, and following it, found him in a box of sticks. "Eddie, oh no, I mean; you're in a box! I was worried that you went back to the Land of Boxes. Are you okay?"

"Don't look at me."

"I won't. Here. Look. I'm turned the other way."

"Bobby, I'm afraid."

"Yes, I know. I'm sorry. I really am. I'm sorry the gate tore your box off. Do you want to go back?"

"No. No. If I were back there I'd be dead. I'm alive. Oh."

His voice changed to a deep sneer. "You should be dead, you failure." His voice returned and he cried, "Bobby, I'm afraid. Help me. Please. Please!"

"I will help you. I will help you as much as I can for as long as you want. Believe me, it's true. I put my life on the line for you, so don't worry, Eddie; I'll stay with you as long as you need me. Do you believe me?"

"Yes. I have always believed you."

"Please, believe me now. Let yourself be afraid. It won't kill you, and fright won't hurt as much as trying not to be afraid."

"Bobby, will I always be afraid? I can't live in fear. I'm afraid to even move."

"I hope not. You just lost your box yesterday. Give yourself some time. Can I look at you?"

"No."

"We'll stay in the woods where no one will see or judge you."

In his father's voice, Eddie said, "He has already been judged and found guilty for upsetting his parents and making them unhappy."

"Eddie listen, we need to get out of here. We are too close to the Land of Boxes. They might come out to get us if they see us. Come on, please, let's get farther away."

"No. No. I can't move."

"At night. How about at night? I won't look at you. No one will see you. Please. We really need to get out of here."

"I'll try. I think, oh," his father's voice interrupted, "he's not going anywhere. Nowhere with you, Bobby, you no-good sonufabitch. He can't get anywhere even when he tries. He's finished before he starts, defeated before the thought of trying."

"Eddie, are you there? Remember me? I lived with you when I was young."

In his voice, "Yeah. I think so." He paused. "Don't leave me, Bobby; I need you. I can't lose my box and be alone too. That would be the end. You won't leave me?"

"No. I won't."

At night wild things roam, and at night we roamed. The sudden loss of Eddie's box left those things in his box with no place to be. They were used to being on their stages. Now, they roamed and fought with each other as they tried to find a home. Eddie, still weak and unsure of what he had done, was at their mercy. He would throw himself on the ground and cry, sometimes even sob about not being loved, and then his voice would change to his father's, and he'd start yelling at himself, "We didn't love you because you wouldn't let us. You weren't good enough to deserve our love. Why would we waste our love on a loser like you?" He'd jump up, look at me with such meanness that at times I became afraid, and scream something like: "Come on, you slow poke. You're always putting me down. Come on, let's see who is the fastest now." He'd then run me ragged for miles.

I'd try to keep up with him for I was afraid he would turn his anger against himself and try to kill himself again or suddenly feel that I, like his parents, had abandoned him. Once, after he sprinted away from me, I found him unconscious on the ground. Later he told me that he was overwhelmed with rage against his father and started screaming and slamming the side of his head into a tree.

Gradually, after part of him stopped wanting to return to the Land of Boxes, his feelings and emotions calmed as they seemed to begin to find a place. We started traveling more during the day. He began to let me look at him. His own voice began to dominate. Then, one day, I felt the hardest part was over and that he would make it without a box. It was in the evening after a day of looking at the shapes and patterns of leaves. We were sitting next to each other, and he was chewing his nails, while I was throwing leaves in the air and watching them float to the ground. After watching the leaves fall many times, he said in his own voice, "Things fall into place on their own. If we only let them, yes, if we only give them freedom, they will fall freely to the place where they belong. I hope they will. I must believe that. Do you believe that, Bobby?"

"Yeah, I do. Everything, if allowed, will find its home. I have to believe that to do what I'm doing."

"If they don't, they will always be trying to find their place. Until they do, they will never give me any peace. Box them in, no, that's not where they really want to be. They don't. They want to get out. But how, but, oh no, how could it have been any different?"

Eddie started crying. I put my arm around him. He leaned against me like a child.

"I wanted to be loved by them. I'd do anything for them. I almost killed myself because they didn't love me. It's easier to die than not be loved. What could I do? What can any child do? We need our parents. Don't they know that? Didn't they need their parents when they were young? I was a great swimmer. I really was. I could have been a champion. I'm not bragging. I could have been."

"I know you could have. You were," I said, "but not with your mom and dad."

"They'd make me so nervous. They made me lose. If they wouldn't have, I could have been the winner they wanted. Then they would have loved me. I used to beat everyone in practice."

"They still would not have loved you."

"Oh, yes, yes, they would have!" Eddie cried.

"I'm sorry Eddie, but they would have found something else wrong with you. I don't mean to hurt your feelings. It wasn't you, it was them. Your parents didn't have much love to give."

"I wish I had been raised by Aunt Iris. Why didn't my parents die in a car crash?

"That's terrible. That is the way I feel, though. I do. Terrible. I'm a terrible person.

"You're so lucky, Bobby. You could fall in shit and come out smelling like a rose. You lose your parents and have someone like Aunt Iris take their place. She was always nice to you.

"I never ever heard her yell at you. That's all I wanted. Is that too much to ask for in life? Is wanting your parents to love you too much to ask? Didn't they want to be loved by their parents? Can't they remember? Couldn't they have remembered how it hurt when their parents were mean to them? Couldn't they have remembered and not been mean to me? Where is the pleasure in passing along meanness?

"I will never have children. I don't want to cause another human being to suffer as I have.

"I need the love now I didn't get as a child. I need it. I won't make it. I can't. I can't make it alone. I'm gonna go back.

"I can't help it. I don't want to, but I've got to box myself into something that will please others. I don't care what it is. I'll even be mean to be accepted. No. I can't. No. No. I can't let myself be naked in front of others. How can it be any other way?

"I'm doomed. We are all doomed.

"No. No. I'm not going back. No more boxes. No more hiding way back out of sight. I want to live. I won't live there again. That's not living. I'd rather die.

"But I need help in staying away from there. I can't make it alone. Bobby, you will stay with me, won't you?"

"I'll be with you. Do you think I'd desert you now after helping you escape from the Land of Boxes and almost getting myself killed?"

Eddie gave me a condescending look and sneered, "What can you do?"

I kept my patience and said, "I can love you. I can support you now, while you stay rid of your box. I'll be your crutch. I know you can't do it alone. No one can. I'll try to help you see that you can be loved without your box. I'll help you see that without it you'll be stronger and not dependent on what others think of you.

"And besides that, I can throw leaves in the air."

I threw leaves in the air. We both watched them fall to the ground.

I spoke in a quiet voice, "No one is here, just us and the woods. We can be whatever we want to be, do whatever we want. We are free. Nature will not judge us. Let nature caress you. Let nature love you. She will, that is if we don't run into a grizzly bear." I laughed.

"Aunt Iris used to say to be yourself because no matter what you become or how many times you change for others approval they will still find something wrong with you. You can't expect others to accept you when they cannot accept themselves. Changing for others will always lead to disappointment, both for yourself and others. So, you may as well be yourself, for really, that's what everybody wants to be, and even if you get criticized for trying to be yourself, underneath it, you will be envied and respected. I don't fully understand this, but I believe it because of Aunt Iris, and that is as you try to be yourself you move closer to being and to others, and you will not feel as alone. I know you are torn. I know your fears, but the worst is almost over. Stay with me, join me, be a part of me. I want you. Together we can be strong."

Eddie said, "I am not strong. I am weak. Weak and worthless.

"You can say all that, but Bobby, you were loved when you were young. That's the difference. I didn't get the love that I needed when I was young. So now it's too late. I'll never get it. No one will ever love me. I'm not worth loving.

"I don't want a box; I want to feel myself but, oh, I can't help it. I automatically box in whatever needs to be boxed in to be accepted. It happens all by itself. I can't stand critical looks, can't even look at others when their look is disapproving. I can't stand the cold, empty breeze that chills me. I want to be a part of others' lives. I don't want to be alone. I'll do anything not to be alone, anything. I need the love I never had to be myself. I never got it, so I'll never, never, but I'm here. I made it this far, didn't I?"

"Yes, you have! You're going to make it! I can tell. It's not over. You can regain the love you never had. I have yet to experience this, but Aunt Iris did. It sounds impossible, but the love we receive is part of our connection with being, and if we can move closer to being, then more love will enter our experience and remove the pain of past rejections and losses. We can regain the love we missed when we were young. What happened happened; what will happen is up to us. We can do it together. I know we can. This can be the beginning of a new life for us. No more boxes, no more evasive fantasy."

"I believe you. Do you love me?"

"I love you as I love myself." I kissed him on the forehead.

"You won't put me down, will you? You won't criticize me when I try to be myself, will you?"

"No. I won't."

"Will you really stay with me?" said Eddie.

"Yeah."

"Even though I shot you in the leg?"

"Yes, I will. It was either taking the risk of getting hurt or not being with you now."

"Let's stay together in the woods. No. Don't. It's a waste of your time. I should just go back. I don't deserve this. I don't deserve your kindness."

He jumped up and yelled, "Yes, yes I do. I do. I'm not going back. I'll kill myself first. I'm gonna be strong. Yes. I will. I'm gonna love myself. I'm gonna get strong and go back to the Land of the Boxes and beat my father." He raised his fist to the sky and guffawed.

Eddie reached down and threw some leaves in the air. "No, I won't go after him. I'm going to stay away from him."

In a secluded area in the woods not far from another town, Eddie built a cabin. I helped him deal with others in purchasing the land, materials, etc.; for it was still difficult for him to be himself with others. He still prefers to be by himself. The pleasure of being with others, which so many take for granted, is still difficult for him to enjoy.

Eddie and I traveled a long way together. We are still traveling together.

Chapter 21

I've never owned a map. During my travels I just wandered about, seeing what I happened to see. I could have been on the Northern Hemisphere, Southern Hemisphere, west of east, east of west, below up or up above below, inside of out or outside of in, behind the front or in front of the behind, past the future or in the future without a past, around the corner or cornered in the round, or anywhere at all; I didn't care. This particular day I was walking on a path toward the sounds of a stream.

The path divided into three at the stream. One to the right toward the ocean, the other left to the mountains, and the third straight across a bridge through a meadow where it disappeared in a deep dark wood. I headed straight toward the woods.

It didn't take me long to lose my way in the woods. For an entire day, I tried to find a way out. I walked east, then north, then west, then south, then all over the place. In spite of man's endeavors, I became convinced that the entire earth had somehow covered itself with trees.

As evening approached, a panicky feeling started crawling up my legs and into my stomach. I didn't want to stay overnight in the woods. There are too many wild things crawling and sneaking around in the woods at night. There are many creatures we have not discovered yet because they only come out at night, and who wants to be in the woods at night to find them? Let them stay there! What difference would it make if we knew about them or not? We know about a lot of creatures, but it doesn't seem to do us or them much good.

All I wanted was to find the edge of the woods. Even a small clearing would have satisfied me. I would have felt safe beneath the stars with a wide open view. But, as dust crept through the trees, I knew I was doomed to spend the night with strange creatures. By this time, I had no idea where I was. All I knew was that I was in the woods somewhere on the planet. I could have been only a few feet from where I had entered or a few feet from an edge.

When darkness had almost filled the forest, when shadows looked like trees and trees like shadows, I took a step to the left in hopes of lucking out and finding the edge before darkness reigned. The trees, the shadows, their spacing looked exactly the same as the other part of the woods I had just turned my eyes from. I turned around only to find the same arrangement. All around, no matter which way I looked, I saw the same trees, the same distances between the trees, and the same arrangement. The panicky feeling began to spread from my stomach to my heart and out along my skin, which began to tingle with goose bumps. I knew I would be saved when I realized that if I looked up I would see different tree tops and branches. For a moment the panicky feeling sank down toward my feet but rose quickly, as though delighted in my mistake, when I raised my eyes and saw in all directions the same patterns of branches. My only hope was that, maybe, things had changed on the forest floor. But, as I lowered my eyes everything in every direction looked the same. Symmetry surrounded me.

Maybe, I thought to myself, I was in a unique area of the world in which everything was the same. But then, sameness was one of the reasons why I started my travels, so it couldn't have been that unique. Even though it was almost dark, everything was vivid. I walked around the sameness, touched the trees, looked at their size, their spacing, and was convinced that everything really was the same. Where do you go when everything around you is the same? Why bother going anywhere? That would be the same as going nowhere. But, then again, I could go anywhere and it wouldn't make any difference. So there was no decision to make, no weighing the pros and cons of which way to go. And there would be nothing to miss if I ventured off in the wrong direction. There would be no wrong direction, no mistake to make. When I came to that conclusion, the panicky feeling subsided.

But something was amiss. Symmetry, I've always thought and have heard, is a basic structure of the universe and the substance of beauty. Scientists, in trying to unravel the mysteries of the universe, look for symmetry. The symmetry of the atom, planetary movements, the equality of action and reaction, the balance between positive and negative forces, day and night, the seasons; everything we see is somehow held up by symmetry. And as for beauty: flowers, snowflakes, eyes, leaves, shells, plants — where beauty is so is symmetry. People even meditate on symmetrical forms in trying to find their own center. Symmetry is the key; it holds and protects the center in which lies the essence of life. And yet, there I was in the middle of symmetry, the central hub around which my world revolved, and I was completely lost.

I thought, if I were the center of a circular symmetrical form, like the center of the eye, and the outside ring was the edge of the forest, then no matter which way I went in a straight line, I would travel the same distance to the edge. Besides that, even if I did get lost, what difference would it make? I'd still be traveling in beautiful symmetry. Forever wandering, wondering, traveling along in beauty, forever surrounded in symmetry; I could stay lost forever.

But if it were really that simple, then how did I get lost and why couldn't I find the edge of the forest? The only reason I could think of was that I was not capable of finding my way out, and once lost, a failure at trying to find myself. Why was I even an adventurer if I couldn't travel where I wanted? How would I get anywhere? Why bother going anywhere? And if I accidentally found a home, I would probably not even know it and still feel lost. But, that was ridiculous because if I couldn't even do a simple thing like find my way out of the woods, then I'd never be able to find a home. And that meant I'd never see Pom Pom again. I'd just wander away the rest of my days until I dropped to my knees and died on the forest floor. I then stopped caring about whether I was lost or found. All effort seemed useless.

I leaned back against the trunk of a huge willow tree. As I gazed upward at the swaying sameness, serenity filled my soul, everything became quiet and peaceful, and I lost all desire to go anywhere. Was content to spend the rest of my life protected by that timeless tree.

I became drowsy, and as my legs gave way, the tree trunk stretched out to a great length and the ground fell away, so instead of falling a few feet to the ground, I fell a great distance through the ground into the depths of the earth.

I landed on a tiny ledge on the side of a cavern. Water trickled down the wall over the edge, making it so slippery that I could barely stand. I leaned back, spread my arms out, and gripped the wall as best I could. The rocks on the walls sparkled and glistened like jewels. I ventured to look over the edge. I felt that if I fell, I would never return. I would not die, I would just not return. It was frightening yet inviting. For a moment, I seriously thought of jumping, for I felt I really had nothing to lose by not returning, but then decided that I'd leave it as a option for later, and in the meantime try to find out where I was.

I raised my eyes and almost fell headfirst into the unknown when I saw Pom Pom sitting on a large ledge across from me. On her right foot was a high-top sneaker; the other foot was crammed into a tiny black shoe. Heavy brown wool stockings ran up her legs to a hot pink miniskirt. On top of the mini, a chastity belt bound her. From the waist up she was naked except for sparkling tassels on her breasts and a 2001 Miss Universe banner. A rosary was wrapped around her hands, which were folded neatly on her lap. I feared her neck was going to break by all the gold jewelry hanging from it. She had a chicken bone through her nose, a heavily made-up face, and eight different kinds of earrings stretching her ears, and to top it all off, a red ribbon bunched together her short, pink hair. A confused, distressed look distorted her appearance even more.

I yelled, "Pom Pom! It's you! What are you doing down here?"

She responded in what seemed like a thousand different languages.

"Can you still speak English?"

With a whimpering monotone, she said, "Yes, I can. I live down here."

"All the time?"

"Yes, this is my home."

"It is?!" I paused. "How'd you get dressed like that?"

"Others told me to dress this way."

"You mean people come down here to tell you how to dress?"

"It seems to happen that way. As soon as they arrive they start telling me what I should and should not be. I guess they want to make me into something."

"You put on whatever they tell you?"

"Yes. I have no choice."

"What do you mean — you have no choice?"

"I don't know. Whatever they tell me to be I become. I have no ideas of my own. Theirs become mine." She then chanted, "I am nothing without something, no one without someone. One and one are three. One alone is nothing."

I said, "There were a lot of people in my hometown with no ideas of their own."

"What became of them "

"Nothing."

She looked so unhappy with the way others had made her up. It was not just sympathetic feelings that made me want to change her, but also feelings of being irritated by her appearance. I tried to fight my own discomfort, tried to replace it with sympathy, but couldn't get rid of it.

I had no idea what she should be. Images of women in my hometown slid through my mind, but I thought, oh no, I couldn't do that to her. Then I thought of Aunt Iris. Maybe Pom Pom should become like her. But how could I make her like Aunt Iris? She was too young to look or be like her. But, then again, age didn't have anything to do with it. Aunt Iris's character is what I wanted Pom Pom to become. But, who wants another person to be like someone else? There's enough sameness in this world.

She spoke again with her weak, dreary voice, "Will you also do something to me?"

"I feel that I should but I don't know what."

"Oh, no!"

"Oh, no! Why?"

"Because when they don't know what I should be, then the only thing they do is tell me what not to be. I shrivel up and fall apart. It's terrible."

"I won't do that. I won't make you any worse than what you are now."

"Thanks. I hope you don't. You should have seen me a few days ago. I'm much better off than I was then."

There was another long pause while I thought about what I should have her become. What a rare opportunity for a man to have — to make the kind of woman he wants. Too bad an abyss separated us. I did exactly what I told her I wouldn't do.

"Get rid of all that stuff on you. Will you?"

She immediately became naked. Soon she began to shiver. I shivered too as I felt to be losing my balance on the slippery ledge.

"A soft blue, silk robe would look beautiful on you."

245

She was magically dressed in the same robe I had pictured in my mind. But instead of looking happy about her new look and comfortable robe, she looked more unhappy and uncomfortable.

"What's wrong?"

"I don't know."

"You don't like the robe?"

"It's okay. I guess."

Her hairdo was still the same.

"Maybe this will make you happy. Let your hair be long and blonde."

Her hair changed to blonde and began to grow. The speed with which it grew shocked me. It flowed down her back, on her shoulders, over her breasts, and onto the ground where it piled up and began to suffocate her.

"No. No. I'm sorry. Just to your waist."

It shortened to her waist.

My right foot slid off the edge. I leaned back, slid my foot back on the tiny ledge, and with arms spread, gripped the wall with all my strength. I felt that at any moment I would be airborne into the unknown.

She looked so good that I wished I could have sprouted wings and flown over to her, but she still looked unhappy. No longer did I feel an urge to change her because of my own discomfort. I thought that by getting rid of all the garbage on her and making her warm she would have felt better. She actually looked worse. She needed something, she needed someone, but it wasn't me. My confidence in my ability to help her started slipping.

I asked, "What is wrong? You look much better. Why aren't you any happier? You look like you're going to cry."

She remained silent.

"Please, answer me. Please, before I fall."

Her voice was so weak that I barely heard her words. "I was hoping you were different. You are the same as the others."

"What do you mean?"

Again there was a long silence before she spoke. "You are decorating me into something that pleases you. What about me? Doesn't anyone care about how I feel, about what I want to be?"

"Pom Pom, I do now. I admit; I didn't before, but I do now. Here, I'll make it all right for you. You will love this. Be surrounded by flowers."

The image I had was that of Aunt Iris when I first saw her asleep on the ground in her garden, and sure enough, Pom Pom was now in the same surroundings, but instead of a woman sleeping peacefully in the midst of flowers, there was a lost woman with tears swelling in her eyes.

As a tear rolled down her face, my right foot slid off the ledge.

I leaned back, pushed down with my left foot as I tried to pull my right foot back to a secure position, but then my left foot started to slide too and then, suddenly, it shot out dropping me on my rear. I clung to the rocks thinking how simple-minded I was to think that Pom Pom needed a change in appearance. As if that would have made her happy. She probably had been made into every possible appearance imaginable. What she really needed, I thought, was a change in her thoughts. Not only that, she needed companionship. I thought for sure that I was on a track that would help me regain my balance.

With a pathetic smile, I said, "Pom Pom, I understand now what you need. You need thoughts. Here, this will dry up your tears. Think of me sitting next to you."

She shook her head then buried it in her hands. My rear slowly slid off the ledge. With my arms outstretched, I dug my fingers into the rocks and hung with my back against the wall as though I were being crucified. Like a typical man, I blamed her for my upcoming downfall.

I screamed at her, "Why are you doing this to me?"

With her head still in her hands, she spoke with a weak voice, "I've done nothing. What have I done? I'm only obeying you."

"I don't believe it. There's something going on here. There's some connection between what I have said and how slippery this ledge has become. You're controlling everything. When you don't like what I say, you make it harder for me to keep my balance. Do you think others are supposed to tell you what to be? I don't care what you are or who you are or what you want to be or what you should wear or what cavern you choose to hide in; it's none of my business. So you can just stop demanding that everyone else decide what you should be. It's not up to us.

"All you care about is how you feel. What about the way I feel? I said.

"Do you think I enjoy dangling over the edge? Do you think I am proud of what I've done to you? I wanted to make you happy with how you looked. I wanted the best for you. And what did I get? Failure! I've failed all along. I couldn't even find my way out of the woods, and now that I'm lost, I'm a failure at helping you. I may as well just fall in the void. I'll never find my way out of here. I'll never find a home.

"I'm gonna push off. Yeah, that's what I'll do — deprive you of the pleasure of dropping me into oblivion. That's probably the only pleasure you get-watching others fall after they fail to meet your standards. I don't care what you want to be. Be what you want to be!"

My words echoed around me as I pushed off into nowhere. For a thin slice of a moment, I felt proud of telling her the way I felt and asserting my freedom by pushing off instead of passively sliding into the deep, dark emptiness, but that moment was followed by an endless feeling of being a fool because she never once asked, let alone demanded, me to tell her what to be. Yet, there I was dangling over the edge yelling at her for putting me in the untenable position of deciding what she should be. In a way I was glad to be tumbling alone where no one could see me.

Out of control, I flipped, tumbled, and twirled. The air became more fluid, not as thick as water, but fluid enough so that I could control my movements by exerting pressure. For quite a while, I had a ball twirling around in the darkness. I got so that I would glide around, flip, glide back, tuck into a cannon ball to speed up my descent, then open up and sail across the unknown. I did things I used to dream about doing while watching birds play in the sky. I took great pleasure in gliding back and forth. Then I stopped all the antics. The fluid felt so soft, so comforting that I slowly turned over on my back and let myself sink through the softness. The sensation of softness soon replaced all other sensations. And if that wasn't heavenly enough, the soft sensation enclosed me completely as time slipped away, and I felt that for no time, all time, I had been sinking in softness without past memories or future expectations, and then the feeling began to fade, and as it did, the separation between myself and my surroundings dissolved. There was only a dull, sinking softness becoming duller and duller, softer and softer, as I slowly sank, like a pebble in honey, into the depths of oblivion.

Chapter 22

I was lying on my back looking up at a curved, gray rock ceiling.

I sat up to find myself on a rock ledge much larger than the previous one. The chamber was large, about a hundred feet across, well lit, and like the other one, seemed to have infinite depth. At my feet, steep stairs lead downward alongside of the jagged rock wall into the darkening abyss. At least, I thought to myself, if I wanted to visit oblivion I could stroll down into it instead of falling.

I stood up, leaned against the rock wall, and stared down the stairs. Both attraction and dread possessed me. The stairs led somewhere, as all stairs and paths do, and that simple fact kindled my adventuresome spirit. But, I was afraid of what I might see down there. Yet oddly enough, this increased my attraction for descending.

So, as one drawn into a woods without any idea of where to go or what to expect, I was drawn down the stairs. Besides, where else could I have gone? Fishing?

After taking a few steps, I saw a man on a ledge across from me.

At first he was hard to see, but as I concentrated on him, he became easy to see, and I wondered why he had been so hard to see before. As I looked at him, I experienced an eerie feeling I was he, or that he was closely related to me, although he did not look anything like me. He was tall and thin. A long scraggly beard hung from his face. His eyes were dark and bulging; his face drawn and hollow, and torn, ragged clothes hung from his body. Above him, a vertical rock jutted out past his ledge. A beam of light, coming from a hole across the cavern, shone through a hole in the vertical piece far above his head, hit a shiny rock, and reflected up onto the ceiling, making it appear, from the man's position, that the light of day was shining through a hole directly above him. The man was frantically chopping footsteps in the sheer rock wall beneath the reflected light with a hammer and chisel. Only one rough step was chopped out.

He would chop for a while, bow and pray, and then jump up and vigorously chop away at the solid stone. Sweat dripped from his face.

Every so often he would glance over at me with a disinterested look.

Although his glance was short, it stripped me of my covering. I trembled, backed against the wall, and shouted, "That light is only a reflection. It's coming from over there. "I pointed to its source in the large dome. "Believe me, it really is. You're wasting your time."

He looked at me without expression, turned, and resumed chopping.

When I pushed off away from Pom Pom into oblivion, I felt that I didn't fall through space but fell through time into timelessness. So now, in this timelessness, the man across from me had only, for his entire existence, chopped out one step.

I leaned against the wall, looked up the stairs to my ledge, then down the dark cavern and thought, "What am I going to see? More lost people? I'm lost enough now. Why should I see others who are even more lost than I? What good will it do me? Maybe I should just go back up on the ledge and try to find my way out instead of becoming more lost by going down. But, oh no, that's not for an adventurer. You're an adventurer? Adventurers don't sit, they travel. And they travel where the road leads, and this road, these stairs, reluctant adventurer, lead downward into who knows where, but where you'll soon find out. So come on, you can do it."

Dismally convinced, I leaned and cautiously stepped downward. The cavern was narrowing quickly. I half-heartedly looked at the ledges on the other side both hoping and not hoping to see someone. I could not have missed the next man even if I had wanted. Toward the front of a rough semi-circular ledge on a church pew teetered a man dressed in a black suit. He was alone. His face was thin and drawn. With his head hung, he was mumbling through a big, black book titled <u>Robert's Ordered Rules</u>.

I stared at him and tried to understand what he was saying. As though he knew I wanted to hear him, he began speaking more and more clearly until I was able to understand. Although, at the time, I felt so lost that I may have formed his mumbles into words.

"Procedure #578: In public always walk with head erect, shoulders back, and do not turn from side to side to look at other people.

Place one foot quickly and firmly in front of the other, not inwardly like a pigeon or outwardly like a duck. With an even stride, move arms slightly in a stiff motion.

"Procedure #579: When shaking hands, always squeeze firmly; not too tight unless you want to intimidate the person; not too loose for fear the other will think you soft-willed and cowardly. Release when you feel the other weaken his grip but not beforehand.

"Procedure #581: Never be friendly to strangers.

"Procedure #582: Reserve your smile until the other person smiles. Do not be the first to smile unless you want something from the other person, otherwise the other will think you are vulnerable and can be taken advantage of. Always control your smile, maintain an even lip opening, reveal only the lower half of your top teeth and upper half of your lower teeth, never expose any of your gums, and never allow yourself to lose control through laughter. Control. That is our primary aim.

"Procedure #583: Upon waking in the morning, immediately jump out of bed, wash face and hands, fully clothe yourself, and make sure all of this is done before anyone sees you.

"Procedure #585: Always respond when spoken to, unless it is someone inferior to you or someone you do not like or someone with whom you are angry."

Each procedure he repeated several times before he continued with the next. After he finished, he turned to the front of the book and read, "Procedure #1: Always act as though you are self-willed and in control. Never appear afraid, hesitant, confused, dependent or indecisive. Never let it be known that you have or follow this sacred book of procedures. Give your life if it be the only way to protect your secret."

He closed the book, let his arms drop to his sides, hung his head, and sighed, "How can I ever remember all these procedures? I can't. There are too many. I can't even remember how to get off of this pew. Somehow move my right foot forward. But how? Straight out? To the side? The left one directly behind the other? But how close? Oh, I can't even remember that. How will I ever go anywhere, do anything?"

He leaned forward, slid his right foot forward, cringed, and then withdrew his foot under his pew.

I pulled a blank piece of paper out of my top pocket and wrote "Bobby's Rules Unordered" at the top, folded it into an airplane, and threw it over to him where it hit him in the forehead and fell on top of his book. For a long while he stared at the plane. Mechanically, he grabbed the plane with both hands, slowly opened it, turned the blank sheet over, and with a disgusted look, crumpled it and threw it to the floor. With a trace of anger he said, "What good is that going to do me? Useless piece of paper."

I felt I should say something. But what could I say? What good did the things I said do for Pom Pom? I stood up, thought for a while, but still was at a loss for something to say or do. Then I felt that I had nothing to say to him because I was as lost as he. I turned away from him as I felt myself being drawn down the stairs.

Wasn't long before I heard someone yelling, "Help me, help me. I'm falling. I'm losing my grip. Help me, please, I'm going to fall. Isn't there anyone to help me?"

I rushed down the steps and spotted a naked man hanging on some rocks with his hands. He was long and thin and strung together with wiry muscles. Water was trickling down over the rocks around his hands, into his face, and over his body. He reached up with his right hand, grabbed a rock that looked like a fancy car, and began to pull himself up with it, but the rock car crumbled into sand, and he fell a short ways onto a small ledge. He grabbed a gold bullion with his left hand. It broke loose and fell into the void, almost taking the man with it. Right above him was a rock in the shape of a handgun.

The man wrapped his hands around the gun, but it too turned into sand, sending him on a long fall. He climbed up the wall again trying to avoid the water, but the water seemed to move with him. With both hands, he seized a stone tablet with words chiseled into it. The tablet crumbled in his hands, and once again, the man fell. On his way back up again, he turned his head, caught sight of me, and yelled, "Lend me your hand! Pull me over! Please, help me, please! I'm loosing my grip. Please. I can't find any strongholds."

I stretched my arm as far as I could; he stretched his, but a few inches kept us apart. With my hands still outstretched, I looked into his eyes and realized the uselessness of trying to help, for I felt, as with the others I had seen, that he was forever lost.

The stairs and the wall opposite me began to curve toward each other. At the top of the stairs, the walls of the cavern were fairly smooth and had few ledges and caves. The walls were getting rougher and had more ledges and caves. After I walked a short ways, my eyes were drawn to a long narrow ledge that extended within a few feet of my stairs. At the back of the ledge next to the opening of a cave, sat a man dressed in a white robe. I could tell, when my eyes met his, that he had been watching me descend the stairs. He stood slowly and walked softly with shoulders slouched to the edge of the ledge. He had fine, delicate features: fair soft skin, blonde thin hair, watery blue eyes, a forlorn narrow face, thin lips, and a tiny chin. A sad helplessness spoke through his features.

His arms dangling at his side, he begged, "Will you help me get out of here? Please. I am paining to get out. Here. This should help us."

In his right hand was a black Bible, in his left, a white candle.

He leaned over the abyss, reached toward me with the candle, but before I could get a grip on it, he let go, and it fell into the dark depths.

He clutched his face with his hands and said, "Oh, no. I'm sorry. It's all my fault. I thought you had it. Stupid me. Please, we can still get out. Help me, please!"

"I don't know. What can I do? I feel helpless, too."

"Oh, but you aren't. You're on the stairs. I'm stuck on the ledge. You can get out of here. I can't. Please. I beg you." He lowered to his knees. "Save me!"

"But don't you belong down here? Wouldn't it be a terrible thing for you to leave. Doesn't everyone belong where he or she is?"

"No. They do not. Many belong in other places; that's why we try to change ourselves. What would be the use of trying to better our lives if we all belonged where we were? Believe me, I don't belong here. Please. I'm begging you. You're my only hope. Please don't think of me as lost. Think of me as wanting to be found. Please, I beg you! You don't know what will happen to me if ..."

He started trembling and turned away from me as he covered his face with his hands. Never would I have imagined what was to follow. A dark, hairy muscular arm emerged below his right arm, another appeared below his left, then one leg and another, and with the legs a massive torso and a beastly head. This new being separated himself

255

from the man and stood over him. The man, with his back to the beast, cowered on the floor.

I fell against the wall.

Deep scars gouged the beast's face. His eyes were bright black, and as he snarled at us with his sharp, pointy teeth, saliva dripped down his chin. He shook from head to toe as he screamed, "You rotten, pathetic sneak! You think you're going to leave without me! Forget it.

"Wherever he goes, I go. He's not going anywhere. No hope does he have. I'll take care of that. Hopeless fool. Look at the coward trembling on the ground! He can't do anything right. He makes me sick.

"Just the sight of him throws me into a rage. Stand up! Stand up! I said—stand up! Stand up and face me!"

The beast yanked the man up by the arm. He grabbed his other arm, tore it off, and threw it over the edge. The man didn't scream or cry or put up any struggle. The beast, still holding onto the man's arm, threw him down, stamped his foot on his chest, pulled that arm off, and threw it into the void. Then he grabbed him by each leg, tore him apart, and threw his remains into the darkness.

Suddenly he became calm, looked at me with vacant eyes and slowly walked back and sat down at the opening of the cave where I first saw the man. He slowly transformed back into the man. He stood up, strolled out to the edge of the ledge, and began saying the same things as before.

Still lying against the wall, I thought — what kind of adventure is this? I'm being led where I never expected to go! I don't know if I can take seeing this. What if I can't? What if I close my eyes and I still see? What will I do? Where will I go? Will I ever, how will I ever find a way out of here?"

I wanted to turn back up the stairs, but was afraid that if I turned around something might rush up out of the darkness and grab me from behind, just as when I was young and would venture alone into Aunt Iris's dark, dusty cellar and part way down would want to turn and run, but was afraid something might get me from behind. My eyes darting along the rugged walls of the cavern, trying but not wanting to see what was in the smallest recesses, I ventured downward holding onto the rough wall along the stairs.

On a small ledge a woman alone was giving birth. As soon as the child came out, she snatched it, cut the umbilical cord, and after wiping off the child, set the child across from her. The child squirmed and cried on the rocks, but the mother ignored her. She reached into her own head and pulled out a picture of her mother. She then reached into the picture of her mother and pulled out a picture of her mother and on and on until she was surrounded by pictures. She studied these pictures, one by one, and then put them back, leaving only the picture of her mother. She then picked up a large wooden mold resembling those sinker molds that are hinged at one end and open and close by means of handles at the other end. After she opened the mold, she meticulously carved out an image. Her child writhed and cried. After she was finished, she put down the knife, lifted her newborn, and dropped the child in the mold and squeezed.

The child screamed. I could hear bones breaking and saw blood flowing out the seams. She opened the mold. Her child was shaking and choking on the blood flowing out of her mouth. Her nose was smashed against her head, her skin was torn off the right side of her face, her pelvis was flattened, her left knee was broken sideways, and her feet were crushed. Her mother picked up the picture of her mother, looked at her child, lifted her broken child out of the mold, and once again, with great care and precision, carved out the mold. She carved for a while, then picked up the picture, carved a little more, stared at her whimpering child, and then slowly, as though unaware of her child's suffering, carved the mold some more. When she was through carving, she placed the child in the mold and squeezed. The child squished out the sides of the mold. The mother opened the mold. The baby's forehead was smashed in, her left eye dangled on her cheek, her chin was broken sideways, and her shoulders were crushed together.

I'm sure more of her was broken, but I turned away. The mother squeezed her child many times until she was deformed beyond recognition. After the last squeeze, she opened the mold, stared at her lifeless child with a critical look, and then in disgust pushed her over the edge. She leaned back and started giving birth to another child.

I cried to myself, "No, no, there has to be more. Do parents just deform their children? That can't be the only thing they do. Press them in a mold and be dissatisfied with the results. Do parents just crush their children's identity? Some parents must love their children. Some must be happy with their children as they are. They must! Where will these stairs end? Will they ever end? How much more lost can these people, can I become?"

I was afraid to step either upward or downward. Looked over at the woman on the ledge; she was squeezing another child. I turned away and continued downward.

I was feeling, more and more as I descended, that I was getting too close to those on the ledges. The ledges were now right across from me, just a little more than a jump away. Yet, at the same time, mixed with feelings of wanting to escape was the desire to go deeper to see what was in store.

It was quickly becoming darker and darker, and I felt, as I looked into the cool darkness, that the stairs would soon come to an end.

They had to. I couldn't keep walking down forever and ever seeing souls lost in every way possible. It all had to come to an end somewhere, somehow. But what if it didn't? What if this was the place in which I would aimlessly wander for the rest of my days. The moment that thought entered my mind, I pushed it out and walked downward in search of the end. After a few steps I hesitated for a moment, fearful that the bottom would be strewn with dead babies and decayed body parts.

Soon I began hearing voices. I stopped, and looked around, but saw no one. As I descended, the voices grew louder. Not far across the abyss in the mouth of the cave a man, a typical man with no outstanding features, was running around in circles as voices jetted around his head.

"Clean your hands." He ran over to the side of the cave and started to wash his hands in the same water that had been flowing over the man far above him. "Clean the floor." He grabbed a metal bucket, filled it with the same water, and started scrubbing the floor with a brush. The voice screamed, "You've got your hands all dirty. I told you not to do that. Why did you do that? Keep them clean!" The man froze in his spot.

A hollow, feminine voice said, "Be strong my son. Make your way in the world. Stand tall and be yourself. Where are you going?

How can you leave me after all I've done for you? Too bad others won't like you."

The man stood up, staggered backward, then forward and smashed his face against the wall of his cave. Blood streaked down his face.

Another harsh voice yelled, "Stand on your own two feet." The man stood there. "Stand on your head." He balanced on his head. "Do them both." The man fell on his side. "Yes, that is much better. You do understand, don't you?"

The female voice returned, "Yes, it would be nice. I wish the best for you. I have to, no one else will. Too bad your best is not good enough."

The man rose on his knees, tilted his head upward, and with his hands clasped together in front of his chest, begged in a weak voice, "What do you want from me? How can I please you? No matter what I do it's always wrong. What are you trying to do to me? How can I have a future when everything you say contradicts what you said before? There is nothing I can do. There is nothing I can become except nothing. I don't want to be nothing. Tell me, tell me, what should I be?"

From deep within the cave, cutting through the other voices, a sweet, hopeful voice whispered, "Please, do what's best for yourself, listen to me. Ignore them. I am your hope, your salvation. Turn away from them toward me. I can make you strong. So strong that when they speak you will not hear them, and if by chance you do hear them, you will not care about what they say. Follow me. I can guide you through the cave of contradiction. Believe in me, and together we shall be free."

The other voices suddenly became louder and tangled with the sweet voice. I could no longer hear it. The man turned toward the inside of the cave, turned away, then buried his head in the bucket of water.

I held my head, stumbled down on the stairs, and said to myself over and over again, "You should listen to the soft voice. Listen to the faint, strong voice. You must, you must. Listen to her voice."

I was so absorbed in repeating those words to myself that I didn't even notice stepping off the last stair onto a flat, rock surface. I stopped in the middle of a dimly-lit area. Sheer rock walls shot up in front of me. A large, round, flat stone, like a giant coin six feet in diameter, was lying up against the wall. Instinctively, almost as though following a plan pressed into my unconscious, I walked over to the stone and rolled it away.

I was stunned with awe. All my fears subsided as I stood at the opening of a golden cave. The floor was smooth, solid gold. The black dome of infinite depth twinkled with chunks of gold. I felt I had found a golden universe. I stood at the opening entranced by its beauty and brilliance. I felt I had found my home.

Cautiously I stepped forward. An icy breeze chilled me. My fears returned. I started to tremble. Slowly I ventured deeper into the gold mine. A short ways in front of me a small human figure was lying on its back. I stopped and looked away. Turned my eyes back toward it. It was still there. I ventured forward until my feet were next to its, and before me, lying dead still on the cold golden floor, was a faceless, sexless child. My vision blurred, I grabbed my head with my hands, and shaking violently, reeled backwards and fell against the wall screaming, "No, no. This cannot be. No. No."

In my screams, I heard the words of Aunt Iris, "Believe what you see. No matter whether it should or should not be, believe in what you see." I opened my eyes and focused on the child. It looked dead.

The barrier I had been building up against the lost souls began to weaken as Aunt Iris's words kept running through my mind. I slowly began to realize that the best thing I could do for myself would be to accept what I saw. I had seen the lost souls; I had seen the sexless, faceless child, but I didn't acknowledge them as being real. As I kept my eyes on the child, my fear and trembling slowly gave way to a profound loss and sadness. I started to cry while saying to myself, "No. No. This does not have to be. You don't have to stay buried away from the world. You can have a life. You can live. We do not just reduce each other and cause each other to become lost. No, mothers do not just deform their children. They also lift them up.

"They also love them. We also help each other to expand our lives. I will not abandon you; I cannot. I cannot help but love you."

Saying these words to myself, I crawled to him on the cold gold floor and sat beside him. He wasn't breathing. I placed my warm hands on his cold chest. His chest rose slightly and became a little warmer. I felt then that it would be possible to retrieve this lost child. With both hands I gently caressed his face and then softly ran my hands up and down the length of his body. Over and over I did this, and each time his body became warmer, and his chest expanded a little bit more. As I was doing these things, I said, "My dear child, you are not worthless; you do not deserve to lie hidden away from the rest of the world. You do not have to remain lost as to what you can become. You are golden. You have potential. Come, come with me. Oh child, who I love with all my heart, come with me out of this darkness into the light of day. Raise up your eyes, look into mine, you can stand tall. You are not a nothing. You are not faceless and sexless and without anyone to bring you to life. You are alive. I know you are. You will have a name, others will know you by your name, and we will be proud of you and your name. You are somebody. Oh yes, warm your heart, precious child, warm your body, come alive, you can. I know you can. Yes, yes, you are. With help you can get out of here. Child, don't worry, I will stay with you. Never again will I abandon you. Yes, you are becoming warmer. Yes. We are believing in each other."

Two small black dots appeared where his eyes would be. I was overjoyed with hope and said, "Oh, yes, yes, you can make it. I know you will." A small line appeared at his mouth, two more curved dots above his mouth, small pieces of skin rose on the sides of his head and his sex began to form. I kept rubbing and talking to him. Slowly his face took shape. The line for his mouth separated and opened. I covered his mouth with mine and breathed into him once, twice, and the third time his chest inflated, and he exhaled. I placed my hands under his arms, picked him up and pressed him to me. He wrapped his fragile little arms around my neck.

I pushed him away so that I could look at his face, and the faceless, sexless child looked more and more familiar. His blue eyes sparkled, his face was rosy, and as he kissed me on the cheek, his tiny body warmed mine.

I stood with him in my arms and said, "Come on, let's go outside. I know now how to find my way out of here."

He wiggled for me to let him down. I placed him on the golden floor. We took each other's hands and left the gold mine.

.

The cavern was now well-lit. We could see all the way to the top of the stairs. We ascended the stairs with quick solid steps.

The man lost in conflicting orders was kneeling in front of the cave repeating to himself what the sweet voice was saying to him, "Listen to me. I may now be soft and weak, but believe in me and soon I will be strong. Stronger than the voices that have gotten you lost in others' confusion. Listen to me, listen to yourself. You are strong enough to find your self."

Upward we climbed. The woman about to give birth pulled a picture of her mother out of her head, threw it over the edge, then leaned back and gave birth to another human being. She gazed at her child with watery, dreamy eyes. She gently picked up her child, and with the umbilical cord still attached, drew her to her breast. We waved to her; she smiled.

The man with the Bible and the candle already had seen us and was walking toward the edge of his ledge. Before we got to him, the beastly man separated from him. For a moment, they stood looking at each other. The man straightened out of his hunched-over position and threw his Bible and candle over the edge. They hugged each other into one man. By then we were across from him. The new man, standing tall, looked me straight in the eye and with a clear, strong voice said, "I don't need to beg anyone for anything. I can leave on my own. Watch out, I'm jumping across." As a cat springs through the air from a still position, the muscular man leapt onto the stair above us. We kept pace with him up the stairs.

The man who could not find any solid places to grip was rapidly climbing up the rocks.

Pieces of paper were twirling past us. The man, who had been trying to find his way in a book of rules, was tearing the pages out of the book one by one and flinging them over the edge. The airplane I had thrown him was sticking out of his top pocket. We waved to each other.

With each step I was becoming more invigorated. When we reached the top, instead of finding ourselves on a small ledge hanging in space, we reached a ramp that lead upward to the hole in the ceiling through which the beam of light shone. I looked back to the man climbing towards the reflection. He had climbed up to the hole in the rock and was looking at the source of light. He dropped his tools, quickly climbed down, ran along the cliff face to the beastly man's ledge, jumped across onto the stairs, then ran up and joined us.

Together the four of us walked up the ramp toward the light outside.

Quietly walking up the ramp, I wondered where I would find myself when I passed through the hole to the outside. The ramp grew wider, the hole got bigger, and when my head passed through the opening, I found myself stretching and yawning in the dim dawn light beneath the majestic willow tree.

I focused on my surroundings expecting to see a plain old wood, but everything was still held in peaceful symmetry. There was no breeze, no sound, no movement whatsoever. I lay gazing at the symmetry surrounding me, feeling found. Slowly the woods came back to being a woods. I gathered up my bag, canteen and binoculars, and without giving thought to direction, strolled directly out of the woods. When above the horizon the sun rose, it found me sitting in a flower-speckled meadow eating wild turnips and strawberries.

After I got lost in the woods, I found myself getting lost more and more. This may sound a little odd, but when you think about it, how are you supposed to be found if you don't get lost? People fear becoming lost, yet, how can you do one without the other?

Every time you get lost you usually see new things before you're found. That's what I like most about being lost. Just the thought of being lost sends my mind off into an excited state of anticipation of what I might find. If you've ever found anyone who was lost, you will notice that after he calms down and realizes that he's found, he'll start telling you of all the new things he saw while lost. And I bet, if he could go off again and become lost with the assurance of being found, that after he told you his tale, he'd no sooner finish than he'd scamper off to get lost again. That's the whole trouble with getting lost — you never really know if and when you're going to be found. But whether you know it or not, you'll be found, so you may as well have a field day getting lost. You may not be found when and where you want, or you may be found out when you're not ready (that could be embarrassing), but in the end, everyone is found.

Sometimes, people are found, but they just don't know it, just as people are lost when they think they're found.

Sometimes, I think you have to really get lost before you can be found. If a friend of yours is a little bit lost, you don't try to find him because you know he'll figure out where he is, and if he doesn't, he won't be too scared wandering around half-lost. You can still make it while being a little bit lost; no one knows the difference. But, if he's completely lost, you become concerned and try to help him be found, and you know your efforts won't be in vain because he'll probably be in a panic trying to be found. But, if he starts to become more and more lost, so lost that he doesn't know which way to turn, then he's starting to get somewhere. Pretty soon he'll be so lost that the only thing that can happen is that he'll be found. Then again, I'm not sure if you really have to go off and become so lost that nothing looks familiar; I think if you sit back and think about whether you're lost or found, before you know it, you'll be calling the police station to find out if you've been found, even though you may be sitting in your own backyard or praying at the altar.

I've never had to call anyone; I've gotten used to getting lost. Sometimes, I never know where I've been while lost. I mean, if you wanted me to take you to the woods where I got lost, you'd probably have a better time finding it than I. I have to admit that since I got lost in those woods, I've gotten lost in quite a few other woods, so now I can't tell one woods from another, which is just fine with me.

Chapter 23

Tall grass tangled around me as I waded through a meadow. All around the grass waved freely in the wind, except for that within a few inches of me. I changed my course, went left, suddenly right, zigzagged in a path that defied all reason, contradicted all logic, ran against everything illogical and unreasonable, and still caught every knotted and tangled clump of grass there was between me and my destination, which was, as usual, unknown. It probably wouldn't have bothered me if that had been the only thing tangling me up, but I was also trying to straighten out my thoughts about my adventures. Before leaving my hometown, I thought, no, I was convinced that it was the oddest place on earth and that every other place I would travel to, no matter how odd, would not be as odd and make as little sense. How wrong I was. I wished breaking through the grass was as easy as breaking through my amazement and bewilderment. The two only seemed to encourage each other. I would just begin to straighten out a few thoughts, feel a little smoothness and understanding, when a tangled wad of grass would wrap itself around my leg, trip me up, scatter my thoughts, tumble me backwards, and leave me flat on my back in confusion. To add to all this, the wind, I swear, blew so hard and loud that it sent chaotic vibrations through my brain so that I could not even hear myself think. I began to blame my confusion on the wind. A smooth brown wave would dash across the grass in front of me. No sooner would it travel a short ways than a few gray lines would charge through it, crash into another wall of brown, and send swirls of browns and grays in all directions. They would then disappear in leaps and bounds. I must have crawled on my hands and knees with my eyes closed for over a mile before I rammed headfirst into the side of a road. Saved by civilization.

I jumped up, swung my arms around, leapt onto the road, ran around, hooped and hollered, and then after being satisfied that I was completely unrestrained, stood on the side of the road with my thumb out.

A few went by pretending they didn't see anyone on the road.

Have you ever, when driving down an empty country road, not seen someone standing along the side? I haven't. Then, a pickup truck came along with a man and a woman in it. It wasn't slowing down. I saw the woman watching me as the truck approached. She turned to the driver.

The truck screeched and weaved to a stop. I grabbed my bag, canteen, and binoculars, opened the door, and almost fell over when I saw Pom Pom reaching her hand toward me.

"Pom Pom!"

She too was stunned. Our eyes sank into each others'. I stood there looking at her. Her long, wind blown hair hung in strands around her face. The brightness and blue-green depth of her eyes dazed me. She looked smooth and full — from her full red lips to her breasts pushing out of the top of her halter top to her smooth stomach and handsome silky legs. As I watched her chew her gum with her sparkly white teeth, I started to get excited. On her lap lay a book titled *Life Without a Banana*.

The man yelled, "Come on. Do you want a ride or don't you?"

I hopped in.

She put life into the silence. "Well hello, stranger. Fancy seeing you here!"

"It sure is. Don't we meet in the strangest places?"

She looked me over and said, "Where have you been? You look like someone whipped you and then when they were all done they whipped you again."

"You don't have to tell me. It was that grass out there. And the wind. I fought that stuff every step of the way. What kind of grass is that anyway?"

"I don't know. Plain old grass as far as I know."

The man next to her looked over at me strangely. His face was round and unshaven and had a wild, ornery look that shone in his devious, brown eyes. He leaned forward and encircled the top of the steering wheel with his hands.

"That guy thought he was pretty slick, don't you think? Charging me for whitewall tires and then putting on blackwalls. We got him though, didn't we? Made a bundle on his labor when I made him take off the blackwalls and put on what I paid for. Slick, stupid asshole." He smiled as though he were the cleverest person in the world.

Pom Pom and I still had our eyes on each other.

She said, "Are you still searching for a home?"

"Yeah. I feel that I'm getting closer."

"You do? That's great. Would you like some company?"

I looked over at her friend, "Well..."

He peered at me, "Watch out, buddy, you might have her tagging along. Rebound time."

With her soft, sensuous voice, which reminded me of our meeting (if you can call it that) in Garbageland, she said, "Come on, Bobby, you wanted me before. All you'll have to do is wait an hour or so in town while I get divorced. Come on, I've been waiting longer than that for you." She rubbed up against me and put her arm around my shoulder.

"That's it, yeah Pom Pom, right here in front of me in the truck. Want me to stop so you can get in the back and fuck him while I drive into town?"

"No. I can wait. Anyway, what do you care? You screwed more women after we got together than before."

"So what?" he grinned. "Men can do that. Women can't. What do you say, partner?"

"Anybody can do it," I said.

"Well, maybe he wants to stop."

"Oh, stop it now." She twisted his ear. He yelled.

"This will be the first divorce on record on grounds of the woman abusing the man. I better watch my mouth; she might knock me around the moment I step out of the truck." He laughed.

"Worse than that, I might not divorce you."

"Heaven have mercy," he sighed.

"Are you two really getting divorced?" I asked.

In unison with smiles, "Yep."

"No, you're not really, are you?"

"Yeah, we are, really." She smiled.

"You don't act like it."

She continued, "Why? Can't you be happy when you get divorced?"

"I suppose. But if you're happy, why not stay together?"

Once again in delightful harmony, they said, "Because we don't want to."

"I don't understand. You should be mad at each other. You shouldn't even be driving there together. Isn't one of you even hurt or angry with the other or feeling rejected?"

"Come to think of it," he said, "I'm hurt." He hung his head. "No, I'm mad." He clutched the steering wheel so hard that his knuckles went white. He floored the truck.

"Oh, you silly fool, slow down," she yelled in his ear. He slowed down.

He hung his head again and began to rub his eyes with his right hand as though crying. "I'm hurt. Oh, Pom Pom, you've hurt me so, and rejected, I feel so rejected that my own mother probably won't like me anymore."

"That's nothing new," she quipped.

"Pom Pom, don't hurt me anymore. What do you want me to do, put a gun to my head? Isn't it enough that I'm getting out of your life? What more do you want? What pleasure do you get out of torturing me so? You know what she said to me last night, buddy?"

"No. I wasn't there, was I?"

He looked at her and said, "Where did this guy come from? Is he your long lost brother or lover or what?"

"Not the former but I hope the latter." She tickled my ear.

"Oh, I can barely force myself to repeat it. It hurt me so badly. Talk about hitting below the belt. When we first got together she did other things to me below the belt. How quickly things can turn into the opposite. But, isn't that the cycle of life. Birth, death, wake, sleep, eat, shit, get drunk, sober up, get up, fall down, marry and divorce. Oh well, yes, once she hugged me, now she hurts me. Last night, when I was putting my all into it, I mean all my finesse and experience I've learned all along the way, she said, 'Here comes my man the plumber who thinks I'm a toilet bowl that needs plunging out.' And then a couple seconds later when I thought I was foreplaying her into ecstasy, she says in a monotone, 'Well, change trades already? Now you're a carpenter gone wild with some sandpaper. As long as you're at it, why don't you become an electrician and make my hair stand on end?' And I said, 'I will, as soon as I push in the plug.'"

She slapped him on the arm.

"I'm not only divorcing her for physical abuse but for mental abuse, too. Look at me, do I look like a straight-ahead, no holes barred, bulldozer of a lover?"

"Say yes," she whispered in my ear as I looked at him.

"Don't say it." He grasped his ears with his hands. She grabbed the wheel as the truck veered onto the shoulder.

"For Christ's sake, you'll kill us with your horseplay. Get me there alive? Don't you think there's life after you?"

"Yeah, but it will be so second rate that it won't be worth living."

"Let me be the judge of that." She said.

"Come on, you guys aren't really getting divorced, are you?"

Once again in perfect harmony, "Yes, we are."

"I don't believe it."

Sam looked over at me with hate in his eyes, "You calling me a liar, buddy?"

"No. I think you're just pulling my leg."

"No, not me, but you'd better watch out before she starts pulling something else." He laughed as though no one else in the world could amuse himself more than he.

"We are, Bobby. We really are getting a divorce." She kissed me on the cheek and whispered in my ear, "You sure have a sweet, innocent face."

"What are you saying to him? Arranging a rendezvous for after our divorce?"

"Maybe. But that's none of your business. Is it?"

"Please, be considerate of my tender feelings, Pom Pom. What pleasure do you take in hurting me?"

She turned to me, and in a soft affectionate voice began, "You see, sweet stuff, we are just being honest with each other. Yes, we still like each other, but we don't want to be together anymore. So, why stay together? I've seen too many people stay together, for whatever reason: 'cause of their kids, 'cause they're afraid to be alone, 'cause they're afraid they'll not find another, 'cause they can't make a decision, 'cause of their fear of rejection, 'cause they think it improper, and that once you're married you're bound by God to stay together the rest of your life even though you're both miserable and destroying each other and making home hell on earth. Life is too short for that. Because, the way I feel, I've got my fears, my insecurities, don't we all?; and that's enough. Why let them spread like cancer into other parts of your life, into other people's lives.

"Life is too rich and wonderful to let that stuff spoil it. And spoil it it will! Don't you think so?"

"I couldn't agree more."

Softly she said, "Yes, you could.

"That's why we're getting divorced. We want to feel free that we can do it. We have a, by most standards, nice relationship. But, we can feel this fear and jealousy creeping in, slowly and steadily like gangrene, so to prove to ourselves that we are free and have control over our fears and insecurities, we are going to get a divorce, and to tell you the truth, we probably love and care for each other more than most married couples. You don't see too many couples separating in order to help each other out, do you?"

"No."

"And besides that," she paused, grinned at her mate, and once again, with a perfect blend of their voices, they shouted, "We're not married."

"What?" I wanted to say more, but their hearty laughter spilled over into my vocal chords. We were laughing so hard that she had to grab the wheel once again. After our pleasures subsided, I said, "Really, you're not married?"

"No, really we're not. But we're getting divorced anyway. Aren't we, Sam?"

"As sure as dusk precedes dawn, Pom Pom. We're going to fight for the custody of the children we don't have, quarrel over who gets what, stop talking to each other, stop seeing each other altogether.

"Then I'll go out every night and get drunk and get in fights. She'll be so lonely that she'll be going to bed with every guy in town. She'll probably, after I take everything we have, have to move in with her parents, and then after we make it as miserable as we can for each other, we'll get married. Get that out of the way first, then our life together will be an easy ride down future's lane, just like this old truck cruising down the highway."

"Yeah, last things first," she said.

"Too bad we don't die before we're born, eh Pom Pom?"

"Maybe we do. Even if we don't, our marriage will, eh Sam?"

"Eh, Pom Pom."

"So let's go on a honeymoon after our divorce, eh Pom Pom?"

"Eh, Sam. Let's take this dreamy little fellow with us too, eh Sam?"

"Whatever you say, Pom Pom."

We pulled into a parking space. Sam jumped out. Before I could find the door handle, Pom Pom pressed me against the door and gave me a long kiss on the mouth and then, half-whispering and half-nibbling on my ear, said, "Meet me later at the cliff dwellings by the lake. Okay?"

She leaned away from me and looked at me closely. There was a sadness in her soft eyes. I pulled her to me, and after giving her the same kind of kiss she had given me, said, "I'll be waiting."

I grabbed my things and slipped off the seat onto the brick-paved road. Pom Pom followed and walked over to Sam. They motioned for me to follow.

"No thanks. Thanks for the offer and the ride into town."

"Are you sure?"

"Yeah."

Taking Sam's hand and swinging it in the air, she led him skipping and hopping across the street toward the courthouse.

Some things have to die before other things can begin. I had that feeling when I left my hometown, although I was still doubtful whether the other thing, whatever it was, had ever begun. I wasn't in the same place and surely not in the same time, but still, that didn't mean anything. My adventures had begun; I was in the midst of them, but leaning against that old truck and looking at the dingy buildings and heads bobbing in and out of engine compartments, I wondered if they'd really begun, or if I was just looking at the same things only in different ways. But then, I thought, maybe I just needed something to eat.

Down the street to my left, I noticed a green cloth awning which read, "Cafe." I trudged down the brick-paved walk, almost falling a couple of times after tripping over the uneven bricks which reminded me of the chaos in the field that scattered my thoughts. Not needing any more of that, I turned my eyes away from the bricks onto a storefront window in which was a male mannequin decorated with a pair of jeans with red arrows pointing toward the crotch and a red shirt with an oval cut in the center. Kept on going past a rock shop where dull, boring speckled rocks were perched on disfigured pieces of driftwood, past an alley strewn with trash and broken glass where a couple ragged men were eating broccoli out of a dumpster caked with grease, past a bank and lawyer's office with beveled, stained glass windows and carved oak doors adorned with engraved brass hardware that almost made me puke; was about to turn my head away when I caught sight of a room full of lifeless, plaster-of-Paris women waiting to have a few strands of hair cut by some clown-faced women, and then reached the cafe where I almost got smashed in the face by the door that was recklessly thrown open by a stocky, red man laughing at a prim, tall, pale man.

The squeaky hinges cut through my ears as I walked into the crowded cafe and sat, without looking around, at a table in the middle.

After dropping my bag, canteen, and binoculars on the floor, I looked up to find a petite, young woman sitting across from me. Her delicate face was framed by her bangs and long brown hair that flowed along the side of her face onto her breasts. With neat, smooth lips she said, "Hi, I'm Nancy. What would you like?"

"What do you have?"

"Oh, no menu? Just a minute." She disappeared and reappeared with a menu. "Here you are." She sat back down. "Looks like you could use a shower."

"More than that."

"What else?"

"A home."

"You too? Housing sure is tight, isn't it?"

"Yeah. I'll have a fish dinner with extra coleslaw."

"Sorry, dinner doesn't start until four."

"Could you get it for me anyway? Please?"

She paused. "Yeah, I'll do it. You look like you need someone to do you a favor."

"Thanks."

I sat there for a few minutes as though the only one there. Didn't notice anything, didn't see anyone, didn't hear them, wasn't even aware of thoughts or disturbances in my mind. Everything was empty and still and fresh. In the distance I heard the pleasing sound of the reggae beat.

It gradually became surrounded by voices and smooth guitar playing. On the wall across from me was a scene of an open air market. Everything looked so real that I caught myself getting up to reach for an orange. More real than the painting were the people in the cafe, which I was liking more and more with each new experience. Everyone was comfortably dressed, relaxed, and engaged in lively conversation. I was the only one alone. There were many couples and groups of couples and a long table of boys and girls next to the front window. I sat back, raised my feet up on a chair, leaned my head toward the ceiling, and slumbered to the reggae beat. As I rested, I felt my attention being drawn back to the wholesome women in the room. It seemed that every time I looked at one in particular, she would turn her friendly gaze toward me. How pleasant they were to look upon. I felt overly welcome; so much so that I almost fell asleep. Instead, I went to the men's room and washed.

When I returned, the cute little waitress was sitting at my table with my dinner. As I was lowering myself into my chair, she said, "How do you like that? I even managed to get you the extra coleslaw you wanted? Pretty nice of me, wasn't it?"

"Yes indeed. As pretty and nice as can be."

"Anything else?"

"No. Not really. How long have you been working here?"

"Since it opened. I own the place."

"You do? And you still wait on tables?"

"Only the ones I want to."

"You have a nice place. I love the atmosphere. Is it always so pleasant in here? Everyone in here seems to be in such a good mood."

"I don't let them in if they're not in a good mood." She laughed.

"Really?"

"Yeah. That's my advertisement. Everyone knows that when they come here, everybody will be in a good mood. And the sour pusses know not to bother coming. It's a great place to meet people."

"So I see."

"If you need anything don't hesitate." She turned to leave, turned back around and said with an inviting smile, "Don't hesitate."

"I don't know the meaning of the word."

273

I looked at my plate and for a moment thought that the food was going to get up and dance to the reggae beat. The food was that colorful and vibrant. The melted butter gave a golden sheen to the silvery halibut. The coleslaw reminded me of shiny speckled stones that used to dazzle my senses as they danced beneath the ocean waves along the shore. And the French fries, you know, French fries, just plain ol' everyday French fries, but these were such a cheerful, golden brown that not only looking at them but eating them made me feel more alive.

I stuck a piece of halibut in my mouth, and felt its soft flesh fall apart in flakes to the soft touch of my teeth. After mashing it up to a fine mooch, I slid in some slippery coleslaw. It just sat there in my mouth, like algae on a rock, and slowly changed from being a mound of mooch to a pile of stringy pieces as the dressing dissolved and slid down my throat. The pieces of coleslaw seemed lost and lonely without the dressing holding them together, so I introduced them to a French fry, bonded them together with some molar action, and sent them down to rejoin the Mayo. Each mouthful was a unique sensation and an adventure in itself.

The whole place was swaying to the reggae beat. Everyone was becoming more cheerful, which I had thought was impossible; the colors on the walls, clothes, my food, everything was getting brighter and deeper, and best of all, the women were looking good. So good that I began to crave feminine affection. And if that doesn't make you feel alive, I don't know what will. My craving wasn't the kind that becomes painful in anticipation, but was pleasurable in itself and made me tingle and hum throughout and through in. My body was preparing itself for something special, something sweeter than dessert.

Nancy reappeared and in a clear, sweet voice said, "Everything all right? I've been watching you. You look like you're having the time of your life over here."

"I am. I really am. I feel so good. I am so glad I found this place. The food is great. The people, the music, everything is just fantastic."

"You look ecstatic."

"I am. Oh, thank you so much. What a wonderful place you have here."

I stood, picked her up, and gave her a hug and kiss.

"Wow, what do you do for a tip?"

"Anything you want."

"You do feel good!"

"I do. I'm ready."

"Ready for what?"

"To leave."

"Oh no, so soon?!"

"Yeah. Sorry. I've got to meet someone."

"Are you sure?"

"If I were sure, I wouldn't be adventuring. I'm not completely unsure, just unsure enough to let myself be drawn. How much do I owe you?"

"You? Oh, nothing. I'm glad more men like you don't come in. I'd go broke. Good luck." She ran her hand down my back.

"Thank you very much." I said with a delightful grin. "You and your place have been a godsend to me."

As I opened the door, the squeaky hinges added an interesting background rhythm to the reggae beat. I walked back past the beauty parlor where the women were being together and pampering each other, and then I slowed down as my eyes were pleased by the fine carpentry and metal work on the doors and entry way to the bank and lawyer's office; past the alley which appeared, in an instant, as an intricate collage of shapes, shades, and colors, and in which the same guys were defying the work ethic by living off society's abundant wastes, to the rock shop where I was stopped by the sparkling colors and forms and by the driftwood's smooth, rounded shapes that were formed by the gentle waves of time, and past the zany outfit in the clothes store that sent me laughing across the beautifully patterned red bricks and back toward the grassy meadow from which I had just come.

Chapter 24

This time the grass was so soft and tangle-free that I thought the clouds must have showered it with creme rinse while I was eating. The patterns of the grass, dancing and shifting in the gentle breeze, massaged my imagination and let it roam freely, which, in itself, made me feel at home. Light golden hues misted with green waved outward to the horizon where they leapt up into the sky, drifted back over my head, and teased my mind with their elusive, soft colors. I skipped and hummed and felt so good that it didn't matter if I ever went on another adventure again or ever found a home. I soon felt that I was millions of miles away from civilization where man had never been, on virgin soil, a natural solitary man in the midst of his wide open, natural home. Although I had been through that same field just a few hours before, everything looked new and shined with life from deep within.

Everything, inside and out, felt good. Each little movement of my body, from digging my toes into the dry, red sandy soil to tilting my head back to watch a hawk soar through the soft blue; ooh, even the quick blink of my eye brought a quick blink of pleasure. I moved just to feel pleasure. I looked at pleasure, smelled pleasure, heard pleasure; every sensation, no matter where it came from, was pleasurable. Oh, how alive I felt, how much a part of life. I knew then what Aunt Iris meant when she said heaven was being a part of life. If I could have been flown to the moon, I bet, within minutes after landing, the moon would have instantly transformed into a deliciously, lush orb that would have rivaled the earth. I couldn't tell whether my delight was causing my perceptions to be delightful or the delightful perceptions were making me feel delightful or if I was simply bathing in a pool of delightfulness that had no boundaries. I didn't wonder about it for long. Things were too delightful to be bothered by wondering why they were so.

Skipping along, sliding through the grass, feeling time was moving forward, I almost sailed over a ledge to my death. I thought the world could not become any more beautiful, but as I looked down, I almost fainted in awe. Who would have thought such lushness would have existed in that arid land? Large pine and aspen trees soared from the canyon floor. Green was sprinkled everywhere with brilliantly colored flowers. Vines hung majestically in the trees.

From my perch, I could faintly see a stream flowing in and out of the thick growth.

Before long, I was upon a spongy overgrown path that lead down into this other world. Lifting my legs while letting gravity carry me down, I bounced down the path about a hundred yards to a small hill. With delicate steps I walked up the hill to the top. As I slid down the other side on my rear, the entire hill quivered.

Hitting the bottom, I jumped up and again bounced along my way. A cool, moist breeze rose up from below and spread a tingling mist all over me. Hot, dry air from above breezed by, leaving me fresh and dry. The two breezes continued to exchange places as I ventured down into the cool, moist valley.

The path lead down to the stream. It flowed over solid rock. I knelt in the stream and took a long, slow drink. The water was clear and clean, and its coolness spread throughout my chest. I followed the path back up above the stream bed onto a dry, rocky area.

Coming up on a porcupine sitting on the path, I yelled and jumped up and down and sounded as fierce as I could, but he only looked at me with an expression that said, "I was here first," so I finally walked around him, then came upon a small herd of deer grazing beside the path. They barely noticed me as I walked past and patted a doe on the head.

I continued following the path as it rose and fell and went back and forth across the stream. Large cottonwood, spruce and aspen trees grew along the stream. Each time I approached the stream, fish darted all around. I walked deeper and deeper into the valley and felt life wrap itself around me. The plants seemed more alive, the colors shined, the shapes were more definite, and the stream was telling me secrets. Everything felt closer in a deep, vague way. The plants brushing up against me felt good.

The stream disappeared in a meadow of tall, silky grass. The large trees forked around the meadow making an oval. I ventured to my right across the stream toward a large south-facing cave in the side of a light red sandstone cliff. In the meadow there were many edible wild plants, domestic vegetable plants that had gone wild, berry bushes, and fruit and nut trees. I stopped a few times to gather some food.

At the base of the cliff was an incline of fallen rocks upon which I climbed to a flat area in front of the large shallow cave. In the cave were ancient dwellings. A thin sheet of water, flowing down the back of the cave, made the rock appear fluid. I was drawn to one dwelling with a short door and a long, horizontal opening across the front. Breathing slowly and deeply, I strolled up to the house and bent through the doorway onto the earthen floor. My head brushed the ceiling when I stood. I walked to my left, placed my bag, canteen, and binoculars on the floor, and, in the side of the cliff, washed my face in a bowl through which water bubbled up from the bottom and overflowed out the back, down the wall, and into a long crack in the floor. I returned to the outside, gathered an armful of soft grass, and spread it on the floor of the house in the sun.

After taking off my clothes, I lay on the grass and let its sweet smell lull me to sleep.

I dreamed I was lying next to a lake fingering the water and watching the ripples spread across it. The ripples turned into waves. I fingered the water again, hopped a wave, rode across the lake, bounced off the other side, and on the way back, jumped on a raft and raced down the lake, which had turned into a river. In a grassy meadow lying on my back, I was picking dainty flowers and seeing a different universe in each one. After examining them, I ran them softly up and down my body, which with one stroke was a man's and the other a woman's. The woman's body gave me more pleasure than the man's. A small deer staggered out of the grass and collapsed on my chest. Her blood ran down my stomach, between my legs, and up inside me. I felt helpless and vulnerable. With all my strength I pushed her off and licked clean the wound in her side. I spoke to her softly while I stroked her head, "It will be okay. It's okay. You will live." She then said, "You can save me. You can. Love me. Help me." With all my strength I picked her up and started carrying her through the grass toward the lake. A large bear-like man appeared and growled, "I'll help you." He pulled a large knife covered with dried blood, grabbed the deer by the head, and just as the knife touched her neck, I yanked her away and began to run with my free arm stretched out in front of me. I could hear and smell him right behind us but was afraid to look back. I stretched with all my strength, slowly left the ground, and soared high above his head. Everything was gray and misty. I began falling. I let her go. She drifted away from me as I fell. I was kneeling on the ground looking at a naked woman trying to crawl out of the narrow hole. She pushed up toward the surface. I picked up a sharp stick and poked her in the shoulder. She fell. Blood flowed down her shoulder. She tried again and I jabbed the stick into her forehead. Blood flowed down her face into her eyes. Each time she tried I rammed her with the stick. I didn't dislike her nor did I like her. I just wanted her to stay where she was. She cried, "Help me. Please don't. Help me." I was stumbling up a rocky, barren mountainside marred with burnt oak brush. The wind blew hard and cold. Out of a cave to my right, a female voice screamed, "Help me. Please don't. Help me." I stopped, listened to her calls for help, and feeling nothing, turned and trudged up the mountain. The wind became colder and stronger, and it started to rain. I pulled the collar of my long, gray coat up around my neck, stumbled and fell over jagged rocks, reached the top of the mountain, and dropped down the other side into a desert of black sand.

Chapter 25

I woke, and while thinking about my dreams which were as fresh and immediate as the air, felt my soul fill with love. I loved my hands, my face, my back, my thoughts, my dreams, the grass upon which I was lying, the cave dwelling, the earth, the air, the movement of my muscles as I raised myself up, and as I looked out the window toward the expansive meadow, I loved the woman sitting on the rocks with her back toward me.

I crawled out through the door, and as I neared Pom Pom she turned, and I said, "Hi, Pom Pom. Well, here we are together, alone. Don't we meet in the strangest places?"

"Yes. I was thinking the same thing myself. Who are you, really?"

"I'm Bobby the Lovegod." I laughed.

"Yeah! Right!"

"Since I woke from my nap I feel full of love. So I'm a lovegod. I am. I love everything. Please don't think I am some kind of sex maniac waiting here to pounce on unsuspecting maidens. I'm not that kind of lovegod or rather devil, but I am Bobby the lovegod. Really.

"Watch, I'll prove it to you." I gave her a quick sample of the lovegod wiggle dance. "And besides that, look around at this lovely, lush island in the middle of the desert. Where else would you find a lovegod?"

"Well," she looked me up and down, "that's good enough for me."

"I thought it would be."

"Pretty cocky, aren't you, Lovegod?"

"I should hope so." I accompanied that with another wiggling tease.

"So should I. Aren't you going to show me your domain?"

"It will be our pleasure."

"Good. You shouldn't be the only one having a good time."

"Don't you worry your sweet, little self about that. I'm a lovegod, aren't I."

"We'll see."

I took her by the hand and lead her down the rocks. After a few steps I stopped, pointed at the rocks, and said, "These are rocks."

She nodded her head. A little farther in the grass I stopped and said, "This is grass." She nodded her head. Some more movement over to an old peach orchard, stopped again, and said, "This here is a peach tree." I picked a peach and gave it to her. "And you see this little thing here?" I pointed to a green, furry thing chewing on a leaf. "I'll prove to you once again to dispel any doubts concerning my lovegod status by informing you that I have named all the creatures. Who else but a god or a man created directly by God could do something like that? This thing's name is Teresa Johnson." A bird landed on the branch and ate Teresa Johnson. "Its name is Brian Johnson. And do you see that thing squirreling up those nuts. Its name is none other than Matilda Johnson."

"They all have the same last name."

"Of course. They are all related. What else do you expect?"

"If they're related, they shouldn't be eating each other."

"They shouldn't! What can be more intimate than to eat another? Hey, there goes Heratio Johnson." I pointed to a mouse running through the grass. "Come on, I'll show you some more of my domain."

As we continued on our tour through a cool clump of aspen trees, the dew from ferns and other low plants rubbed off on us and made my skin tingle and perk up, which was something I needed. I told her the names of the animals we saw, and her face shone with the same excitement as those riding cross-country on a bus. The forest became thicker, the underbrush more lush and green, and soon we heard the stream.

She yanked my arm and said, "If this is your domain, Lovegod, then you must have control over this. Gods have control where others do not. That's why they're called gods. How do you control this place? What do you do to insure this remains lovely? You must have set down some commandments or rules for your own and others' conduct."

"You mean the dos and don'ts?"

"Yes. You just don't let desires run wild, do you?"

"Well, let me see. I never do what I don't and I've never not done what I didn't do and before I do something I never wonder if I shouldn't do it and after I do something I'm more than willing to do it again. So, I guess I do what I do and don't what I don't."

"But how do you know everything you do will be good and enhance the beauty of this lovely place?"

"How do I know? I don't have to know. I don't even have to think about it. All my desires are desires of love. I'm a lovegod."

"So you do let your desires run wild?"

"I wouldn't say they run wild. They run. They run me. And I don't think I'm wild, do you?"

"Not yet. Although, for all I know you could be holding yourself back."

"Oh, no, never. At least not now. It's hard to explain, really. You see, I'm new at this. I've only been a lovegod for a few minutes. But you know, now that I feel about it, I may have been a lovegod for a long time and have never known it. All I feel is love and what I'm loving. I don't feel any anger, frustration, sadness, confusion, envy, possessiveness — nothing but unified love. So why should I worry. Everything I do will simply be lovely and not hurt anything."

I fondled a few succulent leaves next to me. "Look at the white puffball clouds floating in the deep blue sky. How beautiful!" I stretched my arms and jumped in and out of the sky. That started to get me excited. I kept on jumping up and down, started dancing, wiggling all over, and singing at the top of my lungs, "Oh, I love the grass and I love the trees, Sam Johnson flying overhead, Delilia Johnson bounding through the fields, oh I love fire, I love myself, I love you, I love to drink wine and dance all night, I love this stream here and oh, oh, oooh." I slid down a smooth clay bank, fell backwards in the stream, and while floating away on my back, waved and sang, "I love watching the world go by while streaming in time."

I used to have and still do have a reccurring dream of floating in a stream with a smooth clay bottom and sides. My dream had become real. I bounced off the soft clay side, flipped, and diving downward, let the forceful stream glide me along the soft clay bottom.

I kept on gliding up and down like a dolphin. Then I floated on my back. The leaves on the trees danced and reminded me of the dancing patterns of human lives. Large gray boulders along the banks, masking some hidden significance and breaking up the web of green and brown, made a mysterious impression on me. Suddenly the stream narrowed, deepened and picked up speed. I flipped over, stretched out like Superman, and was pulsated along as the stream narrowed and widened, and then it became so narrow that my shoulders scraped the sides, and with great force I was shot out into the air, awhoopin' and ahollerin', and fell a long way into the lake. I swam toward a sandy cove.

While I was being carried along, Pom Pom was walking through the woods toward the lake thinking to herself, "Why am I here? Why am I meeting this guy alone? He's cute. He's got a cute butt. What nerve he had walking out of that cave dwelling with no clothes on. I wonder if he's affectionate. It cracked me up when he was naming all the animals Johnson." She laughed to herself. "He does seem different. He is. After I heard about him escaping from the Land of Boxes with Eddie, I wanted to know him even more. Now is my chance to get to know him. I better get to know him now; who knows when I'll see him again. But, I've always managed to see him in an unplanned way. And all that stuff he said about me talking through my grandfather — that is just wild. But I like wild men. Yeah, I'm here because I want to know him. But, Pom Pom, be careful. Let's not bounce from one guy to another. They all seem nice at first, but then later, as you get to know them, they are not that nice and they hurt you. Be careful. He may not be different in the way you want him to be."

She sat on a dead log on the shore and watched me swim toward her. I glided up to her, and still lying in the water, rested my head on my hands. She smiled and said, "I thought you said you never hold yourself back?"

"I don't. I was letting my desires carry me along."

"Oh yeah! It seems to me you were just looking for an opportunity, or more like an excuse, to let yourself get excited over something."

I stood up and said, "Well, excitement is always a possibility that with a little help and encouragement becomes an actuality."

She looked me in between the legs and said, "So I see."

I crossed my legs, covered my penis with my hands, and pretending to look embarrassed, said, "Some things just can't be helped."

"I can help it."

"I wish you would. I could use some help."

"Couldn't we all. I need help."

The feeling of making a serious mistake seized her. She felt that she should stay away from men for a while, get some distance between her and her relationships so that she could understand them better instead of falling into the same old trap. How can I get out of here, she thought, without hurting his feelings and ruining all chances of ever seeing him again?

Her body stiffened. Her face became pale. A helpless fear glazed over her eyes. I began to ache. My muscles even started feeling sore. I walked out of the water to her, and after taking what felt like a surfboard into my arms, said, "It will be all right. It will. It really will. Love will make everything all right." I could feel her quivering on the inside, her shallow, rapid breathing, and then she gradually began shaking all over as her breathing became even more erratic.

I thought for a moment she might crumble into the sand, and then, as though she were having an orgasm, her whole body started to convulse, and after each convulsion I could feel some of her tension being released until she was limp. I had to hold her up.

She began to cry and said, "I'm sorry; I must leave. I'm so embarrassed. Please forgive me."

"Please don't go. Why are you going?"

"I just have to. Please don't ask why. Don't be mad at me."

"Come on, give it a chance. Forget I'm even here. This place is enchanted. Believe me, it is. Everything feels so close. I want to find a home but now I don't care. I'm just happy with how close and real everything is. No, really, don't look at me like that. Come here and sit down and feel. Come on, please don't leave. Trust me. I won't hurt you. Here, come here. I'll prove it to you. I won't bother you. Come here. Sit back down on this dead tree, please? I don't want you for anything. I just want you to feel the enchantment. I'll even leave you alone." I dove into the lake and swam away.

Pom Pom was stunned that I swam away. She relaxed, and moving her foot back and forth through the sand, thought about how close everything felt. She had felt, while following the same path as I into the Land of Love, everything become more alive and closer to her, and in feeling that way she felt more attracted to everything and everything became more lovely. And as she sat free to do as she pleased and watched me swim in the lake, she felt the valley surround and protect her, and she felt love fill her up. What had happened to me was happening to her. She felt love for everything: the sand, the dead tree, the lake, the sky, her life, me, and most of all, she felt love in her passion for living, which was enjoying a rebirth since her escape from the Land of Boxes.

"I want to do everything with passion," she said to herself, "and right now I want to passionately swim with that lovegod out there."

She took off her clothes, folded them neatly on the dead log, turned to go in, turned back, threw her clothes on the grass, and took the plunge.

I was swimming underwater watching fish swim in and out of crevices in the rocky sides of the cliff. Her shadow floated through mine as she swam beneath me, surfaced, and said with a smile, "I'm sorry for what happened back there. Thanks for swimming away. I just, well, I'll tell you, I was afraid I was bouncing into a trap with another man. I've always felt comfortable with you, even though I don't know you. Who are you really?"

"I'm not really a lovegod. I'm a he-devil."

"Come on. Really, who are you?"

"Here. Swim over here. There's some rock ledges we can stand on."

Holding her I said, "I'll tell you a story Aunt Iris once told me. It's a story about how the universe was born. God and the Devil used to make love only to themselves. All of God's offspring would live forever, and as a result, limit creation. The Devil's offspring would always die before they were born. After God saw this, she said to the Devil, 'Let's love each other, and by sharing in each other, we will give birth to a child. We will teach this child everything we know and it will live long and prosper. We will name our child Universe.' That's where the saying comes from, 'Every person is a world unto himself.' It comes from the old tale that every offspring of God and the Devil is a universe unto itself. Without God and the Devil loving each other, there would be no birth and death, no day and night, no summer and winter, no stars in the night, no symmetry, and no love between a woman and a man."

"Hmmmm, interesting."

"And what's more is that love switches their sex. That way both can enter into and know each other. That's why sex for the woman is empty when the man does not let her inside. Anyway though, the devil is usually a male. So I'm a he-devil while you're a she-god. A lovegod."

"Why is God a woman?"

"Because God is creative."

"So," she said, "I'm a lovegod or a she-god. This place is enchanted. I've never felt this way before. I care about what you said and I also don't care. How can I feel both things? And I think it's corny, but true.

"I've been thinking about you ever since I met you in the park. I never left that night. I needed to leave with someone. It was a setback for me when you failed to show up. I was so disappointed. I sat by myself in the park and cried."

"I'm sorry for making you cry."

"That's sweet of you. You don't have to be sorry. It wasn't your fault."

"Yeah, I know. I just said that to make you feel better."

"Thanks. I'm okay now. I heard what happened. How's your leg?"

"Fine. I ran through the park on the way out of town to see if maybe you had come early. I was disappointed too. I've been thinking about you too. When did you leave?"

"Shortly after you. Now that I look back it wasn't that hard.

"Passion pulled me along. Now it all comes back; I really wanted to tell you about passion, oh yes, but I had to leave, oh yes." Pom Pom paused for a moment, then words poured out of her. "The lack of passion in my life was killing me. I didn't really care to cheer for most people. I was trained to do it. Besides that, most people don't care about themselves. They don't want to try to cheer themselves up.

"So why should I care for them? They'd just as soon live their fake, varnished-over lives and do what they're supposed to do, and if nobody really bothers them or they don't experience great discomfort, they'd just as soon do as they're told until they die. Because if someone else didn't tell them what to do, they wouldn't know what to do.

"They'd wake, sit at the edge of their bed, wonder what to do, and if hunger pains didn't move them to get a job so they could stuff their faces, they'd just sit there in a vacant gaze until they dropped to the floor in a heap and decayed into dirt. I may not know what I want to do with my life, but what I do, I want to do with passion." She relaxed with tears. "I don't want to, I don't want to, I don't want to be dying and think that all I've done is live the life I was supposed to live. You know, then I will feel that I have not lived, just as I feel now that I have not lived. Life is passion. I know it is. I know it is! If I know anything, I know that.

"Don't you think so? How can we live without passion? Even when I eat, I don't want to eat just to keep alive. I want to enjoy feeling the fruit in my hands, take pleasure in sinking my teeth into its juicy interior and feel its life sustaining mine. There is something truly passionate and mysterious about eating. We live by consuming life, by life consuming itself. Life lives by passionately loving itself. I want to love myself. I don't want to be afraid to show myself to the world. I want to be proud of myself, of what I really am. How can I be proud in this get-up?" She looked down. "Oh, I got so carried away that I forgot I took off my clothes." We laughed.

Her eyes were bloodshot. Mascara had wept under her eyes. She looked at me then lowered her eyes. I put my arms around her waist, drew her to me, and said, "Pom Pom, you should be proud of yourself. You should be proud that you do not want to live an unlived life. I am proud of you. Aren't you being passionate now?"

She looked up, smiled, and her vitality broke through as she said, "Yeah, I guess so. But I've always thought that passion should be pleasurable." She laughed, ran her hands up the back of my legs, and pressed her sex against mine.

I kissed her and said, "Let's go up on top of this cliff near the stream. There's some nice soft grass up there."

"That sounds lovely."

We dove in together. I swam beneath her and blew bubbles along the length of her body. She dove under, placed her hands on my waist; I held her under her arms, and together we spun through the water.

We let go of each other as we bubbled up to the surface. I dove under; she followed. We rolled around and played like that on our way over to the shore.

We walked out of the lake holding hands. She stopped, placed her other hand on my shoulder, and as I put my hand on the small of her back, she said, "I'm glad I stayed. I almost left."

"Yeah. I thought you were going to."

"What would you have done?"

"Let you go."

"You would have? But don't you want me?"

"Yes, oh yes. But not if you don't want me."

We kissed.

"I do want you," she said. "But as much as I want to be passionate, to be spontaneous, I can feel myself holding back, even in this enchanted Land of Love. I've been hurt in love. My relationships always seem to be the same. That's why I'm hesitant with you."

"I won't hurt you. I can't. I'm a lovegod."

"I thought you were a he-devil."

"Yeah. I'm that too. What don't you like about your relationships? You seemed to get along well with Sam."

By this time we were walking up the side of the hill toward a plateau.

"He can be fun. We were just goofing around trying to make things work when we knew, well I knew, that they couldn't. He's a baby boss. I always get with those types. He's helpless. He can't do anything by himself. All he does is his job. He can't wash his clothes, can't wake himself up in the morning, can't fix his own food, can't initiate a conversation about anything that matters, can't even drive to the store by himself; he has to have me with him. He can't even be alone in the house for a few hours without getting drunk. And he thinks his cesspool of helplessness is a throne. He's always bossing me around. He doesn't like it when I go out alone with my friends. "He's got to be there. I'm his slave, wàs, that is. But, he's the real slave — a slave to his dependency. If I ever have a child I'll make sure, especially if I have a son, that he is independent. I won't raise a baby boss to be a drag on another woman's life.

"But, I was a part of it. Can't blame him for the way I was. I was born a cheerleader. Used to make me feel good to take care of a man, and when I wasn't, I'd feel worthless and guilty. That's not love. It isn't love to help keep someone dependent.

"What really hurts me, this has happened with most men I've known, is that, men — they stand around gawking at us women, making dirty comments, trying to think up something clever. They think it's flattering. It's not, it's humiliating. They act as though we should be grateful to go to bed with them cause they're such great lovers.

"Why is it that after men come, is it that they feel they've had sex with their moms? Is it because all we are is a way for a man to release himself, and afterwards all he can do is turn away in shame because all we've done is replace his hands and leave us alone feeling his shame and disgust? How can I feel passion for a man who treats me that way? How can I love him? How can I love a man who treats me like a slave, has no respect for my goals and ambitions in life, who starts hating me when I don't do what he wants, and only cares about his needs. I can't. I've tried to. I want someone I can love, someone who is kind. I have a lot of love to give."

"Yes, you seem like you do." We were now standing on the soft grass looking across the lake to the ocean. She sat down. I laid my head on her lap and said, "I was serious when I said I was proud of you. You understand a great deal."

"Why thank you." She blushed.

I said, "You know, we all are squeezed in different molds. Men in one kind, women in another. But, essentially, there isn't much difference in the sexes. Don't we want the same things? Don't people want to love and be loved, have a roof over their heads and food in the refrigerator, be free to express themselves and realize their talents, feel their work is meaningful and their life is worth living, have friends and be respected. We are all human beings, aren't we?"

"You're the kind of man I could love. It isn't enough to be loved. Everyone talks about the need to be loved. But are we just passive blobs waiting to be loved into the human form? I don't want that. I want to actively love. I want to be passionate in living. Then my sex, as part of my life, will be passionate. Who will there be to give love when all everyone wants is to be loved? To only selfishly want love, you dry up the person who is giving. I should know. I have given and given and given until my love has turned into resentment. But you, my lovegod or he-devil or whoever you are, you aren't a taker. I can tell." She paused, looked deeply into my eyes, and said, "Yes, you are a man I could love."

"I hope so. And if I'm not what you want, I'll become whatever you want."

"No, you wouldn't! Would you?"

"No. I'm just teasing. Take me as I am or don't take me at all."

She smiled and said, "I'll take you now with whipped cream and later with chocolate.

"I'm still holding myself back. I should be able to extend myself in the Land of Love. Yes, I'll say it; I love you. I felt I would love you the moment I saw you. Something came alive in me for you then. It feels so good to have told you that. All that stuff I've been saying about love and passion, my mind has been on it since I saw you. Now, finally, that we're alone, I can tell you because I know you feel the same way." She paused. "You do, don't you?"

"I sure do. You know when I fell for you?"

"When?"

"In the Land of Boxes when I saw you trying to get rid of your box."

"I still want to get rid of it. Here, I'll give it to you."

I was still lying with my head on her lap. I looked up at her; her dreamy green eyes were swimming in water. I was full of love for her. Before, with other women, I could not have been naked for so long without becoming eager, but with her, I wasn't in a hurry. I felt I had been in her by her childlike way of expressing her innermost concerns to me. I was content to look at her, hear her voice, watch her expressions, and feel closer and closer with each passing moment.

She looked at me with tenderness. I felt that she genuinely loved me.

I kissed her stomach and immediately wanted to be as close to her as I could for as long as possible. I turned, ran my right hand along the side of her breast to her back, and as I pulled her toward me, she slid down, pressed herself to me, and made me feel at home. Soon we were found in each other's love.

Chapter 26

Most of that day we enjoyed in the orchard. Toward evening we returned to the lake.

We were sitting next to the falls with our legs dangling over the edge of a cliff watching swallows weave their invisible patterns in the air. They slowly moved along the lake, a few at a time, until there was only one swallow left, free to fly wherever she wanted without fear of tangling with a fellow bird.

Pom Pom looked at me and said, "What do you think, lovegod, can we only be free when alone? Do we have to give up our freedom to not be alone? Why can't we be with others and feel free? Now I feel both free and not alone, cause I'm really with you, but this is not real.

"In real life, I lose my freedom when with someone. So what am I to do, which is more important — to be free or to be with someone?"

"Why can't you be with someone and also be free?" I asked.

"It's not just me but everyone I see, really, maybe it's just because I was born and raised in the Land of Foxes, no, I mean the Land of Boxes, but everyone has a plan for everyone else. No matter who I've been with, they have a role for me to play in their life's plan. It's never what I have in mind, and I must admit, I have a plan for them too. So we try to force each other into roles, all for the sake of not being alone. But, even that can turn on itself.

"Sometimes, I'm the loneliest when I'm with someone. It's the contrast of what I feel should be that makes me feel lonelier than if I were by myself. Lately with Sam, although on the surface it seems we're close because we can still joke around, I feel like we're in plastic bubbles, passing back and forth, bumping off each other without making contact. It's all so useless; isn't it? With someone, without someone, we're still alone.

"Sometimes, it's such a contradiction, you're supposed to feel close, feel joined with another living breathing human being, like when we made love today — I felt that way; but sometimes with Sam, when we were drifting apart in our plastic bubbles, I felt my loneliest when we were making love — that's a joke, when we were screwing. I'd feel that he was intruding into the only place where I could be myself, into the privacy of my inner self. Yet, at the same time, I wanted him there, not really him, but someone. That's what's painful when there's no one you really want." She put her arm over my shoulder and said, "Things have changed now. I want you."

"You have me."

"You mean I had you."

"That too, and you can have me for dinner if you want."

She slapped my shoulder and frowned, "Come on now, I'm serious. These are delicate feelings you're dealing with." She smiled and kissed me. "I love it when you joke with me."

"That's not all you love."

"Yeah, I know. I love you."

We kissed and touched and then she said, "I remember, that's an understatement, I'll never forget; it was such a realization for me; my friends and I had planned a surprise birthday party for one of our friends. She had just gotten out of the hospital, so it was a-happy-you're-better-birthday party. I was really excited about it. She's my best friend. I had been looking forward to this party for weeks.

"This guy I was with then starts getting jealous about me spending all this time and effort on the party. He never said so. He would have never admitted to it. So one night I was late to meet him for dinner — not by much — just ten minutes or so. I apologized and everything, but he gces on and on about how I didn't have respect for him, made a fool of him by letting him sit at a table alone and all this other nonsense, and so he says he's not going to the party with me. I was crushed.

"That's how he wanted me to feel. And he thought that I wouldn't go alone. Nothing in the world would have stopped me. So I went alone, which was for me—'cause I've always got a guy — really different. And just to get under his skin, because he really wanted to ruin my night, I dressed to kill.

"For some reason that night I felt very independent, tightly contained within myself. Sometimes when you go places alone you can feel more lonely by taking on others' perception of yourself as being alone, like a kind of magnification, but that night it didn't matter to me what anyone thought. I was standing alone watching everyone — the couples together, the games, the come-ons, the teasing, all that stuff, and I felt removed from it all, and it all seemed so phony; that they were together having fun when really it was to cover-up their loneliness. They were all lying to themselves and the world that they were not alone. And everything they did was an attempt to bury the truth under tons of lies. People's lives are lies."

She stood and cheered,

"We are living lies.

Lying to ourselves till we die.

And from our deathbed we shall see

That our filled lives were empty."

Then repeatedly, with her hands cupped around her mouth, she yelled, "Living lies." Her voice echoed around us.

She burst out laughing, placed her hand on my penis and said, "Come on lovegod, lie with me about your love."

"Whatever you say. I am your slave. My purpose is to please you, for that will make me free."

"Does this please you?" She caressed my face with her hands and gave me a warm kiss.

"Yes. But first, tell me, what is this lying business you're getting so excited about? I want to know more. Boy, if you get this excited over a lie, I'd like to lay a few truths on you."

"You can lay anything on me."

I softly ran my hands up and down her spine and kissed her breasts.

"That's all, Lovegod? Please don't stop until you're finished."

"Come on, you ornery thing. You should talk about stopping before finishing. You've got me on the edge. Please, I can't take it. Finish me off."

She jumped up and started to push me off the cliff. I grabbed the smooth rock, but kept on sliding.

"Have mercy. Please. You shouldn't treat your lovegod this way."

"Oh lovegod, I'm sorry. I'll get you off the way you want."

She sat behind me with her legs along the sides of mine, ran her fingers up and down my penis until we had erected an extremely healthy, ten foot hard-on. She withdrew her legs behind my back, and I thought — how wonderful, Pom Pom is going to come around front to extend my mighty ten footer into a monstrous twenty footer with some poignant oral instructions — but suddenly she jerked her hands back, and with a smooth thrust of her legs, sent me flying head over head off the edge of the cliff, and as my lovegod luck would have it, I landed on my head.

After bubbling up to the surface, I floated on my back, and while waving my demon in the air, wondered how many women I could take for a ride on my magic wand.

From below I yelled up, "How can you resist?"

From above she yelled down, "I can't."

She disappeared and then reappeared as her lovely form arched through the air, hit the head of my dandy dick, and when they both hit the water, every man's dream sprung up and bounced me about fifteen feet out of the water. She swam up to me and said, "Is that the way you wanted to get off?"

"Not exactly, but it will do."

"You're lucky you landed in deep water."

"Yeah, I know. I'd hate to be the first and only man impaled on his own prick."

"I wouldn't like to see you hurt in any way."

We were both treading water. My wonder wang rose about five feet out of the water then disappeared. Pom Pom reached down to find my sex as it should be and said, "What happened?"

"I couldn't feel anything because everything was so stretched out. Anyway, where would I ever find a woman with that much depth? And how could I make love to the woman I love? But enough of that. I want to know more about lies. Let's swim over to the sandy cove where we can lie together."

As we were walking out of the water, she pulled me to her and said, "Let's stay here. It is so beautiful in this spot."

It was. The red cliffs streaked with bands of white wrapped around and dropped behind us to a small, sandy beach. From where we stood, we could see the distant sand dunes and the ocean. The sounds of the sea softly caressed our ears. A few stars twinkled in the deep blue twilight sky. The cool evening air floated around us, and then warm air, flowing off the sun-baked cliffs, breezed by and warmed us.

The cool and warm air kept exchanging places just as they had when I entered that magical land. I really felt that I was in another world, which shocked me because the only way I felt I would ever do that would be by leaving the planet.

We held each other as close as we could. She lifted her head off my shoulder, leaned back, and said, "How do I know the origin of my feelings? I want you. I feel so close to you. I don't want to sound like a worn out cliché, but I feel at one with you. I'm free but not alone. I wish this were real. It's the enchantment of this place. I feel like I'm in a dream. So how do I know? Are my feelings of aloneness covered up or am I really a part of everything? And I feel such a strong desire for you. Why is that? Is it because of my genuine love for you, or is it because I want to lose my loneliness by becoming absorbed in your life?"

"I don't think this place is unreal," I said. "The cold separateness of everyday life is unreal. The closeness and love we are feeling is the possibility of what we can become. I truly believe that. We are getting a glimpse of what our future is, of what it is to feel at home both in ourselves and the world. I feel so happy now. I feel that I'm going to find a home.

"It's so nice standing here with you, feeling your skin against mine, feeling your stomach and breasts move against mine as we talk, hearing your thoughts. I could stand like this with you for a long time.

"It's feeling the love in this enchanted land that makes me feel at home. Aunt Iris used to say that love bonds us to life. Now I know it's true. We need to share in more love than what our parents gave us. I said that to Eddie after we escaped from the Land of Boxes. I wasn't sure about it then, but now I feel it in my heart.

"Somehow we have to move ourselves into more of love's flow, then we can be anywhere with anyone and feel free to be ourselves. What you are doing, I believe, is part of it. It's your love for yourself, your love to live a passionate, free life and honestly look at the cause of your enslavement to others, instead of reacting defensively to your loneliness, that is the beginning of it. So, my lovely friend, I believe you can be free and with others. Being with others doesn't have to mean being tied into the roles others have for you, for they don't tie you, your fear of experiencing separation from life does. So, what do you think about that, my love?"

"I think, oh, feeling you so close it's hard to think."

I kissed her neck, glided my hands down her back to her hips, pressed us together, and said, "Does that help?"

"All depends on what you're trying to help. While I have hold of this thought, oops, there it goes. Who wants to think when feeling like this? I feel the best I've ever felt. I am so much in love. Here it comes, I better say it before it leaves again.

"What you've said is what I've been feeling about passion.

"Passion is living actively. It's the same feeling I've been having, I think, that you call becoming more a part of life. When I asked you if we could be free and not alone, I wasn't sure, but now I know we can. Since I went to that party alone, I have pretty much stayed in that way of perception. I'm not looking to you to end my loneliness, I'm looking to myself. That, in itself, makes me feel much freer and more able to give to those I love while not looking for what I can get from others." She looked closely at me.

"I couldn't agree with you more."

"Yes, you could."

She gently showed me the way home and made me feel more than welcome. But for some reason, perhaps because I was tired of thinking, I felt playful and went soft. She looked concerned and said, "What's wrong, lovegod, don't I agree with you?"

"Oh, yes. Nothing could be more agreeable. I'm just demonstrating to you what is known as the lovegod control."

"Hmmm. So that's what you call that."

She firmly pressed herself against me as she held my cheeks and drew me farther inside. Still soft and confident, I got a bored look on my face and stared off into the distance. I felt a few sensations but nothing to get excited about. I started whistling a tune. After the third note, I puckered to produce a long note, but quite by surprise, a chirp popped out as my desire disagreed with me and started to agree with her. I splashed some water between us to try to cool off. Waves of pleasure repeatedly waved through me, but before they made it to the shore, they crashed and crumpled against the wall of my lovegod control. Sticking out my chest, I rocked my shoulders back and forth and got a cool triumphant look on my face.

She ran her hands along my back to the sides of my head, and after giving me the sweetest kiss I had ever felt, I said to myself,

298

"You'd got to have the devil in you to resist this." Together we circled upward, higher and higher, exploring each plateau to its fullest before moving on. I felt we were going to fly over the top, but somehow she held us right below it, pushed it away, lifted us higher, edged us closer and closer until I felt I could not absorb anymore pleasure, but no, she didn't let us go. Becoming tighter and tighter, like the string on a bow, I felt that if the archer would not release me soon I would snap. She pressed her soft lips against my ear and whispered, "What's wrong, lovegod? Why aren't you coming?"

Being a man and wanting to take credit for a lovely situation, I somehow uttered, "It's my lovegod control."

"Well, how does your lovegod control like this?"

At that moment I was convinced she wasn't a she—god but a pure she-devil when she gently rubbed my ass and started tickling my balls.

I started laughing, burst over the top, shot out of the water, and fell back quivering and flopping around like a spastic fish. Our love slowly spread throughout the lake. I floated on my back in the warm water with my arms and legs spread. I felt her hands and held them.

It was almost dark. The deep, dark blue sky sparkled with its millions of stars. The sky descended, absorbed the lake, and encircled us. We were floating in an oval. Slowly we floated out of time into a pool of timeless tenderness. The universe stopped. We were in lovegod heaven.

I stood up in the shallow water, lifted her into my arms and whispered, "Let's go before it gets dark."

She sighed, "I'm with you."

Hand in hand we walked on the warm sand. Every so often a cool breeze would interrupt the warm, moist air and cause us to quicken our pace and get closer to each other. We turned to our left, climbed over red sandstone, and continuing the way we had come through the woods and meadow, arrived at the cliff dwelling where I picked her up, carried her into the house, and laid her on the soft grass bed.

She lit a fire and spread the fruits, nuts and vegetables we had gathered that afternoon on a small wooden slab next to the bed. She leaned over and gave me a long, soft kiss. Everything was still in quiet, except for the crackling of the fire. We ate slowly and fed each other without talking. We were content. The food, in spite of the faint light, appeared bright and exceptionally real and close. I picked up a pear, and its color and fine composition pressed upon my senses as never before. It was as if I had never seen a pear before. I bit through the tight, green skin. Its sweet juices slid through my teeth and spread throughout my mouth, bringing it alive with flavor. I examined the pure white, sparkling flesh. Small droplets, reflecting light from the fire, sparkled like diamonds. Still lying on my back, I slowly raised the pear above my head and felt as though the top of my head was being lifted off, and my feeling of self began to spread out, not in the physical world, but out into a great vastness. I felt light, as though I were losing my body, and my mind just kept on opening, and the solid feeling of self was became thinner and thinner until I wasn't sure who I was or where I was. I became afraid that I might dissipate so much that I would not be able to recollect myself, but at the same time I felt so peaceful and light and intrigued by the experience that I just let go. Everything drifted out of me into the vast emptiness: without a mind, or a body, just an awareness, an uncaring observer in the thin constellations of myself.

Faintly I heard Pom Pom say, "Bobby, are you all right?" Seeing her face above mine, I spoke to her from the deep, blue void, "Yes, I'm fine. Just wonderful." I looked at her as though I were seeing her for the first time. My eyes on her, I felt my scattered self come back together in a new way, but part way through, the closing stopped.

I waited for everything to return and the lid to close, but it didn't.

A whole new world was left open in which I could roam. To talk to Pom Pom, I had to pull my awareness out of the other world into this world. I took my attention off her and felt my awareness drift naturally into that vastness as though that was where I truly belonged. I guess once a lovegod, always a lovegod.

We continued as we had, eating quietly and looking at each other, and then she said with her soft, low voice, "You know, when I came here I thought about how nice it would be to have a little romantic affair with you, a sweet, little lift in my stagnant life.

"But, I've been thinking about how I really felt since our talk by the lake, and it really was, well, partially it was that I didn't want to go away alone. Another part was that I really did want some tenderness and love, but I really didn't want to face the fact that I was alone. It's so quiet now, so still, and I feel that aloneness even with you here. I wonder if I could take it if you left or if I'd rush out after you. Oh, God I hope, I really do, that I don't return to fleeing into others' lives."

She continued, "It's hard, but not as hard as it once seemed. I don't want to go back. Let's just stay here forever. Come on lovegod; you're an adventurer, aren't you?"

"Yes. That's why I don't want to stay."

"Why?"

"There are other places I want to explore. This place has helped us look at our place in life in a more real way, but, I mean, that's all. It has opened our eyes in a very nice way and that's about it.

"There's no future here. Everything stays the same. It has brought us so close to life, so close to what it takes to feel close, that we are able to look at our loneliness and separateness without being threatened by it. Now it's time to leave and develop this same closeness in our lives. We can do it."

"Do you really think so?"

"Yes. I didn't before," I paused, "but I do now!"

"You really think I can?"

"I think so because I think you won't like going back. You'll begin to hate it when you see that you're lying to yourself. I feel you're strong enough to stand alone. I really do. You are a strong person. It takes strength just to think the thoughts you're thinking."

I pulled her down and kissed her affectionately. After leaning back up, she said sleepily, "I don't know really. Right now I don't care. I hope you're right. I'll find out soon. Won't I?"

"Yeah, you sure will."

"What about you? Will you go back to living a lie?"

"I hope not. Ever since I escaped into the clouds (I had told her my adventures), I decided that I'll never find a home in fantasies. I've been trying to accept my feelings of loss and of not having a home. Being with you here has made me all the more sure that I'm moving toward the place I want to go. Where this place is or what it will be like I have no idea; but nevertheless, I am more sure now than ever that I'll make it."

"That's very nice." She leaned and kissed me. "In some ways we are inseparable."

"Yes, I believe we are."

We ate some more, and the longer I looked at her the more familiar she appeared. I felt that I had known her for a long time.

Then I began to see myself in her. The more I looked at her, the more I wanted her. I stopped eating and watched her every movement: the way she picked up a nut, split it, held it in her long fine fingers, slowly lifted her arm, opened her full lips, closed them around the nut drawing it in; the soft, rhythmic movements of her jaw, and her knowing eyes that were lovingly gazing into mine. With each of her movements, I felt myself wanting to move in the same way. She stopped eating, and we looked at each other for a long time. Her watery green eyes still on mine, she slid down and drew me inside. We moved slowly, kissed each other tenderly, and in the warm mist, eased each other into vivid dreams.

I dreamt I was flying with a wounded deer in my arms. The sky was a clear blue, the earth below a bright green. I looked at the deer's face, and it was Pom Pom's. I glided downward, went to ease her onto her feet, but she was gone. I looked all around. Could not find her, but could feel her close by. I felt she was watching me. I parted the grass and saw her eyes looking into mine. They disappeared. I jabbed at the woman in the hole in the ground and was overwhelmed with grief and began crying and wondering what had ever made me be cruel to her. I looked down. Her forehead was bleeding; her torn hands clutched the jagged sides of the hole, and her bare shoulders were gouged and covered with blood and torn skin. She looked up at me with pain and fear. I reached down, grabbed her under her arms, and in one smooth motion, pulled her out of the hole and held her in my arms. Our quivering subsided as I said, "It'll be all right. No more. We're together now. Never again. I want you. I'll never cut you off from me again. Never." I felt I had committed a terrible crime. I was standing on ragged rocks. The sun was down; the wind was raging all around. Suddenly, I heard cries from the cave, "Help me. Please, help me." I felt I had to save her before something terrible happened to both of us. I raced back, fell a few times over rocks, and as I approached the cave, her crying became louder and more urgent. I stopped and trembled at the cave's entrance and walked inside toward her voice. I touched her face and carried her outside. The once barren ground was now lush. Before I was able to set her down, she stood, and looking very much like Pom Pom, took me by the hand into the cave. The cave was lit and the ceiling sparkled with diamonds. She led me to the back of the cave where the floor was satiny soft. Pulling me down with her, she laid me on my back, sat next to me, and said, "It's not so bad in here, is it?" I smiled and stared at the ceiling. The diamonds smoothed out, became fluid, and began to wave back and forth, and then they turned into water and flowed down around us without getting us wet. I pulled her down on me, held her against me for a moment. She rolled and sat up. She was relaxed and familiar. I touched her leg, examined it closely, and then her knee and down to her foot and then back up touching her everywhere, feeling and seeing everything fine and delicate about her. At times, being so involved in knowing her, I couldn't tell whether I was touching her or myself.

We were floating in endlessness; her softness surrounded me. I felt as though I was melting into her and enjoying a comfort I had never known before. A familiar rise, another and another, each one making our softness a little firmer, and as this was happening, I felt her withdraw from around, now next to me, touching me everywhere, rising up with me, taking me with her, and then suddenly the diamond waters washed us out into the daylight. I awoke looking into Pom Pom's ornery, dreamy face.

I whispered in her ear, "Who are you anyway?"

With a rhythm she said, "I'm a she-devil of a he-god lover."

"Tell me, my lovely she-devil of a he-god lover, you must roam in mysterious realms; can we communicate with each other in dreams as we do in real life?"

"Yes."

"Then I truly am in love with you."

"Yes, I know."

Forms fading, boundaries dissolving, divisions melting, we slowly descended into deep oblivious sleep.

When I woke, I felt rested and content as I used to at Aunt Iris's; nowhere to go, no one to see, no reason to get up, but wanting to get up because I was alive. Slowly and quietly I tried to move away, but just as I was about to stand, Pom Pom wrapped her arms around me and pulled me to her.

"Where do you think you're sneaking off to?"

"Not away from you, that's for sure."

"Good," she smiled.

We kissed and played around a little, and then I said, "Come on. Let's get up. It's a gorgeous day."

In the middle of the day while we were sitting on the rocks in front of the cliff dwellings, she said, "It's time for me to go. It was lovely getting to know you. I will never forget yesterday or today."

"Neither will I. What do you plan on doing."

"I'm returning but not going back. I'll tell Sam how I feel, collect my belongings, and then I want to, I guess, be with you."

"You guess?"

"Well yes, at least now that's how I feel, but after I leave I may feel differently. It's not that I don't love you; I'll always love you. It's just that maybe I should be by myself for a while instead of being with another man. I feel like I've been living in a cave and have finally come out. I don't want to lose that, but I do want to see you."

"I want to see you, too. Our meetings have been unplanned, at least in the, oh well, you know what I mean. Let's plan our next meeting."

"Let's. Where?"

"How about over there," I pointed beyond the sand dunes to the ocean, "at the source of life?"

"Yeah, that sounds lovely."

We kissed. She turned and walked away. When she reached the meadow, she waved and blew me a kiss. I waved back and did a short version of the lovegod, wiggle dance. She smiled, waved again and headed back the way she had come.

With each step, her feelings of closeness fell away, yet she still felt free and strong. Up on the ridge she looked down upon the Land of Love, and with equal clarity she looked into herself at her separateness, and next to it, her tender feelings of being joined to everything. Both were equal, yet changed. She turned away, then turned back toward the Land of Love. She did not want to leave. She wanted to stay there with me, but knew that would only be hiding, that she needed to return to her situation in life with her new feelings and perceptions. Holding her fond memories of the Land of Love close to her heart, she turned and walked to where she was living.

By this time, I was swimming on my back across the lake with my bag, canteen and binoculars on my chest. I was thinking, as I too was feeling the enchantment fall away, that I needed to find a home not in the world but in myself — just what Aunt Iris had told me many years before. Then, no matter where I went, what I had or with whom, I would always feel at home. It would be nice to find a place where others cherished life and felt similar to the way I did, but still, I couldn't look to them for a home, just as I couldn't look to them for meaning or to not feel alone. I gathered up my experiences in the enchanted Land of Love, held them in the forefront of my mind, just as Pom Pom had done, and decided to use them as a gauge as to whether I was moving toward or away from a home.

I reached the other side where the lake slipped through a slit in the canyon wall. After climbing through the slit, I stood on a ledge on the cliff's face and watched the water fall a long way onto protruding rocks and spray into a pool. I looked beyond the sand dunes to the sparkling sea and forward to seeing Pom Pom.

As I strolled down the zigzag path in the face of the cliff, I thought about Pom Pom: her desire for passion, her courage in wanting to be free and live a full life, her soft warm touch, her kind eyes, her innocent, experienced love, her love for me, her delicate way of approaching and withdrawing, her playfulness; and when I reached the bottom, I knelt next to the pool, spread my hands on the ground, kissed our dear mother earth, and thanked her for blessing me with feminine affection.

Part IV

Chapter 27

I stopped to rest on a large rock near the stream that flowed out of the pool toward the ocean. Next to the rock a spring bubbled up, cut along the side, and flowed down into the stream. I filled my canteen from the spring. Although the experiences of closeness in the Land of Love had fallen away, I kept them alive by thinking about them. I was excited about joining Pom Pom at the ocean. Together it would be much easier and more enjoyable finding a home. I also longed for a companion.

I pulled out my only picture of my parents and started thinking about what my life would have been if they had lived, my life after they died, my life with Aunt Iris, her great influence on me, our talks, especially those at the ocean, her death, and my life afterward. I felt that after my abrupt landing on the mushroom, I really did stop fleeing from feelings of loss. If I hadn't, I wouldn't have entered the Land of Boxes and helped my cousin save himself, nor would I have ventured down those stairs and seen those lost souls and helped bring that child back to life, and without those previous adventures I would not have ventured into the love and vitality in the Land of Love with Pom Pom. I felt that the momentum of my adventures had moved me onto the threshold of finding a home.

I heard someone walking through the brush toward me. Looking up, I was pleased to see Aunt Marty. She was dressed in a loose, blue dress. Her hair was braided.

She smiled, sat next to me, and said, "How are your adventures going?"

"All right," I said.

"You sure have traveled a long way for not getting very far," she laughed. "All kidding aside, you've made good progress. I'm proud of you. Iris would be very proud of you."

"Yes, she would. I wish she were here now." I paused. "I've been thinking about my adventures. Yeah, I have moved forward some. But you know, I'm done looking for a home on the earth. I've really wandered around too much. I'm going to quit traveling but not adventuring. I'm going to move but not on my feet, going to move without moving, be a motionless mover. I'll go farther that way. Hey, how'd you know I was adventuring?"

"I've been reading about you."

"Reading about me! What are you talking about?"

"I've been reading *Adventures of Bobby*."

"What?! Here, let me see that."

She handed me *Adventures of Bobby*. I paged through it.

I couldn't believe it! There were my adventures. I turned to chapter twenty-seven and said, "Have you read this chapter?"

"No, I haven't. I was just going to start it."

I turned to the end of the book and realized that I had found a home. I got excited and said, "So I do find a home! I really do find a home!"

"Yes. In this edition you do. Would you like me to read the rest of your adventures to you?"

The idea that my adventures were already recorded in a book seized my imagination. To have my own adventures read to me! I wouldn't have to live it? I could just sit and hear it; wouldn't have to move at all. But if it was recorded, then I must have already lived it. But how could I have done that? Then I began to think about Aunt Iris's idea of traveling through various parts of our lives in time in any direction, and I thought, have I been adventuring at all or just been seeing old adventures of mine? This perspective could be a new adventure entirely or a new dimension to my old adventuring. Maybe I've been walking around for nothing. Instead of rambling about to who knows where, I could just stay seated and hear how I found a home.

"Yeah. Sure. I'll hear it."

She began to read, word for word, the beginning of this chapter.

I still couldn't believe it. There were my feelings, my thoughts, my descriptions in a book I had never seen before. Then when she got to this word right here, she put the book down and said, "Come on, Bobby, let's live it."

"Oh, I don't know; I'm pretty comfortable sitting right here on this rock. Although, I could use a cushion. You wouldn't have one with you, would you?"

"No." She laughed. "Are you sure you wouldn't rather live it?"

"No, I'm not. Why do you think I should live it?"

"Because by living you'll really find a home but by hearing you may not."

"But haven't I already found a home, and hearing about it will be just a reminder?"

"What if you haven't found a home? Do you think you'd be looking for one if you have already found one? And what if, after you hear the tale, you still feel you haven't found a home, but after you have lived it, you know for sure that you have?"

"Yeah, that's something to consider. Why don't you read on while I think about it some more?"

She read to this word right here. I said, "Could you tell me a little bit about what's going to happen? Maybe skim it and tell me the highlights?"

"No, but I can tell you that you have moved some and now seem ready to move much farther."

"You mean I can stay seated right here and still find a home?"

"No. You'll have to walk some but not much."

"Are you sure? How do you know?"

"Well, to be honest, I peeked through the rest of the book."

"So you do know."

"A little. I know how this chapter begins."

"How does it begin?"

"It already has. Do you want to live it or not? Try to decide. It's getting dark. If you want to live it, we should get going. What do you want to do?"

I couldn't decide. I was still fascinated by the idea that I may have already lived it, by the idea that maybe this was proof of Aunt Iris's idea of traveling through the many times of our lives. If after hearing it, I felt I had already found a home, then that would be proof. It was a risk. And I've usually preferred a risk to a sure thing. That's part of being an adventurer. But then, with my parents' picture still in my hand, I started to think about Aunt Iris and the day she died, and I began to feel, as painfully as I did before I got sick, feelings of loss and of not having a future. I knew then, in the midst of those feelings, that I hadn't found a home, and even if I had found one in the future, I wouldn't find one now by hearing about it but only by living it, whether this was the first, second, or thousandth time."

"Are you deciding or falling asleep? If you want to go, we'd better go now.

"You know, I'm not acting alone. Before Iris died, she told me that I should take you on this adventure when I thought you were ready."

I said, "Okay, let's go."

She led me down to the stream. At the stream the path divided into three — right, left, and straight over a bridge. We turned right.

The moon, a few days from being full, shone plenty of light for us to find our way. The air was fresh and crisp; dew was forming on the grass; the sky was clear. This walk was quickly becoming one of the most enjoyable in all my travels. We kept on making many sharp turns as though going through a maze. During our little venture, Marty was quiet. Her step was quick and decisive; I trusted she knew where she was going. I had to. I didn't have the faintest idea where I was. That didn't bother me though. I was used to it.

The path ended at the base of a sand dune. My mind was exceptionally clear. I felt relaxed, refreshed, and ready for anything. The whole area was well lit by the moon. I swear, when I looked up at the moon, the man on the moon winked at me.

"We're almost there. I advise you to take in as much as you can. It's not often someone gets to see directly what you're going to see."

She smiled at me kindly. She put her arm on my shoulder and led me down dark stone stairs that were located against the base of the sand dune. Down the long winding stairs we went, downward and downward, on and on, ducking and bending so as not to scrape ourselves on the protruding dark gray, jagged rocks, until we came to a tunnel that sloped gently upward. The tunnel was highly polished. The floor was perfectly flat and smooth. In contrast to the dark gray rocks of the stairs, this tunnel was cut through light gray granite streaked with blue. Colorful drawings of animals, including man, in all kinds of situations were drawn on the walls and ceilings. They reminded me of petroglyphs I had seen in the Land of Love. I felt an affinity towards these figures, and the more I examined them, the more I seemed to understand the story they were telling. Although, the different scenes didn't follow each other as in a story; they followed each other as in a dream.

Then I began to notice fine lines, forming the outline of doors, running through the figures.

"What's behind those doors?"

"You'll see in a minute" ·

It was shorter than a minute. We only took a few more steps before she turned and opened a door to our left.

"Here we are, Bobby. Come in."

I entered the room and felt that I had been there before, and then, an eerie feeling of always having been there began to enclose me. I staggered back in a daze. How could this be? As I looked around, things began to appear more and more familiar. I tried to remember where I had come from, but my memory was disappearing. This room I had always been in; had never been anywhere else. In front of me was my stiff-backed chair, next to it my old table. I rigidly walked over to the closet against the wall to my right and opened it.

Yes, there were my trowels, plaster knives, and various kinds of cements and plasters. The bed must be behind me against the wall. I turned around; there it was. An oppressive, hopeless feeling fell off the ceiling and wrapped itself around me as the thought of the wall entered my mind. I turned around to the front of the room hoping that it would be different, that it had changed in some futuristic way, but no, there it stood cracked and covered with gray, white, black and brown patches. Patches overlapped each other and covered the entire wall. It was a mess. That was what I had to wake up to every morning.

No, I didn't. I wouldn't. It wasn't going to happen to me again. I turned to run out the door, but it was gone. So was Marty.

For hours I covered every inch of that wall, traced every crack; it was all in vain. No exits.

I slumped to the floor and held my head in my hands as I did on the roof of my only car one night while stargazing. Doomed. Don't ask me how, but with my head in my hands, slumped against the back wall like a defeated man, I knew where I was.

Chapter 28

I was in a room with four walls. The patched wall in front of me had things behind it that were always trying to break through. I was alone, separated by walls, but not completely alone. On each side wall was a door leading to rooms like mine. These rooms had doors leading into other rooms, and on and on, forming a tremendous circle of rooms. No one knew how many rooms there were; there were probably millions. I've never heard of anyone leaving his room in one direction and returning from the other. The patched walls lined the circle, so that everything threatening to break through came from the inside. No matter where you went, who you saw, you were held in by a wall and surrounded by rooms filled with worried, anxious people sealing their walls. That's all we did — seal, seal, seal. We called ourselves Sealers. Our entire existence consisted of keeping our walls sealed.

Day in, day out, patch here, seal this up, rush over there, patch another crack, oh no, two cracks are forming at once, hurry, hurry, something may break through! There was not a moment during which something was not trying to break through.

Sealers never sleep through the night; they can't even sleep for an hour. Something could break through by then. They only take short naps every once in a while. And these naps are usually not very restful, for Sealers sleep with one ear open to hear the possible cracking of plaster. Quite often they are driven out of their sleep, as one frightened out of sleep by a nightmare, by the sounds of cracking and crumbling plaster or by terrifying sounds from behind the wall.

The things pressing inward threaten Sealers' existence right down to its foundation. Sealers don't know why they are devastating, but what is never doubted is how dangerous they are and what destruction they'll cause if they are ever let through the wall. All you need to be convinced of this is to see the fear on a Sealer's face when something threatens to break through.

This fear made sealing the number one priority in their lives. All else was of lesser value. If your friend or child was in great pain or in a life-threatening situation and helping him meant that something might break through, there were no second thoughts or doubts about what should be done. There was plenty of justification for taking care of yourself first. There wasn't much love among Sealers, although the word was used a lot.

Different things come through the wall. What remains the same is that the same thing always presents itself in the same way and breaks through in the same spot. Some things that come through are objects, people, animals, or parts of a person or animal. Often, after a patch bursts off, a picture will be there. Similar to this are floating images. Images float out of the wall and swirl around its victim's head. The only other way is sound alone or with its source.

Sealers have nothing to look forward to. What could be in the future? Every day was the same as the one before, the same as the one to be. Life was a skipping record. Patch, seal, patch, seal, and hope it'll hold while you wait for more cracks to appear. One moment was a lifetime. The only thing to look forward to was a wild dream of someday maybe escaping or of the things behind the wall going on a permanent vacation. There was as much luck in that as what was real becoming unreal.

You may wonder how Sealers kept on going in their dead-end existence. Each day stared them in the face — the wall, its cracks, the fear; you'd think it would be in the forefront of their minds, but no, it wasn't at all. They shoved it back as far as they could. They were extremely adept at anesthetizing themselves to the hopelessness of their existence. They did not see what surrounded them. Life was too bad to be true.

In trying to forget, they concentrated all their energy on practical activities: sealing methods, different techniques, new compounds, etc. They held regular meetings and conferences on methods of sealing, progress in the art of sealing, research into new cements and plasters, and anything else they could wall themselves in with.

Life was their walls. It was an accepted fact that life was maintaining a sealed wall: nothing more, nothing less. Nothing else existed, especially the notion that perhaps there was more to life.

Yet, not all were successful in numbing themselves to their existence. Every once in a while the facts of their existence would slip through a crack in their mind and come up front to disturb even the most active and successful Sealer, and when it refused to be driven back, a Sealer became vulnerable to being overwhelmed by what was behind the wall.

The thought that distressed me the most was that I knew Sealers were born into their rooms. How this happened I did not know. But I knew it was true. They didn't build their rooms nor did they alter them. They died where they were born. And what troubled me the most was that I was a Sealer. I was one of them. But I refused to believe that I was born there or would die there. Where I was born or would die I did not know.

For a moment I thought that maybe it wasn't true. Maybe if I opened one of the side doors I would be somewhere else. I knew better, but have you ever thought that maybe, just maybe, something may not be true that you know is true? That's how I felt.

Just as I had known where I was, I also knew that I had a mate. I slowly walked over to the side door on my left, reluctant to open it for fear of being disappointed, but was disappointed anyway when I saw Masonis patching her wall.

"Hi, Masonis."

"Hello, dear. How are you? Gotten much done this morning?"

"Oh, yes. See you later."

I closed the door, went over to the other one thinking that I might as well give it a try. What the hell. There he was, Professor Cleanwall, meticulously tidying up his patchwork. I tried to close my door before he saw me.

"Hello, Robert."

I was feeling a little queasy before I opened the door, and the sight of Professor Cleanwall and the sound of his nasal voice made me feel much sicker. I vomited on his floor.

"Sorry about that, Cleanwall."

"Ugh, Robert, what's wrong with you? Did you purposely come over here to prove to me how disgusting you can be? No need for that! I was convinced of that the first time I saw you. Clean it up! Hurry! Clean it up right now!"

I quickly closed the door without cleaning up my mess. I got my plaster and cement out of the closet and put them on the floor in front of my wall. I began doing what I had no choice in not doing. A crack was forming to my right; I took some cement, didn't bother to walk over to the crack, and haphazardly flung it at the crack. It splattered nowhere near the crack. The crack began to widen; another was forming beneath it. I threw more cement at the crack. Missed.

Feeling beads of sweat forming on my forehead as I missed with another shot, I walked over to the cracks and sloppily sealed them up.

The lack of a choice was what enslaved us to our walls. It would not have been as bad being walled in or even having to patch a wall that was crumbling, but to have to patch a wall continuously because of an undefined, very real fear was what made us prisoners. And I thought I was free! Free to go anywhere, be anything, but no, not there; I was not free at all.

For days I had a strong feeling that I could escape. There was no evidence for it; had never heard of a Sealer leave his room, yet I still felt there was something else for me. You see, by this time, I had lost all memory of my past. If you had asked me if I had ever been outside, gazed at the stars, sailed, or adventured; I would have looked at you with a blank expression. All I knew was that I had spent all of my born days in a room patching a wall. Perhaps it was a leak in my sealed memory, or my not wanting to believe that sealing was all there was that gave me the idea that there was something else.

Sometimes, it helps to believe in something even if it will never come true. Although, who is to say something will never be?

While I was yearning to find a way to this vague idea of there being something else, I neglected my wall, which put me on edge most of the time. Why do something when you think it not worth your while?

Would you fix a meal and then go out to eat? I wouldn't. I let the wall develop large cracks, carelessly sealed up those that made me most anxious, and threw plaster and cement willy-nilly all over the wall. But, I could only be that way for a short while. Soon it would all seem so useless, hopeless, and the more I thought about there being something else the less likely it seemed to be. I would then give up completely, return to conscientious sealing, and work on my wall until I could no longer bear it. This cycle of neglect and repair I went through continually. Why, tell me, why continue doing something that is the same for all time; when one day, no, one second is a lifetime, when nothing is missed whether you blink your eye or your life?

During thoughts like those, I would neglect my wall and return to wondering and dreaming about there being another kind of existence.

My fellow Sealers thought something was seriously wrong with me, especially Professor Cleanwall. Although, he thought something was wrong with everyone but him. According to them, I was stricken by some unknown malady that would send me into days of despair and neglect. When I wasn't afflicted, I was an efficient, thorough Sealer. It was just this sickness I had that prevented me from having a good life. Little did they know my affliction was my strength.

One day while I was doing a lot of staring into space, pacing around, and flinging plaster and cement all over my wall; Cleanwall entered my room and started talking. He must have been talking to me for a while before I heard him.

"…let your wall become such a mess. You have the worst wall here. Stop that, Robert. You are not that way. You do not have to give into it."

"Give into what?"

"You do not fool me, no, not for a second. You go along with what others say about having something wrong with you in hopes that everyone will leave you alone, but I have read about Sealers like you.

"Everyone has gone through similar periods you go through. They are usually not stupid, often quite intelligent, have much potential, yet fall into days, weeks, and sometimes years of behaving like imbeciles. The reason was that they wanted a different life, and in their wanting, convinced themselves that life could be different. Do not fool yourself, Robert, this is life. I know. I have studied it, wanted it to be different, and searched for a long time when I was young. It was a wasted period in my life. This is it and this is all there is. No one I have ever heard of, no one, has changed his existence. There have been a few who, ah…" He paused and then blurted out, "No one has escaped."

"What were you going to say?"

"Nothing of any import."

"Come on, Cleanwall, as long as you are telling me what is and what is not, tell me everything. Come on, speak up. You're never at a loss for words."

He turned and waddled toward his room. I quickly grabbed him by the arm. He turned and peered at me past his puffy cheeks with his beady, ice blue eyes.

"You can't just mention something like that and drop it. It's not fair. There have been a few who have done what? Is something else possible?"

"Oh, confound it. I should not have said a thing. Okay, I will tell you. It is not much. I wish I had never mentioned it. Knowing you and the frames of mind into which you get yourself, you may try it.

"A few Sealers, thank God there have only been a few, have driven themselves into a state of complete hopelessness. In wanting a different life, they have refused to live in the only one there is, and in so doing, have left no avenue for escape when they finally realized the truth that this is the only existence there is, and, at that point, they have gone through their walls. It is suicide. You know what lies behind the wall."

By this time he was shaking, beads of sweat were forming on his red face, and his voice was quivering. He put his hand on my shoulder and pleaded, "Robert, I know we are disinclined toward each other, but if you ever consider doing what they have done, come see me first."

"They've never come back?"

"No! Not one."

"Cleanwall, what you said, how much do you know? You know they went through, but were they desperate when they did it? Were they ending it? Do you know that or is that your own interpretation?"

His tiny eyes glazed over with scorn. "Why else? Tell me! I am warning you for your own good! I did not have to tell you. Why else would they go behind there?"

His pudgy finger quivered at my wall. Sounds of plaster cracking came from his room. He scurried his fat, little body back to his room.

I sat down in my chair, ignored my wall, and thought about what Cleanwall had said. So, some Sealers had gone through their walls and never returned. Where did they go? Somewhere in the inner circle from which everything comes. Suicide, Cleanwall said. Staying here was suicide as far as I was concerned. What did I have to lose. I had already lost yesterday. What difference would it make if I lost tomorrow? Behind the wall — sounded terrifying. What had they to gain?

If they weren't ending it, then what were they after? To go in that great circle, to see all those things threatening and controlling Sealers' lives, what could be gained?

Chapter 29

Thoughts of what Cleanwall had said circled in my brain for days. I could think of nothing else. A few times when a crack would appear, I'd try to look into it, but as it widened, the usual fear would grow inside me, force my hand into the cement, and make me seal the crack.

More than anything I wanted to know why others had stepped through. If not to end it, then what were they after? It had to be what I was after. What else could it be? Sometimes, well, to be honest, quite often I can talk myself into almost anything if I want it enough.

I continued to neglect my wall. It was the longest time I'd ever spent in the neglectful part of my cycle.

I figured that the only way to find out was to try to get myself in the same frame of mind Cleanwall had said those other Sealers were in before they went through their walls. That wouldn't be hard. I was close to it already. I wasn't afraid to try. I doubted I'd get in such a state that I'd want to end my life. Unlike my cousin Eddie, I have never been a victim of suicidal desires. For some reason, I felt that when I got into that state something would break or open up, a clearing of some sort.

It lasted longer than I had expected, not that I had anything else to do. Has a waitress ever lost your order? You sit there watching every plate of food come out thinking it's yours, but no, it strays away to someone else who gobbles it down. That's what it was like for me. Every day I would think to myself — this is the day something will happen. Nothing would happen. But, I didn't give up.

I didn't forget about escaping and seal myself by patching. Now, when I look back, I wanted to know more than I've wanted anything in my entire life. You could say I was pure desire.

Then, one day while I was sitting in my chair drawing mandalas, the activity on my wall subsided. At first I didn't pay much attention to it, but then, it was obvious that something different was happening. That lifted up my head. No new cracks were forming. The ones that had begun to form stopped expanding. All was quiet. My first thought was that they had gone on vacation. Then, in an instant, a crack appeared in the center of my wall. Very odd, I thought to myself. Cracks always start out small and gradually enlarge. While I was wondering about that, a sweet hopeful melody flowed out of the crack, swirled around my head, and floated me out of my chair toward the crack. Tiptoeing across the floor, I felt in a trance as I leaned over to look in that crack, but before my eyes reached it, the patching instinct erupted and forced my arm to slop a glob of cement over the crack. The melody ended; cracks began to form, and I was at it again.

Never before had a crack appeared in that part of my wall, nor did such a sweet melody come out of any of my cracks. The development of new cracks was common, in fact, it was an unsolvable problem.

Sealers were constantly being plagued by new dangers. Yet, I felt different about this crack. I wanted it to appear. The sound it emitted comforted me; it had been a hopeful sound.

I soon found that it would appear whenever I sincerely wanted a way out. In that frame of mind, my thoughts developed a certain rhythm, and as I followed that rhythm, I would soon find myself listening to the sweet melody, which seemed to enhance those same thoughts. For a while I didn't bother to go near the crack. Just concentrated on the melody. And after a while the melody would fade away and the crack would seal itself up. That was the other unusual thing about that crack. Cracks never sealed themselves.

One day the melody fused itself so completely with my thinking that I couldn't tell the difference between the drift of my thoughts and the movement of the melody, and then I gradually began to hear a voice in the melody. At first the words were barely audible. They slowly became louder and clearer until I could plainly hear them calling me, "Come see what lies beyond our wall. Come see, come see, come see me." I was reluctant to go. The old Sealer fear of what is beyond the wall rose up in me. But, the call was hypnotic. Seeing was a risk, and although I had no memory of being an adventurer, I still had the desire, so the risk very much indeed attracted me.

Without taking a chance there'd be no change; I'd be stuck in the same old sameness. As before I floated down to the crack, but this time I controlled my patching instinct, and upon gazing through the crack, I saw myself sitting in a large, soft, comfortable chair in front of a wall covered with far fewer patches than mine. I turned around and smiled at me. I felt myself slip through the crack, drift through an empty space, and merge with my likeness. I was ecstatic. I wasn't concerned about the cracks that were forming; I felt confident about patching them. Patching them wasn't of any interest to me. I was occupied with some vague, exciting ideas of how I was going to pass through that wall. I stood up, still in that frame of mind, quickly and easily patched the cracks, and sat back down again. No new cracks were forming; the patches were holding well. I had so much extra time.

Then, I felt myself being drawn back. I wanted to stay, tried to will it, but it was of no use. After being detached from my likeness, I drifted back through my sweet hopeful crack while keeping my eyes on him. I patched the few cracks that were forming and sat in my stiff, hard chair.

I was dazed. What I had dreamed about, hoped for, doubted, was true. There really was a different way of existing. You didn't end it by going through your wall; you began something new. I could be with my likeness in a new room, a soft chair, without being concerned about sealing but planning a future. Future. The sound of the word pleased me. I would have definite plans not whims or hunches or unfounded, wishful thoughts. I'll never forget that moment as being the beginning of my finding a home.

I had to tell Masonis. After slopping some cement on developing cracks, I rushed over to see her. She was inspecting her wall with a magnifying glass. She was almost as bad as Cleanwall in keeping a neat, clean wall. I grabbed her bony shoulder and turned her around.

"Masonis, listen. You won't believe what I just saw. You know, oh, boy, you won't believe it. It's amazing. It has all come true, it really has. We're going to have a future together. A future, do you hear me?"

With a quizzical look staring out of her dark, recessed eyes past her thin, pointy nose, she said, "What are you talking about? I've never seen you so excited."

I described to her what had happened as best I could. During my explanation, her eyes got bigger and bigger, her thin lips became thinner, her usually pale cheeks flushed, and by the time I finished, her arms were tightly folded and pressed against her frail body.

"I saw you. I couldn't figure out what you were doing down at that crack. I even called to you, but you didn't answer.

"Bob, I can't believe you did that. How could you ever think about it being real? Don't ever think there's anything worthwhile

323

behind our walls! It's boundless with horrors! Why do you think we keep them sealed? Because we've got nothing else to do with our lives? Sealing saves us! Face the facts; your dream is just a dream. It will never be anything else then that. I'm afraid for you. Please tell me you'll never look in that crack again."

"You don't understand. Have you ever seen a crack go away by itself? And have you ever heard of something coming out of a crack that wasn't dangerous but soothing? Come on, tell me."

"No, I haven't, and I don't care to hear about it either. It's a trick. It's baiting your naive heart. You just wait. It'll call you more and more; you'll spend more time staring through that crack, and then, one day, you'll fall into a trance while staring through it, and the things behind the wall will know they've got you and come crashing through. Believe me, that is what will happen."

"Say that will happen. So what? What difference would it make when our future is our past? Right here," I clicked my fingers, "that's our entire life. That moment. Looking through that sweet crack, seeing myself at a different wall with fewer things coming through, that was worth more to me than what my life has been.

"Anyway Masonis, don't just disregard what I saw. Think about it. That won't hurt, will it? Something has happened that I've never seen happen before. It is worth something. It really is. This is our chance. We could have a future together."

Her sudden anger jolted me. "We do have a future together! We have had a future together! What is this crazy talk about a future? What is tomorrow? Tomorrow is in the future. It hasn't happened yet, has it? Tomorrow isn't yesterday."

"It is when it's the same."

"But it isn't the same. We'll patch different cracks, we'll say different things to each other, we'll..."

"We'll still be sealing our walls as always. Our life is dead monotony. Time has stopped here, you know that. There's no forward movement."

Suddenly her anger passed. She looked at me with her sad, brown, sunken eyes; a deep hopelessness was wandering in the shadows. She stood and stared at me without focusing. Then she turned and returned to patching. I felt I had said too much in my enthusiasm.

As I look back, I think it was my desire to want a way out, more than anything else, that convinced me that what I saw through my sweet hopeful crack was a possibility. I could see no feasible way of getting over to my likeness, nor was I sure that being over there would be much different from where I was. Floating through did make me feel different, but was it because of the place or because I wanted to feel that way? I would still be stuck behind a wall. Nevertheless, I felt it was a beginning to not being trapped at all. For some reason, once I got over to that other wall, I felt something would happen that would allow me to leave it.

Since I had convinced myself there was something else, I detested having to patch my wall. Before it was a waste of time, but now, it was an obstacle. What was the point of maintaining something I was only going to leave behind? Both efforts were contradictory. How could I do one and the other? My patchwork became sloppier. I almost let a few things poke through. Although, as much as I hated to patch, I still couldn't help myself.

For a long time after I saw the other wall, my sweet hopeful crack failed to appear. Every few minutes I would go over to its spot to see if it was beginning to form or if it had gotten stuck.

Nothing. No melody, no voice, no one called. The sweet crack's absence began to wear on me. My old despair of being doomed forever was hard enough for me to endure, but now that I knew my fate wasn't sealed, my despair drove deeper and gripped me harder, for I feared my sweet hopeful crack would not return. I thought in the rhythm of the melody as much as I could. Didn't do any good. I paced around, hit the wall where the sweet crack had appeared in hopes that something might loosen up, thought all kinds of strange things under the idea that the melody might have changed, and tried a few other things I'd rather not mention. My choices were limited. Just how much can you do walled inside a room?

I had to do something. The thought that the hopeful crack would never return started to haunt me. At the time, my scheme made perfect sense. I couldn't see any flaw in my logic. But, since I've left that place, I've realized that many things that made perfect sense in there do not make much sense out here.

Convinced myself that in order to go through to another wall, I would have to stop sealing. By not sealing, I figured that my sweet crack would appear and open up to where I could step through. Just as wanting had given me a hopeful crack, doing would give me the rest. I was beside myself when I began to carry out this plan.

Cracks were appearing, opening wide; cement was popping off the wall, but I refused to give into the desire. It wasn't easy. My eyes began to twitch. My arms started going through the patching motions.

I quickly wrapped them around me, paced in front of the wall; my head jerked about as I saw more cracks form, and I finally had to force myself to march to the back of my room where I crouched into the corner. I couldn't see anything but could hear cries from behind the wall. I held myself tighter. I was afraid it was already too late. The next thing I was aware of was sitting in my chair, tired yet relaxed, and my wall was completely sealed. I couldn't believe it! It had worked! Didn't have to patch my wall!

It happened differently than I had thought. I had expected to be with my likeness. I hadn't walked through to my likeness; my wall had changed. My excitement was dulled by my being in the same room. Nonetheless, things were different than what they had been.

As I turned to rush over to tell Masonis, I saw her standing in our doorway. She was pale. Her alabaster hands gripped the doorjamb.

"Masonis, did you see that? Did you? How long have you been there? It worked. I don't have to patch my wall anymore. Refused to do it. Took care of itself. Somehow, I don't know, but, who cares? It worked. You must have seen it. You've just got to hold yourself back from sealing. I just stood there, controlled myself, and then..."

"I saw you."

"You did? Wasn't it amazing?"

"What are you rattling on about? You patched your wall. I saw the whole thing. You were trembling in front of your wall, then you went back and huddled in the corner, and then like a robot, as though it wasn't you, you very mechanically walked out to your wall, grabbed your tools, and patched faster than I have ever seen you patch. You don't remember, do you? I can tell by the look on your face. Fool yourself but you can't fool me. Look at your hands."

A cold chill rippled up me. The blood drained out of my face.

"That must have been there from before. I've always got cement on my hands."

"Why would I lie to you, especially about something like this?

"I'd be happy if you didn't have to seal your wall. Ever since you looked through that sweet crack of yours, I think that's what you call that damn thing, you haven't been yourself. You think you can do things that just cannot be done."

She came towards me. Her face softened, her movements were more relaxed, she put her hand on my hip and whispered, "I shouldn't be saying these things, but I don't like our existence anymore than you. Do you think I enjoy sealing my life away? The same thing every day, nothing to look forward to. But face it, because if you don't, you'll only make yourself miserable. And how do you think that'll make me feel?"

"I can't accept that. I just can't. I couldn't continue if it were true. If what you say is true, then my sweet hopeful crack would never have appeared. You know, it didn't appear by accident; I wanted something like that to happen. I feel, I really feel, I willed it!"

She burst out laughing. "So you willed it, huh? As if we don't have enough cracks to contend with, you willed some more. I suppose you will all your cracks. If you want to end it, why not stop willing?"

Without thinking and in a distracted tone of voice, I replied, "Not willing is what makes the things behind the wall dangerous."

"I give up! I really do! I give up! You don't care about me and about what we have between us; all you care about is this obsession of yours. It's a fantasy. Nothing you say is real! We have our walls; we patch them, and you, you, you're the one who patched your wall. Go on, ruin yourself. Don't think I'll be a part of your crazy scheme. I want nothing to do with it. You should feel the same way.

"Don't you care about what it'll do to me? There's not one good thing that'll come out of it. You'll see. If I didn't know any better, I'd say you were being self-destructive."

She stepped back, scowled at me and sneered, "So?"

"I've got to try something. I can't go on as I always have. If I could, I would but I can't."

"So it's beyond your control?"

"Give me some time. I'm not sure about much right now. I think I heard some cracking over at your wall."

She rushed to her eternal duty. I was glad to see her leave. I didn't feel like talking. There was too much to think about.

I continued with my plan of not patching my wall. Each time I felt the urge to patch, I would fight it. Many times I had to go to the back of my room or in the closet. Cracks would be forming, cement breaking loose. I'd be afraid and then find myself sitting in my chair or lying down across from my neatly patched wall with cement on my hands. And I was always disappointed. Each time I expected to find myself relaxing in a soft chair in my new room, but just the opposite was happening. I was becoming increasingly nervous and agitated. I began pacing around my room, looking into drawers and in the corners. Then I started to experience lapses in time. At first, when I would be holding myself back from sealing, I would notice it was, say, three o'clock. Next time I would become aware, it would be seven or eight. As the days passed, these lapses in time became longer and longer and ceased limiting themselves to when I was trying to prevent myself from patching. I would be pacing around or just sitting, and all of a sudden, it would hit me that a day or a week had gone by. At first, I thought it somewhat interesting that a week could sneak by without me, however, that didn't really bother me. My whole life could have slipped by for all I cared. But then it occurred to me that I did have to know, for if I was to get through to that other wall, I would not be able to make it by losing weeks and by not knowing where I was or what I was doing most of the time. One week quickly extended to a few weeks, then I began losing longer periods of time. I mean long. Months. Before I knew it, there was very little time I could call my own. Just as when I had gotten sick, I didn't want to believe my scheme had veered off on its own course.

You know how, sometimes, you can mentally step out of your skin and watch yourself as though you were another person? Well, one day when I thought I should do something before it would be too late, I watched myself pace around, walk to the back of the room, and feel the overpowering desire to patch rise up in me, spread throughout my limbs, quickly take complete control over me, but unlike before, instead of trying to hold it back, I let it do with me as it wished.

I watched myself march over to my cements and trowels, pick them up, and quickly and efficiently patch my wall. I stepped back inside my skin. It was over.

I dropped on my hard chair. Maybe Masonis was right. What had I accomplished? Nothing. How did I expect to deny the desire the threats behind the wall created in Sealers? Those things ruled our lives. It wasn't as if Sealers had nothing better to do. They were forced to do what they did. Why did I think that by not sealing I could escape from sealing. Many times Sealers become hurt or seriously ill, but no matter what, they still try to maintain their walls. The strong desire is what sustains, or from another angle, destroys them. And I had spent all that time learning that, learning what I had already known.

I looked up at my wall. It needed to be sealed. I couldn't raise myself up, couldn't go back. But I had to. I couldn't face the fact that I was a prisoner trapped in my lonely room. As I stood up, the trapped feeling seemed to tighten around me like a hangman's noose. I rushed over to the place of my sweet hopeful crack. The entire area was sealed with Never Worry Anymore Cement.

Masonis was standing in our doorway. She was pale, thin; deep dark circles depressed her eyes. At first I thought she had come down with a serious illness. I quickly threw some cement on my cracks, ran over to her, and said, "What's wrong? What has happened to you?"

She stepped back, scrutinized me closely with an anxious look, and then suddenly threw her arms around my neck, and cried. I had to hold her up.

Through tearful voice, she said, "You're back. It's really you, isn't it? Talk to me. Say something, please."

"Yeah, it's me. I know I haven't been myself lately, but it's over now. I'm back. All of me."

"Promise me, please, promise me you'll never do anything like that again. I couldn't take it. All I've done is worry about you. For the last half year I thought you'd never be yourself again."

"What, half a year! I knew I was losing time, but a half year all at once!?"

"You didn't know?"

"No."

"You really didn't! You were a different person. As time went on, this person occupied you more and more. You hardly talked to me, acted as though you didn't know me, never were concerned about my welfare; all you did was patch.

"That's all you did. Even when there was nothing to seal, you still sealed. You even stopped pestering Professor Cleanwall. You were stiff, like a robot, very precise, mechanical; as though you were driven. You've been like that for over half a year. I thought, oh, what does it matter, you're back."

"I'm glad it's over too. I feel terrible about what I've done to you. It wasn't worth it. Are you all right? Have you been sick?"

"Just sick over you. All I've done is worry about you all the time. Maybe now you'll listen to me. It didn't do you any good, did it? You're still here. You always have had to patch, whether you knew it or not."

"I have, haven't I?"

"You sure have. I've got to go. Go seal up your wall completely, and I'll do the same to mine, and then we'll have time to talk to each other. We have to talk about this."

"All right. I'll come over when I'm done."

On my way back, I took a closer look at the place where my sweet hopeful crack appeared. What was unusual was the Never Worry Anymore Cement. I rarely used it. Masonis used it a lot. And the patchwork was her style. I sealed my wall fairly well before going over to see her.

As I approached, she came towards me, took my hands, and sat me down across from her. She held my hands for most of the time we talked. She looked much better.

"It sure is nice to see you again, to talk with you, feel you, see that ornery grin of yours. You know, for a while I thought I would never see you like this again. You don't know how much I've missed you."

"I can see it in your face. I would like to say the same to you, but I don't remember missing anything, not even me."

"I'm not just thinking of myself. Bob, I really care about you. "Before, when I tried to talk you out of trying to get over to your likeness, I sounded as though I were only thinking of myself. But, I'm more concerned about you. Have you thought of what could have happened if you hadn't regained yourself? You would have remained a mechanical robot. And then, even if it would have been possible for you to pass through your wall, how could you have done it? You weren't in control of your faculties. And besides that, all you wanted to do was patch, not go through. You even patched your sweet hopeful crack. Have you thought about that?"

"Yes, I have. That's one of the reasons I ended it. Even so, I can't see much difference between being a robot my whole life and sealing away my whole life. They're the same. I wonder, those who are very efficient Sealers without much personality, have they tried what I did and never got out of it. Or maybe they've just become their desire."

She said, "There's a lot of difference, a whole lot, between being a driven robot and what you are now. You're in control now, you can smile, you can talk to me. We could not talk like this before.

"Believe me, you're not just one single-minded, tunnel — brain Sealer."

"I guess so. But, I don't know if I am in control. Everything I do seems to be in reaction to what I have no control over."

"I see what you mean. Still, the rest of the time you're in control. Like now, what you re saying, thinking; it's what you want to say and think."

"I guess."

"You're really not sure about much, are you?"

"No. Would you if you had done what I did? I'm very doubtful now. I don't think I can get out of here."

After I said that, despair rose out of the past and blackened my hopes. All effort seemed useless.

"Why continue going up and down the way you do? When you come down, you come down so hard. Each time you seem to fall farther down.

"Honestly, if I thought we could go through, I'd be with you, but I know we can't. So why set ourselves up for grave disappointments over something that cannot be done? Can't you see what you're doing to yourself? You're depressing yourself over nothing. For your own well-being, Bob, try to accept our existence. It's not that bad once you do. Really, can't you remember what you used to be like? You were never like this. You always patched well. You invented new cements and ways of patching. Everyone looked forward to your presence at the committee meetings. You had a bright future. Now, you don't do any of that. Sealers are concerned about you. Can't you remember?"

"Unfortunately, I can. What I'm doing isn't something that has happened all of a sudden. It's been coming on for a long time."

Quietly to herself she said, "Maybe it is a disease." She paused before continuing. "While you were gone, Professor Cleanwall and I talked about you quite a bit. He has been concerned about you too. He told me about what he had said to you. Now, hold it. Come on. Listen to me. Give him a chance. He's not stupid. I know you don't think much of him, but you can't deny that he knows a great deal about walls and what can and cannot be done with them. One of the things he said was that if Sealers have been able to go through their walls, then why haven't they ever come back? It only seems logical that if they know how to go through, they would want to go back through to prove that going through is possible and to help others, if going through is really worthwhile.

"From that he concluded, and it makes sense to me, that they don't go through to another wall, but get stuck and are destroyed. Doesn't that make sense to you?"

"It sort of does."

"You aren't convinced, are you?"

"I'm not convinced about anything except that I'm sitting in this chair. Although, he could be right. He is knowledgeable."

Her face brightened. "Seriously, Bob, what if it happened to you? It could. What if you got caught behind your wall and were destroyed? Is it worth it?"

"Not if that were to happen."

She was getting more and more excited. She moved closer to me.

"That's not the only way you could get stuck."

"I'm stuck now."

"No. I mean, you were almost stuck before. In fact, you were stuck there for a while. It very well could happen that your sweet crack could make you think of doing something else that could really get you stuck so that you wouldn't be able to seal. If it weren't for our strong desire to seal, you would have quit sealing your wall, and the demons behind your wall would have seized you. As I said before, I think you're being tricked. You asked me to think about the possibility of going through; I have; now please think about what I have said. I have thought a lot about it. Please!"

"I have been thinking about it too. I'm afraid you may be right."

Her excitement and enthusiasm were sneaking past her self-control. She was easy to read. Her face glowed, her eyes were dreamy, her hand began to heat up my leg. I could tell she was having a hard time keeping herself in her chair. And all I could think of was how strange it was for two people going through life together, seeming to want the best for each other, to have such extreme, opposite reactions to the same circumstance. Masonis was over-flowing with joy. I knew she was thinking that things were going to return to how they used to be. We'd be together. I'd be my old self again. We'd enjoy each other again. It was probably the happiest day she had had in a long time. Not so for me. I felt as though my life were coming to an end. Going back to what I was was the worst thing that could have happened to me. I couldn't bear to think about it. I wanted to forget about everything: the sweet hopeful crack, my plans, everything. I wanted to sleep for the rest of my life. I could see no future. All my hopes and dreams were fading. There was nothing to keep me going except the dumb, blind sealing instinct.

We heard a pop and the sound of cement hitting the floor. We walked over to our doorway from her room. My sweet hopeful crack had freed itself from the Never Worry Anymore Cement. We looked at each other; her glow was dimming, while I could feel my despair easing. I didn't know what to do. Was it a trick? Was it worthwhile? Would it really free me? What would it do to Masonis? Then, the melody swirled out, around, and through my brain.

"Isn't that melody soothing? If anything that sound speaks of another place. Have you ever heard anything like it before?"

With twitches and head jerks, she responded, "What melody? I don't hear a thing."

Light-headed and feeling somewhat in a daze, I felt myself being carried down to my sweet hopeful crack. Through it I saw my likeness leaning against his wall and smiling gently. There weren't any traces of cement or tools on or near him. He turned slowly and freely, stretched his arms above his head, and then let them glide down to his side as he came around to face me. Never before had I seen a Sealer go through those movements. It never would have occurred to any of us. He did it four times. Each time he lifted his arms, I rose up inside myself and then circled around back down as he ended his rotation. My mind was clear; anything was possible. Energy surged through my body. I felt I could walk right through to him. He seemed to move right up in front of me. I felt I could easily reach through the crack and touch him. He spoke to me saying, "Don't be discouraged. You're doing fine. You see," he pointed back towards his wall, "there is a different way to be."

Before I could speak, the crack closed up.

I looked over at Masonis.

"Don't tell me anything. I don't want to know. Think about what I said. You owe me that much." She spun around and stormed into her room.

Now, more than ever, I was convinced of another way to exist. I was sure of it. And I was sure I could go through to a new wall.

What made me hesitate was what it would do to Masonis. What would happen to her after I would be gone? Could she take it while I tried to go through? What if there were more episodes like the last one? I knew she couldn't endure many more. Yet, I had to continue. I had to try. Once you see what I saw, you have to follow, or else you begin to feel your life fall back through itself into a black hole of nothingness. Why should I end my existence just because she was afraid of changing hers?

She was afraid to take the risk, to challenge her life. Still, I didn't want to leave her. If there were only some way I could have convinced her, made her want to realize that there really was a different way of existing. The thought of leaving her behind, stuck for the rest of her life in dead monotony without anyone to help, was what troubled me more than anything. I didn't feel guilty for what might happen to her; wasn't responsible for the way she chose to react. Although, now when I think about her, I think she had sunk below being able to create a choice.

These concerns were being pushed aside quickly by another scheme developing in my brain. At the time of conception, it seemed flawless; didn't seem anything like my previous plan.

My new plan went like this. What we know about something is the image of it in our mind. The thing itself cannot be known. In the process of perception, from sensing the object to the development of the image in the brain, many distortions probably occur. What comes through the wall may not be dangerous at all. Somehow, its image takes on a dangerous characteristic, or perhaps, it is something altogether different from what it is perceived as being. What I was driven to patch really might not be dangerous at all. What I originally planned to do was to alter the image in my brain to match the object coming through the wall. But that was impossible. So, I settled on just changing the image to something that was not threatening. I decided to start with a few changes, and then, little by little, progress to where I wouldn't have to patch anything.

Before I put my new plan into action, I thought I'd better practice. There was more danger involved in this plan than in my other one. To successfully maintain one's wall, a sealer has to know what type of cement to use on what crack and how much of that cement to use. Although Sealers rarely, if ever, see the things come through, they know instinctively by the way the crack appears, the speed at which it spreads, and the section of the wall where it appears; how much and what kind of cement to use. By not perceiving all this, a Sealer could easily confuse his patchwork and bring a downfall upon himself.

I stared at my tiny pointing trowel and tried to see it as a silver key. The grayness seemed to be shifting toward silver, but it was still a trowel. For hours I tried to see it as a key, but its form would not alter. My scheme was failing before it had a chance to begin. It then occurred to me that it wasn't necessary to see it as something different; all that had to be done was to believe it was something else, and it would gradually become that thing. I refused to use the trowel as a trowel. Next to where I entered the room I set the trowel, believing it was a key and planning that soon the door would appear and I would be able to unlock it and leave.

After thoroughly persuading myself it was a key, I put my scheme into action.

Midway down my wall, a little right of center, a crack appeared. It expanded as cracks always do. I began to experience the same feelings as I had when I refused to patch, although, as the crack widened, I became very much afraid in anticipation of what might come out. I glanced at the crack, turned away, hoped it hadn't widened anymore, and looked back only to be met by what I didn't want to see.

The urge to seal was getting stronger and stronger. Tried to control it until the thing broke through. Through the crack a blue cloth emerged and drooped down the wall. I tried to believe it was brown burlap, but its blueness insisted on piercing through me. It would not change. I couldn't make myself believe it was something other than what it was, and as I strained my mind as much as I could, I was overpowered by the desire to patch and watched myself, as I did to end my previous plan, be carried over to where I stuffed the blue cloth back behind the wall and sealed up the crack.

Chapter 30

Something was different. I stepped back and wondered what I was afraid of. Was it really the blue cloth? What's so fearful about a blue cloth? My fear seemed to be shifting around as a rock loosens up in the bottom of a river. It moved about in me from the cloth to the wall and then separated itself from everything. For a brief moment, it was alone, naked, without attachment, and for that moment, I was not afraid. I wondered, were the things behind the wall something to fear, did they actually instill fear in me, or did I place fear on them? If I didn't, then what was it about them that terrified me and made a slave out of every Sealer? Whatever it was, it was deeply embedded in me, as much a part of me as any other part. It couldn't be eliminated — nor could its offspring — the desire to seal — by toying with images. It was there to stay, no matter what I wanted to believe.

When I returned to my function in life, it went much smoother.

My feelings of doom, of being eternally trapped, were not as strong nor was the fear that sustained them. I didn't have any plans of escape. Yet, I felt somehow I would come across some that would succeed. My previous plans, although they had failed in their original intent, had not been a waste. They had taught me something. I accepted my fate as a Sealer, not as a fate that was sealed, but as something I had to be for a while. There was no use fighting it or pretending it wasn't there. Sealers' fear had become a curious mystery to me. In wanting to understand it, I was glad it existed. That, in itself, shocked me.

And so, day in day out, I patched my wall and pondered my new perceptions. I was content to do that. I didn't even bother to examine the area of my sweet hopeful crack.

Each time I would go over to see Masonis she would be slowly patching her wall. Her movements were without her usual liveliness.

From our doorway, I'd say, "Hello," or tell her I wanted to talk to her, but she'd only look at me with her cold, hurt eyes and turn away.

This went on for quite a while until she began looking into my room through our doorway. She'd look; I would feel her presence, but as soon as I'd look her way, she would walk away. One day, while still keeping her distance, she said, "All you've been doing is patching. What's wrong? Can't think of any clever ideas?"

"I haven't tried. Have you?"

"No. But then I don't practice at being a fool. You've accomplished a great deal, haven't you? After all that effort and disappointment, not to mention the pain you've caused me, you're back sealing just like the rest of us. It was worth it though, wasn't it?"

I didn't say anything.

"I thought you wanted to talk to me? Now you won't bother to answer a simple question?"

"You don't really want an answer."

"Why do you think I asked it? To hear myself talk?"

"No, to express your anger and frustration."

"Wouldn't you be angry? Tell me, Bob, wouldn't you?"

Her arms dropped to her side.

"Yes, I would," I said.

"It's not just anger. I'm hurt. You've proven to me how little you care."

"That's not true. I do care about you."

"Then why do you hurt me so? You don't hurt someone you care about. Or maybe you do."

"You don't understand."

"I understand."

"I tried to improve my life. Is there anything wrong with that?

"You couldn't see that though. It didn't work, but I tried. It was worth it. Just because you couldn't accept it, wouldn't budge out of your way of reacting, you got hurt. Am I to blame for that?"

"So you're saying it's my fault. I can't believe you! I've done nothing but be concerned for you. And this is the thanks I get — blame. Is there anything wrong with being concerned for someone you love who is doing himself harm? Is there?"

"No."

"I've always felt that what has kept us together is our caring for each other. You don't want me to care about you anymore?"

I went over to her and tried to touch her, but she moved away.

"Bob, answer me. You don't care anymore, do you?"

"I do. Honestly, I do. It's just that, oh, I don't know. Can't you see you shouldn't worry about me? I mean, it's not coming out right, but I think we're thinking of two different things."

"What do you mean by that?"

"If you really cared about me, you wouldn't condemn what I've done. You would have encouraged me. You care about me as I was and as I am, not about what I can become. You see, going back to what I was is, the worst possible thing I can imagine, but for you it's the best."

"It's that hair brain idea of yours that's poisoned your mind! I wish, I do, like I told you before, that what you say were true. It's not that I don't care, it's that we perceive life differently. I see it for what it is, but you've distorted it with a false dream. That's what worries me. You believe your dream is true. I wouldn't worry if I didn't care about you. This is life. Right here in our rooms. Do you think we are here but are supposed to be somewhere else? Then we would be there and not here. And I do care about you, as you are, and I'm afraid for you, for what you might become because it will only be less than what you are now. Bob, what's wrong with you now? Why can't you be what you are? There's nothing wrong with you now."

"I'm trapped. I'm unhappy. Oh, I don't know. I'm all confused now. Things haven't seemed so bad. I do seem more able to accept this life."

"I've noticed that. You seem to be more content."

"Well, I am, sort of."

"But you still seem preoccupied."

"I am. Been thinking about this fear that controls us."

"Don't think about that!"

"Why?"

"Nothing to think about. You'll only become more afraid."

"I haven't yet."

"Did I tell you about the new cement?"

Her manner changed instantly. Seriousness withdrew as a superficial gaiety replaced seriousness.

"No."

"It's called Instant Cement. It's not strong like Never Worry Anymore or Super Deluxe Eternal Holding, but it dries the moment you put it on the wall. It's good to use when a lot of cracks are forming.

It seals them until you have the time to put on something stronger. It won't dry in your hands. Just on the wall. You should try it."

"Does it save any time? You know, with all the new types of cements that are supposed to make life easier, we still don't have any more time for ourselves. Haven't you ever noticed that?"

"I don't know. Still, it's fun to work with. It's different. It's something new to use."

"Not interested."

She started talking to me as though I were a child. "Come on, sweetie pie, let me see a little smile. Come on. It's not all that bad, is it? You can do it, come on now."

I faked a little grin.

"There we go. Keep your chin up and smile. Life will get better. I just know it will."

"Yeah," I said, "things could get better than they ever were before."

Her face lit up after I said that; her eyes even got a little bit dreamy. "We've been away too long. See you later."

Our walls separated us.

It still didn't bother me to go back to a life of sealing. It would have if that was all I did, but I was still intrigued by our fear. I still couldn't decide whether we were actually afraid of what was behind the wall or if we placed our fear on it. The uniqueness of what came through an individual's wall made me think we placed our fear on it, but the fact that everything came from the same place swayed me the other way.

I couldn't settle the difference. I wasn't getting anywhere.

Days passed, weeks, months; and my yearning to get out of there once again began to grow. A new scheme snuck into my mind without me hardly being aware of it. While thinking of our fear, it became a little less fearful. What Masonis said was really true; for most Sealers thinking about it only made it worse. But, I thought, perhaps I only have to think about it long enough and begin to believe it's not fear, and I'll stop being afraid. I'll just begin to believe that I'm not afraid of what is behind the wall. I'll refuse to acknowledge my fear as fear, no matter what its origin.

I proceeded half-heartedly with this plan. As before, I stood in front of my wall and let the cracks appear. A few appeared and began to spread. I could feel myself becoming anxious, and the resemblance between this scheme and my two previous ones hit me so fast and hard that it made everything seem ridiculous, and I fell on my knees laughing. I couldn't control myself. Everything was funny: our existence, the monotony, the trapped feeling, our wasted lives, the things I agonized over, even my despair. I laughed about them all.

You can imagine how long I laughed. What a relief it was.

I didn't care about a thing while laughing. I experienced so much pleasure in not being serious that I would have been happy just to have laughed my life away. If I didn't get out, it didn't matter because I could laugh about it. And for some reason, by laughing I felt more assured of going over to my likeness.

Sealers never laugh. There is no reason to laugh. They never have the feeling of laughter. Serious, serious, serious — that's what they are. What was there to laugh about? Except for when I laughed, I never heard anyone laugh nor did I hear the word used. Those who did laugh were strange, misfits, outsiders.

I expected Masonis to be upset with me, but she didn't say a word, although Cleanwall had a few things to say. He sternly marched into my room while I was still laughing. He stood there for a while as serious as a stone, eyes staring, mouth held tight, but when he realized his presence wasn't going to end my laughter, he started yelling, "Robert! Robert! Gain control of yourself. Robert, calm down. Control yourself!"

I stumbled over to him, and not laughing quite as hard, squeezed his fat, little cheek and said, "Come with me, Cleanwall. I'm going to get you to laugh. Come on, ol' boy, spit that seriousness up. It's like gas in a baby. Makes you fuss and cry."

I patted him on the back and stuck my finger in his side. He shoved me.

"Come on, Cleanwall. Now don't get mad. Oh, I see you're mad already. It's only fun. How can you get mad at a little fun? Here let me show you something."

As I reached toward him, he backed away and squealed, "Don't touch me. You stay right there. I can help you, Robert."

341

"Help me? You can? Help me do what? Escape from this prison?"

"Listen to me, Robert. Try to calm yourself. Breathe deeply. That's it. Follow my breathing."

His cheeks and stomach puffed out each time he inhaled, and when he exhaled, his skin turned a pale blue. I playfully followed his breathing a few times, then broke it apart with laughter.

"Robert, Robert, don't let it get the best of you."

Still laughing, I replied, "I think it is the best of me. It's got itself."

"Now you just listen here! Listen to me!"

I pursed my lips together, bound myself with my arms, sat down, and frowned. "Okay, I'm ready. See, I'm in control."

"That's more like it. Now, I know this will be hard for you to hear, but hear it you must. There are some things about ourselves to which we cannot admit, for they are painful and conflict with the image we have of ourselves. I am afraid that what I am about to say is of that very nature."

"Go on. I can handle it."

"You have fallen into illusion, Robert. What is real is too painful for you, and in reaction, you have replaced the real world with an illusionary world. I have been meaning to say something to you about this matter, but have not been able to find the appropriate time. Now, I feel I can wait no longer. You have not gone into it completely; there is still a chance for your return. Do not give into it, Robert. We can help you."

"How?"

"You must realize what you have done. That way you can prevent it when it starts again. You see, Robert, illusion violates reason. By maintaining a logical mind you will be able to stop yourself when you begin to slip into your illusionary world. If what you are doing or believing does not fit into the logical scheme of our existence, then you know something is amiss. Let me give you a pertinent example. Behind one's wall lies dangers, which threaten one's existence. If these are allowed to break through the wall or if the wall were to no longer be, then one's existence would end. Therefore, it is necessary for one to maintain one's wall in order to ensure no contact with the dangers behind it.

"Clearly you can see how this applies to your predicament. Your illusion is plain to see when tested against this logical sequence, for it is not contained within it. It lies outside, and consequently, becomes what it is. Do you follow me?"

Still holding myself back, I replied, "Yes, sir, I do. But, may I comment?"

"Yes, what is it, Robert."

"All is fine with your reasoning except for the beginning. Logic certainly does follow the order of events in the real world, but it is bound by the knowledge of those events. A new set of events changes a logical sequence. Now, what you call illusion I call a new set of events, a different way of perceiving our existence. You, on the other hand, say that those perceptions of mine violate reason, whereas I believe they can be incorporated. You start with the assumption that the things behind the wall will always present themselves as dangerous. That leads to our being a prisoner behind our walls. Now, if that premise were to alter by perceiving those things as harmless, then a different logical sequence would result. Simply put, it would go like this: no dangers, no need for a wall, no need for an existence of sealing, freedom. And so, in regard to your statement that I can guard against falling into illusion through reason, I will summarize by stating that reason is second to perception, for new perceptions alter logical sequences, consequently, in contrast to you, reason will limit me, hurt me instead of help me.

"Well, how's that Cleanwall? I can even talk like you. If I can do that, then I can do anything." While saying this, I started losing control so by the end I was laughing uncontrollably.

"Robert," he screeched, "do not make fun of me. I have come to you with complete sincerity and earnestness, and you show no regard for my feelings by toying with me. Stop that laughing. Stop it right now. You are in far greater danger than you realize. Listen to me. Sealers do not laugh!"

I staggered sideways to my wall, patted it, and said, "Good ol' wall. You ol' sonofabitch. You've got me trapped in here. But not for long. Isn't this wall a beauty, Cleanwall? I bet you've got one just like it. Too bad we don't have tourists; we could give them a piece to take home with them. Everybody needs a wall, don't you think?" I kissed my wall and continued, "Oh, you lovely thing. You are my protector, my strength, the keeper-away of evil, my stronghold against invaders. You big bastard. Till death do us part. Fat chance of that for you. I'll leave you behind one of these days. Slip through away and leave you without a purpose because I'll have a purpose. Come on, Cleanwall, wouldn't you rather laugh than lecture?"

"So, you call my help a lecture. I am insulted. You are laughing at me!"

"Not only you."

"At me, Professor Cleanwall. How dare you! What gives you the right? You are beyond help. I once thought, unmistakably so, that you had intellectual possibilities. How could I have been so wrong? I pity you."

"What you can't get with reason, you'll try to get with an insult. Is that how intellectual minds function?"

"You know nothing of the life of the mind. A few words will be sufficient to set you straight."

I interrupted him. "You know, Cleanwall, because of your grand idea of yourself, you think others are privileged to hear you speak. I'd say that was an illusion. Anyway, I still haven't heard you laugh."

I quickly grabbed his hot, red cheeks. He slapped my hand away, jumped back, shook his finger at me, and was about to say something when again I reveled in uncontroliable laughter. He scurried back to his room. I laughed for a long time after he left.

Around that time Masonis began having trouble patching her wall.

Cracks were forming faster than she could patch them. Her hands were shaky; she gradually became weaker, wasn't napping well; dark circles around her eyes sunk to her mouth, and she was losing her skill in sealing. It was just enough for her to keep patching without having to mix the cements, carry them, take care of her tools, and do all the other necessary tasks. I started doing those tasks for her. At first, there was little to do, but as the days passed, she gradually became incapable of doing anything except seal, and at times, I feared she would fall behind. Her patchwork appeared very difficult for her.

She couldn't decide what to use where or how to apply it. Her quickness reversed itself to sluggishness. She rarely ate, lost a lot of weight. I was worried she might get sick and die.

I should mention here that only the individual Sealer could seal his or her wall. Another Sealer could help in preparing the cements as I was doing for Masonis, but an outsider could not know what kind of cement to put on what crack, how much to put on, the succession of layers, (for sometimes combinations of different cements were needed to seal a crack), the type of patchwork to be used, and other details necessary to proper sealing. Each Sealer had instinctual knowledge only about his own wall. Although he did not know what pressed inward behind his wall, he somehow knew the power with which the dangers pushed. Sealers knew much more than they admitted.

I had to put my plans aside. Maintaining my wall and helping her took all my time. My ambitions began to fester in my mind; I felt they would rot and die there. There seemed to be no end in helping Masonis. She wasn't getting any better; she had, in fact, sunk and remained at a level where she barely managed to maintain her wall. I tried to help her, to find out what was wrong, but she rarely responded. It seemed to be too much for her. I began to hate helping her, dreaded going over to her room, and then I started to hate her and wish that she would die if she didn't get better. I felt guilty for feeling that way. She didn't seem to want to get any better.

She appeared to be content.

One day after leaving her room, I collapsed in my chair from which I could see through our doorway. In the depths of my sleep, I was jarred. Rising up to the surface, I opened my eyes, glanced around, and began to sink back down when an image halted my descent. I rose back up to see if it were true. It was. I went over to her.

"Oh, Bob, you missed it. I was my old self again. It was wonderful. For a moment I was sealing just as I used to. If only my strength would stay. Why won't it stay? What will happen to me?"

Her eyes watered, her mouth quivered, and her face contorted.

"I didn't miss anything. I never thought you'd do anything like this to stop me."

"What are you talking about?" Her eyes darted around the floor as though she were looking for something.

"You know."

"No, I don't."

"You've been faking it. There's nothing wrong with you. You've been acting helpless in order to prevent me from following my plans."

Her entire body began to shake. "What are you saying? Do you realize what you're accusing me of? How can you say that to me in my condition?"

"I'm not accusing you of anything. I saw you! While you thought I was asleep, you decided to catch up on your eating and sealing. I saw you. There's nothing wrong with you! I feel sorry for you. I really do. How long did you think you could fake it?"

"I'm crushed. You've hurt me before, but this...I can't bear it." She slumped to the floor.

"Go on. Play it to the end. All those lectures you gave me about caring, about how I didn't care for you but you cared for me; do you call what you're doing caring?"

"Stop it! Stop it! Can't you see what you're doing to me? Help me up, please. Help me." She reached up towards me with her arms.

Back I turned to my room.

There was nothing left between us. I had hoped, in spite of the resentment I felt for having to help her that she would someday want to try to understand what I was after. That would have been enough.

If she had just tried. Even if she didn't agree, talking and arguing about it would have sustained the bond between us. Both the deception and her method of trying to prevent me hurt me; I thought she'd never come to that, but what made me feel separate from her was that she would have preferred to reduce both our lives, more than they already were, in order to prevent me from following my plans. It would have been the end for me. She would have sacrificed anything, even life itself, to keep me with her. What's the purpose of staying together if it leads to that? It's not too bad not knowing what you're living, but once you know and believe something quite different is possible, for whatever reason, and feel that your dream may never be realized, then that unfulfilled want is conscious every moment. It meets you in the mirror every day where it reminds you that you're not living.

That's the despair in it. It's not as though you're missing out by not getting a sweater you wanted or a mate or a handful of sweets; it's life itself you're missing out on. And that was what Masonis wanted me to miss. She would have never said that for she thought she was keeping me from ruining myself. According to her, life was what she was living. Although, I've always had my doubts about that; not only of her, but of all Sealers. What they failed to perceive was not what just happened to not be there, but what they kept from being there, just as their life's work was keeping things behind their wall. Those things didn't keep themselves sealed.

My frustration and discouragement fell away from me, allowing my withheld eagerness to carry me along. I couldn't wait to put another plan into action. I didn't have to wait long. As I walked back into my room, I was overjoyed by the sweet melody. My likeness was waiting for me. It had been such a long time — too long. I bent down to gaze through my sweet hopeful crack. Cement slammed across the side of my face and onto the crack. I jumped back. Masonis heaved a whole bucket of Never Worry Anymore Cement all over my sweet hopeful crack. The cement wouldn't stick and kept sliding down the wall. Her body was shaking, her face red, and she was screaming through her tears.

"Stick, goddamnit. Why you lousy no good crack." She flung the bucket across my room and started kicking the crack. Then she swung on me. "I hate you, Bob. Just looking at you disgusts me. I never wanted your help anyway. I never wanted you. I hate you. Kill yourself. I don't care. Go on. Be an asshole and look through your crack up your ass. Go on. It's waiting for you, the goddamn thing."

She kicked the crack a few more times. "Go on, look in it. Oh, you're afraid to let me watch you. Is that it?"

I said, "Leave me alone."

"I won't."

"What are you going to do, Masonis, stand there the rest of your life?"

"What do you care if I do?"

"Why don't you give it up? I don't want what you want for me. It's as simple as that. So give it up. You don't really care what happens to me. You've already proven that. All you're thinking about is yourself."

"I don't need to worry about you," she screamed. "You can't do anything right anyway. You'll be here forever."

In response to that I turned away from her toward my sweet hopeful crack. I heard her stomp back to her room. The melody eased my mind; I began to feel light again. My concerns faded as I looked through and saw my likeness smiling as usual.

He came up close to me and said, "It shouldn't be long now. Soon, I hope, we'll be together. But first, there are some things you have to do. Watch me and do what I do."

Midway down his wall, a little right of center, a crack began to appear. He sat down on his soft chair where he watched it widen. The same blue cloth I tried to see as brown burlap began to droop down the wall. He walked over to the blue cloth, grabbed it, pulled it out of the wall, carried it over to a table in the center of his room, and put it down. He picked it up again, fondled it, examined it closely, touched it to his face, kissed it, and set it back down. He then turned to me and said, "Try to do that. If it becomes difficult, think of me. Whatever I do you can do." The crack sealed itself.

Never before had I seen or heard of anything like that. Pull the things out of the wall—was that was all I had to do? It seemed too simple of a solution. But, it was more than simple; it was frightening.

My entire wall subsided in activity except for the place of the blue cloth. The crack began to form; I was doubtful. It widened, and the urge to seal began to build. The cloth peeked through. I was overcome by the patching instinct and rushed at it with Super Deluxe Eternal Holding Cement. I pushed the cement in the crack as far as I could, smoothed it out all along the length of the crack, but the crack only continued to widen, and the cloth, covered with cement, hung down the wall. Hands shaking, beads of sweat rolling down my face, I grabbed the cloth between my thumb and index finger, held it away from me as far as I could, and rushed over to my table where I let it drop. Like a wary animal, I paced around the table keeping my eyes on the cloth. Vague, dreadful feelings began roving in me. I wanted to run and hide, burn the cloth, do anything so that I wouldn't have to see it. I thought of my likeness and felt less afraid. I cautiously touched it as though it were hot. My whole body trembled inside. I couldn't do it; I couldn't bear to have it in the room with me, but I knew, if I wanted a future, that I had to do what my likeness had done. I placed my hand on the blue cloth. Tears swelled in my eyes. My head began to throb. I picked up the cloth, rubbed it between my hands, and dropped it back on the table. The dreadful feelings subsided. I felt I had better get away before those haunting feelings the cloth had awakened in me rose to the surface. I walked to the far corner of my room. My sweet hopeful crack summoned me. I rushed over hoping to be comforted.

This time my likeness had a concerned look on his face. I could feel him look right into me as though I were transparent. After looking around in me for a while, he smiled and said, "You're doing fine. Feel whatever these things make you feel. You've always been feeling them. Here's another thing for you to pull out."

He stepped aside and pointed to the place on his wall where we pulled out the blue cloth. A plain, blue blouse hung out a crack above the cloth crack.

"Do with the blouse as you did with the cloth."

The dreadful feelings were still moving about in me as though they were looking for a way out. I carefully walked over to the appropriate place on my wall. As soon as I arrived, the crack began to form and the blue blouse emerged. I cautiously pulled the blouse out of the wall and marched it over to the table where I dropped it on the cloth. Suddenly, I felt extremely sad and alone. I didn't know why the blouse evoked those feelings, but I was overwhelmed with them.

I leaned on the table, buried my head in the blouse, and cried. Still crying, I picked up the blouse, examined it, and turned it around, inside-out, wondering what it was that made me feel sad, and dropped it on the table. Slowly I walked back to my chair and sat down, but was shoved up on my feet by vague, dreadful feelings, which were becoming stronger and more restless.

Pacing around my room, I heard the soft, sweet melody float out of the crack, but it failed to lure me. I didn't want to have to pull anything else out of my wall. I wanted to make it over to my likeness without having to pull anything else out. And then I seriously considered, not without startling myself, that I might be better off staying where I was rather than doing what had to be done. It would be easier. Life over at the other wall might be the same as where I was except for having fewer cracks to patch, and I would be spared from feeling what I didn't want to feel. But, I soon dismissed it, knowing full well that a future was just beginning to unfold, and I sincerely wanted, in a deeper part of myself, to feel what I didn't want to feel. I knew a future could not be without feeling.

I gave myself over to the melody. It took hold of me completely as it did when it first floated me over to my likeness. He was fondling the blouse and cloth. He looked up knowing I was there. He turned his head back down, continued examining the cloths, and then looked up at me again, smiled, turned, pointed toward the wall, and said, "We have to keep up the momentum. It's already beginning to carry you along. Let it take you wherever it wants. It knows better how to get you over here than you do. It's already starting to bring you over. Do you believe me?"

A sudden chill of excitement danced through me. That was the first time he had ever asked me a direct question. I felt a connection I'd never experienced before. It just wasn't a one-way street from him to me; I could make contact with him too. "Yes," burst out of me.

He grinned our ornery grin and continued, "See the patch above the blouse crack, you know the one, the one you always seal with Super Deluxe Eternal Holding Cement; pull it off and listen to what comes out of the crack. Listen to it fully. Let it penetrate you. And after that, when you've accepted it as much as you can, go over to this place on your wall," he walked over to the area below the cloth and blouse cracks and pointed to a long vertical crack that ran to the floor, "and when you're ready, this crack will open up wide enough for you to step through."

His face lit up, but quickly turned serious as he said, "Remember, try to forget about what should and should not be. What you'll see behind the wall is something that really happened to you. By thinking it should not be, it remains and continues to happen and controls you in spite of your wanting not to be controlled. If it gets too difficult for you in there, try to think of me and what you're doing. You're not going back there to stay. On the contrary, you're going back to free yourself from what keeps you from finding a home. I'm happy for you. We'll be together soon."

He smiled with affection. The crack closed up. I was left alone with myself.

I sat in my chair doubtful of what I had to do. My roving feelings began to die down; I seemed to be sinking back to the life I hated, and then it occurred to me what my likeness had said about the momentum. I jumped up and quickly walked over to the Super Deluxe Eternal Holding Cement patch, which I thought would have to be pried off with a crowbar, but to my surprise it popped off when I merely touched it. A deep, angry voice yelled at me over and over again, "They're dead. You're gonna have respect for them. Say goodbye. Go on. Say goodbye. See 'em. See 'em. They're your parents. You don't say goodbye, and they'll never forgive you. Say it. Say it. You'll never see them again."

I crouched down and covered my ears with my hands. All those dreadful, haunting feelings became charged and raced around in me like caged animals. I ran to the back of my room, started kicking the cabinets, and part crying, part screaming cried out, "No, no, let me go. Let go. No."

I was afraid to move, to do anything other than what I was doing. Gradually, the voice lost some of its menacing character, and I was able to listen to it for what it was and stop my screaming and kicking. It still frightened me; my insides were churning, but it wasn't devastating. Somehow, I thought, this voice is linked to the blue blouse and cloth. They all go together. That whole section of my wall goes together. I walked over to the wall as though being led by the hand, waited for a long time as the voice diminished, and when I could no longer hear the voice, the vertical crack appeared, opened up; I quickly turned, waved goodbye to Professor Cleanwall, and stepped through my wall.

I saw myself sitting next to my mother's mother in the back of a funeral home. She was a delicate woman of small frame; her face with few wrinkles was of a light complexion, and her mouth was small and fine as the rest of her features. She always spoke to me in a soft voice. Next to her sat my burly grandfather, a hard-looking man with coarse rough skin and dark, overbearing eyebrows that hovered above his sunken dark eyes. His mouth was permanently set in a bitter frown, and deep wrinkles, almost scar-like in appearance, gouged his cheeks and forehead. My grandmother was crying. She had been crying for days. The rest of my relatives, sad and forlorn looking, were standing or sitting in chairs along the walls.

I felt detached from them, from the room, from everything around me. When my relatives looked at me or talked to me, they seemed far off in the distance. Even when they touched me, I failed to feel the closeness of my mother's touch.

My grandmother picked me up onto her lap and spoke to me slowly, "Bobby, you should go see your mother and father. Soon they'll close the caskets." She broke down crying very hard, regained herself, and continued, "You haven't gone over to see them. It's been two days now, and you just sit here. You should see them."

I flung my arms around her, held her tightly, pressed my head into her bosom, and with a frightened voice said, "They not Mommy and Daddy. Mommy and Daddy coming back. They say so. They coming back."

I began to cry.

She leaned me away from her. Tears hung on her face as she looked into my eyes. She shook her head back and forth, and in a soft cracking voice, which I could barely hear, said, "No, no, they're not." She then drew me to her breast, which heaved heavily.

Suddenly I was yanked off of my grandmother's lap onto the floor by my grandfather. He scowled at me and yelled at my grandmother, "He's not going over there. Can't you see that. You're too soft on him, just like I used to tell Clare. She was always hugging him, kissing him, letting him have his own way. He's gonna show respect to his dead parents."

He jerked me into the air. I leaned back, dug my heels into the carpet, looked back at my grandmother, but she could only look at me with her sad, bloodshot eyes before I was yanked into the air and dragged across the rug. He was cursing me all the way. "You little spoiled bastard. I'll show you how to behave. Goddamn little shit."

I was screaming and crying and trying to kick him in the legs. One kick hit him solidly in the chin. He stopped, slapped me across the face; I turned to mush on the floor. I could feel myself being lifted up over something and shoved downward. I opened my eyes and saw a woman lying down surrounded by flowers and dressed in a plain blue blouse and skirt. She wasn't my mother. My mother never slept during the day in front of other people. She didn't wear red on her lips or black around her eyes; her skin was always a pale white or tan, not pink, and even when she did sleep she never looked like that. She always had a peaceful look on her face as though she were being happily entertained by pleasant dreams. And her hair, it wasn't a dark brown glob on top of her head; her beautiful, golden brown hair flowed around her face. A hand grabbed me and shoved me face first onto this woman's face. Her cold, hard skin sent chills through my body, and I started sobbing. My grandfather was yelling in my ear, "They're dead. You're gonna have respect for them. Say goodbye. Go on. Say it. See 'em. See 'em. They're your parents. You don't say goodbye, and they'll never forgive you. Say it. Say it. You'll never see them again." I tried to push away, knocked her hair off, and inches from my face was her caved-in skull, blue and purple, with a massive stitch zigzagging across to the back of her head. I screamed. Everything went black.

As though in a spotlight, everything around him turned dark. He could see no one, yet everyone could see him. He was all alone.

Touched, he felt no one; spoken to, he heard nothing; held, he was by himself. The sad, little boy abandoned in the world early in life, not knowing anyone, deserted by his parents. Why did they do that to him? It wasn't fair. Didn't they care about him? Didn't they love him?

I was sliding down toward him. I tried to hold onto the floor, but it was cold and hard to my touch. An icy breeze drifted through me. I started to shiver. As I was being drawn closer to him, I had difficulty in feeling myself separate from him. It was as though my feelings of my self, of feeling myself in my body, were beginning to slip away, and what I perceived him to be, I was becoming. If there were just something nearby to hold onto; I looked around, there was nothing. I could see him and a little bit of me. I felt myself go into him or him into me; I was not sure, and then I began to cry out, "Mommy, Daddy, where are you? Come back! Come back! Don't leave me alone."

I was being powerfully driven into a cold emptiness. A terrible fear and dread waved through me as I felt I was to remain there forever. Suddenly, the thought flashed through my mind that I wasn't this child. He wasn't me. I had grown up. I struggled to try to feel myself as being older, but I could not. I was the child. My parents had abandoned me. Then I thought of my likeness, and as though looking through a fog, I saw him standing by his wall. He smiled and motioned for me to come over to him. I tried but could not, and then darkness filled in the fog. I became the child.

Intense feelings rapidly waved over and through me, crisscrossing, leaving and then returning with shaking power, changing their intensity and direction as they met, mixed, and then separated like raging currents beneath a waterfall. Being helplessly tossed around, I heard a torrent of conflicting orders echoing around me: memories of aunts and uncles tumbled through; they were passing me from one to the other, telling me different things, expecting different things, ordering me around, not liking me; a strong wave of isolation shoved me away and brought to the surface an image of myself after my parents' deaths, crying out at night for my mother and father from a strange room and hearing the distant, harsh voice ordering me to shut up or else they would come upstairs; I pounded on the floor, and cried out, "Why'd you desert me. Why'd you leave me all alone? I never did anything to you," and as I was being driven about by this rage, I felt a small current rise up and down in me. Each time it rose it became stronger, and images of my parents began to appear with it; I began to realize that they really were dead; they had not abandoned me on purpose, they loved me in their death. I felt I was their thoughts when they died and that they cried out before they died that they wanted me, wanted to stay with me, and when they died I was on their minds. A ravaging, rough current powered its way through everything, and I saw my parents in their coffins, and they were dead.

They had died. I cried for them and myself, and sunk into a pool of sorrowful feelings for them, myself and everyone in the world, for I felt that everyone, in one way or another, had been abandoned, and in reaction, had abandoned his or her own self. I lay there like a waterlogged stick, rocking to and fro, crying deeply, breathing deeply.

Then, gentle currents began to sway me. I let them take me wherever they wished. They began to become more solid, less fluid, and gradually took form. Weaving through these molding currents was a strong, steady feeling of wanting to be close, held, kissed, of cuddling up to someone soft and warm; and I felt myself being touched and held, and what felt like a hand wrapped itself around my side, picked me up, and placed me on what seemed like a lap. As the one hand held my side, the other stroked my forehead, and soft lips kissed my cheeks.

Images began to form, and I gradually saw my mother, at first vaguely, but clearer and clearer until I was looking up at her while she was holding and kissing me. Next to her sat my father with one arm around her and the other on my leg. I gazed into my mother's loving, soft brown eyes, then let mine wander to her thick, light brown eyebrows, her soft clear skin, her delicate bone structure, her soft pinkish mouth, her calm kind face; and I felt loved and wanted.

As I snuggled into her, I felt a single current rise up through the turmoil and gain in power. Unchallenged and confident of its own power and pushing all else aside, it carried me out of the surging currents into a swiftly moving stream. As I was what may be called waking up, for any better explanation because I really wasn't waking from a sleep, although in a way I was waking up, I felt softness surrounding my sides and back, and I knew, as I was becoming more aware of my surroundings, that I had finally found a home.

Chapter 31

When I finally realized where I was and what I had just done, I jumped out of my soft chair and ran over to the part of my wall where I had stepped through. The cloth, blouse, and long vertical cracks were gone, and so were a lot of other cracks in that section. Ran my hands over that part of the wall. It was smooth and solid — showed no signs of ever having been cracked. I could feel, instinctively, that there was less power behind my new wall. I stepped back in awe. Just couldn't believe it! I had made it through to my new wall. And even though I was still in a room, I didn't feel trapped.

Feeling someone else's presence, I turned to the left and expected to see Masonis, for it hadn't completely sunk in that I was in a new room, and was stunned when I saw Pom Pom walking through a wide, arched opening between our rooms. She was wearing a plain red dress. She looked refreshed, relaxed, and as lovely as ever. I ran to her. "Pom Pom, I can't believe it! You're here!"

She smiled. "Yes. And so are you." We embraced. "Isn't this fantastic?"

I said, "It's more than that. How long have you been here?"

"Not long."

"This is incredible, Pom Pom! Not only have I stepped through my wall, but I'm with you too. And we are next to each other. I'm so glad I left my hometown to search for a home."

"So am I. It seems like an eternity since I left the Land of Boxes."

"I wonder where my likeness is? I thought I'd be with him. Have you seen someone around here who looks like me?" I glanced around.

"No. You're with your likeness, only in a different way."

"I think I know what you mean. Anyway, right now I'd rather be with you."

"I know." She drew me to her and whispered, "Dreams do come true, don't they."

"They sure do."

"How did you get here? Were you led here or did you step through?" I asked.

"I stepped through just as you." ·

"Pom Pom, it is so nice to touch you, to see you, to know that we're together. When I said to you, as I was leaving my hometown, that I felt I'd be seeing you somewhere in the future, I never thought that," I paused, "we'd find each other like this, but, I must have thought it somewhere; it was a dream, our dream speaking to me. Dreams, reality, life, who cares? We have a future together. It is so good to see you again." I held her.

"After leaving the Land of Love, climbing down the cliff along the waterfall, all the way along I thought of you." I started to tell her about my adventures after leaving the Land of Love, but she was so excited that she kept on interrupting me with her tale. Her excitement kept on spilling into mine, and mine into hers, and back and forth as we kept on breaking into each other's stories. I don't think I ever enjoyed talking as much as I did then. We were beyond ourselves.

She cruised with her words. "I was trapped in a room with men on both sides, and when I'd look through their rooms into other rooms, all I'd see is men and mothers. There were so many men; what a joy it could have been," she laughed, "if they had been nice. They weren't of any help. I had to fight and argue with them just as you did. And when I finally stepped through my wall, I saw things I'd known before; other things were completely new as with you, but it wasn't like with you, mainly one traumatic event. There were many things that had happened over a period of time that slowly crushed my will, slowly molded me into a cheerleader, slowly turned me against myself. My mother told me that my dog — I loved my dog; we went everywhere together — had wandered off one day and never came back. I searched for him for months. My older brother told me at the time, but I couldn't believe him; I saw this clearly when I stepped through; my mom had him put to sleep because it wasn't proper for a girl to always be playing with a dog. I played with my dog because she wouldn't let me play with other kids. She was afraid I'd copy their bad manners. Once I took off my cheerleader outfit, put on regular clothes and went out and played in the mud. It was so much fun. I was kept in my room for a week after that and was never allowed to wear anything but my cheerleading outfit. Never allowed to be sad, never allowed to complain, never allowed to cry, never allowed to do anything but smile and cheer for others. Never allowed to cheer for myself. Even when my mother divorced my father, (which I found out behind the wall was the other way around; he divorced her for not wanting to smile all the time), she acted as if nothing had happened. Nothing bad ever happened to her.

"All you had to do, she used to say, was to think happy thoughts and your life will be happy. She never talked to me about my dad leaving, never asked me how I felt, just kept on telling me to smile and cheer.

"She'd make me cheer for hours and hours, and my legs would ache so much I could barely lift them, but she'd make me cheer and smile and laugh, and at night, behind the wall, underneath my covers, I'd cry for myself, for my father, for my dog, for my childhood. You lost your parents, Bobby. You are not alone. I lost mine, too. Most kids in the Land of Boxes, probably in your hometown too, didn't have parents even though they all lived in the same house together."

"Yeah," I said, "lots of kids in my hometown were without parents. Kids weren't kids, they were trophies that could be dressed up and made to perform. And if the trophies didn't perform as they should, then they weren't wanted anymore. Like my cousin Eddie, instead of his parents bringing him to life, they almost brought about his death."

"But, you know, Bobby, it goes back a long way. I can get angry with my mom, but there's so much more. You know, what pressures she was under, what her parents had done to her, things she had no control over. We're all in this together, we are, really. Time makes a difference and then it doesn't. We all hold each other in, you know how it's done. Was it them? Was it me? Does it make any difference?

"Getting through our walls is what makes a difference. And what made a difference was feeling those things passionately. I had known them before, somewhere, but this time I felt them through my entire being.

"I cried, I really did, just as you, but to say I accept them doesn't reach the depths of my experience. Those experiences are a part of me now, they are me, they exist; and cheerleading my life away will not make them go away. They will never go away, although, in a way they have because it doesn't hurt anymore to think about them, and I'm not interested in thinking about them. They were past, and I'm not in the past anymore. I'm in the future. And the best thing about this, besides being with you now, is that I'm not interested in cheering. I don't need to cheer for my mother's love, I don't need to cheer to fit into other's definition because those needs and desires that grew out of what I experienced behind my wall are now gone. I feel that I've gained some of the love I never had before. Now, I'll cheer because I genuinely care and I'll cheer for those who cheer for themselves, who want to go through their walls, who want to be passionate about themselves, about life. That's the greatest thing — being passionate for life, to want to feel more alive. I've just about gone crazy over wanting a man, like when I was waiting for you in the park that night, but not near as passionate as I am for life. It is so good to be alive!"

"It is!" I said. It really is! I've always had my doubts about whether it was worth it or not, but not anymore. It's amazing where a search for a home will lead. I'm so happy to have found a home!"

By now my memory had returned, and I started thinking out loud. "I thought when I was trapped behind the wall that there was no other place like it. Even though, because I had lost my memory, I had nothing to compare it to, I still thought it. But it really wasn't.

"Trapped in that room was only bringing me face to face with the prison my fears of loss had erected around me. Aren't we all trapped in one way or another. Trapped in fears, lies, the day to day routine; trapped in a protected, vulnerable, constrictive world, in boxes, in guardedness, trapped in, what Aunt Iris used to say, keeping nonexistence at bay. What a waste. Nothing is gained. Just trying not to lose more of what has already been lost."

"All for nothing. It can even get worse than that."

"What do you mean?"

"I have been here longer than you and have had the time to look through the walls in both directions, and the opposite of what we did also happens. Everything is in motion, especially our lives. It's terrible, but rooms can become smaller, walls can get weaker, more cracks can form, and the dangers behind the wall can increase in both number and strength. We are fortunate to have moved forward because if we hadn't, not only would we be wasting away, but we'd be making things worse when we thought we were making them better."

"I know what you mean. The results of endeavors are often opposite to what is desired. But, I'm not sure that somewhere along the way the unwanted results are not foreseen. We all seem to have the ability to reflect upon what we've done and see what those efforts have produced. I just don't know. As Aunt Iris said, it's hard to know what's going on inside others."

Suddenly, I was seized with concern for Masonis. I rushed to the back of my room and opened a window through which I could see my old room. Masonis was shaking terribly, dropping her tools, rushing over to our doorway, staring wide-eyed into my empty room, and rushing back to her wall where cracks were forming faster than she could seal them.

She darted from one crack to another, spread a little cement, but before she was able to finish, she rushed over to another, slopped on a little cement, and ran to another. Cracks bolted all over her wall.

Some things began to poke through: clothes, pieces of furniture. Frantically she tried to shove them back behind, but it was of no use.

She stepped back; her face was contorted by horror as the things behind the wall began to break through. She froze in her spot, her bony hands gripped her face. She began to scream and cry as a floating image of her drunken, naked uncle came toward her. She raced to the back of her room where she curled up with her head between her knees. Her wall began to crumble. Ridiculing laughter echoed around her, and harsh, piercing voices were yelling, "You can't do anything right, you can't do anything, you're no good, no one loves you, you're unlovable. He never wanted you, no one has ever wanted you." Between these and the echoing laughter, other soft, seductive voices were imploring her, "Suffocate yourself, cut yourself off, bury yourself, lock yourself away." Her room was slowly becoming darker as her fears coming out of her wall were becoming more radiant and lifelike.

At the upper left section of her wall a picture of herself tied in a chair broke through, below it a paddle spun through the wall and quickly began twirling around her head, and then, the mid-section of her wall bowed inward, patches flew everywhere, and it imploded as an array of floating images rushed at her: a floating image of her crying and confessing in front of a statue of the Virgin Mary, her being scolded and locked in a dark closet, her as a baby crying and screaming and being picked up, slapped, and thrown to the floor, a scene of her nailing me to my old chair, a shadow sliding across the floor, and a scene of her crying for help as her parents turned and walked away.

And through all this, I could hear her mother yelling over and over again that she was a mistake and wasn't wanted. More things kept pouring through that hole. They tore down the rest of her wall. They swarmed around her like angry bees. Cleanwall walked across my old room with determined steps, and the Sealer on the other side headed toward her other door. I screamed at them, "No, no, don't do it. Don't lock her in. Give her a chance." They didn't hear me.

They locked her in from the outside.

I could barely see Masonis. She was still huddled in the back of her room. Her fears were swirling around her. Through the voices, I could still hear her screaming. A door flew open in the back of her room. She was pulled through the door. The door slammed before her pains could follow. They began pressing with great force against the back wall, which appeared to be weaker than her old wall.

I dropped to the floor and cried. It wasn't fair. Sealing one's wall for an entire lifetime wasn't fair. What did we do to deserve it? But, this, no, this should not happen to anyone. So what if she was afraid of having a sweet hopeful crack, so what if she didn't want to take a risk, so what if she was afraid to be alone, so what if she perceived the wall and her existence as she did; was that so bad as to have her wall cave in on her? Was that such a mistake, if it was a mistake at all, that her fears should have overwhelmed her?

Pom Pom sat beside me and put her arm on my shoulder. We sat there together for a fairly long drift of time. Every so often I would raise my head to look at her. In the dark pupil of her eye, I saw the same sadness I was feeling. She had known it, and yet, surrounding her sadness as color surrounds the pupil, was an unrepressible vitality. Each time I looked into her soft green eyes, I was seized by her vitality, held for longer and longer periods of time until I began to feel it without looking at her. It eased my distress around Masonis. Her vitality wasn't overpowering or nullifying it; it was complementing my sadness. Often, when tragedy sweeps through the life of someone you love, it can overwhelm you, blacken your outlook on life, surround your mind so nothing else can enter, and be the beginning of your own downfall. But this vitality I was feeling, whether it was from her or me, assured me that what happened to Masonis was only one aspect of our existence.

Pom Pom turned toward me, gently lifted my head with her hands, and said, "It happens to many of them back there. You've never seen it before, have you?"

"No. I've heard of it and was told how others lock the Sealer in, but no, oh no, never."

"It's painful to see," she said. "It reminds us of what can happen."

"It shouldn't happen."

"I think that many times myself."

"Has it happened to anyone you cared for?"

"Yes," she said.

"Does it ever happen here?"

"Rarely. Once in a while it starts to happen when someone stops trying to pass through, but that isn't very often. We don't let others stop for too long."

She smiled, laughed a little, and continued, "But what makes me sad is that if someone stops here, he is usually back at it again after others help him get through whatever is holding him in, but back there it's not understood. No one knows why, how, or what to do if it starts. You know, I've heard that sometimes one person can start a chain reaction. That's why they're locked in."

"No! Really!"

"I'm afraid so."

"That's terrible! Oh, I don't understand! Why do we have to be this way? You know, really, whose bright idea is this? I'm happy to be here in another room, but that wall," I pointed at my new wall, "why do we have to live behind it?"

"It protects us."

"I know that. But why are there things we have to be protected from? Why did my parents die? Why was I left alone? Why was my grandfather cruel to me? Why didn't my relatives understand me?" I began to cry. "Why, can you tell me, why do these things have to happen?"

"I don't know, Bobby. I wish I did for your sake, but I don't.

"All I can say, maybe this will help, is that the best we can do is try to be kind to each other and remove the walls we have built up while being hurt because sealing walls causes us to be cruel."

"Yeah, I know. Trapped in our room, fearful of something breaking through, no way to escape, someone comes along, but no, what if he brings something forbidden into our room or reminds us of something that has been sealed away or will do things that will cause something to break through? They can't be let in as they are. No, first they need surgery. Cut them up, shut them up, remove the bad parts, glue on some plastic, screw on a few nuts and bolts, make sure they behave properly, and if not, don't let them in, get rid of them, kill them if need be.

"I'm happy for you and me, for what we've done, and what you said has been comforting, but still, even though I understand how we are cruel, the mechanics of it so to speak, I still want to know why life has to be this way. Why does hurting and limiting each other play such a large part? I don't expect you to know, I wish you did, but, well, I guess maybe I'll find the answer in another adventure.

"Somehow, it seems that cruelty helps move life forward. If it weren't for the cruel things done to us and to those around us, we would not have ventured to where we are now. Yet, still, why has the scheme of life been set up this way? I wonder if it is always set up this way or if there are many set-ups, just as I believe there are many universes and many aspects of time, maybe there are many aspects of life, and from here, after we die, you and I will move on to a kinder place."

"I don't know, Bobby. But I do know we don't have to wait that long. There are pockets of peace and happiness right here on this planet."

She wiggled her hand into my pocket.

"You never miss an opportunity, do you?"

"Not if I can help it." She smiled.

"Anyway, I was just thinking out loud. A habit I got from Aunt Iris. You would have liked her. I wish you could have met her. In many ways you are both alike. That's one of the reasons I'm attracted to you."

"I wish I could have met her too. I have, in a way, met her through her influence on you. Maybe that's why I love you so much."

She kissed me.

She continued with a soft, sincere, slow voice, "We can cry over what happened to us, we can cry over what happens to those we love, but for us who have stepped through and broken out of cruelty's vicious circles, love is what matters, love is our future. How can we love being sealed in a room worrying and fretting our lives away about what might come through a wall? And when we meet someone, how can we really love that person when the thought that jumps into our minds is whether or not he or she can be fitted into our plans? And when they can, is it love to give them a bit of guarded acceptance?

"Enough of this talk! I'm so excited. It's always been easy for me to get excited, but never this easy. No more living a lie, no more living an unlived life, no more cheering because I'm supposed to or afraid not to, no more faking passion. I'm passionate. I'm passionate for you, for life, for another moment. Your home is moving forward into a future, my home is being passionate. If I could get my hands on life, I'd give it one big, glorious kiss."

She jumped up and cheered:
"Lovers of life
Everyday.
Without much strife
We found our way.
Through our walls
We have grown.
Gave it our all
To find a home.
Happy to be alive.
Happy to cheer.
Happy to be beside
My old fears."
Still standing in front of me, she said, "How's that for a new cheer?"

I laughed and said, "That's great. Your moves are smoother than before."

"Oh yeah! You haven't seen anything yet."

"Mmmmmmm," looking her up and down, "I don't know about that.

"I'm still in a daze," I said. "I can't believe where my adventures have led me, led us. We're together, through our walls; this is too real to be true. I feel more alive than ever."

She leaned away and said, "We celebrate every time someone passes through, either from here or to here, or if we hear of someone passing through somewhere else, we celebrate. Everyone is getting in a festive mood around here. Pretty soon we'll all get carried away by it over to you, and, oh, I'm getting so excited! So, don't be surprised.

"See you later." We kissed.

With pleasure I watched her as she strolled back to her room and gazed through her sweet hopeful crack.

For days, I was still in a daze as memories of my parents, their funeral, our house, my neighborhood, relatives, feelings, and thoughts slowly drifted into my mind, pieced themselves together, and formed a whole new aspect of my life I had never known before. Many things I had always wondered about were now being cleared up. I just lay around on my soft couch, sat in my soft chair, spent little time on my wall, and watched my mind rearrange itself. And with every new piece, I felt, oh, what should I say — I felt thrilled to life. I really did.

It was a time for a celebration.

One day while looking at mandalic designs on my walls and thinking about how simple my life had become, how I didn't have to worry about keeping a wall sealed, how I didn't have to wonder and wander about finding a home, and how, if I kept my life moving forward, I didn't have to be concerned about right and wrong because, like a lovegod, my actions would be an expression of my being becoming closer to being; my new neighbors started coming into my room bringing food, talking excitedly, waving their arms around, teasing each other, laughing, joking. This went on for a couple of days. We talked about our future plans, the circumstances under which we had passed through, the different things we had experienced, what we planned on doing with all our extra time, plans on rendezvousing later at other walls, the end of sealing, and other topics like that. Towards the end of the celebration, sitting in a circle with Pom Pom beside me, we sang:

"The sweet crack reveals a future.

This we know for sure.

All we have to do

Is step through, step through.
Step through to a thinner wall
That beckons with a call
From the sweet voice encouraging you
To step through, step through.
As you follow your sweet voice,
You'll be left with little choice
Of what else there is to do
Than to step through, step through.
Soon you will come to see
The end of walls for you and me.
Wide open spaces, content friends.
A future without a beginning or an end.
Step through, step through.
La lee la, dee da do."

Partway through the song, Pom Pom nudged me and said, "Look through your sweet hopeful crack."

Again, as the first time I ever heard the melody from my sweet hopeful crack, I glided feeling completely taken over. Through my precious crack I saw my likeness smiling and standing next to a wall with far fewer cracks than my new wall. He walked toward me and exclaimed, "You made it! Now we can live! This is just the beginning for us. Please, follow me." As he turned toward his wall, a huge vertical crack opened in front of him, and when he was about to step through he turned toward me, motioned with his hand for me to follow, and stepped through. Hand in hand we walked through to another wall.

The previous wall faded away. Another crack opened up, and we stepped through to another wall spotted with fewer patches. Through another wall, then another; the walls were less cracked, losing their patches, becoming translucent. Rooms were becoming larger, more comfortable and colorful. The song was rising in pitch and loudness. Holes began to appear, larger and larger, and then we stepped through the last wall to where I could see and be forever. He faced me, spread his arms far apart, and twirled around a few times. The song ended. The whole process quickly reversed itself to where my likeness was leaning against his wall grinning our secretive smile. Lightheaded, I stood, teetered back and forth, and sat next to Pom Pom. Everyone else had left.

Chapter 32

For a long while I sat next to her thinking about what I had just seen. And then, I began to yearn to go outside, especially since my memory had returned. Wanted to feel the grass, smell aromas in the air, hear the birds sing, feel the wind blow, see the sun — just plain be outside. Now it wasn't that I wanted to go scampering off into another adventure as though I wasn't satisfied with my latest, I just wanted to go outside. I had been inside long enough. I looked back to see if maybe my new room had a back door. It did. The outline was not easy to see; you had to know where to look, but it was there.

I jumped up and ran to the back of my room. At first, I was leery of trying to open the door for fear that it might not open, but then, I decided if it didn't open, I'd break it down. To my pleasure it swung to a soft touch. I stepped out into the hall feeling free and more than ready to leave. The intriguing figures were still along the wall, and way down to the left was a stairway leading up and out.

I was ecstatic. I raced back into my room and exclaimed, "The door! It's there! I opened it! We can leave!"

Pom Pom said, "I was waiting for you to discover that."

With a hesitant, questioning voice I asked, "We can leave any time we want, can't we?"

"Sure can."

"And we can come back any time, can't we?"

"Yes, we come and go as we please."

"Oh, good! I want to leave here; oh, how I want to leave, but I want to come back, too. I want to make it through more walls.

"Passing through has made me happy enough, but no, oh, this is fantastic; I never imagined that I'd be able to leave. I thought I'd have to step through all the walls before I'd get to go outside, and by that time, it would take so long, I'd be dead. Oh," I looked to the back of her room to see if she had a door and continued, "this is quite an adventure! Come on. Let's go outside."

"Yeah, let's go."

I grabbed her hand and headed towards my door. She let go and said, "I've got to go out my door. I won't be able to go through yours. I'll meet you in the hall."

It made perfect sense. I was surprised I didn't realize it myself.

Hand in hand, we strolled down the hall toward the stairs. Every few steps, a figure or scene on the wall would seize my attention, draw me over, and carry me along. I understood them more than before.

When we reached the stairs, my heart began to shake my ribs and my body felt as though it were being electrified, which was a pretty unusual experience for me. I couldn't wait until we reached the surface.

I sprang off the top stair, sank into the wet sand next to the stream that gushed out of the bottom of the sand dune, stumbled forward, almost fell on my face, but somehow managed to keep my balance. The crisp air, the warm sand on my feet, the sensation of losing and regaining my balance, the warm rays from the sun, the ocean breeze blowing across my face, oh, they felt so good. I never knew feeling could feel so good, except of course, in the Land of Love.

Everything felt close and alive. Everything must have been alive because they livened me right up.

On our way down I saw a woman and child playing in the surf. As we got closer, I recognized Aunt Marty and her grandson. I was happy to see them. After she had abandoned me in that room, I wasn't too pleased with her, to say the least, but now I was thankful. Without her, I may not have been able to move as far as I did without moving.

When we reached the sea, Pom Pom and I waved to them, and I yelled, "Hi, what a surprise to see you! How's the water?"

She yelled back, "Come on in, it's refreshing. Come on."

I stepped into the water, but before taking another step I noticed colored speckled stones, about the size of marbles, rocking to and fro in the gentle waves. I felt them with my hand, pushed them around, and lifting a handful out of the water, examined them more closely. They were all a different arrangement of colors, each and every one; they fascinated me, but then as they dried, they became dull, lifeless, and lost their uniqueness. I dropped them into the ocean where they immediately began to shine. My eyes were drawn to a pale white stone. After looking around for more white stones, I returned my gaze to the solitary, white stone. I was mesmerized by it. Quietness filled in the spaces. Alone, the white stone was rocking back and forth, back and forth. Then the other stones joined in the rhythm. These stones no longer appeared as individual stones but as one dancing, multi-colored mass. As my eyes drifted up the shoreline, the rhythmic colors extended with it. The waves and whitecaps lapped over the colors and made their dance more lively and varied, and as I looked out into the sea, the rhythmic colors joined with those waves and whitecaps, all of which moved together to the same movement, and as I gazed toward the horizon I could not tell whether the water was waving up or the sky was waving down. They seemed to be playing with each other, exchanging places, and when I turned my head toward the shore, the golden sand, glittering as the wind shifted the particles about, matched and joined with the rhythm of the stones, sea, and sky; and as I looked farther inland, I could feel the pattern following me, extending its lines, weaving into it the next thing I was about to see, and sure enough, the bushes and small trees were swaying in the wind to the same rhythm and became a part of the expanding, dancing pattern. I gazed outward, spread my vision to take in everything around me, and unable to distinguish one thing from another, the entire world appeared as one immense, pulsating pattern of colors and forms. Then everything began to swirl; my mind began to whirl; I became dizzy, stumbled and staggered along the shoreline like a drunken sailor, tripped over a piece of driftwood, and fell into the sea where I let the undertow carry me out to Marty and her grandson.

Bubbling up to the surface, I was met with laughter. Those two were like a couple of mischievous kids. Wouldn't have thought one was an older woman. They were swimming all around, pushing each other, splashing, catching waves, and making all kinds of noise. I was too tired to join in the fun so I just floated on the surface. They swam over to me and alternately began bobbing up and down. Each time they'd come up for air, they'd manage to utter a line of verse. Among the gurgles, my partly submerged head, and the sounds of waves, I had difficulty hearing what they were saying. This is what I think I heard:

"Don't stay too late; don't leave too early.
What you've done you'll do again.
What you'll do is already done. .
Every father is a son.
Ha ha ha, hee hee hee;
Come with me
To the edge of the sea.

371

No sooner is it late than the latter is too soon.
At night we all kiss the moon
Who shines upon us like the sun.
Who knows, maybe he's his cousin.
Ha ha ha, hee hee hee;
Come play with me
In the deep blue sea.

What you've seen you'll see again.
But will it appear to be the same?
It may be blue; could be green
Unforgettable, as real as a dream.
Ha ha ha, hee hee hee;
Swim underwater with me
In the clear blue sea.

Travel when you're young.
Travel when you're old.
Tomorrow might be yesterday.
Yesterday could have been tomorrow.
Ha ha ha, hee hee hee;
Come flip around with me
In the waves of the sea.

Travel on the earth; travel underground.
Travel on your feet; travel in your mind.
All ways can be sublime.
Ha ha ha, hee hee hee;
Travel with me
To the distant sea.

Travel in your bed.
Travel in a chair.
Never leave the house
And travel everywhere.
Ha ha ha, hee hee hee;
We don't need a boat

To float upon the sea.

Adventure here, adventure there.
Adventures can be found anywhere.
Something new may be old.
Secrets are waiting to be told.
Ha ha ha, hee hee hee;
Listen closely
To the sounds of the sea."

When they finished, we were close to shore. I let the waves rock me in as Marty and her grandson swam back out and started playing with Pom Pom. I scraped the bottom, crawled up on the warm sand and immediately fell into a sound sleep.

The next thing I remembered was the sensation of being kissed softly. I opened my eyes to be pleased by Pom Pom's vibrant face looking down upon me. Her blond hair hung in strands around her oval face, accentuating her high cheekbones and full lips.

We looked at each other for a while without moving or speaking. I then said to her, "I feel more in love with you and closer to you than in the Land of Love. Can you believe it?"

"I sure can. My feelings for you are more intense too."

"Do you want to be together, or are you still thinking of being by yourself?"

"I want to be with you, at least for now."

"Now is long enough for me. Here, take my hand. Let's go for a walk."

On our way over a few small sand dunes, I asked, "Did I ever tell you about the time I became a lovegod?"

"No, I don't remember hearing about it but I most certainly remember feeling it."

"You do?"

"Oh, yes!"

"Would you like having it felt to you again?"

"That sounds very lovely. I wonder if it will feel the same now as it did then. You know, feeling has a way of being enhanced by passion."

"Yeah, I know. That's one of the nice things about finding a home."

Softly she whispered in my ear, "How do you know?"

Softly I whispered in her ear, "The same way you know." We smiled our secretive smiles.

On our way back to the ocean, we saw Marty and her grandson walking along the shore holding hands. They saw us and waved.

We waved back, and I shouted, "Where are you going?"

Marty yelled, "We're going home."

Pom Pom and I sat at the high tide mark and watched them stroll around a curve and out on a peninsula. Have you ever stared at something for a long time, just that one thing, and have that thing fill your entire vision? Well, as I was watching them walk onto the peninsula, I was staring at them in that way, not blinking, not moving my eyes at all; and the golden sand, waving in the heat of the sun, blended into the blue waves and sky, and the two figures kept on appearing out of and disappearing into that pulsating, golden blue. They were becoming smaller, being absorbed for longer and longer periods of time, and then they disappeared; and all I was aware of was the undulating, golden blue.

I blinked my eyes, rubbed them, strained them, shook my head, but they were gone. Pom Pom placed her hands in mine and pulled me up.

Hand in hand we strolled onto the peninsula and joined them.

That was the beginning of my greatest adventure, at least one of them. Ha.

The End?

Printed in the United States
1138600004B/22-36